BLOOD

DIVIDED

BLOOD
DIVIDED

The Felserpent Chronicles:
Book Two

KATIE KERIDAN

Published by SparkPress, a BookSparks imprint,
A division of SparkPoint Studio, LLC
Phoenix, Arizona, USA, 85007
www.gosparkpress.com

Published 2023
Printed in the United States of America
Print ISBN: 978-1-68463-220-6
E-ISBN: 978-1-68463-221-3
Library of Congress Control Number: 2023904877

Interior Design by Stacey Aaronson

To everyone who's ever had a dream and wondered
if they should go for it— this is your sign.
Do it!

1

Sebastian tried to close the door quietly behind him, but the wind caught it, slamming it shut with a bang that did nothing to improve his mood. Hopefully his mother hadn't heard. With any luck, she was writing new music, too lost in her own world of sharps and flats to care about noises around the drafty old house.

"Sebastian?"

Sebastian cringed as his mother's voice drifted down the stairs. So much for sneaking in without her noticing.

"Welcome home, sweetie!" his mother continued. "Grab your snack and come up to your room."

Sebastian glanced at the thick slices of bread covered in blackberry jam his mother had left on the counter, then walked past without reaching for the plate. For once, he didn't feel like eating. Forcing one foot in front of the other, he made his way through the white-washed kitchen, past the dining table that took up most of the small living room, and up the creaky wooden stairs. Reaching the open door of his bedroom, he froze— a black suit he'd never seen before was hanging on his closet door, and his mother was rummaging through one of his dresser drawers.

The fire inside him roared to life, stealing the air from his lungs as flames curled around his small fingers. He couldn't breathe, and his heart began to pound. He knew from experience panicking would only make things worse, so he desperately tried to remember the mental tricks he'd been taught, focusing on something observable around him and taking evenly spaced breaths, relaxing enough to pull the fire back inside.

His mind, however, refused to focus and kept returning to the reason he'd been reluctant to come home in the first place. His teacher had said she was going to call his mother. Normally his school didn't care if students fought. But when injuries were worse than simple cuts or bruises, the parents of the student who'd caused the injury received a courtesy notification . . . mostly so that if the parents of the injured student appeared at their house, angry and demanding retribution, they'd be prepared.

What if his mother was so mad he'd broken his classmate's arm, she was packing his things and sending him away? What if the new suit was for wherever he was going?

His mouth went dry as the fire hungrily stole the little air he'd been able to draw in, flames spreading over his palms, his skin unharmed by the dancing red light that would happily destroy anything else it touched.

His mother turned from the dresser, a smile on her face, but at the sight of Sebastian fighting to control his pyromancy, her smile instantly faded, and she hurried around the bed to kneel in front of him. Placing her palm against his chest as he moved his fire-engulfed hands away from her, she gazed into his eyes as she took slow, deep breaths, encouraging him to do the same.

"Focus on your breathing," she instructed. "Everything's fine, and I'm right here with you. In and out . . . don't think about anything else, just in and out."

After a moment, Sebastian's body relaxed enough for him to pull the fire back inside, and his chest loosened, allowing him to breathe freely.

His mother brushed his hair off his damp forehead with a worried expression. "That hasn't happened in a while. Do you want to talk about what upset you so much?"

8

Unable to continue looking at her, Sebastian dropped his gaze to the ground. "Did my teacher call you?"

"She did," his mother replied, and Sebastian let out a shaky exhale even though he'd expected as much. "She said you got in another fight today."

He nodded, keeping his eyes on a crack in the hardwood floor. His mother hated when he fought.

"Was the other boy teasing you?" she asked softly.

He nodded again.

"About your Cypher?"

Sebastian shook his head. "About my reading. I got called on to read out loud."

Thinking about the other boy's laughter, something twisted painfully inside him, embarrassment turning to anger. "It's not my fault the letters get all mixed up on the page!" he snapped. "I don't do it on purpose!"

Deep down, Sebastian didn't believe fighting was always a bad thing, as he'd sent a very clear message today, mainly to the boy who'd teased him, but also to everyone who'd witnessed the fight . . . they each knew what to expect should they ever tease him about his reading.

At the same time, he hated upsetting his mother.

His mother offered him a smile, but he could tell she wasn't truly happy because her eyes looked sad even as her mouth rose upwards, and that made it difficult to predict what she was going to say next. The best fighters were those who could anticipate what was about to happen, since by predicting their opponent's moves, they avoided being surprised. Sebastian hated surprises and did his best to anticipate everything he could, but it was more difficult when it involved feelings rather than fighting tactics.

"You're growing stronger and learning new skills every day," his mother said, "and I want to make sure you control your abilities, rather

than them controlling you. I know it might not feel like it, but you always have a choice in how you behave."

"I just wanted him to stop teasing me," Sebastian said, hanging his head and wishing he could disappear beneath the floorboards. "I didn't mean to break his arm."

His mother pulled him into a hug. "I know, honey." As she stroked his hair, Sebastian wrapped his arms around her neck, burying his face against her skin. While he didn't like admitting it, given that he was seven years old, he felt so safe in his mother's arms.

There was still the problem of the new suit, though.

Pulling back from his mother's embrace, Sebastian searched her face for some hint of what was happening. "Are you sending me away because I fight so much?"

His mother's light brown eyes widened, and her mouth fell open. "Sebastian, no! Why would you think that?"

He gestured to the suit, his fears spilling out one after the other. "Maybe I'm too much like Father. Maybe I can't control myself, and you're worried it's not safe to be near me."

He thought back to all the times his father had hit his mother, making her cry and even bleed, then quickly pushed the memories aside, lest the fire inside him get stirred up again. His father had hit him too, once, and the next day his mother had packed two suitcases and said they were going somewhere safe. They'd left Vartox and moved far away to the territory of Doldarian, and even though Sebastian normally despised unexpected changes, he'd found himself eager to start over in a new place where no one knew his father, a place where his mother could be happy, and where he wouldn't feel angry and get into fights all the time. He and his mother had settled into the old farmhouse and Sebastian had enrolled at a new school . . . the same school where he'd broken his classmate's arm just a few hours earlier.

He clenched his hands into fists before adding, "Maybe I'm going to live somewhere else, and I'll need that suit wherever I'm going."

His mother's eyes filled with tears, and he wished he'd never come home from school. He couldn't stand to see her cry, especially when it was because of him.

His mother quickly ran her hands across her face, wiping away the tears as they fell. "You're right about your father not controlling his temper, but that's not because he couldn't, it's because he refused to even try. That's where you are nothing like him, Sebastian. I know you try."

She cupped his face in her hands and leaned towards him, the usual happy shine returning to her eyes. "I love you more than I have ever loved or will ever love anyone in the entire world. I would never send you away or leave you. It won't always be easy, but it will always be us. I promise."

Sebastian nodded, relief washing over him. "So, where am I going in that suit, then?" Excitement stirred in him now that he knew nothing bad was going to happen.

"You mean where are we going," corrected his mother, a smile stretching across her face.

Sebastian's Cypher, Batty, suddenly materialized on the edge of the dresser. "We are going to have so much fun!" the fruit bat exclaimed, flapping his wings excitedly.

"Dunston and Rennej invited us to the symphony next week to celebrate my birthday," explained Sebastian's mother. "When I mentioned needing to get you a new suit, given how fast you're growing, they sent over this one to see if it might fit. I believe Rennej bought it for Devlin a while back, but he never wore it."

"Will you be playing in the symphony?" Sebastian asked.

His mother shook her head, causing her shoulder-length blonde hair to sway. "That's what makes it such a wonderful present! I'm so used to being on stage, it's going to be a treat to just sit there and listen without any responsibility."

Sebastian wrinkled his nose. "I doubt any of the musicians will be as good as you," he said, causing his mother to laugh before reaching over and plucking a cloth toy animal from his bed. She tossed it at him and he giggled, letting the cotton-stuffed owl bounce off his shoulder instead of swatting it away like his reflexes urged him to do.

"I'm sure all the musicians will be wonderful, and I could likely learn a lot from any of them," remarked his mother politely, but he could tell she liked the compliment because she couldn't quite suppress a smile.

"Of course," added his mother, "the symphony is all the way in Jaasfar. Dunston suggested we use his intersector, but I reminded him I know I someone who's quite skilled at making portals and might be willing to help."

Sebastian grinned. "I can do it."

His mother ran a hand through his hair. "Of course you can. Now, tell me about the rest of your day while we start dinner."

Sebastian never tired of talking to his mother. She was always interested in everything he did and made it seem like he was the most important Daeval in her world, which, given that it was just the two of them, he supposed he was. Following his mother downstairs, he recounted everything he could remember from school, washing vegetables as directed and occasionally stirring something on the cookstove.

Batty kept trying to sneak bites of everything, even though he was a Cypher and didn't need to eat, and when he grabbed a noodle from the pot Sebastian was watching, Sebastian pointed his wooden spoon at the bat's protruding belly.

Cut it out! he ordered through their mental connection.

Batty studied him, a sly look creeping over his face before he burst into what were obviously fake tears and sobbed how no one loved him.

Sebastian's mother immediately scooped him up and hugged him to her chest before offering him a piece of watermelon-flavored rock candy. The bat grinned as he slurped up the treat, even as Sebastian clenched his teeth and wished yet again he'd been paired with a more respectable Cypher.

Sebastian and his mother enjoyed a quiet dinner and were just discussing dessert when a sharp knock sounded at the front door. His mother exchanged a look with her Cypher, a hummingbird named Verbena, before rising to her feet and crossing the room. Even though she flashed Sebastian a quick smile, he thought she looked more worried than excited. They never had visitors, except for the Dekarais, and they always knew when to expect Dunston and his family.

As his mother opened the door, she gasped . . . right before Sebastian's father swept past her into the room.

"Just the two Daevals I've been looking for," his father said with a wide smile.

Sebastian knew how quickly that smile could turn into a snarl. And how a snarl could turn into his father hitting his mother until she couldn't stand and had to see a healer, even though she never told the healer the truth about how she'd been injured.

His mother quickly closed the door as Sebastian went perfectly still, trying to blend into his chair even as his heart pounded so loud, he worried his father would somehow hear it and berate him for it. His father despised any signs of what he considered weakness; even if Sebastian felt scared, he was never to show it. As his mother hurried towards him, he caught a glimpse of his own fear reflected in her eyes. At the realization that she, too, was afraid, his fire roared to life, thawing his previously frozen limbs and propelling him to his feet. It was his job to protect his mother now. Unfortunately, when he tried to move in front of her, she quickly shoved him back.

"Don't," she whispered firmly. He couldn't see her face, but he heard the tremor in her voice as she said, "What are you doing here, Malum?"

His father chuckled. "Did you really think I wouldn't find you, Grace?"

She straightened her shoulders. "I was never trying to hide. You could have come and seen your son at any time."

Peering out from behind his mother, Sebastian watched his father walk towards them, tall and lean with hard muscles under his tailored black suit earned from years of hand-to-hand combat. His brown hair was slicked back, and his dark eyes stared out over high cheekbones.

He looked down at Sebastian's mother, and the anger in his gaze sent fear flickering alongside the fire in Sebastian's veins.

"I had hoped some part of you would be happy to see me," he said.

Grace shook her head. "Not anymore. What do you want?"

Malum strode towards the large wooden table. "To discuss our son's future."

Grace wrapped an arm around Sebastian's shoulders and gently turned him around, guiding him back to one of the mismatched chairs they'd purchased at a rummage sale their second day in Doldarian. Once they were seated, his father pulled a thick envelope from his jacket pocket and set it on the table.

"It seems," began his father, "aside from reading, Sebastian has been doing very well in school, particularly in mathematics, potions, and physical activities."

Grace frowned. "How did you get a copy of his progress report?"

"I am his father," retorted Malum. "The school sends me updates, same as you."

Sebastian wondered if the school would have done such a thing if they'd known he and his mother didn't want anything to do with his father.

"You came here to congratulate your son on his grades?" His mother's brow furrowed.

Malum responded with a disbelieving snort. *"Don't be ridiculous, Grace."*

Sebastian's mother glanced at him, clearly worried his feelings had been hurt by his father's response, but he gave her a tiny smile to assure her he was alright.

His father then set another envelope on the table. Sebastian couldn't see all the words but the crest was dark red and stood out in stark contrast to the white envelope.

His mother must have recognized the insignia, though, because her eyes widened and she shook her head. *"No,"* she said. *"Absolutely not."*

Sebastian looked to his father for an explanation.

"I showed your last few progress reports to some colleagues of mine, and they've decided to offer you an incredible opportunity." Malum glanced back at Grace, who was resting her forehead against her fingertips, her elbows on the table the way they weren't supposed to be during meals. *"It's an honor they even agreed to test him."*

Sebastian's heart lurched as he pictured sharp needles and cold measuring instruments. *"Test me for what?"*

His father's eyes narrowed, making Sebastian wish he'd kept his question to himself. His father's movements were usually efficient and controlled, but he could move with near-impossible speed when he chose to. Part of what made him so frightening was not being able to anticipate how he would respond to things. One act on Sebastian's part might elicit no more than an eye roll, while another would provoke a tirade, and Sebastian had never been able to discern a predictable pattern.

"Don't sound so scared," his father ordered. *"It's embarrassing."*

As Sebastian sank deeper into his chair, his father adjusted his tie, and when he spoke again, his voice was slightly nicer. *"You've been of-*

fered a chance to train with an elite squadron in the Nocenian military. If you qualify, you'll go to a special school where you'll learn more about fighting and weapons and war than you ever dreamed of."

Sebastian's ears perked at hearing words like weapons and war. But glancing at his mother, it didn't seem right to get excited about something that was clearly upsetting her.

"They'll make him a monster," Grace said, lifting her head and glaring at his father. "He'll be nothing but a weapon to them."

Malum held his mother's gaze. "He needs to learn to use his gifts. He's already stronger and faster than others his age. This is a chance to secure his place in Nocens, to be recognized and respected. Don't you want that for him?"

His mother shook her head. "Not like this."

Malum rubbed the bridge of his nose. "Grace, we discussed this when you found out you were pregnant and insisted on keeping him . . . he belongs where he can make the best use of his particular abilities."

While this wasn't the first time Sebastian's father had made it clear he'd never wanted a child, his words still stung, although Sebastian did his best to keep his reaction to himself.

Sebastian's mother glared at his father, and if she'd been a Pyromancer, flames might have exploded from her eyes. "He belongs with me," she said in a low voice Sebastian had never heard her use before.

Malum stood up, and Sebastian tensed as his father rested his palms on the table. "He belongs where I say he belongs. Don't forget who actually makes the decisions here."

His father walked over until he was standing behind his mother's chair, and Sebastian watched his mother stiffen, her eyes not leaving the table as his father leaned down so his mouth was beside her ear.

"Surely there's some part of you that's glad to see me," he said in a quiet voice that was somehow more disconcerting than if he'd begun yelling. His mother closed her eyes and seemed to be concentrating on breathing.

Malum nuzzled her ear with his nose. "Don't forget you're still mine, Grace. You belong to me." His voice became lower, and Sebastian didn't miss the slight growl running through his next words. "I could take you upstairs right now and show you exactly how much you still belong to me."

Sebastian held his breath as his mother shivered. In a voice that sounded much braver than she currently looked, she said, "You're wrong. I'm Sebastian's mother, and that's it. I'm not yours anymore."

Sebastian watched his father's eyes flash with anger as he straightened. Thankfully, he didn't turn over the table or throw anything; instead, he made his way to the front door and when he turned around again, his usual smirk was back in place.

"Well, then, you won't be disappointed to know I can't stay," he said. "I just stopped by to let you know the evaluators will be at Sebastian's school tomorrow." His eyes were hard as he looked from Grace to Sebastian, and Sebastian wished he could open a portal and escape with his mother to someplace his father would never find them. "I don't need to tell either of you what will happen if you fail to comply with them." As he opened the door, he said, "I'll be back once they've made their decision."

And with that he was gone.

2

❦

KYRA

*O*pening my eyes, I focused on the familiar lighting fixture overhead, the bronze rods and crystal pendants just visible in the early morning light peeking through the curtains. I wasn't in an old farmhouse in Nocens. I was in my bedroom, in my apartment, safe in the Aelian capital of Celenia. I focused on taking deep breaths, steadying my pulse as the fear thrumming through me began to dissipate.

What kind of dream was that?

Sebastian and I had shared dreams before, but they had ultimately turned out to be memories of our past life together as Kareth and Schatten. Was what I'd just experienced also a memory, one that belonged exclusively to Sebastian?

Sebastian hadn't shared much about his parents, other than they were dead and he was convinced his mother had died before her time—a conviction that turned out to be correct—but if the dream portrayal of his father was to be believed, no wonder Sebastian hadn't spoken about him. Forcing Sebastian to comply with his wishes, threatening those he should have been protecting, physically hurting his own wife and child . . . how dare that man get away with such things!

Aurelius's voice interrupted my rising ire.

"Given that I couldn't sense your thoughts," intoned the

lynx from the foot of my bed, "I take it you were sharing a dream?"

Pushing myself up into a sitting position, I ran my hands over my face and nodded before meeting the lynx's gaze. Aurelius's chin was resting on his oversized paws, and his whiskers were turned down. It still irritated him that the mental connection he enjoyed with me as my Cypher—my assigned lifelong advisor—didn't extend to seeing the dreams Sebastian and I shared or hearing the conversations we had through our bracelets. While Batty had never mentioned being bothered by such an exclusion, Aurelius directly equated having information with being able to take care of me. When offering advice, he couldn't stand thinking he'd somehow failed to account for all possibilities, worried his lack of knowledge might somehow negatively impact me.

I told the lynx what I'd witnessed, my voice scratchy with sleep, then fell silent, tucking my hair behind my ears. I could certainly relate to being worried over an upcoming test, but I couldn't imagine ever being afraid of my father; even when he'd been upset with me, he'd always made it clear he loved me. In fact, he'd spent his last breath telling me he loved me. I pressed a hand against my chest, as if the small act could stop the ever-present ache from spreading. My heart felt like the village of Aravost after the earthquake, torn apart by jagged cracks, but while the destruction caused by the natural disaster had been repaired with hard work and spells, my own devastation wouldn't be healed so easily . . . if ever.

Had it really been almost a month since my father had died? Some part of me thought if I walked into my childhood home at just the right moment, I would see him, his long black hair tied back with a ribbon as he excitedly showed my mother a handmade gift he'd received from a patient. I would hear him doing an array of character voices while reading a story to my younger siblings, smell the citrus and sandalwood scent he wore on special occasions, and watch him smile with pride as I demonstrated how I'd mastered one of his healing techniques.

I tried to hold on to the happy images, so different from my last moments with my father, but I was powerless to stop the flood of more recent memories from rushing through me. There I was crouching beside him, holding his hand as he struggled to form his final words. His torso—and the wooden beam protruding out of it—was covered with his golden blood, shimmering in the sunlight cutting through the dust-filled air. My sob-laced screams became increasingly hoarse as I tried unsuccessfully to heal him, until I fell silent and curled up near his unmoving body, my life upended and my family broken in a way I'd never imagined possible.

Ironically, it was my father's death that revealed me to be a Recovrancer, able to enter Vaneklus, the realm of the dead, and recover the shades of those who'd died before their time. While I'd eventually learned my father had died at his appointed time, knowing that didn't make the loss easier to bear, and I gazed down at my sheets, wishing I could pull the covers over my head, go back to sleep, and wake up in another life where my father still lived.

As always when I thought about my father these days, however, grief wasn't the only emotion to fill me. I had always viewed the two of us as having an exceptionally close relationship, but discovering he'd visited Nocens, interacted with Daevals, and undertaken the study of silver blood without telling me made me question how well I'd truly known him. How could he have kept such things from me? And even worse to contemplate, what else did I still not know about the man I'd looked up to and tried so hard to emulate? Obviously it wasn't his fault he couldn't answer my questions, but why had he left behind questions in need of answering in the first place? I wanted to cherish my memories of my father, but I wouldn't be able to sort out my feelings for him until I possessed all the available information, regardless of how terrible some of his secrets might turn out to be.

"I'll reach out to Flavius again today," offered Aurelius in what I knew was an attempt to be comforting. "Perhaps he's back in Celenia for reassignment."

Flavius was a timber wolf who had been my father's Cypher. When the Astral a Cypher was paired with passed away, the Cypher was given two choices: They could bond with another Astral after a suitable grieving period, or they could choose to forgo another bond, although that meant losing the immortality they gained by serving as lifelong guides. I had so many questions I needed to ask the wolf, but they all revolved around one thing . . . had my father been involved in experimenting on Daevals in Rynstyn?

"You're certain there was nothing of the facility in Sebastian's dream?" asked Aurelius, pricking his black tufted ears, his voice hopeful I might have remembered something I'd forgotten to mention earlier.

I shook my head, still hating to think of Sebastian being tortured by my kind. "What I saw must have happened before he was taken to Rynstyn. I didn't see any of the experimentation facility."

While most of me was grateful I hadn't seen what Sebastian had endured in the mountains of Rynstyn, a small part of me wished I had . . . perhaps I might have seen my father and settled the question of his involvement in the Daeval experimentation program once and for all. Of course, even if my father didn't appear in Sebastian's dreams, his absence wasn't proof of his innocence, as he could have started working at the facility after Sebastian's time there.

"Or it could mean just that," countered Aurelius, following along with my thoughts. "Your father won't appear in Sebastian's memories because he wasn't involved in that program. I still don't see how he could have been. He was one of the most compassionate and trustworthy Astrals I ever had the pleasure of knowing."

While I appreciated Aurelius's ongoing belief in my father and secretly hoped he was right, I also had to be realistic.

"My father had a suppressor medallion, one of the rarest items in Aeles, purposefully designed to hide silver blood from the Aelian Blood Alarm," I said, ticking off the facts as I knew them on my fingers. "He was working on a project with Senator Rex involving Daevalic blood. Sebastian is a Daeval who was kept prisoner at an Astral facility and even though it was thirteen years ago, he wore something very similar to a suppressor medallion . . . while my kind tortured and studied him."

I stared directly into Aurelius's eyes, the same deep blue as my own. "Those can't all be coincidences. Is it normal to be unable to reach another Cypher for so long?"

Aurelius twitched his whiskers. "Losing the Astral you've been paired with is never easy," he said gently. "Every Cypher grieves in their own way, and the process cannot be rushed. I suspect Flavius has simply been keeping his own company and hasn't wanted to be disturbed. When I reach him, I'll let you know."

I nodded and smoothed a hand over the sheets, wishing I could soothe my frustration as easily. "Only Flavius knows for *certain* what Father was doing, but in the meantime, hopefully I'll learn more by working with Senator Rex."

Of course, I wasn't only working with Senator Rex to uncover the truth about my father . . . I also needed to obtain proof of what Astrals were doing to Daevals to shut down the experimentation program, and shame pricked the underside of my chest at my selfishness. Whether or not my father had been involved in the experimentation program wasn't *nearly* as important as the fact that the program existed and needed to be stopped. The only reason I knew of it was because Sebastian had been taken there and tortured for two years as a child; to shut it down, I needed evidence beyond the word of a Daeval, evidence no one in my realm would be able to ignore. Acquiring such evidence meant getting Senator Rex to trust me enough to invite me to see the facility for myself, and while everything in me loathed the idea of pretending I was interested in studying silver blood, I would do whatever it took to end the program.

The wide gold bracelet on my wrist suddenly vibrated, and a smile sprang to my face, momentarily pushing all other thoughts from my mind. Aurelius rolled his eyes before hopping off the bed with a huff and stalking out of the room. I pressed my fingertips against the bracelet as a small black dragon appeared, swimming a graceful loop around the cuff before sinking out of sight.

Good morning, I said to Sebastian, hoping he could hear my happiness at speaking with him.

I'm guessing you saw my dream. His harsh tone caught me off guard, slicing straight through my excitement.

What I knew of Sebastian—as well as what I remembered of him as Schatten—was that his brusqueness was often a mask to hide his fear.

In this instance, he was afraid of having me see his most personal memories.

I did see it. There was no point in pretending otherwise. The bracelets we wore, forged for us over a thousand years ago, allowed us to intimately experience each other's thoughts and feelings. While we'd both easily refamiliarized ourselves with certain aspects of the jewelry, such as communicating using only our minds, other powers inherent to the bracelets were less familiar and far more uncomfortable, particularly for Sebastian, who hated feeling as if something about him had been shared without his consent. *I'm so sorry,* I added. *It's probably my fault you had that dream in the first place.*

As a Recovrancer, I had the power to recover shades who died before their time, but the ability also seemed to work in more subtle ways, such as causing those around me to resurrect forgotten or purposefully ignored memories.

You can't help it, Sebastian was quick to point out. *It's part of who you are . . . who you've always been.*

I smiled. This was the man I remembered, always ready to come to my defense, even against accusations I levied at myself. Questions danced on the tip of my tongue, but it also wasn't my past we were discussing, and I didn't want to push Sebastian to speak about things he didn't wish to share.

Do you want to talk about it? I asked gently.

No. Today's your internship orientation . . . what's on your schedule? He clearly wanted to change the subject, and I was fine to let him, as his childhood memories were better discussed when we were together than in two different realms.

Thank you for remembering, I said, and I felt a pleasant tingle speed through Sebastian at my words. *I'm excited, but I'm also nervous. I'll feel better once I know more, like where in the* Donec Medicinae *I'll be located and what my specific duties will be.*

What time will you be finished?

Is that your way of saying you'd like to see me? I purposefully kept my tone light to make it obvious I wasn't asking the question seriously. While I'd grown up with siblings and was used to teasing, Sebastian had been an only child. On top of that, given his unusual childhood, he hadn't enjoyed opportunities for traditional socializing, meaning he often struggled to differentiate between a joke and a challenge. *I should be done around five Aelian time, and I'd love to see you!*

Let me know when you're finished, and I'll come get you, he said, missing my attempts at encouraging him to share his feelings rather than simply issuing dictates.

Because you'd like to see me? I prompted. I understood Sebastian was more comfortable giving orders than discussing emotions, but if we were going to be in a relationship, there was a lot he needed to learn about communication.

Of course because I'd like to see you, he replied, and I envisioned two red streaks spreading over his sharp cheekbones. *You're aware of nearly every thought and feeling I have. You know I miss you. There's no reason for me to tell you something you already know.*

I smiled at Sebastian's admission, partly because I did know he missed me, but also because his reasoning was so in keeping with who I knew him to be.

I do know you miss me, but I still think it's important for us to say things like that, I explained. *It's wonderful how we can sense what each other feels or thinks, but I don't want us to assume we always know what the other means. I'd rather us just communicate like we'd have to if we didn't have these bracelets.*

Sebastian considered my words.

If it's important to you, I'll try.

It involves you, so it couldn't be more important to me, I assured him. Throwing back the covers, I made my way into the kitchen and selected a muffin from the container my mother had left. She and my siblings had come with me to Celenia and stayed a few days as I settled into my rented apartment, ensuring I had everything I needed to start my internship, and while I normally enjoyed spending time with them, their presence had also meant time away from Sebastian. I couldn't wait to see him again.

Looking out the window at the brightening sunlight, I realized something . . . if it was morning in Aeles, that meant it was evening in Nocens.

My heartbeat sped up as I thought about why Sebastian might have been sleeping during the day.

Are you getting ready for work? I asked hesitantly.

No, he said, and I let out a soft sigh of relief, even though I knew we couldn't avoid a conversation about his chosen occupation as an assassin forever. *I was going to try and find some information on the missing Daeval children. Hopefully I can uncover a lead or two.*

Silver-blooded children had recently gone missing in Nocens, including a teenage boy named Gregor, whose body was later found in an alley, completely drained of blood. I'd suggested any Daevals who participated in his autopsy look for trace memories, information stored in the body that would offer details on where, when, and how Gregor had received his injuries. Sebastian had passed on my suggestion to some powerful Daevals he knew, but I hadn't heard if anything had been discovered. Looking at the spelled clock on the wall, I decided to ask about it later.

Be careful in your reconnaissance, I admonished Sebastian. *I'll let you know how orientation's going a little later.*

You know I'm always careful, he replied. *And I look forward to an update.* He hesitated, then added, *I mean . . . I look forward to talking to you.*

I look forward to talking to you too, I smiled, appreciating his efforts.

It felt odd ending the conversation without telling Sebastian I loved him, as we'd always ended our conversations that way in our past life. But even though we'd done it before, we weren't at that point in our current relationship. As I felt the connection between us sever, I gazed at the white marble countertop, trying to reconcile who we'd been with who we were now.

"I'm going to see Sebastian after work," I informed Aurelius, curled in a tight ball on the sofa.

He grunted, keeping his eyes closed. "What a pleasant event to look forward to."

"We have a lot of things to talk about, particularly with Batty and Nerudian," I chided him. At the mention of the fruit bat and the dragon, Aurelius groaned and moved his paws over his eyes, although I knew his disdain was intended almost entirely for Batty. In this life, Batty was Sebastian's Cypher, but centuries ago he had been my royal advisor, back when Aeles and Nocens had been one realm and I'd been half of the Felserpent monarchy. Batty had worked tirelessly over the centuries searching for Sebastian and me and ensuring we ultimately found one another, but that was only the first step towards a much larger goal . . . which meant completing internship, figuring out the truth about my father, and shutting down the Daeval experimentation program *weren't* the only tasks clamoring for my attention. "Now that Sebastian and I remember who we are, it's time to start reuniting the realms and bringing peace between Astrals and Daevals again."

Back when Sebastian and I had been Schatten and Kareth, Astrals and Daevals had known nothing but bloodshed, living in constant war with one another until our marriage and the signing of the Blood Treaty, which brought peace to the realm. Most Astrals and Daevals alive today didn't know the realms had ever been united, and I had no idea how we would convince them of the worthiness of such a thing, but I was certain Batty would have thoughts about what to do next.

"Batty's also worried Tallus has returned," I reminded Aurelius, causing the lynx to shake his head, although this time his reaction was purely out of concern for me. What I recalled of Tallus—both what he'd done to Schatten and me and what he'd orchestrated after seizing control of our kingdom—made him a vile enemy to consider. It wasn't enough that he'd divided Aeles-Nocens . . . he'd then decreed no one with silver blood could remain in the newly established realm of Aeles. The Daevals who hadn't immediately relocated to Nocens had suffered the terrible consequences of his hatred: Daeval husbands and wives had been dragged from their homes in the middle of the night, and silver-blooded children had been stolen from their parents' arms, never to be seen again. In some instances, entire families had been subject to public executions.

I swallowed down the memories, some clearer than others but all of them awful. Leaning forward, I rested my forearms on the counter.

"I'm not certain Tallus is an immediate threat, though," I confided to Aurelius. "Shades don't normally remember anything from previous lives. The only reason Sebastian and I remember being Schatten and Kareth is because of the binding spell I cast." Hopefully Batty would know if similar spells existed. "We also need to know if there's a way to recognize Tallus, since shades hardly ever look the same from one life to the next."

Lowering my head into my hands, I massaged my forehead. As if that wasn't enough, I still needed to determine if I could recover Sebastian's mother. Given that recovrancy was outlawed in Aeles, unfortunately such a feat would have to wait until I was back in Sebastian's cave where I didn't have to worry about someone accidentally uncovering my secret.

The magnitude of everything I needed to accomplish suddenly washed over me, crashing down and threatening to overwhelm me, and even as I did my best to avoid drowning in my worries, an anxious groan escaped my lips. I had so much to do and not nearly enough hours to do it. I needed to be in multiple places at the same time, learning entirely different things, most of which needed to be kept secret, at least for the foreseeable future. How in the falling stars was I going to do this?

Something bumped against my knee, and I looked down to see Aurelius standing beside me. Lowering into a crouch, I gazed into his eyes, holding myself together even though it would have been so easy to fall apart.

"Place one pebble in a river and it might be washed away," the lynx said. "But keep placing pebbles in a river and eventually, you'll change the course of the river."

I wrapped my arms around my Cypher, burying my face in his silky white fur, clinging to him as much as to the words my father had said in an Ash Festival speech.

"Thank you," I whispered. "You're right. One thing at a time."

It wasn't going to be easy, but things that mattered rarely were. I thought back to what I'd told Demitri a few weeks ago, about how perhaps the challenges I was facing had come to me because I was capable of changing things for the better. I'd changed things for the better before, back when I'd been the Felserpent Queen, and I'd overcome seemingly impossible situations as Kareth. Much had changed since that life cycle, but one thing remained the same—no matter the obstacles, I would never stop trying to do what I believed to be right.

3

⁊⊙⁊

SEBASTIAN

*S*taring up at the stone ceiling, I berated my need for sleep, as well as my tendency to dream. Why in the burning realms did I have to have *that* dream, of all the things my mind could process while my body rested? I'd been purposefully vague about my parents to Kyra, and she hadn't pressed me to share information, but how could she not have questions after what she'd seen?

Of course, what she'd seen wasn't even close to the worst of what I'd experienced as a child. Hopefully those nightmares didn't reappear any time soon.

Batty materialized on the footboard of my bed, and I scowled, refusing to meet his gaze.

"Perhaps it is best if Kyra sees what happened," the bat offered, scratching the golden fur around his neck with the tip of a wing. "It is certainly easier than you explaining things, given that you refuse to speak about them."

"Just because she and I are connected through these bracelets doesn't mean I want her to know everything about me!" I all but shouted.

"You're connected because you bound your shades together centuries ago," Batty corrected me. "The bracelets merely offer you a unique way to communicate."

I rolled my eyes before untangling the sheets from where they'd become wrapped around my legs, an unwanted reminder of my flailing during the nightmare. Once I'd freed myself, I hopped out of bed and hurried out of the alcove that served as my bedroom.

"Kyra will not think less of you because of what she sees in your memories," the bat called as I made my way to the kitchen and put together enough food to pass for a meal. "If anything, they will help her understand you more."

I hated when my Cypher was right. Logically, I knew Kyra would never use my past against me. At the same time, I couldn't instantly overcome years of life experience insisting that sharing personal information simply gave someone ammunition to attack me with when I least expected it.

Unused to having so many feelings stirring inside me—and conflicting ones, at that—I sped through washing my plate and utensils before dressing in my usual black breeches, tunic, and boots.

"I'm going to Vartox," I said, slipping my weapons belt around my waist, "so while I'm gone, do something useful and make sure everything looks nice for when Kyra comes over."

The bat clapped his wings so vigorously, he almost fell over backwards and let out a grunt as he righted himself. "I shall make every last crystal shine! Will she be spending the night?"

I'd been on the verge of opening a portal, but the bat's words made me pause. Kyra and I were in a relationship now, and folks in a relationship often spent the night with one another . . . in fact, they often lived in the same house. Was Kyra planning on spending the night? She'd stayed over before, but out of convenience, and certainly not due to any romantic attachment.

Then again, in a past life, the two of us had been wildly in love and even married, spending every night together. Of course, things were different now, since *we* were different, but the longer

I considered Batty's question, the more I found myself having a positive reaction to it, which was surprising, given my preference for solitude.

"I don't know," I finally replied. "I didn't ask her." Certain I would most likely regret my next words, I nevertheless asked, "Do you think she's expecting to stay over?"

"I think it is always wiser to ask than expect," replied Batty, flying over to perch on the back of the sofa. "Hence why talking about things is so important. But I shall make sure there is plenty of planterian food for her, regardless of whether she sleeps over or not."

I nodded my thanks, conjured a portal, and stepped through to Vartox.

The stars were winking brightly across the sky as I made my way to one of the larger taverns on Diafol Way, the main thorough-fare running through the capital of Nocens. It was still relatively early, but I had the entire night ahead of me, as Kyra wouldn't be done with internship for several hours. While I doubted I would uncover anything realm-shattering on my first night of reconnaissance, I had to start somewhere. That meant being out around others who liked to talk, and while socializing was a necessary part of information-gathering, it was also the part I liked least.

Stepping inside the tavern, I noted the exits and skimmed the crowd to see if I recognized anyone. Daevals filled nearly every available space, laughing as they sat at tables made of por-ous volcanic rock or enjoying the privacy of curtained booths. A line of patrons pressed towards the shiny black basalt bar running the length of an entire wall. A handful of others made their way to the secluded rooms reserved for the most affluent customers, those who preferred to take their drinks, perception-altering substances, or other forms of entertainment in private.

I slipped through the churning mass of bodies until I reached the bar, ordered an ale, and claimed a seat abandoned by its previous occupant. Thankfully, there was no music tonight, as that would have made the headache-inducing din even worse. Sipping my drink, I made small talk with the Daevals who rotated in and out on either side of me. While I knew a handful, having purchased information from them before, no one reacted suspiciously to any of the baited topics I mentioned.

Swallowing the last of my ale, I drummed my fingers against the bar, considering. There was one other Daeval I could try contacting, someone who seemed to have an ear pressed against every closed door in Vartox. While his information was often of no consequence—I didn't care what color a government official had repainted her dining room or who a certain socialite was sleeping with—every now and then, he passed on something useful.

The only problem was, acquiring such potentially useful information meant spending time with Devlin.

It wasn't that I disliked him, exactly . . . it was that being around him was always such a production. I preferred anonymity and working from the shadows, whereas Devlin lived in a perpetual spotlight and worked hard to ensure Daevals across the realm knew his name.

Sighing, I pulled my peerin from my pocket, running my thumb over the hinged coral-colored device. I was already in town; I might as well contact him, and hopefully the Fates would favor my efforts.

"Sebastian! Over here!"

Glancing around the tavern, my eyes finally landed on the

shouting Daeval, and even though I'd asked to meet him, I still briefly considered opening a portal and disappearing. But, no matter how much Devlin irritated me, I wouldn't do such a thing, primarily because he was my best customer's son, but also because I supposed he was the closest thing I had to a friend, besides his sister, Eslee.

Voices dropped low as the other patrons noticed the Daeval, and the crowd between us parted as he made his way towards me. The gasps and muffled exclamations I heard would only feed Devlin's already oversized ego. His carefully styled brown hair was brushed back on the sides, making it easy to see the multiple gold hoops in his ears that matched the one in his left nostril. He was wearing black leather breeches and a sleeveless tunic made of such thin blue silk it left little to the imagination. Numerous inked drawings crawled over his bare arms, and his butterscotch eyes, identical to Eslee's, glowed brightly in the dim lighting.

He stopped before me and grinned broadly, ignoring the semicircle forming behind him, curious or awestruck onlookers trying to catch a glimpse of the infamous Daeval. He stuck out his hand, and I shook it; at least he knew better than to try and hug me.

"Now, this is a surprise!" he said. "I can't even remember the last time you let me know you were in Vartox; usually I hear about it from someone who saw you disappearing through a portal. I was starting to think the only thing you liked about my invitations to get a drink was ignoring them." He gave me a knowing smirk. "Who were you here to see this time—my father or uncle?"

"Neither," I replied, prompting him to raise his dark eyebrows. "I'm here on reconnaissance."

"That sounds serious. You might need more than just a drink." He gestured for me to follow him.

I sighed but fell in after him, already rehearsing the excuse I would make to leave after we'd spoken a while. Waving, smiling, and calling out to those he knew, Devlin made his way to a roped-off door guarded by a large Daeval with numerous scars on her face. She dipped her head at Devlin and pulled the rope aside, allowing the two of us to enter a sumptuously furnished suite. As the door closed behind us, I was grateful it muffled the noise from the main chamber of the tavern.

Devlin dropped down onto a plush red sofa and let out a satisfied sigh before reaching for an ornate black and silver opium pipe laid out among other paraphernalia on a small table. Inhaling deeply, he closed his eyes and let out a slow breath. As he blinked his eyes open, his pupils pulsed, and although he offered me the pipe, I declined, preferring to keep a clear head any time I was in public. He rolled his eyes before taking another long inhale.

"I don't know that I've ever seen you out without an entourage," I said.

Devlin chuckled and placed the pipe back on the table. "Eslee's meeting me here later with some of her friends. But if they take too long, I'm sure I'll find someone to entertain me." A predatory smile spread across his face, and I scowled at him. I'd never liked his casual attitude towards sleeping with women. Then again, as long as the encounters were consensual, I supposed it didn't really matter how many partners he'd had.

"And speaking of being entertained," he said smoothly, "who was the Astral I saw you with a while back at Uncle Caz's? Eslee said her name was Kyra but didn't know more than that."

I told him the same story I'd told his father and uncle. "I was looking for something in Aeles, and an Astral accidentally fell through my portal. Caz helped me get her back to her realm, but we stayed in touch."

Devlin clearly knew there was more to the story, but he wisely kept his questions to himself. "I've always wondered how different

Astral women are from Daeval women . . . besides their blood, of course."

The fire stirred inside my veins even as I forced myself to shrug. I didn't like when someone took an interest in something that belonged to me.

Kyra is not an object in your possession, scolded Batty indignantly through our connection. *She is with you because she chooses to be.*

I ignored the bat in favor of crafting a response to Devlin. "Well, seeing as how I only know one, I certainly can't tell you anything interesting about Astral women." I was careful to sound nonchalant; if Devlin thought he'd gotten under my skin, there would be no end to his needling.

"When are you seeing her again?" he pressed.

"Devlin, I reached out to you against my better judgment. Don't make me regret it."

Devlin studied me for a moment before correctly interpreting I had nothing further to say on the subject of Kyra. He then turned his attention to a large brass hookah constructed of exceptional filigree work and motioned to the bowlful of unlit coals.

"Would you mind?" He flashed me a bright smile.

I rolled my eyes but nevertheless sent a flame toward the coals, quickly heating them as Devlin added small pieces of fruit to the water base before tipping a pouch of tobacco into the bowl.

"So," I said, needing to gather some kind of information to make this evening worth it, "what are you up to these days?"

Devlin was two years older than I was, but at twenty-two he still acted as if the sole purpose of his life was to attend galas, purchase expensive clothes, and spend family money. He took absolutely no interest in the family business, which I knew irked Dunston to no end, but I also knew Devlin's mother indulged him the same way Dunston doted on Eslee.

Devlin began recounting his recent exploits, and I paid only partial attention to his long and dramatic recitation. When he mentioned how someone had recently approached him to act as a patron for a new, privately funded orphanage, though, I couldn't contain a derisive snort.

"I know!" he agreed. "It's completely ridiculous! As if anything about me screams *the patron saint of needy children*! Why wouldn't he go to my father?"

I assumed because Dunston was seen as a shrewd businessman you crossed at your own risk, whereas Devlin was known for spending enormous amounts of money on frivolous pursuits. I would never say such a thing, though, and merely shrugged.

Devlin rearranged a pillow behind his back. "Besides, aren't there enough orphanages in Nocens? Why do we need more?"

"Did you tell the man that?"

"Of course. Then he gave me some speech about how all the orphanages here receive government subsidies, which means there's a lot of oversight and rules and sometimes that actually hinders helping the children."

"So, he wanted you to fund an orphanage with no oversight that doesn't answer to anyone because that would be better for the children?" I frowned at the absurdity of such a thing.

"That's what it sounded like," nodded Devlin. "To be honest, I was worried there was a lot the man wasn't telling me. And the last thing I want to do is bring down the wrath of my father for investing in a business deal the government turns out not to like."

"What do you think was really going on?" I leaned forward, resting my forearms against my knees.

Devlin took a long inhale from the hookah before responding. "I was worried it might involve something even *I* would consider unsavory—which I know is saying something—some sort of underage brothel or child labor program. I don't know, exactly, but . . . something was wrong. Also," he made a face, "I was rather inebriated at the time, but I could have sworn there was something off about the man. You know that tingling sensation you get when you sense golden blood? I thought I felt that, but no one around me seemed bothered, so it might have just been me."

Something was certainly wrong, but I suspected it wasn't what Devlin was thinking. If I was an Astral looking to get my hands on Daeval children, a privately funded orphanage with no government oversight would be the perfect way to ensure unrestricted access. The children could be taken to Aeles for experimentation without anyone being the wiser when they never returned.

Of course, even though the logic was sound, that didn't mean it was correct . . . but there was no harm in looking into it.

"Who approached you about this?" I asked. Devlin gave me a puzzled look, so I added, "If this man finds someone to fund his project, and the government gets wind of it, there's a good chance either your father or uncle will hire me to take him out." I was pleased with my ability to concoct such a believable story on the spot. "I want to be ready when the time comes."

Devlin ran a hand over his jaw. "He probably said his name at one point, but as I mentioned, I was somewhat inebriated . . . possibly more than somewhat. He approached me when I was at Tarfann's a week or so ago but didn't leave any contact information, so I don't know how to get in touch with him."

I filed away the name of the eatery, then let Devlin talk about other, less consequential things before I stood to take my leave. As I did, his Cypher, a large black panther named Onyx, suddenly materialized. He and Devlin shared a long look as they communicated silently, after which Devlin turned to me.

"Eslee and her friends are on their way. Why don't you stay? There'll be plenty of opportunities to enjoy yourself."

"I've got other matters to attend to," I said, even though it was unfortunate I'd miss Eslee, as I'd always preferred her company to her brother's. "Tell your sister I said hello, though."

"Only if you let me meet Kyra the next time she's here," he grinned, and while I knew he was mostly teasing, a part of him was also serious. I wouldn't put it past Devlin to make up an excuse to start spending time at Caz's office, hoping to bump into Kyra while she was using his uncle's special intersector. Thankfully, the suppressor medallion back in my cave allowed me to portal in and out of Aeles as I pleased, making Caz's intersector unnecessary.

Thinking about Devlin's fascination with Kyra, I realized something . . . she was going to be spending all day at internship, working alongside other interns, as well as supervisors, at least some of whom might, like Devlin, develop an interest in her.

That was entirely unacceptable and as soon as I got someplace where I could hear myself think, I'd contact her and learn exactly who she would be working with.

4

KYRA

 I ran my hands over the skirt of my dark green dress, straightening the fabric that always reminded me of the forest before glancing around the spacious auditorium. We'd begun orientation with a few introductory games, followed by a tour, and now it was time to hear from our first speaker. The other interns were all Astrals I'd gone to school with, although I hadn't seen most of them over the summer, and I'd accepted their condolences on the death of my father as best I could. I thought I'd spoken with everyone when Hymnia Narsis turned around in the seat in front of me, sympathy sweeping over her heart-shaped face.

"I'm sorry about your father," she offered. "He was so kind. My mother's still wearing a black mourning ribbon for him. I don't know if you remember, but he helped heal her a few years ago after her sister passed away . . . she was so despondent, some days she couldn't even get out of bed. We were really worried about her, but of course your father knew exactly what to do, and we'll never forget him."

"Thank you," I smiled, even as my chest tightened. It wasn't that I disliked such condolences—I was glad folks remembered my father so fondly—but each time someone shared a memory about him I was forcibly reminded he wasn't just a building away in his office, waiting for me to have a break so we could get scones, or in a nearby auditorium, giving a lecture to a crowd of rapt listeners. He was gone, and I would have to navigate every day of the rest of my life without him. I struggled to draw a full breath, and the circular walls wavered in my peripheral vision, making it seem like they were moving towards me. I glanced towards the door, wondering if I should go collect myself in the hallway, when a loud buzzing noise suddenly rang out.

It sounded like a horde of cicadas had awakened in the room, and everyone quickly reached for their peerins. The government didn't often send out mass communications but when they did, it was important. My pulse quickened as I flipped open the hinged copper lids and scanned the scrolling text.

"There's been an avalanche!" Hymnia exclaimed. "In the southern part of the Wystern Mountains."

Even though the avalanche had occurred hundreds of miles from my mother and siblings, it had still occurred in the province where they lived, making it far too close to home. I sent a quick message to my mother and felt a wash of relief when she responded, assuring me everyone was fine. As I told her I'd call during my first free period, I couldn't help thinking how my father had died in a similar natural disaster. Earthquakes and avalanches had been unheard of in Aeles up until a month or so ago, and while I understood there was no controlling them, I wished I knew why they were occurring or at least how to predict them. Contemplating the possibility of my family moving to a province that hadn't experienced a natural disaster, I read the government communication again. Soldiers had been dispatched to aid in rescue efforts and while not all citizens were accounted for, the search would continue until everyone was found.

The door in the side of the auditorium opened, pulling me from my thoughts, and as the other interns quieted and peerins were put away, I focused on Lionel, the internship coordinator, making his way to the podium. I had interacted with him a few times during the internship application process and had always found him unfailingly polite, as well as quite knowledgeable.

"Greetings, interns," said Lionel, setting down the portfolio he'd been carrying before grasping either side of the white quartz podium. "I'm sure you've all heard about the avalanche. Please know the government is doing everything they can, and we'll keep everyone updated on the rescue efforts. We don't know what caused the avalanche, just as we don't know what caused the earthquake last month, but the brightest minds in Aeles are working on it, which means answers will surely be found."

That was good to know and helped alleviate some of my anxiety. I had no idea how to protect my family from things even the government couldn't explain, but at least this was one problem I didn't have to solve by myself. Astrals with specific knowledge of the realm would uncover what was happening and either fix it or provide guidance on how best to be prepared in the future.

The other interns nodded, and Lionel drew a deep breath, which served to soften his serious expression into a smile he almost seemed comfortable giving. His brown eyes shone with sincerity as he gazed out at the gathered crowd.

"In the meantime, I hope you all had an enjoyable break, just as I hope you're all ready to dive into your new assignments. Congratulations on your placements; as you know, they were extremely competitive this year."

The gold bracelet on my wrist vibrated, and my stomach dropped. Why was Sebastian reaching out so soon? Had he uncovered something looking into the kidnapped Daevalic children? Was he hurt? Heartbeat quickening, I pressed my fingertips against the jewelry while trying to appear as if I was simply rearranging my long sleeve.

Are you alright? I whispered, even though I was speaking in my mind and didn't technically need to lower my voice.

Of course. I just wanted to see how you were doing.

I was relieved to hear he was safe and while I appreciated him working to express himself more clearly, this was also a terrible time to attempt a conversation. I didn't want to appear uninterested in Lionel's speech, and I also didn't want to miss anything important the coordinator shared.

Do you know when you'll be finished yet? Sebastian's voice drowned out whatever Lionel was saying.

We're just now hearing from supervisors and support staff. Even though I'd spoken quickly, I still missed the next words Lionel said. Pausing to listen, I was glad to hear he was reviewing things I was already familiar with, such as dress codes and timeliness. *I'll let you know as soon as I have an exact time of departure,* I assured Sebastian, and thinking that would be the end of it, I was surprised when he spoke again.

This isn't one of those places where they expect you to be at the office day and night, is it? I've heard of jobs like that in Nocens, and you can't do that.

I stiffened, not liking the way he'd said I *couldn't* do something, but we could discuss that later when we were together. I started to say as much but Sebastian wasn't done.

Have you seen anyone you know? Will you be working near Demitri?

Lionel must have asked a question because roughly half the interns raised their hands. My stomach did a somersault, and I tried to slow the panic spreading through me. I *hated* trying to do two things at once and ultimately failing to do either successfully. While I loved how easily Sebastian and I could communicate, for the first time I realized there could be challenges associated with him being able to contact me at any given moment.

I haven't seen Demitri yet, but we're meeting later at a café, I said as fast as I could while nodding and catching every other word Lionel said about detailed documentation.

Burning realms, Kyra! Sebastian's snarl was so loud, I jumped in my seat, earning myself a handful of odd looks from the other interns around me. Feeling heat rise to my cheeks, I sank down in my chair as I stared at the wall behind Lionel.

I was going to bring this up later, continued Sebastian, *but I don't think it's a good idea for you to spend time alone with Demitri.*

I let out a controlled exhale, counting to five as the breath left my lungs. I wished Sebastian knew Demitri would never be a threat to our relationship. Of course, I couldn't tell him why without revealing something incredibly personal about my best friend. While I could never predict what would be shared through our bracelets, the jewelry seemed to limit itself to memories, thoughts, or feelings directly involving Sebastian or me, which meant so far I'd managed to keep Demitri's secret to myself. I also wanted Sebastian to believe me about Demitri because he trusted me, not because my best friend's romantic interests ran exclusively to men.

I'm meeting Demitri at a café, I explained, *which isn't the same as being alone with him. I'm going to ask him about using different locator spells to find any other suppressor medallions that might still be out there.*

While Demitri and Sebastian both knew about the suppressor medallion I'd found, I hadn't told either of them how I'd *actually* come to possess it, discovering it in my father's medical kit. Even though they deserved the truth, I couldn't bear to tell them—especially Sebastian—without knowing what my father had been using the medallion for.

I understand this is important to you, I continued to Sebastian, *and I want you to feel comfortable with what I'm doing when we're apart, but I really need to pay attention to what's being said right now, so can we discuss this more when we're together?*

Fine, sighed Sebastian, and while it was obvious he didn't like my answer, I appreciated his willingness to postpone what was clearly going to be a difficult conversation. *Let me know how you're doing later, alright?*

I will. Touching the bracelet, I severed our connection. It seemed I'd turned my focus back to the auditorium at just the right time because Lionel's smile widened as he clasped his hands in front of his chest.

"Now, while I appreciate your attention, that's more than enough from me. We are so very honored to have with us this morning one of our esteemed senators who, even though he's still relatively new to bureaucracy, has already made quite the name for himself."

Lionel's voice grew louder.

"He has a particular interest in the protection of Astral culture and stemming the ever-present tide of corruption from Nocens. He's sponsored over twenty laws and campaigned vigorously on issues including improvements in Astral health, the preservation of historical Aelian artifacts, and increased cooperation between government and military research. I'm fortunate to work with him on a daily basis as his personal assistant, and I can attest he is truly the future of our government and our realm. Interns, please join me in welcoming Senator Tenebris Rex!"

Lionel began clapping enthusiastically as the door in the side of the room opened and Senator Rex strode in, waving and smiling. He came forward and shook Lionel's hand, clapping him on the back as he did.

I joined the other interns in their applause and tried my best to smile, even though Lionel's comment about "corruption from Nocens" was painful to hear, especially since I knew it to be blatantly untrue. If Astrals would interact with Daevals instead of barricading themselves behind the Blood Alarm, my kind would realize how wrong we'd been about those with silver blood.

Lionel grabbed his portfolio and slid into an empty seat as Senator Rex turned to address us.

"Whenever I need to feel especially good about myself, I ask Lionel to introduce me at a speaking engagement," he said with a mischievous smile. "He has a notable tendency for exaggeration, and his descriptions always give me something to strive for."

The senator's glacial blue eyes moved slowly over the audience as he spoke, and when they met mine, they flashed with recognition, and he dipped his chin slightly. His reddish-blonde hair was longer than the last time I'd seen him, the curls more pronounced, and the white pearls on his gold jacket gleamed like miniature moons.

"I'm so pleased to be here with you today." His expression turned wistful. "I remember sitting in those seats, wondering what internship would be like and where I might find myself in a year or two. For me, there was never a choice other than politics . . . it has always been my calling and my duty. And while I know the mundane toil of government work isn't for everyone, some of you," he smiled directly at me, "are just beginning what I imagine will be incredibly lustrous careers here in Celenia."

I smiled back, hoping he was right. Completing internship was the next requirement for following in my father's footsteps and becoming the *Princeps Shaman*, the highest-ranking healer in Aeles. Not only did I want to know everything I could about healing to help as many patients as possible, I also viewed holding the public position as another opportunity to lessen the antagonism between Astrals and Daevals. In fact, my first order of business after being named to the position would be hosting a conference and inviting healers from Nocens to attend, allowing us to share what we each knew of healing.

Senator Rex spoke a bit more about the various educational opportunities available to interns and offered his support anytime someone wished to speak about career possibilities. He then shifted his weight, straightening his shoulders as his expression became more serious. I bit the inside of my lip, hoping he would conclude his speech and send us on our way even as apprehension stirred in my chest.

"Now, perhaps more than ever," said Senator Rex, "we are in need of your new perspectives and impressive talents. While Daevals have always attempted to enter our realm, their attacks have become more serious of late. Those with silver blood are nothing like us, and no matter what well-meaning Astrals with questionable sympathies might say, there will never be a chance for peace between Aeles and Nocens because Daevals simply won't have it."

What attacks was the senator talking about? The last time the Blood Alarm had gone off had been because of Sebastian, but that hadn't been an attack. Did Senator Rex have information I didn't, or was he making things appear worse than they really were?

"Many Astrals believe the military will be our salvation when it comes to winning the war against Daevals," Senator Rex continued, "and while our soldiers are certainly important, there are those in the government—like myself—who believe winning battles of an intellectual nature is just as important, if not more so. After all, we fight for our beliefs, making what we believe a singularly motivating force not to be underestimated."

Judging by the murmured agreements and vigorous nods rippling through the interns, the senator's words had struck a chord. Everyone's attention was fixed on him and glancing at the interns on either side of me, I momentarily wondered if they were blinking.

"Perhaps one day," Senator Rex's voice grew louder, "we won't have to tolerate the evils of Daevals anymore. Perhaps one day we will fulfill our grand purpose and put an end to their destructive ways. Perhaps one day we will bring about a true peace . . . a world without pain, without loss, and without suffering . . . in short, a world without a drop of silver blood!"

The interns around me leaped to their feet, clapping excitedly, many whistling or cheering. The senator certainly had a way of bringing folks together, and as the applause swelled, my heart pounded out a staccato beat; fighting down my rising anger, I forced myself to join the standing crowd.

I felt terrible doing so, betraying the man I'd been married to a lifetime ago and was currently romantically involved with, but I also didn't want my first day as an intern to be marked by publicly disagreeing with a senator . . . especially a senator I was going to be working with. Looking around as I pantomimed a few claps, my heart sank. How in the falling stars was I going to change Astrals' minds when they were so eager to despise Daevals?

Senator Rex flashed a pleased smile before gesturing for everyone to sit back down.

"I'm certain you all have more important things to do than listen to me prattle on," he said, even as several interns loudly assured him otherwise. "Thank you for your attention, and enjoy the rest of your orientation!"

Lionel quickly stood and led the group in another round of applause before calling out instructions on where to go next.

As I gathered my things and made my way towards the door, someone tapped my shoulder, and I turned to find Senator Rex smiling at me. Part of me wanted to jump to the defense of Daevals and tell the politician exactly how wrong he was, but I recalled the writings of Caritas, the Gifter of Charity: "Praise in public; criticize behind closed doors." Arguing in a packed auditorium the first day of internship wouldn't shift Senator Rex's thinking about Daevals . . . if there was even a chance of altering his perspective, it would happen by speaking privately with him. Plus, I didn't want him to change his mind about letting me work on whatever Father had been doing with silver blood, so despite my feelings, I returned his smile.

"Ms. Valorian," he offered a slight bow. "Lovely to see you, as always. How's your orientation going?"

"Senator Rex." I returned the bow. "So far, your welcome speech has been the most memorable part."

While my words were true, I hadn't intended them as a compliment, but Senator Rex beamed as if he'd won an award. "I'm so pleased I can always count on your support when it comes to the health and well-being of our citizens," he said. "I wanted to let you know Healer Omnurion has gone to aid in healing those injured in the avalanche. I'm headed there now to offer whatever support I can, but we're both looking forward to meeting with you next week." He took a step closer and lowered his voice. "I've blocked out plenty of time in your schedule for you to pick up where your father's research left off."

My heart beat faster, and I nodded. While I was grateful Senator Rex was eager for me to join his project, his obvious interest in comparing gold and silver blood was more than a little unnerving.

"I'm looking forward to it," I replied. "If there's anything I need to do to prepare, please let me know."

"Simply your presence and your enthusiasm for research will be more than enough," assured Senator Rex. "Now if you'll excuse me, I must be off, but enjoy the rest of your day."

Apologizing for not being able to stay and speak with the

other interns crowding around him, Senator Rex strode out the door. As I watched him leave, a voice behind me said, "You should be pleased at what an impression you've made."

I turned to find Lionel standing there, hugging his portfolio and smiling proudly at me. "You notice Senator Rex didn't go out of his way to speak with any *other* interns," he pointed out.

"I'm excited to be working with him," I said, which was true even though it wasn't the whole truth. Specifically, I was excited to have the chance to exonerate my father of any wrongdoing. Given that Lionel was the senator's personal assistant, perhaps he might let something useful slip, since he clearly enjoyed talking about the man, so I added, "Senator Rex certainly seems very knowledgeable about Daevals."

Lionel nodded enthusiastically. "He's exceptionally well-educated. I don't know how he managed to gain so much experience in the field, especially since he's not even thirty, but he certainly knows our foes."

It took a concerted effort on my part to keep from grimacing at hearing those with silver blood referred to as "foes," but I managed and quickly took my leave. While I knew my experiences with Sebastian, as well as the memories of our past life together, had changed how I thought about Daevals, I hadn't realized just how *much* I'd changed until this morning. I no longer fit neatly into the life I'd led before learning the truth about myself, and while that gave me a unique opportunity, it was also one more loss to grieve.

5

KYRA

*S*tepping outside, I closed my eyes and inhaled deeply, letting the warm Aelian sunshine bathe my face as a gentle breeze stirred a nearby wind harp, producing a low, melodious chime. Making my way down the wide steps, I hurried across the courtyard, sunlight striking the opals beneath my feet and scattering colorful rainbows across my path.

The banners of various *Donecs* fluttered overhead, and the ever-present sound of water filled the air, flowing down intricate sculptures to form shallow pools or bubbling from fountains small and large. The immaculate city shone: Pearl, gold, and glass glimmered everywhere my gaze fell. The wide boulevards in Celenia were lined with life-sized statues of the Gifters, and I paused by one of my favorites, Acies, the Gifter of Wisdom.

Closing my eyes, I offered a silent prayer.

Please help me navigate internship and being around those who despise Daevals . . . especially while I'm counting down the hours until I'm reunited with the Daeval I was married to in a past life.

Opening my eyes, I smiled my thanks to the Gifter, then pulled my peerin from my bag and rang my mother. Her blue-grey eyes looked tired, and I couldn't imagine she'd slept well since losing my father, but her smile was broad and her auburn curls danced around her face as she assured me she hadn't even felt the avalanche.

"I had no idea until the government sent out the communi-cation," she said. "Seren and Enif are at school, but I spoke with each of them, and they're fine."

"I'm fine too!" called my youngest brother, Deneb, from somewhere out of sight.

"Are you planning on coming home for the weekend?" asked my mother. "I assumed with internship starting you'd have meet-and-greets or parties or other fun things to do, but we always love seeing you."

I hated purposefully deceiving my mother, but given every-thing that had happened with my father, I thought it best to give her a little more time before I shared the truth about Sebastian and our past life together, not to mention our current relationship. I also had to admit that sharing life-altering revelations with those who knew me best was more intimidating than I'd anticipated.

"I do have a lot going on this weekend," I said, trying to avoid an outright lie, "so perhaps we can all do lunch or dinner sometime next week!"

After agreeing to coordinate a visit in the next few days, I ended the call as Aurelius materialized beside me. He'd been vis-iting with other Cyphers while I'd been in meetings, but thanks to our connection, he was aware of all that had happened.

I think you would do well to be cautious around Senator Rex, he said, speaking into my mind rather than out loud. *His speech today, and the way so many interns agreed with him . . .*

He shook his head, and I let out an equally frustrated sigh.

Most of them were probably just acting like the bigoted Astrals we've been raised to be, I said. *But I was surprised by his comments at the end; usually the propaganda the government spreads is about maintain-ing our separateness from Daevals. It's a huge leap to go from isolating ourselves to bringing about a world without a drop of silver blood.*

Your sister's Cypher mentioned something to me a while back. Aurelius ran a paw over his ear. *Do you recall how, when Senator Rex and Adonis came to hear your story about falling through a portal with a Daeval, Sappho made quite the disruptive entrance?*

I nodded. Sappho was my sister Seren's Cypher, and I easily remembered how odd I'd found the sea snake's behavior, appearing out of nowhere and slithering over Demitri's feet, even though she knew he was terrified of snakes.

Sappho later told me something about the way Senator Rex was speaking to you bothered her, prompting her disruption, explained Aurelius. *She felt like he was trying to coerce you into agreeing with him. Now, while I don't believe the old legends about snakes hypnotizing folks, I've lived long enough to know reptiles are particularly sensitive to spells associated with mental manipulation. Have you ever felt anything like that when speaking with the senator?*

No, but I've always been focused on other things, so I could have overlooked it. I studied the lynx's face closely, thinking back to how the other interns had responded to the senator's speech. *Do you think he uses some sort of mind control spell on whomever he's speaking to?*

It pains me to admit this, but I'm not certain. Aurelius pinned his ears back against his head. *I believe Sappho felt something, and what occurred with the interns was certainly disconcerting, but without more information, we can't reach any meaningful conclusions. Just be cautious around the senator.*

I'll be cautious around anyone working for the Astral government, I said, and while Aurelius nodded, I could tell he was still unsettled.

It'll be fine, I assured my Cypher. *I just need to work with Senator Rex long enough to find out what Father was doing and get the evidence we need to shut down the experimentation program. Then I'll work exclusively with Healer Omnurion and focus on becoming the* Princeps Shaman.

I cannot imagine it will be that simple, sighed Aurelius, *but in the meantime, Halo's asking where we are.* The lynx gave himself a good shake before pricking his tufted ears. *Shall we continue with more pleasant activities?*

Demitri was already sitting at a table under the blue and gold striped awning of Bevand's, my favorite café and where I'd first told him about my accidental foray into Vaneklus while trying to save my father. He jumped to his feet when he saw me, making his chair tilt and upsetting his Cypher, Halo, a red-tailed hawk. Running forward, I let myself settle into the welcome familiarity of my best friend's embrace; no one gave hugs like Demitri.

"It's been forever since I've seen you!" he exclaimed, giving me a final squeeze before we settled into our chairs. Demitri had already ordered a chocolate coffee for me, and I appreciated the whipped cream piled generously on top.

"It's been too long," I agreed, wrapping my hands around the warm mug. We'd spoken through our peerins a few times over the past week, but it was unusual for us to go so long without getting together. "How are you? How's work?"

Demitri rolled his eyes and shook his head, causing his light brown hair to fall across his forehead before he brushed it away with his fingertips.

"Work has been one thing after another," he complained. "Originally the theme for autumn was going to focus on messages about caring. We were going to feature the Gifter of Charity and encourage citizens to create art, music, plays, and literature depicting the virtue of helping your fellow Astral. But last week my supervisor said plans had changed and the message from the *Donec Auctoritus* was going to focus on protecting ourselves from the corrupting influence of Daevals." He scowled. "Now all the artwork we've created has to be changed to feature the Gifter of Protection, and it's not as if Praesidio and Caritas are inter-changeable!"

I took a sip of my drink, quickly wiping away the white froth that clung to my nose. I'd been so happy at seeing Demitri, I had temporarily pushed Senator Rex's speech and the interns' reaction from my mind, but now the apprehension I'd felt for most of the morning resurfaced, churning alongside the chocolate and coffee in my stomach.

"Why do you think they made the change?" I asked. "Do you know who ordered it?"

"No. But it must have come from very high up for an entire campaign to be scrapped. As for *why* they made the change . . ." Demitri's voice trailed off as he raised his sandy-colored eye-brows. "It could be because a Daeval successfully bypassed the Blood Alarm and made it into Aeles for the first time in centuries."

I pressed my lips together and lowered my gaze to the mosaic tabletop, not liking Demitri's tone even though I suspected he was right and Sebastian's recent actions were, in fact, to blame.

"Only a handful of Astrals know about that." I felt as if I needed to make some effort to defend Sebastian, even if it was a losing battle.

"But those few Astrals happen to be very powerful," argued Demitri. "I wouldn't be surprised if the directive came straight from the upper ranks of the military."

"Or from Senator Rex," I said, careful to keep my voice low. "He seems to be single-handedly stoking anti-Daeval sentiments." I told Demitri about the senator's speech, and he listened closely before nodding.

"I think a lot of Astrals are feeling even more opposed to Daevals than usual," he said.

I pointed at a nearby bulletin stand, where the moving headline on the daily paper assured readers that a new government study definitively proved at least some Daevals were cannibals whose appetite waxed and waned with the moon.

"Because the government is encouraging those feelings," I said, "and not only encouraging them, but inciting them. It's one thing for government officials to want to uphold the status quo and keep us separate from Daevals; it's quite another for them to be calling for a world where Daevals aren't even allowed to exist. How are things supposed to get better if Astrals are told we're too different to get along with Daevals and led to believe they're evil creatures who can't be trusted?"

"Speaking of evil creatures who can't be trusted," Demitri flashed me an obviously fake smile, "how's our favorite cave-dwelling fire-wielder?"

"The correct term is Pyromancer, and Sebastian is fine. In fact, I'm seeing him tonight."

Demitri frowned.

"The two of us are in a relationship," I reminded him. "It's normal we'd spend time together."

"Are you planning any more near-death experiences this weekend?" His frown deepened, and his voice was sharp. "I should clear my schedule."

"Demitri," I said softly, reaching out and laying a hand on his forearm. Admittedly, his first time meeting Sebastian had been traumatic . . . I'd been gravely injured while working with Sebastian to retrieve Rhannu, the sword that had belonged to him as Schatten. While Sebastian had ultimately burned the poison from my body, Demitri still hadn't forgiven him for exposing me to danger, no matter how many times I insisted I'd made my own decision in going after the sword.

"I can't in good conscience say you shouldn't be with him," Demitri admitted. "I'd be a bigger hypocrite than I already am if I didn't stand by my belief that everyone should be allowed to court or wed whomever they like. But I still don't trust him, and I worry about you. I'm trying, I really am, because I love you and I want you to be happy, but it's just going to take a while."

I appreciated Demitri's honesty, and while some part of me wished my best friend would accept Sebastian without question, if I put my own feelings aside, I could understand his concern. I wanted to tell him the history Sebastian and I had together, but it seemed like something the two of us should discuss before I shared such a revelation, so I steered the conversation away from Sebastian.

"I'm in desperate need of your spell-casting expertise," I said to Demitri. "What do you know about locator spells? I know there are different types, but I don't know what distinguishes one from another. I'd like to locate something without alerting everyone around me when I've found it."

According to Laycus, guardian of the realm of the dead and my begrudging recovrancy mentor, seven suppressor medallions had been created hundreds of years ago. While I didn't know why they'd been created, or by whom, they allowed someone with silver blood to be in Aeles without setting off the Blood Alarm. I suspected any that still existed were housed in the experimentation facility in Rynstyn, although I didn't know for sure. I couldn't exactly go digging through random drawers and cabinets searching for them, and the only locator spells I knew were simple ones from childhood that were far too obvious to be used surreptitiously.

Demitri arched an eyebrow, aware there was more I wasn't choosing to share, but before he could ask questions his body froze even as his eyes widened.

"Don't look now," he whispered, barely moving his mouth, "but Adonis is behind you, and I think he's headed this way." His expression soured. "His new military partner is with him too. Do they have to go everywhere together?"

I pretended not to notice Demitri's jealousy, as I was actually happy to see the soldiers; besides my best friend, they were the only other Astrals who knew about Sebastian, meaning I could be around them without constantly needing to watch what I said. Adonis had met Sebastian while helping him heal the injuries I'd sustained recovering Rhannu. His assigned military partner, Nigel, had also met Sebastian, back when he'd sent the Daeval to his untimely death in the unicorn sanctuary. Taking a calculated risk, I'd told the soldiers about Sebastian being tortured by Astrals in Rynstyn as a child, and while both men had been shocked to learn what our kind were capable of, they'd readily agreed to help determine if such experimentation was still taking place and if so, to try and end it.

Two figures in dark blue uniforms came to a stop at our table, the gold trim on the soldiers' sleeves and pants glinting in the sunlight.

"Well, isn't this a nice surprise!" declared Adonis, grinning broadly at Demitri. While it could have been my imagination, I thought I saw his smile falter briefly as his gaze landed on me, although I couldn't imagine why. "And . . . Kyra. Is it just the two of you?"

I nodded but quickly stood and moved my chair to make more room. "Please, join us."

"We wouldn't want to interrupt," Nigel started to say right as Adonis said, "Thank you! Don't mind if we do," before grabbing a chair from an empty table and seating himself.

Nigel also pulled up a chair, and I nudged Demitri's foot under the table.

"It's nice to see you, Norman," Demitri said. "Were you and Adonis out protecting the good citizens of Aeles?"

"It's Nigel," corrected the soldier with an easy smile, even though I had no doubt Demitri misremembered his name out of a desire to pretend he didn't exist. "Actually, Adonis and I just came from a briefing and were going to grab coffee before training drills."

"How wonderful," remarked Demitri. While anyone else would have thought him perfectly pleasant, I'd known him long enough to recognize his smile was forced.

"How are you both?" asked Adonis, ruffling his wavy mahogany hair and making me wish not for the first time my own stick-straight locks didn't refuse any attempts at curling. He grinned at me. "I haven't gotten any panicked messages from Aurelius requesting my healing abilities, so I'm guessing you're alright." He glanced between Demitri and me. "I was thinking of hosting a dinner this weekend where we could all catch up. Would you two be interested?"

"I can't this weekend," I replied, given that I would be spending it with Sebastian while training with Laycus, "but how about in a week, next Gwener?"

"That works for me," nodded Demitri.

"Next Gwener it is!" smiled Adonis. Leaning in closer, he added in a low voice, "If you'd like to bring Sebastian, he's more than welcome."

Adonis and Nigel both knew about the suppressor medallion that allowed Sebastian entry into Aeles, and I'd told them the same story I'd told Demitri . . . Sebastian had worn the medallion during his imprisonment in Rynstyn and had kept it after escaping.

Demitri made a face. "I can't think of a better way to ruin a dinner party!"

I shot him a reproving look before turning back to Adonis. "Thank you. I really appreciate that. I'm seeing him tonight, so I'll pass on your invitation, and I'm sure he'd love to come."

"That's wonderful you're seeing him!" Adonis's smile widened, and his sea-green eyes positively glowed. While I knew he was open to learning more about Daevals, I hadn't expected him to be so welcoming of one. His reaction made me happy, as well as hopeful . . . if a member of the Aelian military could overcome years of indoctrinated prejudices and judge a Daeval like Sebastian on his actions, rather than his blood, anything was possible.

"Speaking of Sebastian," I continued, still speaking quietly even though the other Astrals in the café were deep in their own laughter-filled conversations, "it seems Daevalic children have been going missing in Nocens." I recounted to the soldiers what I'd already told Demitri about Gregor. "Sebastian is worried it's the same program responsible for torturing him, so he's looking for information."

Adonis picked at the gold trim on the cuff of his jacket. "I'm trying to get a sense of who we can trust in the military . . . anyone who might be open to the idea of repealing the Blood Alarm or who thinks we've gone too far in isolating ourselves. It's slow going," he admitted, "but we're definitely not alone. I've spoken to quite a few Astrals who don't agree with the government's position on Daevals—with the government's position on a lot of things—it's just a matter of getting them to publicly go against everything we've been taught our entire lives."

I was going to ask what Adonis meant about Astrals disagreeing with the government's position on things besides Daevals, but he glanced at the spelled timepiece hanging near the counter.

"We should be getting back, Nigel," he said, rising to his feet.

"But you didn't even get your coffee!" protested Demitri.

Adonis gave him a lopsided smile. "Another time. It was nice seeing you, though. I'm looking forward to dinner!"

Demitri offered a shy grin, and we said our goodbyes as the

soldiers took their leave. I didn't miss the way my best friend's eyes lingered on Adonis's retreating back, his expression flickering between longing and frustration before he tossed his head and slipped his well-practiced mask back into place.

I reached across the table and covered his hand with mine. It had to be terrible, feeling the way he did about Adonis while knowing he could never tell the other man about his feelings, given that such relationships were outlawed in Aeles. I couldn't imagine what would be worse . . . for Demitri to tell Adonis how he felt and risk Adonis reporting him to the authorities, or for him to tell Adonis how he felt and have Adonis somehow reciprocate the feelings, both of them knowing they could never be together the way they wanted.

"I'm sorry," I said. "It's not fair. I would change it if I could. I *will* do everything I can to change it once I'm the *Princeps Shaman* and the realm will listen to me."

Demitri's expression softened, and he took my hand in his, giving it a gentle squeeze. "I know you would . . . and will. Thank you. I can't imagine being named to the position will be easy if your platform is based on advocating for equal relationship rights and establishing peace with Daevals, but hopefully the fact that you're the best healer in the realm will count for something."

His smile was genuine, even if his eyes were still sad, and I smiled back before purposefully directing the conversation to less important things. For a few moments, it was nice to pretend like nothing was out of the ordinary in my life, even though such a fantasy couldn't have been further from the truth.

6

SEBASTIAN

*A*fter leaving the tavern, I considered my options. I still had the majority of the night to pass until Kyra could join me. There wasn't anything I could do to track down the man Devlin had spoken with, and I didn't want to accept a contract and find myself in the middle of something when Kyra became available, forcing me to postpone seeing her for any length of time. Plus, my thoughts kept returning to her so often, I doubted I'd be able to focus on even the most straightforward assassination or interrogation. Normally recognizing I wasn't functioning at peak performance would have irritated me, but tonight I was surprised to find I wasn't particularly bothered.

That is what I would call growth. Batty's voice grated in my mind. *I've told you for years there's more to life than working; it's nice to see you are finally starting to listen to me.*

What I felt had absolutely nothing to do with Batty and everything to do with Kyra, but there was no point explaining that.

What do you know about Shthornan? I asked the bat. After Kyra and I had recovered Rhannu from the realm of the dead, I'd spent hours reacquainting myself with the sword and noticed marks carved into the blade. The marks were runes, shorthand for the ancient Daevalic language of Shthornan, and while I'd read and spoken it as Schatten, I couldn't recall any of it now. I remembered certain things about my former life so clearly, particularly anything involving Kareth, it was frustrating when I was unable to recall other things. I knew the binding spell wasn't intended to keep all our past memories intact, and I was lucky to possess the ones I did, but it would have been nice to remember more about my life as a feared Daevalic warrior.

I want to start deciphering the runes on Rhannu, I added, *so if you know any Shthornan and can be useful, now's the time to speak up; otherwise, I'm going to LeBehr's to see if she has a dictionary.*

Batty suddenly materialized on the back of a nearby bench, and I stifled a groan. He could have simply answered my question, but I'd made the mistake of letting him know I wanted information he might possess . . . and that made it less likely I'd demand he return to the cave as I normally would if he tried to join me in public. The bat's presence made me appear far from formidable, and I preferred not to be seen with him.

"I do not always like being seen with *you,* either," huffed Batty, crossing his wings over his rounded belly. "You constantly glare, you never wear anything that isn't black or grey, and you're completely hopeless when it comes to your hair, but I bear it the best I can. You could try doing the same."

I clenched my jaw and crossed my arms over my chest, then realized I was mimicking the bat's posture and quickly shoved my hands into the pockets of my breeches . . . which were, admittedly, black.

"Now, as far as my knowledge of Shthornan," said Batty, his dark eyes shining in the light of a black and red street chandelier. "While it is not my first language, I am more than proficient. In fact, you might be surprised to learn I am fluent in Shthornan, as well as the ancient Astral tongue of Praxum and four other languages."

I *was* surprised, and even marginally impressed, and while I tried to squash my reaction before Batty was aware of it, his smirk made it clear I hadn't acted quickly enough.

"Yet even with my extensive knowledge," continued the bat, "I do think a dictionary or book would be helpful, particularly something that illustrates how runes are formed and how they can be combined."

I nodded and opened a portal to LeBehr's bookstore, stepping out in front of the squat wood and plaster building I knew as well as my cave. Everything in Vartox was so opulent, the shop was sorely out of place: The burgundy paint was fading, the trimming along the roof buckled, and the windows were layered with dust and grime. LeBehr occasionally talked about updating the store, but I preferred it this way, unchanged since I'd first visited with my mother as a child. Batty flew past me, barely missing the crooked sign out front as he glided through the open doorway, and I shook my head before following him.

LeBehr's Cypher, Mischief, was in her usual spot on the floor guarding the entrance to the bookstore, and she hissed at me as I carefully stepped over her, which was good; there were few omens worse in my realm than being ignored by a cat. LeBehr popped out from behind a tall stack of books leaning precariously to one side and smiled at me.

"By yourself tonight? Where's Kyra?"

I explained about her being on internship, then asked, "What do you know about Shthornan?"

What LeBehr knew never ceased to amaze me, and I hoped this time would be no different. Pursing her lips, she ran a hand through her short white hair, causing it to stand up in odd directions that somehow looked completely normal on her before snapping her fingers and darting out of sight. The purple silk shawl draped over her shoulders floated behind her like a short cape, and she returned a few moments later holding two books.

"Most Daevals today don't know our kind used to speak an entirely different language," she said, "so books on the subject are almost impossible to find." She winked. "Unless you happen to be me, of course."

She offered me the books, and I carefully turned the pages of what were clearly very old volumes, studying the odd-looking symbols. One of the books appeared to be an illustrated children's tale, while the other was thicker with more words and numerous figures turned at odd angles.

"I'll take both," I said, causing the shopkeeper to grin. As always, I appreciated she didn't ask questions about why I wanted these particular books, although I suspected the steep price I paid for the volumes included such courteous behavior.

Assuring LeBehr I'd visit again soon with Kyra, I left the bookstore and returned to my cave, heading straight to my weapons vault. Batty materialized on a worktable, pulling a bag of caramels from a pocket in his wing and stuffing far too many in his mouth.

"I cannot work on an empty stomach," he grinned, and I did my best to ignore his slurping as I retrieved the scabbard holding Rhannu. I also gathered the drawings I'd made of the runes on the blade, having used my finger to trace each one before copying it down on paper.

"As I recall, different words activated runes that caused Rhannu to do different things," said Batty, smacking a few times to loosen the caramel threatening to seal his mouth shut . . . which some part of me thought wouldn't be the worst thing to befall the creature. "One rune would cause the blade to become so hot, it melted whatever it touched. Another would cast a circle of protection impenetrable to spells or other weapons."

A memory appeared in my mind. "I caused a minor earthquake once, activating a rune that made the blade vibrate when I stuck it in the ground." Kareth had come running out of the castle to make sure I was alright, but thankfully the only real damage had been to a tower of sticky buns one of the cooks had prepared for the evening's dessert . . . the shaking had toppled the edible arrangement and infuriated the chef, although Kareth had quickly calmed her down.

It was odd not knowing when I was going to suddenly remember something about my previous life, but I was grateful anytime a memory resurfaced.

I opened the thicker of the two books from LeBehr's, and at the sight of so many unfamiliar words, my stomach tightened, instantly taking me back to being a child struggling to learn to read. In the dream I'd shared with Kyra, I'd broken my classmate's arm after he teased me about my reading. I could still hear the boy stuttering in a cruelly accurate imitation of me, and I tightened my grasp around the book as the fire stirred in my veins. I'd eventually mastered reading and even come to love it, but it had taken *years* of focused practice on my part. I glanced from the book to the rune-covered papers before me. Perhaps this was a bad idea. I hated feeling dumb because I was unable to decipher marks on a page.

Batty suddenly grabbed a small pot of ink and dematerialized, only to reappear on the ground a few feet away. Unfastening the lid, he dipped the tip of a wing into the ink and drew a symbol on the ground. I was about to yell at him to stop messing around when he pointed at the symbol.

"This is the first letter of the Shthornan alphabet," he explained. "Whether it sounds hard or soft in a word depends on the letters both before and after it." He demonstrated the possible sounds of the letter before tilting his head to one side. "Shall I continue, or would you prefer I stop *messing around?*"

"I'm listening, aren't I?" I glared at him, hating that I needed help with this and hating that my infernal Cypher was the only one capable of helping me. At the same time, and likely *only* because Kyra was somehow rubbing off on me, I realized the bat was actually being useful . . . he, more than anyone, knew what being teased about my reading as a child had done to my self-esteem.

Unable to make my mouth form the words, I nevertheless muttered, *Thank you,* causing Batty to stand up straighter as a surprised grin crossed his furry face.

While it was slow going at first, reacquainting myself with the Shthornan alphabet was immensely helpful, and I soon turned to the children's book from LeBehr's, combining individual letters to form words Batty helped me sound out when I became stuck. By the time I opened the second book I'd purchased, I found myself able to read the text as easily as if I'd known Shthornan all my life . . . which, I supposed, I had, at least in one life.

Reaching the back of the book, I thumbed through the pages of runes, which had apparently been developed as a shorthand for the language, meaning once I knew what a certain line or shape meant, I was able to determine the mark's name and bring it to life.

Ready to test out my recovered knowledge, I opened a portal to the forest surrounding my cave. I didn't want to explore Rhannu's powers indoors and accidentally bring down my entire dwelling.

Turning around in the open space between the towering firs and gnarled oaks, I inhaled the pine-scented air and considered how best to practice with the sword. While there were no Daevals for miles, I didn't want to harm any animals that might be nearby, and I had no idea how to limit Rhannu's reactions. I cast an orb of light overhead, illuminating the space around me. Gripping the sword hilt tightly, I decided to start small, although

I first cast the strongest protection ward I knew around myself.

"*Frry'doe*," I said, and a rune began to glow bright gold against the silver blade. Extending the sword, I pressed the tip against a small rock, then watched as the stone exploded into tiny pieces. The fragments hadn't come anywhere near me, but was that due to my protection spell or powers inherent to the sword? Removing the protection spell, I said the rune's name again and pressed the sword tip against another rock. As the minuscule pieces of stone flew into the air, they arced outwards, as if there was an invisible shield in front of me.

"*Dieargryn*," I said, causing another rune to glow a rich golden hue. Again, I pressed just the tip of the sword into the ground and was shocked to see the stones, bushes, and trees around me start to shake. I quickly pulled the sword from the dirt, not wanting to cause an actual earthquake, but thoroughly impressed I could have done so.

I spent the rest of the night trying out different runes, and eventually returned to my weapons vault, where I gathered up pieces of scrap metal and placed them in a large bowl.

"*Toe'dye.*" Touching the end of the blade to the pile of metal, I watched as what had been solid melted into a bubbling puddle of liquid.

This was incredible! While Rhannu was a perfectly balanced sword and a lifetime achievement for even a master sword maker, the fact that I could do so much more with it than simply block or parry exponentially increased what I was capable of with the weapon. I couldn't wait to show Kyra, who would no doubt be impressed.

And speaking of Kyra, she ought to be finishing up at internship any moment now. My heartbeat quickened with an anticipation that might have been excitement, but I so rarely felt excited about something, I wasn't entirely sure. Wiping down Rhannu, I secured my weapons vault and showered before changing into clean clothes. I then did something I almost *never* did and studied my reflection in the mirror. Were my grey breeches and black tunic appropriate for picking up Kyra? I never cared what I wore, as long as the clothing didn't hinder my movement, but that was *before*, and I suddenly realized I was unconsciously dividing everything in my life into *before* and *after* Kyra.

"You know," said Batty, lying on his back on a rocky ledge, "I could take your measurements to a tailor and have some things made for you, should you choose to expand your wardrobe. I'm also certain Eslee would be more than happy to take you shopping, although it might be helpful to have a sense of what Kyra likes to see you in."

Thankfully, I was saved from answering by a familiar vibration on my wrist, although I did file away the bat's suggestions for future consideration. Touching my fingers to the bracelet, a warmth that had nothing to do with my pyromancy spread through my torso as I heard Kyra's voice.

I'm done with orientation, she said, and I could sense she was smiling. *When do you want to pick me up?*

Now. What are the coordinates?

7

⟨⟨⟨⟩⟩⟩

SEBASTIAN

*S*tepping through the crackling doorway, the first thing I saw was Kyra smiling at me. She rushed forward, wrapping her arms around me and hugging me tight. I closed the portal and as she looked up, I pressed my lips against hers.

I knew from firsthand experience using Rhannu caused time to run differently, or at least appear to run differently, but kissing Kyra had the exact same effect . . . everything around me slowed to the point of becoming completely still and nothing existed in that moment except Kyra, me, and my awareness of how good she felt in my arms.

When we separated, her cheeks were flushed. "I'm so glad to see you," she said. "I missed you."

"I missed you too," I replied just as Batty materialized on my shoulder.

"We have both missed you!" he exclaimed, leaping onto Kyra's chest and hugging her with his wings. A snort came from behind me, and I turned to see Aurelius shaking his head and glaring at my Cypher. Not that I blamed him. The bat had terrible timing.

Luckily, Batty was quickly distracted by a container of muffins on the counter, and Kyra set him down before giving him one filled with chocolate and hazelnuts. She then reached over and tapped a finger against the medallion pinned to my shirt.

"We should reset that so we don't set off the Blood Alarm. May I borrow a knife?"

I pulled a small dagger from the holster near my boot, conjuring a flame to sterilize it before handing it to Kyra, who pressed her thumb against the blade until she drew blood. Holding her thumb against the medallion, she carefully spread her golden blood over the surface. During my time at the Astral experimentation facility, I'd worn a collar with a similar medallion, and my captors had reapplied their blood to it every seven days, ensuring my silver blood stayed hidden and didn't trigger the Aelian Blood Alarm. Kyra and I weren't certain if this medallion functioned the same way, and while I hated that she had to hurt herself for me, if I was discovered in Aeles, we'd both face far more painful consequences than a small cut.

Kyra applied a healing spell to her thumb as I slipped the dagger back into its holster. She then gestured around the room.

"Welcome to my apartment." Her smile turned somewhat shy. "Would you like a tour?"

I nodded. Seeing where Kyra lived provided additional insight into her life, and now that her life included me, I wanted to know everything I possibly could.

"It's not very fancy," said Kyra matter-of-factly, "but since I really only sleep here, I don't need much."

The walls were painted a light grey that made the small space feel cozy rather than confined, and the dark blue sofa and overstuffed chairs were decorated with white pillows. The room smelled faintly of lavender, and large windows let in the last sunlight of the evening, as darkness was falling in Aeles. White bookshelves took up two entire walls in the living room, and a large painting of the ocean before a storm hung over the sofa; I liked the way the white-capped water rippled beneath heavy thunderheads. The small kitchen was divided from the living space by the white marble counter Batty was sitting on, and a compact table for two sat in the corner near the front door. Thick rugs featuring bold geometric patterns blanketed the floor.

"My home province of Montem is renown for their carpets," explained Kyra, "so it's nice to have these here with me in Celenia."

Making sure the soles of my boots were clean, I walked forward and examined Kyra's books, pleased to see we owned many of the same ones. I'd never thought about what Astrals read or if copies of the books in LeBehr's shop existed outside of Nocens, but apparently at least some did. In addition to books, there were numerous pictures on the shelves, some moving, some still, and Kyra pointed out members of her family. There were also a handful of pictures featuring her and Demitri, which I did my best to avoid.

"The bedroom and bathroom are through here," Kyra said, leading the way.

I let my gaze move slowly over the bedroom . . . the grey walls were edged in white trim, and there was a standing tripod telescope near a door that must have opened to a balcony, as well as a desk and matching dresser made of pale wood. Kyra's bed was smaller than mine, covered with blue pillows and a fluffy white comforter. A colorful patchwork quilt was folded in half at the foot of the bed, and Kyra touched it affectionately. "My grandmother made this for me when I was a baby. She made one for each of my siblings too. She passed away a few years ago, but it's a wonderful keepsake."

I nodded and, not for the first time, wished I possessed something that had belonged to my mother. I was fortunate Batty had managed to retrieve my childhood captum after her death, allowing me to watch recordings on the monocle-like device, but it would have been nice to have her cello or some of the sheet music she'd written.

Shaking my head to clear it, I refocused on Kyra's room, not wanting to reminisce about things I had no power to change.

"It's definitely you," I said, looking around the room again.

"Is that a good thing?" Her voice was uncertain.

"Of course. It's peaceful and well-organized . . . and pretty. The kind of place you don't want to leave." Normally I wasn't given to such descriptiveness but knowing Kyra could sense just about all of my thoughts actually made it easier to share certain things with her. As a smile appeared on her face, I silently congratulated myself on my choice of words.

"I'm glad you like it," she said, rocking up on the balls of her feet.

Glancing back at the bed, my vision was suddenly awash with memories from my past life with Kyra . . . incredibly *intimate* memories involving a bed and clothing strewn across the floor.

Rubbing the back of my neck, I tried to study Kyra without her noticing, but she was already looking at me, her red cheeks making it obvious she'd recalled a similar memory, if not the exact one I'd unintentionally revisited.

Part of me wanted to open a portal and disappear, even though I knew I shouldn't feel embarrassed. Kareth and I had been in love and had enjoyed every aspect of our lives together. But that life was so far removed from the relationship I had with Kyra now—the relationship I was working to build—that it left me confused. In the bodies we currently inhabited, we hadn't done more than kiss . . . it was far too early to be thinking about other things, even though I couldn't deny I very much *liked* thinking about other things involving the woman before me.

"This is all so confusing." Kyra hid her face behind her hands before lowering her arms to her sides. "I don't know whether to go hide in my closet or take off my clothes and pull you into bed."

I certainly hadn't expected that, and my surprise must have been obvious, because she ducked her head so her long black hair partially hid her face.

"I didn't mean I would actually *do* that, I just . . . I remember doing it before," she said, looking as if she, too, wished she could open a portal and disappear.

Even though part of my mind was still thinking about being pulled into bed by Kyra, I tried to collect myself.

"It's incredibly confusing," I agreed. "I see those memories, and I'm not certain how to act, either."

Kyra ventured a glance at me. "Really?"

"Really." I stepped closer. "I see what we had before—what we spent a lifetime building—and I know it's not going to happen again overnight, but it's hard not to worry I'm doing something wrong or not doing enough to get us back to where we should be . . . or where I want us to be."

For a moment, I worried my words hadn't made sense, but to my relief, Kyra visibly relaxed, her posture softening as the redness faded from her cheeks.

"Sometimes I feel things for you that scare me," she admitted softly. "I know why I feel them, but it also goes against everything I was raised to believe about relationships to feel so strongly for someone I haven't known very long . . . even though I've actually known you longer than anyone else in my life."

"There's no rush." I tucked her hair behind her ear before resting my hands on her shoulders. "We know what we had, and as long as you want it, I'll do everything in my power to give you that again in this lifetime."

Kyra nodded before tilting her head back and pressing her mouth to mine, and the heat in her kiss made my head swim in a way I'd only read about. I was breathing faster when we finally pulled apart, and my entire body yearned to explore Kyra's dark skin with nothing between us, memorizing every freckle, curve, and ticklish spot.

Difficult as it was, though, I refocused my attention, letting my pulse slow and my head clear. My father had always gotten his way through force—verbal, physical, or a combination of the two—and I *never* wanted Kyra to feel like I was forcing her to do anything with me. Of course what I wanted to experience with my former wife wasn't wrong and was far different from the selfish things my father had desired, but I would never put myself in a position where I might act similarly to him. I would let Kyra set the pace and only go as far as she felt comfortable.

I might not have known much about being in a relationship, but I was not my father, and I would do whatever it took to ensure I never became him.

8

SEBASTIAN

*B*ack in the cave, Batty proudly informed us dinner was waiting in Nerudian's cavern.

"I want to look up something in *The Book of Recovrancy*," Kyra said, "then dinner sounds wonderful."

I followed her to my dresser, where I'd cleared out a drawer for her to use. While I'd been the one to find the recovrancy book at LeBehr's, I'd later given it to Kyra in exchange for helping me find Rhannu; it was spelled to respond to Recovrancers and shared more with her than any other reader.

"I want to know if there are time limitations on recovering a shade from Ceelum," Kyra explained. "Back when we retrieved the unicorn horn, we had to use it by a certain phase of the moon, and I don't want to miss recovering your mother because I got the timing wrong."

My heart slammed against my rib cage at the mention of my mother, but I merely nodded, still hesitant to believe there was really a chance Kyra might somehow be able to bring her back to the land of the living.

Kyra opened the book and laid her palm flat against the first page, deep in thought. After a moment, she lifted her hand, and the thick pages began to turn of their own accord before fluttering to a stop. Kyra read the words that appeared before her:

If a shade chooses rest over immediate rebirth upon entering Death, the shade will be ferried to Ceelum. A shade can remain in this part of Vaneklus for as long as they please. With regards to recovering a shade from Ceelum, no particular timetables need be followed, but know that the shade may choose to leave and make their way to Karnis for rebirth at any time.

Kyra closed the book with a relieved exhale. "I still want to try and recover your mother as soon as possible," she assured me, "but it's nice to know I have at least *some* time to learn how to do it."

"Thank you." I couldn't begin to imagine how difficult recovering a shade who had died thirteen years ago would be, but I also knew if such a thing was possible, Kyra would do it.

Kyra smiled at me before replacing the book. She then reached out and took my hand as we made our way down the moonstone-embedded tunnel to Nerudian's cavern. Aurelius followed us, no doubt glaring daggers at my back, but as long as he wasn't actively advising Kyra to stay away from me, I could handle his sullenness.

A light up ahead began to glow brighter as we neared the tunnel's end. Shortly after moving into the cave, I'd discovered veins of turmaxinase gas snaking through the thick rock walls, and I'd piped it into various lighting fixtures I'd set up throughout the underground space. Batty must have turned on the lights in the dragon's chamber, and the heavy sconces filled the cavern with a soft light that warmed the towering pink quartz walls.

Nerudian was peering out from his treasure-filled canyon, his large yellow eyes sparkling as a toothy grin that was entirely out of place on the fearsome beast spread over his enormous mouth.

"Hail the Felserpent Queen and King!" he rumbled, his deep bellow vibrating all the way down to my bones. "Allow me to offer my most sincere congratulations to you both."

While I knew the dragon's words were true, hearing myself referred to by such a title was more than a little uncomfortable, like wearing a tunic that was too tight in the armholes. As I let the words roll awkwardly over me, Nerudian swiveled his head towards Kyra, who walked forward and stroked his black nose.

"Thank you for all your help," she said. "Knowing who we truly are changes everything."

Nerudian nudged Kyra affectionately, then used his head to gesture towards a table that had been set up near the edge of the chasm. Batty appeared on the table, nearly upsetting the tall red candles serving as a centerpiece as he gestured proudly at the covered platters.

"Dinner is served!"

Kyra's expression was both impressed and appreciative as her eyes met mine.

"You didn't need to go to so much trouble!" she exclaimed. "This is so thoughtful."

Running a hand through my hair, I found myself in the regrettable position of having to tell Kyra I hadn't gone to any trouble and was now sorely wishing I had. While I'd been looking forward to seeing her for days, I hadn't thought about what might make her happy beyond seeing me. Vowing to do better in the future, I opened my mouth just as Batty spoke.

"Sebastian wanted the cave to look especially nice for you," he said, his oblong black ears wiggling, "and I was more than happy to help him."

Kyra flashed me a smile then walked over to the table and kissed the top of Batty's head before seating herself.

That was well done, I admitted to the bat.

I have many ideas I can share for the next time she comes over, he grinned.

Aurelius trotted past me and used his head to push a chair closer to Kyra before hopping up beside her. I assumed Batty had included the chair specifically for the lynx, because there was no other reason to have three seats. I took the final chair and Batty waved a wing, making the covers disappear from our plates. Aurelius leaned forward and sniffed Kyra's food, probably making a remark about potential food poisoning because Kyra shot him an unhappy look before placing her napkin in her lap.

While I knew Kyra only ate planterian food, it didn't escape my notice that Batty hadn't included any meat-based dishes for me.

You have all next week to eat whatever you want when Kyra is back in Aeles, noted the bat. *Do you really want to spend the limited time you have with her eating things that will make her sad?*

Of course I didn't want to upset Kyra, and even though I didn't like feeling as if I'd somehow let Batty get away with something, I refrained from further comments about the food.

"I'm so glad we're all together," Kyra smiled. "I have so many questions!"

"Where would you like to start?" asked Batty. Kyra offered him a piece of carrot, which he happily accepted, and a bowl of sugar suddenly appeared beside him; dipping the vegetable in the bowl, he coated it generously in the white grains before gulping it down in one large bite.

"Let's start with reuniting the realms," replied Kyra eagerly.

"I think we ought to start with whether or not Tallus has returned," I said. Our former enemy's reappearance would affect Kyra's safety far more than anything to do with the realms, and without meaning to, I flexed my left hand, wishing I could run Rhannu through the foul betrayer's chest and be done with him once and for all. Tallus's list of crimes was long and blood-soaked . . . scheming to prevent Astrals and Daevals from living in peace, murdering Farent, one of my closest friends, right in front of me, and dividing Aeles-Nocens into two realms, not to mention hunting down and killing any Daevals who remained in Aeles after the division.

"Tallus is only dangerous if he remembers who he used to be," Kyra said. "We only remember our past lives because of the spell that bound our shades together, so it's highly unlikely for him to return with the same hatreds he had before."

"*Highly unlikely* is not the same as *impossible*," warned Batty. "If there is one spell to preserve memories, we must assume there are others."

I nodded, for once agreeing with the creature. It was always better to expect the worst and plan accordingly.

"I have spoken to Laycus," Batty continued. "He last saw Tallus's shade sometime between twenty to thirty years ago—exact times are difficult to pin down in Vaneklus—and while it's possible Tallus is resting in Ceelum, I think it is more likely he has been reborn. Shades always return as the same blood type, and since Tallus was an Astral, he will be somewhere in Aeles. Unlike having golden blood, though, simply because Tallus was a man in one life cycle does not mean he will continue to return as a man. That choice is up to the shade at the beginning of each rebirth."

Kyra's eyes widened. "I can't believe Laycus was so forthcoming!"

Batty smiled. "I have known him longer than I've known Nerudian. I also know better than to appear in his realm empty-handed . . . or empty-winged." He raised a wing and giggled, but didn't expound on what he'd given the Shade Transporter in exchange for so much information.

"While I have no actual evidence Tallus has returned," the bat refocused himself, "I think we would be wise to assume he has, if for no other reason than *you* two have finally returned together, and he has always sought to oppose you at every opportunity."

Batty lifted the bowl of sugar and flicked his long tongue over the crystal-white grains. "What do you remember of Tallus?" he asked, rubbing his nose as he glanced from Kyra to me.

I sifted through my past life memories, recalling a man with black hair and green eyes, much more comfortable wielding words than weapons, although the few times I'd sparred with him, he'd been competent enough with a sword.

"I don't have many memories of him," I shook my head, "aside from our final moments together and the knowledge of what he did after we were forced to flee." I looked at Kyra as her blue eyes darkened; she was clearly remembering the same awful things I knew of the man. "Hopefully I'll recall more, but I can't predict when memories are going to resurface."

"He was an Astral historian," said Kyra. "I think I interacted with him a few times while I was training under Gathalia, before I became queen, but I don't recall anything specific . . . it's more like a feeling than a memory. I do remember him at castle festivals and holiday celebrations, though; he was always social and seemed to know everything about everyone."

"Tallus was indeed a historian," nodded Batty. "No one knew more about the blood feud between Astrals and Daevals than him . . . he lost his family during a Daeval raid on his settlement when he was very young." Batty turned to me. "You were not involved in the raid," he said, which made me feel somewhat better, although it also would have explained Tallus's hatred towards me. "He oversaw the drafting of the Blood Treaty, but he never supported improving relationships between Astrals and Daevals. In hindsight, I believe he was always searching for a way to undermine your reign, but I did not become aware of his intentions in time to prevent his terrible deeds."

The bat scratched the golden mantle of fur around his neck. "He was also incredibly secretive about his particular gifts. I suspect he had the ability to see the future, or at least some part of it, but I do not know for certain. Of course, shades do not always return with the same abilities, but we should keep it in mind."

"According to Laycus, it's highly unusual Sebastian and I returned looking like our former selves," said Kyra, spearing a large mushroom. "Is there any chance Tallus will look the same, as well?"

"There is always a chance," shrugged the bat, "but it is far more likely he'll look completely different."

"Then how will we recognize him?" I drummed my fingers against the white tablecloth.

"I do not know." Batty shook his head. "If he remembers his past life, there is a better chance he will recognize the two of you and reveal himself at a time of his choosing."

The fire stirred in my veins at the thought of Tallus walking alongside Kyra in her realm without her even knowing it, and I tossed my napkin beside my plate.

"You have to give up internship."

Kyra blinked at me.

"I can't protect you in Aeles," I explained. "Here, I know you're safe."

"I appreciate that," she replied, "but I can't just sit around your cave all day. I have responsibilities, and—"

"—Someone else can handle them," I insisted. "It's only until Tallus reveals himself. You'll still have plenty of time to complete internship and become the *Princeps Shaman*."

Kyra set down her fork. "We're not even certain Tallus has returned and is in a position to reveal himself. And it's not just about me completing internship. Working with Senator Rex is our best chance of learning where the experimentation facility is located, which is the first step towards shutting it down."

I'd assumed Kyra knew finding the facility would be the easiest part of ending the heinous Astral project, but clearly this was an example of when it was better to talk things through instead of making assumptions about what the other knew.

"I haven't been waiting to end that program because I don't know where the facility is," I told her. "Batty was with me in Rynstyn . . . he knows exactly where the facility is."

Batty nodded.

"And," I added, "even if he didn't, Adonis told us he found military records mentioning the facility. I'm certain he could find coordinates. The challenge has always been getting inside, obtaining evidence of what Astrals are doing, and getting back out."

Kyra tilted her head to one side. "You're saying you know where the facility is located . . . and you have a suppressor medallion that lets you bypass the Aelian Blood Alarm. Why haven't you gone back and destroyed everything?" She held up a hand. "I'm not asking because I'm surprised you've been able to control yourself. You know I don't think Daevals are like that. And I'm certainly not advocating violence . . . although I suppose it's possible you're rubbing off on me."

One side of her mouth rose in a quick smile before her expression turned serious.

"If I've learned anything these past few weeks, it's that everything doesn't always fit neatly into a *right* or *wrong* category," she continued, and conflicting emotions swirled across her face. "I can't stand the thought of someone hurting you. I want the Astrals who tortured you punished. And if *I* want that, and I wasn't even the one to suffer . . . if I endured what you did and suddenly found a way to enact revenge on those who'd hurt me, I don't know if I could stop myself from taking justice into my own hands."

It was odd hearing Kyra conflicted when it came to any sort of violence, especially given how much she despised what I did for a living, but I appreciated her working to see things from another point of view. I, too, had changed over the past few weeks, considering things I previously never would have and realizing I could still be surprised by what turned out to be the truth.

"I've certainly considered going back and burning everything to the ground." I studied the flame of a candle as it flickered and swayed. "But destroying a building or two isn't the same as ending the program. I could turn the entire facility to ash, and whoever's in charge would just start again somewhere else. Sometimes you have to postpone a battle in order to win the war, even if it's a battle you want to fight and would most likely win."

Kyra mulled over my words before letting out a deep exhale. "Alright, well, even if I don't need to find coordinates to the facility, I still can't quit internship and leave Aeles."

"Why not?"

Kyra brought her gaze to mine. "Remember when I told you about finding the suppressor medallion?"

I nodded.

"I didn't tell you the truth," she cringed. "At the time, I didn't know you, so it seemed wise to keep some things to myself, but now that we're together, you should know . . . I found the medallion in my father's healing kit."

Tears pooled in her eyes, and Aurelius leaned closer, rubbing his head against her shoulder.

"My father was working with Senator Rex on a project comparing gold and silver blood." Her voice was thick with pent-up emotion. "There's a good chance my father knew about the facility in Rynstyn. I . . . I . . . ." A tear streamed down her face, and she gratefully accepted the handkerchief Batty quickly pulled from a wing pocket and offered her.

"I didn't want to tell you until I knew more." She dabbed her cheeks with the handkerchief. "If my father was involved, he might have played a role in what you experienced in Aeles. I didn't want you to hate me." Her last words were little more than a whisper.

"We have no proof of your father's involvement," Aurelius said, clearly wanting me to hear him, as he hadn't confined his remark to telepathy.

While some part of me—the part that had been Kareth's closest confidante—wished Kyra had told me sooner, I also couldn't fault her . . . as someone who regularly parceled out the truth to suit my needs, I understood her desire to acquire incontrovertible evidence before sharing it.

Kyra shifted in her chair, pulled out a captum, and touched the single lens a few times before offering it to me. I placed the monocle-like device before my eye, studying the moving images for a familiar face, even though I knew recognizing Kyra's father would present a challenge to our relationship I wasn't certain how to handle.

"You didn't react to the pictures of my father in my apartment," she said in a tight voice, "but that was also before I told you the truth about the medallion, so you might not have been looking closely." I watched as the man before me described brewing a healing potion, noting his long black hair and dark skin, similar to Kyra's, as well as his amber eyes and frequent smile.

After a few seconds, I handed the captum back.

"I've never seen him before," I assured her, and while I thought that would settle things, tears reappeared in Kyra's eyes as she shook her head.

"Just because you didn't see him doesn't mean he wasn't involved! Working with Senator Rex is the only way I can know for sure. I can't just up and leave Aeles, Sebastian. I can't." She quickly hid her face behind her hands as she began crying again.

Aurelius glared at me before gesturing towards Kyra with his head, and Batty caught my eye before pantomiming a hug as Nerudian sniffled loudly. I quickly rose and made my way to Kyra, pulling her up and wrapping my arms around her, which seemed to have been the right thing to do, even though it took her a moment to stop crying.

"We are not our parents," I said, hoping she heard the sincerity in my voice. "There's nothing you could tell me about your family that would change my feelings for you." I thought how hard I worked to be different from my father, to the point that I'd paid a Nocenian magistrate a significant amount of money to change my last name as soon as I'd been old enough, taking my mother's surname instead of my father's. "You saw my dream," I added. "I don't want to be judged on my father's actions. I would never judge you for your father's."

Kyra let out a shaky exhale before raising her gaze to mine. "Thank you for taking it so well," she said. "Aurelius has been trying to get in touch with Flavius, my father's Cypher—former Cypher—but hasn't been able to reach him, which means the poor wolf is probably still grieving. Until I can speak with him, working with Senator Rex is the best way for me to either clear my father's name . . . or accept I didn't know him as well as I thought I did." Anguish filled her eyes, but she drew a resolute breath. "Working with the senator is also our best chance of getting inside the facility and finding the evidence we need to end that experimentation program for good."

If anyone stood a chance of getting in and out of the clandestine facility without arousing suspicion, I supposed it would be an Astral working for the Aelian government, but I wasn't so certain that Astral needed to be Kyra. I also wasn't certain having evidence of what Astrals were doing to my kind would be enough to end the program, given that the fact it still existed meant it was supported by at least some very powerful golden bloods.

Kyra turned to Batty. "I'll keep doing what I can to get an invitation to visit the facility, and since we can't force Tallus to reveal himself, it sounds like we'll just have to be patient and keep our eyes open. In the meantime, what can we do about reuniting the realms?"

9

SEBASTIAN

"Tallus used the *Fragmen Incanta*, or Breaking Incantation, to physically divide the realms," said Batty as Kyra and I returned to our seats. "In Aeles, the eastern borders of Rynstyn, Iscre, and Aravost used to be connected to what are now the far western edges of Nocens, specifically the territories of Brengwyn, Dal Mar, and Jaasfar. The breaking of the realm allowed the sea to fill the space between the two lands, but the natural state of Aeles and Nocens is to be together. They are not meant to exist separately, and I would not be surprised if we continue seeing signs of their increasing instability."

"What kind of signs?" asked Kyra, reaching for her water glass.

"Earthquakes, floods, avalanches, snow when it should be warm, droughts capable of drying up rivers . . . I'm surprised the realms have managed to survive apart this long." Batty shook his head sadly.

Kyra stiffened and set down her glass. "Laycus said my father died at his appointed time, which means that earthquake in Aravost was supposed to happen, but do you think it could have been the result of instability in Aeles?" Her eyes widened. "There was just an avalanche in Montem too. Do you think it's also related?"

"I do," Batty replied in a far more serious voice than I was used to hearing from the creature. "And I expect more such disasters to occur the longer the realms are apart, which is another reason we must reunite them." A piece of red licorice appeared in the bat's grasp, and he dipped it in the bowl of sugar before continuing.

"When the realms were united, your home was in a place called Velaire. The ruins of your former castle exist in Aeles, in the province of Montem, north of the Nebosa River and west of the Umbra Pass."

Kyra narrowed her eyes while wrinkling her nose, a gesture I recognized indicating she was deep in thought. "I've been to the area you're describing with my father to heal patients, and I don't recall any ruins. There's a sacred grove the Gifters of Aeles once visited in corporeal form, but it's off-limits to visitors."

Batty nodded before shoving the last of the sugar-covered candy into his mouth, and Kyra's eyes widened. "Are you saying the story about the Gifters and a sacred grove isn't true?"

"That story was created to keep anyone from excavating your former home," said Batty, pushing himself up and crossing the table to gently pat Kyra's hand. I knew how she felt. Over the last few weeks, I'd seen one after another of the formative beliefs I'd grown up holding proven to be no more than myth.

"The Gifters may be very real indeed," Batty assured Kyra, who appeared positively crestfallen, "and this does not mean they never visited Aeles, but they have nothing to do with what I am describing."

"So, I'm assuming we have to visit these ruins," I prompted, ready to know what would be expected of me so I could decide exactly how difficult it was going to be.

"Yes," nodded the bat. "You and Kyra will need to return to your former home. You will need to establish who you are, but that won't be more difficult than the blood sample you gave when retrieving Rhannu."

Kyra smiled at me. "We'll make sure you aren't wearing a suppressor medallion this time." While I knew she was trying to make light of the situation, her smile faltered as she spoke.

Recalling how she'd nearly died at the hands of the spelled creatures I'd created to protect Rhannu from being taken by anyone but myself—spelled creatures that had appeared because the medallion had hidden my blood and therefore my identity—I reached across the table and took Kyra's hand.

"We'll be much more prepared," I agreed. "I won't let anything happen to you."

"I know," she said. "I won't let anything happen to you, either." Determination shone from her eyes and—given that she had single-handedly recovered my shade following my untimely death—I knew she meant every word.

"Once there," continued the bat, "you will need to take Rhannu and insert it into the *Cor'Lapis* stone."

The name didn't spark any recognition, even in my past life memories, and when Kyra looked confused, I couldn't keep my annoyance in check. "You expect us to dig around in ruins hundreds of years old and find *one* particular stone?" Even by the low standards I maintained towards Batty, this was ridiculous.

"Yes," he said. "The *Cor'Lapis* stone is the heart of Aeles-Nocens. It was used in the foundation of your castle."

"We didn't know that and it was *our* castle!" I exclaimed. "How do you know?"

"Because I ensured the stone was included during construction," shrugged the bat. "But that is neither here nor there. What matters is finding the stone."

"If the castle was destroyed, couldn't the stone have been destroyed too?" worried Kyra.

"The fact that Aeles and Nocens continue to exist is proof the stone still exists," assured Batty. "If it was gone, both realms would have ceased to function, and we would not be having this discussion. The *Cor'Lapis* lies somewhere in the ruins of Velaire."

"Once we reach the ruins, do you know how to find the stone?" I asked.

"Yes, but the difficult part will be entering the ruins." Batty dipped the end of a wing directly into the bowl of sugar and shoveled a small pile into his mouth. "The last time I checked, there were spells in place to send an alert whenever anyone stepped beyond a certain point."

"Probably cast by Tallus at some point," scowled Kyra.

Batty nodded. "After placing Rhannu in the *Cor'Lapis* stone and applying your blood to it, you will then need to recite the *Ligarum Incanta*, or Binding Incantation. The combination will exert a healing effect, reuniting the realms if not rejoining them physically."

"I don't recall seeing that incantation written anywhere." Kyra glanced at me nervously.

"It is recorded in the Chronicles, and that book is spelled to be indestructible," smiled Batty.

"Well, that's a relief." Kyra returned the bat's smile. "Finally, some good news!"

"Yes," said Batty, "now all we have to do is find the book."

"What do you mean, find the book?" I demanded. "We escaped from Tallus with the Chronicles! What happened to it after that?"

"It was lost in the centuries following your deaths," the bat sighed. "I did my best to keep track of it—Nerudian and I both did—but things happen you cannot always control."

Nerudian nodded vigorously before bringing his head beside the table, the breath from his nostrils immediately extinguishing the dinner candles. "A few hundred years ago, miners discovered the cave Batty and I were sharing in Brengwyn. Batty came to warn me, waking me and allowing me to escape without being discovered, but, alas, the book was not so fortunate."

"I tried to stop the miners," offered Batty apologetically, "but I was unsuccessful." His wings drooped. "The book changed hands—and realms—so many times, I do not know what became of it."

I rolled my eyes, and Kyra shot me a look. "You saved Nerudian's life," she said to the bat. "That's far more important than any book."

"I *did* manage to snatch a page from the Chronicles," Batty said with his usual dopey grin, reaching into a wing pocket and withdrawing a folded piece of parchment, which he handed to Kyra. "Now that you remember who you are and what you must do, we can take it to LeBehr; if anyone can track down a long-lost book, it is her!"

Kyra gazed at the parchment in awe, her eyes moving back and forth as she read the hand-written words. "I wrote this," she said. "It was a few years into our rule . . . and our marriage . . . it mentions the fifth anniversary of the Blood Treaty."

She stroked the paper reverently before handing it to me. I looked at the writing, still as dark as if the ink had been applied yesterday, before returning it to Batty. Part of me thought it would be safer in my weapons vault than a pocket of his wing, but he'd managed to keep it safe this long, so I remained silent.

"Speaking of things that were lost," Kyra said, "in the past life memories we've seen so far, we each had two bracelets. Do you know what happened to the others?"

Batty exhaled loudly before wrapping his wings around himself.

"As Kareth, you died first," he said gently. "I knew the

bracelets were too valuable to leave unattended, and I suspected Tallus might seek them out, so Nerudian removed them. Laycus agreed to keep them safe in Vaneklus until they were needed again. Time passed, and when Schatten died, Nerudian removed his bracelets, as well. I took them to Vaneklus, but when Laycus opened the box containing Kareth's bracelets, we discovered something terrible . . . the bracelets had disintegrated and were little more than two piles of golden dust."

He rubbed a wing beneath his nose. "Rhannu could safely be stored in Vaneklus because it was created using the very essence of the realm. Your bracelets contain gold from Aeles-Nocens, but they also contain meteorite from the heart of a fallen star, and apparently such a substance cannot withstand the inevitable decay of Vaneklus's atmosphere. We were horrified at our discovery, so Nerudian stored Schatten's bracelets in his treasure trove, which he could make invisible to all but other dragons when he chose."

The bat finally raised his head. "I never imagined such a thing could happen. It is my fault the bracelets were destroyed, and I could only hope when you both returned, *together*, your connection would be strong enough that it wouldn't matter how many bracelets you wore." He managed a wobbly smile. "At least I was right about that. They obviously work fine with you each wearing only one."

"You don't need to apologize for anything," Kyra comforted the bat, reaching out to stroke his back. "It's because of you we each even have one bracelet to wear."

I wasn't entirely certain the bat wasn't somehow to blame, but something vibrated in my pocket, and I pulled out my peerin. I'd been so focused on picking Kyra up I'd forgotten to put it in the drawer I relegated it to when I wasn't working. Flipping open the hinged lids, I checked the message, thinking it might be Devlin recalling more about the man who'd wanted to start an orphanage.

The message wasn't from Devlin, though. It was from Caz.

"Is everything alright?" asked Kyra.

"Caz sent a message saying none of the Nocenian healers have been able to uncover trace memories on Gregor's body." My eyes skimmed the words floating across the chormorite lens. "He's arranged a meeting with the top healer in Nocens, and he'd like you to try and teach him to find the memories. If it's something Daevals are unable to do, Caz would like you to examine Gregor's body yourself."

Kyra nodded. "Of course. I can't imagine it's a skill exclusive to my realm, but I'm more than happy to help. If Gregor was injured in Rynstyn, I might be able to learn more about the experimentation program . . . perhaps see some of the Astrals he encountered there." She fell silent, obviously knowing there was a chance she might see her father in the memories stored within Gregor's corpse, before tossing her head and straightening her shoulders. "And after we help Caz, we can go to LeBehr's and start the process of finding the Chronicles."

"That seems like a lot for one outing," I frowned. I'd planned on spending every second of the weekend alone with Kyra and certainly hadn't expected to dive into something as monumental as reuniting the realms within our first few hours together.

Kyra gazed intently at me. "We promised to come back together when the time was right to reunite the realms. We're back, and we're together, so it's clearly time."

"Yes, but we also need to be mindful about how we do it," I cautioned. "Even if we had everything we needed and managed to sneak into the ruins of our castle and reunite the realms this instant, that's not the same as bringing peace between Astrals and Daevals. If everyone suddenly finds themselves living in one realm, it'll be chaos and violence. I wouldn't be surprised if one side started building a wall to keep the other side out."

It would no doubt be Astrals building said wall, but I didn't see the need to say such a thing and possibly offend Kyra.

"The way I see it," I added, "reuniting the realms is only one step . . . but what then? Do Astrals and Daevals really want the chance to live peaceably with one another? Will they be open to forming a new government where silver and gold blood are equally represented? Will each blood type want to keep whatever land and laws they currently have? How will we prevent war from immediately breaking out?" My mind was racing, doing what it did best and imagining worst-case possibilities. "Also, what about us? Will we come out and tell everyone we were the ones who reunited the realms? Will they believe us? Will we attempt to rule Aeles-Nocens again? I can't see either realm welcoming a monarchy."

The more I spoke, the more Kyra's face fell.

"I hadn't thought of all that," she eventually said.

I couldn't stand seeing her unhappy and I hated feeling like it was my fault, even though I hadn't done anything but point out very real issues we needed to consider. I searched for something to say to make her smile again, but she spoke first.

"We don't know that LeBehr will be able to track down the Chronicles . . . what if we go see her and find out one way or another? If she can do it, we can have her start the process, and while she's working on that, we can start figuring out answers to all the questions you just asked." She held my gaze. "Would that work?"

Batty raised a wing but didn't wait to be called on. "I think that is a very good *compromise*," he said, looking directly at me.

Ignoring the bat, I couldn't deny Kyra had a point. Acquiring the Chronicles was only one piece of a larger puzzle, and even if we didn't need to solve it immediately, it made sense to be prepared when the time eventually came.

"I'm fine with that." I wasn't aware my muscles had tensed until Kyra smiled and I felt myself relax, my fire sending a pleasant pulse of warmth through my veins.

"When do we need to leave?" she asked.

"Not for a few hours. I know it's night in Aeles, so if you want to sleep for a while, we have time."

"Sleep would be glorious." Kyra stretched her arms overhead before rising from her chair.

We said goodbye to Nerudian and returned to my living quarters, where Kyra grabbed the bag she'd brought with her from her apartment and headed down one of the numerous tunnels to change. I took the opportunity to let Caz know Kyra was willing to help, and he sent the coordinates to a morgue in Vartox where we'd meet in a few hours. He also mentioned how happy he was to hear Kyra and I were in a relationship, and since I'd never shared that particular development with him, I assumed Batty had told his Cypher, who had in turn told Caz. If there was anything that bat loved as much as sweets, it was gossip.

That settled, I glanced towards the alcove that served as my bedroom, my heartbeat speeding up.

10

SEBASTIAN

*T*he last time Kyra had spent the night, she'd slept on the sofa. But that had been before we'd known who we were and the past we'd shared. Would she still want to sleep on the sofa? Would she expect me to give her the bed? Or, now that we were in a relationship, were we supposed to share the bed?

Of course you will share the bed, Batty said, materializing on the counter near the sink.

You don't know Kyra will feel comfortable doing that, I retorted. *And you don't know I feel comfortable sharing a bed with her!*

You are more than fine with it. The bat's confidence in knowing my innermost feelings made me clench my jaw, even though I couldn't say he was wrong. I scrolled through a few job-related messages on my peerin before returning it to a drawer and was contemplating what to say upon Kyra's return when I heard her bare feet on the stone floor.

I couldn't remember the last time I'd felt so nervous. My hands trembled, and I frowned at them. There was no place in my life for weakness of any kind, and I crossed my arms to hide any further signs of anxiety as I turned to face Kyra.

When I'd picked her up, I'd been pleased to see she'd already had a bag packed, indicating she intended to sleep over, and while part of me had wondered what she'd brought to sleep in, I was mostly grateful she hadn't chosen anything revealing. She was wearing blue and white striped flannel pants and a dark blue shirt with long sleeves. Placing the dress she'd changed out of on top of her bag, she crossed the distance between us.

"I know it's technically daytime outside, so if you have other things to do, I understand," she said.

"I could rest," I shrugged, glancing at my bed without entirely meaning to. Kyra followed my gaze, then looked back at me.

"I'm fine to take the sofa again. It'll be just like old times."

She was wrong . . . old times would involve the two of us sharing a bed, taking turns holding each other and enjoying how perfectly our bodies fit together.

"Do you *want* to take the sofa?" The abruptness of my question caused Kyra to startle.

"I don't mind taking it," she began, but I shook my head.

"I know that. But things are different than when you were here before, so . . . do you want to sleep in the bed?"

"You don't have to give up your bed for me," she replied, missing the point I was admittedly doing a terrible job of making.

Running a hand through my hair, I forced myself to be clearer. "We could share the bed. We could both be in it . . . at the same time."

Kyra's eyes widened, and a hint of red spread over her rounded cheeks. Thinking perhaps I'd gone too far, I quickly added, "But we don't have to. It was just an idea. If it makes you uncomfortable, we can—"

"—I'd love to!" Kyra interrupted. "I don't know about doing . . . *more* . . . just yet, but I'd love to share the bed, if you're alright with it."

I nodded mutely. Even if I'd had the first idea what to say, I didn't trust my mouth to form the words. In my line of work, you were at your most defenseless when you slept, meaning you had to be incredibly careful about who you closed your eyes around, yet here I was *voluntarily* offering to put myself in a potentially dangerous position! It was odd wanting things that felt so out of character for who I knew myself to be, and the only thing I could think of was that some part of me knew I'd done this with Kareth before, making it safe to do again.

I usually slept partially or completely unclothed, but that clearly wouldn't do, so I made my way to my dresser and pulled out a clean shirt and sleeping pants.

"I'll go change." My voice sounded deeper than usual, but hopefully Kyra hadn't noticed. Quickly swapping out the clothes down one of the tunnels, I returned just in time to see Kyra pulling back the dark blue comforter and top sheet, running her hand appreciatively over the bedding.

"I never imagined you'd own such soft sheets," she marveled. "These are amazing!"

"What did you think I slept on?" I made my way to the opposite side of the bed.

She smirked. "Nails and broken glass and pieces of sharp metal. But I'm glad I was wrong. Do you have a side you like to sleep on?"

I shook my head. I usually slept in the middle, taking up as much space as I wanted.

Kyra hesitated, glancing out of the alcove towards the sofa where Aurelius was curled in a tight ball before touching the gold bracelet and prompting me to open the connection.

I've never spent the night without Aurelius beside me, she said, her brow furrowing.

Multiple thoughts fought for my attention. Was Kyra saying she'd never spent the night with a romantic partner? We hadn't discussed any previous relationships either of us had been in— although there would be nothing to share on my end, as I'd never courted anyone—and while I hated to think of Kyra even smiling at someone else, much less doing more with them, she *had* lived nearly nineteen years of her life before reuniting with me. While part of me naturally wanted information, the rest of me didn't know if this was the right time for such a discussion.

Do you want him in the bed? I ultimately asked. I didn't allow my own Cypher to sleep in my bed, but if the lynx's presence would make Kyra more comfortable, it seemed like something I should consider.

Outside of childhood sleepovers, I've never spent the night with anyone before, so I'm not exactly sure what I want. Kyra's cheeks reddened. *He says he's fine to take the sofa, but it just feels so odd.* Turning back toward me, she added, *He's always been wonderful about giving me privacy when I've asked for it . . . I've just rarely asked. Obviously, this was always going to happen at some point, but it's definitely going to take some getting used to.*

Based on Kyra's responses, I still had questions about whether she'd been intimate with anyone even if she hadn't spent the night with them, but such questions could wait, if they needed to be asked at all. Whatever she said wouldn't change the way I felt about her. There was a difference between wanting information because you were curious and wanting it because it would affect subsequent actions and decisions, and I always tried to be aware of that difference.

I want you to feel good about what we're doing, so let me know if there's anything I can do, I said, which must have been a good response because Kyra smiled broadly and thanked me before crawling between the sheets.

I set an alarm using the spelled clock beside the bed, but inwardly my mind was leaping from one question to another. Was I supposed to get under the covers too? Was Kyra expecting me to hold her? Or was that too much, too soon? Perhaps it was enough to simply be close to her. There was something so right about looking over and seeing her where I slept.

Swallowing hard, I stretched out on top of the covers, making sure there was still plenty of distance between the two of us.

"Aren't you going to be cold?" she asked, no longer using the bracelet to communicate.

"I'll be fine."

Kyra rolled onto her side, gazing at me, so I mimicked her movement and turned so we were facing one another.

"I feel silly being nervous about this," she said. "It's not like it's the first time we've shared a bed . . . but it also *is* the first time we've slept beside each other in these bodies."

"I don't want to make you uncomfortable."

"I don't want to make you uncomfortable, either," she agreed. "I know how you feel about someone being near you or touching you, and I never want to assume that just because I used to do those things, it's alright for me to do them again. I think we just need to tell each other how we feel, even when it's awkward."

"I want you to touch me," I said, immediately wishing I hadn't sounded so eager. "I mean, I want to get comfortable with you touching me. I'll tell you if I start thinking about something from my past, but I want this," I assured her. "I want you here, with me."

Kyra's smile was so dazzling, I was momentarily frozen by it.

"I want to be here with you too," she said. "Do you remember when we first met?"

I nodded, doubting I would ever forget the first time I'd laid eyes on my bride-to-be. Kareth and I had agreed to marry in order to bring peace to Aeles-Nocens, an Astral and a Daeval who had never seen one another before, much less interacted. I would have done anything to protect my kind and ensure an end to the constant fighting, even marrying someone I might not turn out to love or who might not care for me. Thankfully, things had worked out far better than either of us had imagined.

"We talked for hours," Kyra recalled. "I was so terrified of what you might expect that first night, but we just started talking and you immediately made me feel better. It worked for us before, so I'm certain it'll work again."

I didn't find talking nearly as easy as Kyra did, but I was able to do it with her far better than with anyone else, and it would certainly be less awkward than lying near one another in silence.

"Is your favorite color still blue?" I asked. "Not a light blue, but a dark one?"

"Yes," she smiled. "Is yours still grey?"

"It is. Although I'm drawn to black too."

"We've both always liked darker colors," noted Kyra. "Do you still prefer night to day?"

"Without question. You too? I remember you loved watching the moon and stars; if you weren't in the library or Vaneklus, you were in the astronomy tower."

"That's right!" Kyra grinned. "Yes, I still vastly prefer night, and I can't get enough of the moon and stars. And speaking of the library, do you remember when we used that cataloguing spell? Books were flying all over the place reorganizing themselves . . . Batty tried to ride one, and it chased him into a corner." She fell silent, both of us recalling the hours we'd spent in the castle library, reading aloud to one another or curled up on a sofa in front of the fire, lost in our own books but still enjoying the comfort of having the other close by.

Not wanting to dwell on the fact that Tallus had burned our books to ash when he'd destroyed the castle, I asked, "And how about flowers? Are stargazer lilies still your favorite?"

"Actually, I think calla lilies are my favorite now," said Kyra, and I stored that away for future use. "Do you still despise music?" A knowing smile tugged at her mouth. "You used to cast a quieting spell around your head before the court musicians played. You'd sit there nodding and acting as if you were enjoying it when really you were enjoying the quiet and probably thinking about military strategy."

I couldn't stop the smile that spread across my face at hearing Kyra talk so easily about our time together.

"I've softened on music . . . probably because my mother in this life was a classical musician."

Kyra's eyes lit up at my disclosure. "I knew from your dream she was a musician, but I didn't know what kind. What instrument did she play?"

"She could play almost anything, but she loved the cello best. She'd practice downstairs after I went to bed, and I'd leave my door open so I could hear her. It was a nice way to fall asleep."

Although I was starting to think lying in bed next to Kyra was an even nicer way to fall asleep.

"That sounds wonderful," yawned Kyra. "You know, I just realized we're on the same sides of the bed we used to sleep on. You always took the left, and I took the right."

"We started out there," I said, "but we usually ended up in the middle, one of us holding the other."

"Left to myself, I'd sleep in the same position all night, but you'd be all over the place," chuckled Kyra. "Every morning we'd tuck the sheets back in and every night, you'd kick them free again." Raising her head from the pillow, she hesitated before saying, "I also remember I used to love to fall asleep with my head on your chest."

"I loved that too." Then, as if my body had suddenly been possessed by some unseen force, I found myself rolling onto my back and gesturing towards my chest. "Do you want to see if it feels like how we remember?"

Part of me was shocked at my boldness. What if Kyra said no? What if I was rushing things and unintentionally pressuring her? I was about to assure her she didn't need to change positions when she scooted so close, her hair brushed the side of my face. I held my breath, not wanting to make her change her mind, but also not entirely believing what was happening.

As Kyra snuggled against my side and rested her head on my torso, I desperately hoped she couldn't hear my heart, which was pounding so loud it felt in danger of exploding at any minute. Wrapping my arm around her, I pulled her closer, momentarily wishing we were both under the covers before I decided this was a very good start.

"It feels exactly like how I remember," she said, draping her arm over me. "Possibly even better."

Lying there, holding the woman I'd loved enough to bind my shade to a millennium ago, I gazed up at the stone ceiling. I wasn't exactly relaxed, as I wasn't used to having someone in my bed, but at the same time, holding Kyra felt so right I couldn't imagine ever wanting to get up.

"I've missed you," mumbled Kyra as she drifted off to sleep. "I just didn't know how much until I found you again."

"I've missed you too." I tightened my grip around her. "Wherever you are is where I belong, and that will never change."

Kyra's breathing slowed and within minutes, she was asleep; I could feel her muscles loosening as she settled against me. I'd always assumed I would die in a fight, but now, lying in bed with Kyra in my arms, I decided if I died that moment, I would enter Vaneklus happy.

11

KYRA

*W*aking up, it took me a moment to remember I was in Sebastian's cave . . . and that I'd fallen asleep snuggled against him with my head on his chest. I quickly lifted my head and ran a hand over my face, hoping I hadn't done anything embarrassing like talk in my sleep or drool on his shirt. Sebastian gazed up at me, lying in the same position he'd been in when I'd drifted off to sleep.

"Did you sleep?" I asked him.

"No," he admitted, "but I didn't want to. I was perfectly content where I was."

I leaned forward and pressed a kiss against his lips before glancing at the spelled clock on his nightstand. It was almost time to meet Caz and the Nocenian healer, which meant I needed to shower. For a moment, I considered inviting Sebastian to join me before remembering we hadn't yet seen one another unclothed in these bodies. While our shared past certainly made some aspects of being together easier, it also presented challenges most new relationships didn't face, such as forcing me to differentiate between things that merely *felt* familiar and things the two of us had actually *done* this life cycle.

Once I was showered and dressed, Sebastian opened a portal, and I pulled my shifter cloak from what I now thought of as "my" drawer in his dresser, settling the garment around my shoulders.

While I loved the swirling pinks, purples, and blues resembling a dazzling faraway galaxy, the colors didn't seem quite right for something as serious as visiting a morgue. Pressing my palm against the velvet, I pictured a dark charcoal grey, the color of ashes, thunderheads, and granite from the mountains in Montem. The cloak fluttered gently as the brighter colors were instantly replaced by a somber grey.

"You used to have a cloak too," I said to Sebastian as I walked towards the crackling portal. His cloak had been beautiful, made from black and grey scales given to him by the Felserpent creature, the last of the Great Beasts, whose duties and title Schatten had assumed in becoming king of Aeles-Nocens. "I wonder what happened to it?"

"It's probably long gone," he said, even though I knew him well enough to recognize the disappointment in his frown. "Just like the crowns we used to wear and the castle we used to live in."

"Crowns can be reforged, and castles can be rebuilt." Batty fluttered his wings where he hung upside down from the chandelier over the dining table. "That cloak is as indestructible as the scales used to create it, so it is simply a matter of finding it. Nerudian has gone to celebrate the birth of a new dragon in his extended family, and he is seeking your cloak amongst the dragon community while he's away."

"That's wonderful news!" I smiled at Sebastian, not missing the flicker of excitement in his dark eyes. "It'll be nice to have something else that used to be ours."

He nodded, then stepped through the portal to make certain it was safe before gesturing for me to follow. As Aurelius and I joined him, I glanced around in awe; even though I knew those in Vartox favored excess and extravagance, the room was still so different from the stark, utilitarian funeral parlors we had in Aeles. Satin-covered settees and leather wingback chairs were grouped around ornate bronze tables, and I could feel my boots sinking into the plush eggplant-colored carpet. An oversized amethyst chandelier cast a comforting light over the space, and soothing abstract paintings hung on the lilac-hued walls, swirls of plum, grape, and periwinkle gently circling one another.

Sebastian closed the portal, then pressed his fingertips against his bracelet, causing mine to vibrate until I touched it.

Keep the connection open in case we need to speak privately, he instructed, and I nodded just as Caz appeared on the intersector across the room. As he stepped off the platinum plate embedded in the floor, another man appeared, but I didn't have time to study him because Caz was hurrying towards me, arms open wide. Tufts of brown curls protruded exuberantly over his ears as if to make up for the fact that he didn't have much hair on the top of his head, and his violet-tinged blue eyes danced merrily.

"My dear Ms. Valorian!" He pulled me into a hug I happily returned. "It's been far too long."

"Please, call me Kyra," I reminded him before lowering my arms and moving closer to Sebastian as the other Daeval stepped forward. He was roughly the same height as Caz, with salt-and-pepper hair and a paunch at his mid-section, but his deep-set brown eyes sparkled as he grinned, revealing dimples carved into each cheek.

"Kyra, may I present my brother, Dunston Dekarai," introduced Caz with a slight bow.

"I can't *tell* you how happy I am to meet you!" exclaimed Dunston, clasping his hands under his chin and causing the numerous rings he wore to clink softly against one another. "It's a great, great honor, Kyra . . . if I may call you that?"

"Of course," I replied. "I'm happy to meet you too. I've heard so much about you from Sebastian."

Dunston grinned before surprising me and pulling me into a

hug. I'd never expected Daevals to be so fond of hugging, and I immediately chided myself for such a negative assumption. Clearly I still maintained at least some incorrect notions about those with silver blood, even though I was working incredibly hard to learn everything I could about Daevals. Having grown up accustomed to physical affection, I welcomed the embrace.

When Dunston finally lowered his arms, I noticed wetness in the corners of his eyes, and he quickly withdrew a red silk hand-kerchief from inside his jacket and dabbed the upper part of his face.

"My apologies," he cleared his throat. "I just never thought I'd see the day. Sebastian's always been so career-focused, but when he told me about meeting you, I thought, well, you never know, and now seeing you *together* . . ." Dunston's dimples became more pronounced as his smile deepened. "I couldn't be happier."

Gesturing towards Sebastian, he added, "Sebastian would never say this about himself, so I'll say it for him—you've got yourself a real catch, Kyra. A *real* catch. He's the top professional in his field. One of the best fighters and tactical minds I've had the pleasure to work with in my not-inconsiderable years. Graduated top of his class, and I always knew he'd do well, but I don't think it's any great secret I've wanted him to have someone to come home to. Seeing you with him . . ." Dunston's voice broke. "Well, I just couldn't be happier."

I was touched at how deeply Dunston cared for Sebastian, feelings that clearly went beyond a standard business relationship. I hadn't expected Sebastian to tell anyone we were a couple, but however the topic had come up, I was thrilled those closest to him were so supportive. Looking at Sebastian, I smiled. "I couldn't be happier either," I said, enjoying the way Sebastian's dark eyes drank in my words.

Caz's Cypher, a porcupine named Alistair, suddenly materialized, followed quickly by Dunston's Cypher, an enormous Komodo dragon named Wayah. After I ensured Aurelius had met everyone, Dunston placed a hand over his heart.

"I was sorry to hear of your father's passing. I only met him once, but he made quite an impression."

"Thank you," I said, feeling the same mixture of sadness and anger that always appeared when I remembered my father's interactions with Daevals in Nocens . . . interactions I'd been completely unaware of until after his death.

I quickly refocused on the situation at hand. "I appreciate you and Caz being here and allowing me to share what I know. I'd like to think my kind are above torturing those with silver blood, but we all know they're not." I interlaced my fingers through Sebastian's. "If Daevals are still being harmed in Aeles, I'll do anything I can to put an end to it."

Dunston studied our clasped hands before turning a questioning gaze to Sebastian.

"Kyra knows about my past," Sebastian said. While Dunston's eyebrows initially shot upwards, his surprise was quickly replaced by a smile.

"Well, this just keeps getting better and better," he grinned. He appeared on the verge of saying something else when Caz held up a hand. "As much as I would prefer to focus on happier things, Minister Sinclair is waiting for us downstairs," he said. "Shall we?"

I nodded and fell into step behind Dunston and Caz, following them and their Cyphers down a dimly lit flight of stairs and through a heavy metal door. As we stepped into the morgue, I couldn't keep from shivering, although my reaction had more to do with nerves than cold. The bodies had been spelled to prevent decay, meaning the room didn't have to be kept at freezing temperatures.

As we entered, a man in an immaculate pinstripe suit

turned to face us, and I didn't miss the way his golden-brown eyes narrowed as they landed on me. I stiffened, and Sebastian immediately moved closer. I felt as if this stranger had scrutinized me, compared me to something in his mind, and found everything about me severely lacking, which wasn't the impression I wanted to make.

Pressing my lips together, I held the man's gaze, refusing to be intimidated . . . or, more accurately, refusing to let him *know* I was intimidated.

"So," the man said in a clipped voice, "you are Arakiss's daughter."

I could hear the skepticism in his tone, the doubt I was anywhere near as capable as my father had been. But I chose to ignore it and held my head high.

"I'm Kyra. Caz told me you met my father a few months ago, when he was here for diplomatic talks."

The man nodded, although the movement was almost as stiff as his carefully styled black hair. "I was sorry to hear of his death. He was different from others of *your kind*."

His upper lip curled into a sneer, and inwardly I sighed. I couldn't fault someone with silver blood for disliking Astrals, but I was tired of the animosity, nonetheless.

Caz stepped forward and gestured towards the man.

"This is Minister Sinclair, overseer of the Meddygol *Adran*, and one of the most respected healers in Nocens. I've worked with him on a few occasions and found him to be a veritable fount of wisdom!"

Minister Sinclair briefly scowled at the floor, making it clear he would have preferred to be somewhere else, and I assumed he owed Caz a favor that was being repaid by his presence here. Dispensing with further pleasantries, the minister returned his eyes to mine.

"Caz tells me you have a way to extract information from a corpse," he all but hissed. "Frankly, I've never heard of such a thing, but then again, I've never been surprised by what Astrals will attempt."

I swallowed down the anger flickering in my chest and did my best to keep any bitterness from my voice. "When the body is injured, a trace memory is created," I explained, "physically recording information about how the injury was made, when it occurred, and where it happened."

Minister Sinclair blinked at me, but through the contempt, I thought I saw a spark of curiosity.

"I didn't know identifying trace memories was exclusive to my realm," I added, "but it doesn't have to be."

Minister Sinclair rolled his eyes. "How kind of you to share your brilliance with us lowly Daevals."

Sebastian shifted unhappily beside me, and I placed a hand against his arm even as I kept my eyes on Minister Sinclair.

"You can insult me and my kind all you want, but I'm not here to fight. I'm here because a Daeval child is dead, and I want to know if Astrals are involved."

"Why?" the minister spat. "So you can inform your government and give them a chance to concoct some ridiculous story absolving everyone with golden blood of blame?"

"My government has no idea I'm here," I retorted, "and I want to know if Astrals are harming Daevals so I can put a stop to it."

Minister Sinclair shook his head. "This is preposterous! Why should I trust a word you say?"

"My father trusted you enough to exchange information," I reminded him. "It might not seem like much, but if there's ever going to be peace between our kinds, we have to start somewhere."

The minister's jaw went slack. "Peace between our kinds?

Why in the burning realm would you even think such a thing?"

I looked at Sebastian before I could stop myself, and the healer followed my gaze, understanding dawning on his face. "Yes, well, it's quite a stretch from having a *personal* interest in Daevals to establishing peace between the realms," he said, each word dripping with condescension. "Forgive me for not sharing your optimism."

I thought about what Sebastian had said, questioning if Astrals and Daevals truly wanted the chance to live alongside one another, and while Minister Sinclair's words stung, I nevertheless pressed on.

"I'm offering to help you understand something you know nothing about . . . something that could benefit everyone in Nocens. I'm not here to convince you my kind are flawless and above reproach. We're not. I'm here to find out what Astrals are doing so I can stop them, and part of that means knowing where Gregor received his injuries."

Minister Sinclair huffed loudly but nevertheless considered my words. After a moment of silence, he shrugged.

"Teach me how to find trace memories." He slipped off his jacket, which he draped over a nearby chair, before unbuttoning the cuff of his long-sleeved shirt and extending his arm towards me. "Injure me."

I winced, not liking the idea of harming any living thing, even one as unlikable as Minister Sinclair. Sebastian, however, had no such qualms and immediately withdrew a dagger from his belt. Summoning a flame to sterilize the blade, he expertly flipped the weapon in his hand a few times before looking at me.

I'm more than happy to injure him after the way he's treated you.

Thank you, I said, *but it's probably better if I do it.*

Taking the handle of the knife from Sebastian, I held the tip of the dagger over Minister Sinclair's forearm. Drawing a breath,

I made a quick slice, ensuring I didn't go too deep, before handing the knife back to Sebastian.

"I'm going to heal you now," I said to the minister, "and then I'll show you how to find the trace memory."

He nodded, and to his credit, he managed not to flinch as I placed a hand above his wrist and summoned my *alera*, the basis of life that formed my connection with the rest of the world. I let the golden light flow out of my fingers, healing the cut until there was no sign it had existed. Minister Sinclair appeared impressed, which made me feel proud, even though I tried not to show it.

"Just by looking at your arm, no one would ever know you'd been injured," I said. "But if you're willing to learn, it's amazing what the body can teach you." Moving my hand off the healer, I pointed to his arm. "Place your hand where I cut you."

Minister Sinclair did as instructed, blinked, then shook his head. "Nothing. Perhaps the ability is limited to Astrals, after all."

"I can't see why it would be." I wasn't ready to give up so easily. "*Alera* functions the same way regardless of your blood type. Try again, and be patient . . . don't assume you know what the body is going to tell you; be open to receive what it wants to share. Since this is your first time doing it, it might take a few minutes."

Minister Sinclair let out an irritated exhale but nevertheless cupped his hand over his forearm and closed his eyes.

"When my father taught me to detect trace memories, he said we often miss them because we're in a hurry to find a problem, make a diagnosis, and apply a cure." I kept my voice low as I watched Minister Sinclair concentrate. "As healers, we want to identify the problem as quickly as possible so we can stop the suffering. We're used to looking for an active issue, something currently causing pain or sickness. Because that's our focus, we don't spend time allowing the body to speak to us, and we miss information about old wounds or illnesses. Follow the *alera* through your body and notice where it might seem interrupted or like it's flowing slower."

I tried to think of other ways to guide Minister Sinclair towards finding something he'd only just learned existed. I'd been doing this for so many years, whenever I touched someone's skin for longer than a few seconds, I saw everything about their past injuries and illnesses . . . but that was me, and a tiny knot of apprehension began to form in my stomach.

Trying to maintain a calm appearance, I added, "I don't know if it will work differently for you, but when I find a trace memory and focus on it, how the patient acquired the injury or illness plays out in my mind like a series of moving captum images. I see what happened, but it might be different for different healers."

Minister Sinclair remained quiet, and I held my breath, desperately hoping something I'd said made sense and would help him find the stored memory. After what felt like an eternity, even though it was actually only a moment or two, he startled.

"I see it," he said, and I couldn't keep from smiling at the mixture of surprise and wonder in his voice. "As clearly as if it's happening in front of me, I see it . . . and not just the injury you inflicted, but others." He blinked his eyes open. "Some of these I'd completely forgotten about." Gazing down at his forearm, he ran a finger over where I'd cut him. "All these years, and I can't believe I didn't know such a procedure existed. What your father said was correct . . . when Daevals come to me, they present a specific issue and I heal it. I never thought to seek information on the body from the body itself . . . which now seems rather ridiculous."

"We heal as we were taught," I said, not wanting him to feel badly about something he hadn't known was possible until just now. "I was fortunate to learn from my father."

Then again, what did it mean about my healing abilities if I'd learned them from someone who had used his knowledge of the body to torture silver-blooded children? I'd always been so proud of what I'd mastered from my father's teaching, but now my pride felt tainted. It seemed every time I revisited a memory involving my father, I was forced to see it differently, my perspective forever altered by what I'd uncovered since his death.

Minister Sinclair unrolled his sleeve and refastened the cuff before bringing his eyes back to mine. I was pleased to see they were filled with far less loathing and something that might have been approaching respect. "Shall we continue on to Gregor, then?" he asked.

I nodded and followed him over to a table, where he lifted a sheet to reveal the pockmarked face of a teenage boy. Folding the sheet down to reveal the boy's head and upper torso, he placed a hand against Gregor's neck. I stepped forward, drew a slow inhale, and gently rested my palm against the boy's thin shoulder.

Closing my eyes, I sent my *alera* into the unmoving body, and even though Sebastian had told me no blood remained in Gregor's veins, I was still surprised at the emptiness I found. It was also odd to touch a body without a shade, and I couldn't help thinking if I'd been a better Recovrancer, I would have been aware the instant Gregor died. Had it been his time? If not, could I have saved him? It was clear I needed to devote far more effort to my training with Laycus.

Focusing on the points of *alera* pulsing in my mind's eye, I let the images unfold before me, and it was only by sheer willpower that I kept my hand where it was instead of jerking it away.

After a few moments, I opened my eyes and gave Gregor's shoulder an apologetic squeeze before looking at Minister Sinclair.

"What did you see?"

The healer's nostrils flared. "The boy was tortured," he replied. "Wounds were inflicted to study his body's healing response, and this continued as more and more of his blood was taken. I . . . I can't . . ." He shook his head, collecting himself before staring at me. "Did you see it?"

"Yes," I replied, wishing I hadn't. "Gregor was experimented on by Astrals . . . in Rynstyn."

Revulsion filled me over what I'd witnessed, accompanied by the tiniest bit of relief that I hadn't seen my father in any of the stored memories. As fast as the relief appeared, however, it vanished as I recalled what I'd told Aurelius earlier, how my father's absence wasn't proof of his innocence. Sebastian's voice pulled me from my thoughts.

Was it the same facility where I was tortured?

Glancing back at him, I recalled what I'd seen of his trace memories. *It certainly looked like it.*

A muscle twitched in Sebastian's jaw, the only outward indication of the turmoil I felt roiling through him.

I turned back to Minister Sinclair. "It appears Astrals also tried to inject Gregor with golden blood. It wasn't compatible with his body, though, and caused severe internal damage." I couldn't fathom the pain such a procedure would have caused and again wished I could have helped the boy, either in life or death.

Minister Sinclair's eyes narrowed. "I saw."

He turned to Dunston and Caz, both of whom wore horrified expressions. Dunston pulled out the silk handkerchief he'd used earlier and ran it over his face before stuffing it back into his jacket pocket. He kept glancing at Sebastian then quickly looking away. He and Caz were the only two individuals besides me who knew about Sebastian's past, and I couldn't blame him for being concerned over the stoic Pyromancer.

"Now we have proof," said Minister Sinclair. "Proof that Astrals had a Daevalic child in their realm, where they tortured him until he died."

"How did he make it back to Nocens, though?" asked Dunston. "His aunt said he didn't have portaling abilities. Why didn't Astrals keep his body to hide the evidence of what they'd done . . . or better yet, destroy it?"

Everyone fell quiet, considering possible explanations, but when no one hit upon anything profound, Dunston spoke again.

"I think our best option is to keep quiet and pretend we know nothing," he suggested. "If Astrals think they're getting away with something, they're more likely to become arrogant, which increases the chances they'll do something careless. If we make it clear we're aware of what they're doing, we may lose the trail entirely, and it could be years before they slip up again."

"And while we're waiting for them to make a mistake, what if more Daeval children are taken to Rynstyn?" demanded Minister Sinclair.

"That's a risk we have to take," interjected Caz. "I certainly don't like it, but we're not looking to stop a few children from being taken . . . we're looking to uncover who in Aeles is doing this. I'm more concerned about destroying an entire operation than preventing a kidnapping or two."

I knew such a plan made sense but at the same time, the kidnapping or two he so casually mentioned involved one or two living *children*.

"Sebastian, what do you think?" asked Dunston.

Sebastian stared at his boots, and as he recalled his own torture in Rynstyn, I found myself struggling to breathe, momentarily overwhelmed by the fear and despair I felt pulsing through our connection. He quickly pushed his memories aside, but I hated that he had to make such a difficult decision. No child should be forced to experience what he'd suffered, but at the same time, the ultimate goal *was* shutting the program down for good.

"I agree with Dunston and Caz," he finally said, and I reached out, taking his hand in mine and offering what support I could.

Dunston dipped his head before turning to Minister Sinclair. "Can we count on your support in this matter?"

"Are you asking me as an official representative of the Nocenian government?" frowned the healer.

"Officially, the Nocenian government has no position on this matter because this matter doesn't exist," replied Dunston smoothly. "I'm asking for your cooperation as one Daeval to another. But make no mistake," his eyes darkened with something that sent an icy chill down my spine. "When the time is right, retribution will be swift and memorable."

Minister Sinclair turned towards me. "How can we trust you won't run to your government and tell them what happened here today?"

"You *dare* question her after everything she showed you?" Sebastian's voice was low, and while the minister's expression didn't change, I saw his throat bob as he swallowed. I didn't blame him . . . I recognized Schatten's voice speaking Sebastian's words, the voice of a king who was used to giving orders and having them obeyed without question.

"I won't say a word," I assured the healer. "And before you suggest I'll keep quiet simply to allow my kind to continue harming Daevals, I hope what I taught you about trace memories and the fact that I'm even discussing this with you proves otherwise."

Minister Sinclair continued to frown as he shrugged on his jacket and fastened the double-breasted buttons. "I agree Astrals are more likely to make a mistake if they believe they're operating without our knowledge," he finally said. "I can't in good conscience remain quiet forever, but I'll keep this to myself for now . . . at least until we've come up with another plan."

"A wise choice, which is exactly what I would expect from someone of your intelligence," smiled Caz, and while the words themselves were kind, I couldn't help but feel as if some sort of threat lingered in their wake.

"Well, I'm needed elsewhere," said Minister Sinclair. Looking at me again, I was surprised to hear him say, "Thank you for what you shared. I won't forget it."

Saying his goodbyes to the others, he strode out of the room and soon disappeared behind the heavy metal door.

12

SEBASTIAN

"*K*yra," said Dunston, "I truly cannot thank you enough for what you did here. I know favor trading is usually Caz's purview, but please know I'm in your debt. If there's any way I can repay you, don't hesitate to have Sebastian let me know."

"Thank you." Kyra smiled. "It was my pleasure."

I expected that to be the end of it, but to my surprise, Kyra ran a hand over her shifter cloak and said, "Since you mentioned it, there *is* something I could use your help with."

My head whipped towards her. What in the burning realm was she about to say?

"Minister Sinclair was right about me having a personal interest in peace between our kinds," she began. "But I don't think you need to be courting someone with different blood to want better relations between the realms. So much good could come from making it safer and easier for Astrals and Daevals to interact. I'm certain there are resources exclusive to Aeles or Nocens that could benefit the other realm. I'd love to share my knowledge of healing with more Daevals, and I have no doubt Astrals could learn a lot from those living in Nocens. I'm not the only Astral who wants a better relationship with your realm, and I'm betting you're not the only Daevals who would be open to friendships or at least business relationships with Astrals."

Dunston and Caz looked at one another, and I knew what they were thinking, given that I had a deeper understanding of their family business than Kyra. The Dekarais made a significant portion of their income through commerce that was strictly off the books in both realms. If more formal, government-sanctioned trade routes opened, they stood to lose the most from peace between Astrals and Daevals unless they pivoted and positioned themselves on the right side of the law. While I could envision such a scenario working, I wasn't certain they'd be willing to change their entire business model.

"What did you have in mind?" asked Dunston warily.

"Someone has to make the first move," said Kyra, "and while I can't do it publicly, I *can* still do it. Could you arrange for me to meet with any Daevals who might be open to better relationships with my kind? I'd love to find ways we could work together to change things in both realms."

"I'm certainly not opposed to new business opportunities," said Caz with a cheeky smile, tucking his thumbs under the lapels of his ill-fitting red and silver jacket.

Dunston ran a hand over his jaw. "The idea has merit," he admitted, studying Kyra. "Something tells me you don't need an official title to get folks to listen to you, but as the next *Princeps Shaman*, you'll wield significant political power."

Dunston was acting as if Kyra's future career somehow boded well for him, which made me think . . . it was one thing for the Dekarais to see me as a weapon to be wielded, but *quite* another for them to involve Kyra in one of their schemes. We'd have to be cautious.

Something unspoken passed between the brothers, and Dunston gave a decisive nod. "I'll do it," he said. "And not just because you're persuasive and I like to make money." He gave me a sad smile before turning back to Kyra. "I haven't always been there for Sebastian the way I should have been, so if I can help ensure his happiness now, I'll do whatever I can."

While I had a good idea what Dunston was referring to, I also didn't want to think about it; fortunately, Kyra spoke, saving me from standing there in awkward silence.

"Thank you!" she exclaimed, hurrying forward and throwing her arms around Dunston. "I can't tell you how much I appreciate your help."

Dunston beamed as Kyra returned to my side.

"We'll throw a party!" he said, his enthusiasm quickly matching Kyra's. "There's no better place to talk politics."

"I'm only in Nocens for one more night before I have to go back to internship," Kyra explained apologetically, "but if that's too soon to get folks together, I'll be back next weekend."

Caz chuckled. "Daevals will drop anything for the chance to attend a Dekarai party. That's more than enough time for invitations to be sent and accepted. Although, sadly, Minerva—our sister—" he added for Kyra's benefit, "is almost always out of town whenever we have a family gathering." He shook his head. "Such a shame."

I didn't like this at all. I'd already shared Kyra with others more than I wanted to, and we still had to see LeBehr. Plus, I hated parties and while it was one thing for Kyra to be around the Dekarais, it was quite another to have her in a house filled with Daevals I didn't know. But now that Dunston and Caz were involved, I didn't see any way out of it, which only increased my frustration.

We made our way back to the reception room and bid the Dekarais farewell as Dunston promised to reach out soon with details about the party. As the brothers vanished on the intersector and their Cyphers dematerialized, Kyra turned towards me.

"I was thinking about what you said yesterday," she offered, "how physically reuniting the realms isn't the same as bringing peace between Astrals and Daevals. You're right that just throwing everyone together would most likely be disastrous, so before we do that, we need to start building relationships. We need to identify those in each realm who want things to change and start them working together. We can't change policies until we change beliefs and opinions."

I knew Kyra always took what I said seriously, but I hadn't expected her to start addressing my concerns so soon or in quite this way. It was strategic thinking, though, which meant I couldn't immediately discount it.

"I don't know about telling anyone who we really are and who we used to be just yet," she continued, "but we don't have to figure that out before we start having conversations with those who are open to change." She studied my face. "When Dunston asked how he could repay me for helping with Gregor, the idea just came to me, but I'm sorry we didn't discuss it first. Are you upset?"

"I was just looking forward to being alone with you," I admitted, staring at a painting of thick purple swirls, circling into smaller and smaller spirals across the canvas.

Kyra stepped forward and slid her arms under mine, resting her head against my chest. "I want that too. But the opportunity seemed too good to pass up."

"It was quick thinking." I returned her hug. "I'm just ready to go see LeBehr so we can go home . . . I mean, go back to the cave."

I'd never referred to the cave as my home before, but perhaps my unintentional slip was further proof of how my life was divided into *before* and *after* Kyra. Thankfully, Kyra didn't comment on my uncharacteristic sentimentality, and I quickly changed the subject.

"We should have a plan for what to tell LeBehr about the

Chronicles and why we're looking for them." I'd never had the book seller track down a lost book for me, and even though she was discreet, it would be difficult to ask her to find a volume over a thousand years old without telling her how we'd come to know of such a book in the first place, as well as how we happened to have a page from it.

Kyra nodded. "The last time we visited her together, she found us a book mentioning the Felserpent King and Queen. You told me before you trust her, at least as much as you trust anyone. Do you think she'd believe us if we told her the truth?"

I thought about how books came alive around LeBehr, communicating with her and sharing information in ways I didn't understand. "She's always been able to learn more than I ever thought possible from books," I told Kyra. "If she can actually find the Chronicles, she'll be able to tell it's authentic. I don't know if she'll believe us, but I know she'll believe the book."

Apprehension and excitement intermingled in Kyra's eyes. "I think it's a risk worth taking."

Batty materialized outside the book shop just as I exited the portal, hanging upside down from the crooked sign and causing it to creak in protest. Aurelius took one look at the store and twitched his thick silver whiskers disapprovingly, but nevertheless followed Kyra inside. While Kyra and I stepped carefully over Mischief, growling up at us from her usual position in the doorway, I was surprised to see the lynx stop near the black cat. They must have engaged in a silent conversation because Mischief suddenly let out a raspy laugh, a sound I'd never heard the Cypher make before. I briefly wondered what the normally pompous lynx had said before shifting my attention to LeBehr, who had popped out from behind a shelf to welcome Kyra.

"Back so soon?" The shopkeeper raised her eyebrows at me. "Given that your last purchase involved a long-forgotten Daevalic language, I can't *wait* to hear what you're in the market for tonight."

"You're either going to love it or think we've lost our minds," I said. "Can we speak privately?"

LeBehr's mismatched green and yellow eyes widened, but she quickly nodded, and Mischief muttered something before rising from the doorway and relocating deeper inside the store. LeBehr waved a hand and the front door swung shut, a lock clicking in place as dark curtains lowered over the windows. The air around us became so heavy I could feel it as the shopkeeper cast a silencing spell, ensuring nothing we said would be overheard by anyone passing by. I'd never seen the store closed no matter what hour I'd visited, and I appreciated how seriously she'd taken my request.

"We need help locating a book," Kyra began. "We aren't certain what information you need in order to do that, but we have a page from it."

Batty pulled the folded piece of parchment from his wing and handed it to LeBehr, who squinted as she delicately accepted it. Carefully unfolding it, she ran her fingertips over the parchment before sniffing the ink and touching the tip of her tongue to one corner. Closing her eyes, she held the paper with both hands and fell silent for a moment before blinking at us.

"The book this came from is very old," she noted. "In fact, this might be the oldest document I've had the privilege of encountering. The spells Batty cast on it are marvelous . . . you could set it on fire, dunk it in water, or take a knife to it and it wouldn't matter. It's indestructible. Nothing could harm this parchment. I'm surprised you managed to separate it from the rest of the book."

Admiration shone in her eyes as Batty shot me a proud grin. Well, it was good to know he'd done something right.

"Lifting the spells was challenging," admitted Batty. "That is why I only managed to grab one page."

"How long ago was the book lost?" asked LeBehr.

"Approximately five hundred years ago," replied the bat. "Give or take a decade."

LeBehr nodded as if she had these types of conversations every day, then turned her attention to the words on the page. My heart began to beat faster, and I stole a glance at Kyra, only to find her already looking at me, apprehension wavering across her face.

LeBehr read both sides of the parchment and when she finally looked up, there was an intensity in her eyes I'd never seen before. "Given that this document mentions the Felserpent monarchy, I take it your earlier interest in the Felserpent King and Queen was not a passing fancy?"

"It wasn't," I agreed.

"I've never heard of a Blood Treaty before," the shopkeeper mused. "I *have*, however, in my illustrious career learned one thing . . . truth is always stranger than fiction." She held up the parchment. "Today I'm breaking my cardinal rule of no questions. What truth do we have here?"

The words stuck in my mouth, and I couldn't force them out, barely able to believe the truth even though I'd lived it. Thankfully, Kyra knew exactly what to say.

"The truth," she said, "is that the Felserpent King and Queen were real. At one time, Aeles and Nocens were one realm and in order to stop the constant warfare between the Astrals and Daevals who lived there, a golden-blooded Recovrancer married a silver-blood Pyromancer, bringing peace with their marriage and the drafting of the Blood Treaty. The history of the realm, along with their rule and how the kingdom was stolen from them, was documented in a book called the Chronicles, and what you're holding is the only part we have left. Sebastian and I were . . . we are . . . the Felserpent King and Queen. We've come back to reunite the realms, but in order to do that, we need the Chronicles."

Batty told LeBehr what he'd shared with us about losing the book, then there was nothing but silence. The shopkeeper looked at me.

"It's true," I said, and while my words were a ridiculously small contribution compared to Kyra's eloquent speech, I had to say something.

"I believe you," the bookseller said with a nod.

Even though that's what I'd hoped to hear, I still couldn't keep from asking, "You do?"

"Of course!" LeBehr adjusted the bright pink scarf tied in a large bow around her neck. "You've never lied to me, and there's no reason for you to start now. But in addition to that, the page agreed with everything I just heard." She smiled at Kyra. "It's clear you wrote this. The page glows when you hold it. Oh, I wish you could see it!"

Kyra appeared momentarily dumbfounded, then made a sound between a choking noise and a laugh as LeBehr pulled her into a hug.

"You're the only one who knows," Kyra said, her voice muffled against LeBehr's shoulder. "Thank you for believing us! It's so hard keeping it a secret, but sometimes it's also hard to remember it's really true, even though we were there and lived it."

After a moment, the two women separated, and Kyra gave me a relieved smile.

"I want to know as much as you're comfortable sharing," LeBehr said as she looked back and forth between the two of us.

And so we told her everything we knew about our pasts, as well as our plan to change the future of both realms.

When we'd finished, LeBehr's eyes were shining, and she looked as if we'd just given her a long hoped-for present.

"Never in my life did I imagine I would be involved in something so incredible!" she exclaimed. "Thank you for trusting and including me."

"Does that mean you can do it?" Kyra asked. "Can you locate the Chronicles?"

"Absolutely," smiled LeBehr, and Kyra let out a happy cry as she reached over and squeezed my hand. "I'll need to brew a potion," the bookseller continued, "which will take anywhere from ten to fourteen days, depending on temperatures. Once it's ready, I'll drink the potion while holding the page, and we'll know exactly where to find your book!"

She handed the parchment back to Batty, who tucked it into one of his seemingly innumerable wing pockets. "I'll reach out when the potion is ready," LeBehr said, "and then we'll be off!"

I didn't miss the way LeBehr had included herself in the plans to retrieve the book, and while I preferred to work alone, in this instance we clearly couldn't succeed without her.

"I meant what I said before," the shopkeeper said to Batty, who was perched on a tall stack of books. "That was *quite* the complicated spellcasting you did. I've read tales of beasts who roamed Nocens ages ago and possessed extraordinary powers— like the Felserpent creature Kyra mentioned—but I've never heard of a Cypher wielding such magic." While her voice was admiring, it was also full of unasked questions.

Batty winked at her. "A Cypher is only one of many things I have been in my life."

I knew from experience the bat shared what he wanted, when he wanted, and no amount of threatening or yelling at him would change his mind. Still, as we left the bookstore, I couldn't help wondering what other secrets the creature kept to himself and for the first time since I'd been paired with him, I found myself wishing I knew more about his life.

13

❧

KYRA

*B*ack in Sebastian's cave, I could hardly believe our good
fortune, and while I wanted to do nothing more than enjoy
time alone with Sebastian, I also knew I couldn't relax while
there were still things I needed to do. Since I only went into
Vaneklus when I was in Nocens, I had to make the most of being
here, which meant practicing my recovrancy with Laycus. After
what had happened with the Dekarais and LeBehr, I was finally
starting to feel like I was making progress towards my goals, and
if the Fates of this realm were feeling favorable, I wanted to make
the most of their generosity.

"I'm sorry there are so many things interrupting our time
together," I said to Sebastian, "but if I can get in some training
with Laycus, you'll have my undivided attention until it's time
for Dunston's party."

To my relief, Sebastian nodded. "Whoever's behind the Astral
experimentation program isn't sitting around doing nothing.
Gregor was proof of that." He pressed his lips into a thin line.
"I'm going to visit Tarfann's and talk to the staff. Perhaps someone remembers something about the man who spoke to Devlin. I
also want to visit some of the charities that look after orphans
and see if anyone has approached them with any unusual offers.
Then I'll be in a better position to relax too."

I smiled and kissed him goodbye, glad he understood my desire to accomplish what I could before stepping away from my responsibilities . . . although the way his lips lingered on mine made it incredibly difficult to let him leave. As his portal winked out of sight, I walked over and retrieved *The Book of Recovrancy*. I then made my way to the sofa, where Aurelius had already claimed a cushion, and adjusted my shifter cloak as I sat down. While I'd learned I could keep myself from becoming soaking wet by focusing on my clothes in the realm of the dead, I preferred not to divide my attention when dealing with Laycus. The shifter cloak somehow kept me dry without me needing to think about it, which was incredibly helpful.

I skimmed the book's table of contents, but as the information I was seeking didn't readily present itself, I placed my palm flat against the page and focused on what I wanted to know: What was the process for recovering a shade who had sought rest in Ceelum?

Lifting my hand, I watched as the pages began to turn, gently flipping forward until they stopped, and I couldn't keep from smiling as black text rose onto the white paper. *The Book of Recovrancy* always showed me what I needed to know, although it never showed me *everything* all at once, as too much information could be overwhelming and more than a mind could bear. Instead, the book shared what it saw fit, and I could easily open to the same page and find different words there each time.

Pulling the book closer, I read:

When a shade departs their physical body, they are ferried onward by the Shade Transporter to one of two places— Ceelum for rest or Karnis to prepare for a return to life in a new body. This is true for those who die at their appointed time, as well as those who die prematurely. Those who die early also face the possibility of a far less pleasant fate . . . while they may be taken onwards, they may also be claimed as the property of the Shade Transporter, at which point they cease to exist in a manner ever allowing for their return.

I stared at a cluster of yellow quartz growing out of the wall across the cavern, and even though part of me was curious, I suspected I didn't *really* want to know what Laycus did with a shade who arrived in Vaneklus before their appointed time. Given how dedicated he was to preventing me from recovering shades who died early, there had to be some personal benefit to him. All the more reason to strengthen my recovrancy skills, so I read on.

Shades in Ceelum are not required to interact with a Recovrancer seeking to speak with them, but if they choose to do so, the shade will appear in the form of the last physical body they inhabited.

That was good to know. While I was certain Sebastian kept a picture of his mother somewhere, I'd also seen her in our shared dream, so I could at least recognize her.

New text appeared on the page.

Recovering a shade who died before their time from Ceelum is perhaps the most complicated procedure a Recovrancer can perform, and the majority of Recovrancers never attempt such a thing, as the consequences can be beyond dire. When a shade enters Death, the shade continues to live; however, the physical body the shade inhabited does not and either decays, is reduced to ash, or meets its demise in some other way. In order for that shade to be recovered, a new body will be required, and many factors must be considered.

First, the shade must wish to be recovered, returning to the last life they lived. Second, someone of the same blood type must die at their appointed time. And third, as the shade who died at their appointed time is ferried onwards by the Shade Transporter, the Recovrancer must perform the Incolens Corpus Novum *spell, directing the recovered shade into the newly vacated physical body. Additional specifications must be met, but these will only be revealed to a Recovrancer once she commits to using this particular spell.*

The danger of such a procedure cannot be overstated, as it is impossible to predict whether or not a shade will adjust to their new body. In some instances, shades ended up losing their minds due to their inability to settle into a different body. In extreme cases, shades took their own lives simply to return to Vaneklus and the familiarity of Death. Family and friends have also been known to struggle with having a loved one return to life in a different body, looking nothing like they did before.

This procedure should be performed only after the most careful consideration, as each Recovrancer is permitted to use the Incolens Corpus Novum *spell once per life cycle.*

A knot formed in my stomach, and I continued to stare at the words without really seeing them. This spell was the only way to bring Sebastian's mother back with memories of the last life she'd lived. Shades didn't usually recall things from previous lives, which meant if Grace journeyed onward to Karnis and was reborn rather than recovered, she would have no memories of Sebastian or their short life together.

But what if I successfully recovered Grace's shade, only for her to fail at adjusting to being alive again, causing her to lose her mind or take her own life to find peace? That would be worse for Sebastian than continuing to live without her.

On the other hand, presenting no less terrible of a possibility, what if I wasn't capable of performing such a difficult procedure? I'd barely begun to explore my recovrancy skills, and while I would work as hard as I could, what if that wasn't enough? Plus, I could only use this particular spell once in my entire lifetime . . . what if something happened to Sebastian, or one of my family members, or Demitri? My blood ran cold, and an anxious shiver sped through me. Who was I to choose who lived and who died?

You are a Recovrancer, that's who, came Aurelius's voice, and I looked at him, gazing at me from the opposite end of the sofa. *But before you become overwhelmed by conjecture, perhaps it would be best to speak with Laycus.*

Thank you, I said, grateful for his ability to know when I needed to be pulled from an impending spiral of worry, *and you're right.*

Closing the book, I gave it an affectionate pat. Regardless of the challenges, at least I knew some of what was required to re-cover a shade from Ceelum.

Relocating to the middle of the cavern a few yards from the sofa, I sat down and ran my fingers over Tawazun and Rheolath, two beads on my *sana* bracelet. "*Bidh me a'dohl a-steach.*" Closing my eyes, I felt myself being pulled from my body before my boots landed firmly in the grey waters of Vaneklus.

The ever-present fog bank hovering over the river slowly parted, and I soon heard oars striking the water, followed by the arrival of Laycus, standing in his black shroud at the prow of his wooden boat. Extending one end of his staff into the water, he drew the boat to a stop before grinning at me.

"To what do I owe the pleasure, Recovrancer?"

"I've been reading." My words prompted the Shade Transporter to groan. "Which means I have questions for you."

"Aren't I the lucky one?" Laycus grumbled before resting both hands on top of his staff and motioning for me to continue.

I told him what I'd learned from *The Book of Recovrancy*, and while he listened, he also made no effort to hide his disdain. I suspected he hated the book because it offered ways to work around him and exposed the limits of his power, but there was no need to point that out.

"I'm going to talk to Sebastian about everything that could go wrong if I attempt to recover his mother," I said, "but if he still wants me to try, I'll need you to take me to Ceelum."

"The last time a Recovrancer asked for such a thing, it was ages before you existed as Kareth," Laycus snapped. "And it ended terribly . . . the shade didn't take to their new body and lived a tortured, miserable existence until they were mercifully struck by lightning and returned here, where they clearly belonged."

"I understand it's a complicated procedure," I began, but Laycus cut me off with a sharp laugh.

"*Complicated* doesn't begin to describe it! To find someone whose time it is to die, then to take the shade of someone who died before their time and tether them inside a vacant body . . . any benefits cannot *possibly* outweigh the risks!"

"It's certainly no more impossible than binding two shades together," I countered, "specifically, two shades with different blood who spent a millennium looking for one another until they were finally reunited."

Laycus's fiery eyes flickered, and I could tell my words had touched him. Gazing down at his boat for a moment, he eventually raised his cowled head.

"If anyone could do it, it would be you." The sincerity in his voice unsteadied me more than if he'd shouted. He must have seen the surprise on my face, because he nodded. "I mean it, Kyra . . . Kareth . . . Recovrancer. If such a thing can be done successfully, you are the only being I've encountered in eons who has a chance of doing it."

It was a rare occasion that I found myself at a loss for words, but I finally remembered my manners. "Thank you for your belief in me."

Laycus dipped his head, then shifted his stance, causing the boat to rock and sending out little waves that lapped at my knees in a not-altogether unfriendly manner.

"If Sebastian wants me to recover his mother, is there anything I need to know to prepare for visiting Ceelum?" I asked.

A smirk stretched across the Shade Transporter's skull-like face. "We'll just have to hope that precious book of yours has a section on that, won't we?"

I frowned at Laycus even as I hoped *The Book of Recovrancy* would, in fact, have such a section. It was maddening how unpredictable he was, one moment giving me an impressive compliment, the next refusing to even attempt being helpful. But such was the mercurial nature of the ruler of Vaneklus, and I would continue to work with him as best I could.

"In the meantime," said Laycus, "what else do you wish to discuss while you're here?"

At least he was open to talking about other things. "How do I know if a shade died at their appointed time?"

"Well, you can always ask me," he replied with a far-too-bright smile.

I gave him a look. "There has to be another way. Remember, you agreed to help me."

"Yes, yes," Laycus grumbled. "Well, for my part, I can see whether or not a shade belongs in Vaneklus. Some might call it an aura, but when a shade appears on my dock, there are two possibilities . . . if it emanates a white light, I know it was that shade's time to die. If there's no such light," he grinned deviously, "then I can enjoy the one pleasure permitted to me in this thankless enterprise."

Certain I'd be sorry I asked, I nevertheless had to know. "What exactly do you do with shades who've died prematurely and aren't recovered?"

"I consume them," said Laycus, "and as I absorb their memories, I experience them, allowing me to feel as if I lived a life outside of Vaneklus."

I cringed picturing the act, but I could also understand why Laycus would do such a thing—thousands of years in the same setting would make anyone desperate to see or feel something new. While I appreciated the Shade Transporter's honesty, his disclosure also prompted a terrible realization.

"Sebastian's mother died before her time." My heart nearly dropped into my stomach. "And she wasn't recovered."

Was I too late? I was prepared to use the most dangerous spell known to Recovrancers, but what good was my power if I couldn't use it when it mattered most? The same helplessness I'd experienced when I'd failed to heal my father began winding through me, reminding me I was lifetimes removed from the powerful queen I'd once been.

"I told you before, the last time I saw Sebastian's mother I was ferrying her to Ceelum," huffed Laycus indignantly. "I don't blindly consume every shade who arrives early on my shores."

That meant I still had a chance . . . although such an act seemed out of character for Laycus, especially when I knew how much he'd disliked Schatten, a dislike that extended to the Daeval's present incarnation as Sebastian. Letting my heartbeat slow as my nerves resettled, I studied Laycus's bone-white face. "Why did you let Sebastian's mother travel onwards?"

"I made an exception, but my reasons are my own," he scowled. When it became clear he would share no more, I tried to put it out of my mind, at least enough to focus on continuing my training.

"Going back to what you said about auras, I didn't see any light when I recovered Sebastian. His death just didn't feel right, but I can't base decisions about who I attempt to recover on feelings."

"You felt it because of your *sana* bracelet," explained Laycus. "Whatever a Recovrancer uses to access Death will tell her whether or not it's a shade's time to die. It's been like that for every Recovrancer I've met. Their instrument—be it a bracelet, a wind flute, bells, or a tuning fork—alerts them to the state of the shade."

"How does my bracelet, or any other recovrancy tool, know if it's a shade's time to die?"

"That is beyond my knowledge," Laycus admitted rather begrudgingly.

I studied the seven beads forming my *sana* bracelet. My father had gifted it to me on my thirteenth birth anniversary, but where had he acquired it? It was almost too overwhelming to think something I'd worn centuries ago as a completely different woman had managed to find its way to me again, but somehow, it had.

"Do you know how certain objects become affiliated with a Recovrancer?" I turned my wrist from side to side. "What makes this *sana* bracelet function for me the way it does?"

"I doubt either of us will ever know the answer to that," said Laycus, "you, because it's not necessary to know to perform your work and me, because my sister simply enjoys spiting me."

"Your *sister*?" I repeated, more than a little taken aback.

"My sister," glowered Laycus. "Suryal. She oversees Karnis and the process by which shades return to the land of the living.

As she is involved with returning shades to life, I assume she is involved with recovrancy tools, but her secrets are her own."

"How does she—" I started to say, but Laycus raised a skeletal hand.

"I will say no more about her."

Even though I was eager to know everything I could about the mysteries of Vaneklus, I also didn't want Laycus to decide he was done teaching, so I returned to the topic of my recovrancy skills.

"If a shade enters Vaneklus and it wasn't their time to die—and you don't consume them—how long do I have to recover them before you ferry them onwards?"

"It varies." Laycus smoothed a skeletal hand over the front of his black shroud.

"That hardly seems fair!" I protested, causing the Shade Transporter to lean towards me.

"What length of time would you deem fair?" For once, his question was sincere as opposed to sarcastic. "An hour? A day? What would seem fair for one shade would be horribly unfair for another. Death comes for everyone and waits for no one . . . even with your abilities as a Recovrancer, all you're doing is postponing the inevitable." He shrugged. "Why bother? Every shade finds their way to me eventually."

"Perhaps, but if it's not their time, it's only right they're returned to their body and given the lifespan they've been allotted. Look at Sebastian."

"I'd rather not," muttered Laycus, but I ignored the barb.

"I recovered his shade, and he used the second chance to make much better choices."

"The only truly *good* choices he's made since his recovery have been accepting his past and choosing a present with you," said Laycus. Sighing loudly, he stared off into the distance. "Although I suppose he does deserve some credit for that."

The way Laycus spoke made it seem as if he'd somehow seen Sebastian's actions in the realm of the living. Of course, he could simply be inferring things since I frequently spoke about Sebastian to him, but I also recalled that he'd come into Aeles-Nocens and spoken with Schatten before we'd been married, meaning he had at least some ability to be connected to the world outside of Vaneklus. There was so much I didn't know about the enigmatic figure before me, but I *did* know he disliked personal questions, so once again, I kept the focus on myself.

"I can't save everyone, can I?" I studied Laycus's face. "Astrals and Daevals will die, even those who aren't supposed to, and even if I'm aware of it—which is something else I have questions about—I won't always be able to put things right, will I?"

"No," replied Laycus, although his voice was gentler than I'd anticipated; I'd half-expected him to taunt me about my limited powers. "Your recovrancy is a gift, because it's not promised to everyone . . . whereas death is not only promised but assured."

"How do I know when someone has died if I don't see it happen, like I did with my father and Sebastian?"

"You learn to live with one foot in life and one in Death." Laycus shifted his staff from one hand to the other. "This was quite the challenge for you before . . . once you were aware of your connection to Death, you almost became overwhelmed by it."

"How did I master it?" Holding my breath, I prayed to the Gifters Laycus would answer.

"You learned to influence the connection within yourself. Think of it as turning a knob . . . you can control the flow of information coming in, increasing it so you're aware of more or decreasing it so you're aware of less. Once you gain an intimate acquaintance with Death, you can never truly ignore its presence, but you can learn to live with it."

"When I was Kareth, I recovered both Astrals and Daevals,"

I recalled. "Do you think I could become strong enough to sense someone dying in Nocens?"

Laycus considered that. "Sensing the death of someone with silver blood will likely be more challenging, given the separation of the realms, but with practice, I believe you could."

If the realms being separate made recovrancy harder, reuniting the realms would allow me to be a more effective Recovrancer, which was yet another reason to keep working at bringing Astrals and Daevals together.

I was about to ask Laycus how to strengthen my awareness of what happened in Vaneklus when I wasn't actually there when an elderly man suddenly appeared at the end of the dock jutting out into the river. Laycus smirked at me.

"My shade or yours?"

Pressing a finger against Glir, the diamond bead on my *sana* bracelet associated with clarity, I closed my eyes and concentrated. Everything inside me felt right, calm and settled and very different from when Sebastian had died.

I opened my eyes. "He died at his appointed time. He's yours."

Laycus gave a pleased chuckle as his boat pulled away, but whether he was proud I'd mastered his teachings or happy to be claiming the newly arrived shade, I couldn't quite say.

14

SEBASTIAN

J returned to find Kyra sitting on the sofa, gazing pensively into space. While part of me dreaded what she might have discovered about recovering my mother, the rest of me craved information, so I took a deep breath, sat down beside her, and listened as she explained what she'd learned from her book and the Shade Transporter. My head swam with the implications . . . how in the burning realm could I make a decision of such magnitude for my mother, a decision that might cause me to lose her a second time due to my own selfishness at wanting her back? And, as much as I wanted to think I wouldn't care what my mother looked like so long as she was in my life again, I had to admit I didn't know how I'd respond to being reunited with her in a different body that had no place in my childhood memories.

"I think the first thing to do is see if my mother is still in Ceelum," I said, using Kyra's Astral terminology, even though I'd grown up hearing that part of Vaneklus referred to as Gabfarr. I rubbed the back of my neck. "If she's there and you can speak with her, you can find out what she wants. If she wants to be recovered, then that's what I want, but if she doesn't . . ." my chest tightened even as I forced the words out, "then I'll respect her wishes, and she can remain where she is."

Kyra nodded, pulling off her boots and tucking her feet underneath her. "Did you have any luck finding out more about the man who approached Devlin?"

"No." I pushed myself up and crossed the cavern to the area that served as my kitchen, filling a glass with water from the sink I'd installed. "Two charity directors described meeting with someone who has to be the same man, but they didn't make any formal agreements and had no idea how to reach him. Whoever he is, he's good at covering his tracks." I set the glass on the counter and crossed my arms. "Speaking of someone who will undoubtedly be good at covering his tracks, I've been thinking about where we might discover Tallus—if he's returned with his memories intact—and I think we should keep an eye on the Aelian military."

Kyra's eyebrows rose. "It would make sense," she agreed. "It's one place where it's perfectly acceptable to hate and kill Daevals." She sighed and sank deeper into the sofa cushions. "Unfortunately, Laycus doesn't keep up with shades after they've left his care, which means he won't know the last time Tallus was reborn. His sister, Suryal, rules Karnis, and *she* would know the last time Tallus returned to life; unfortunately, I have no idea how to contact her or if contacting her is even possible, and I don't think Laycus will be inclined to help."

"If we're assuming Tallus has returned, then based on what Laycus told Batty, he would be a man or woman somewhere between the ages of twenty and thirty." I walked over to the dining table and rested my hands on the back of a tall chair. "How old is Adonis?"

"Almost twenty-one, but you can't possibly think—"

"—What if he's only pretending to help you shut down the experimentation program?" I pressed. "What if he's really just trying to get close to you to see if you're Kareth returned?"

"That's absurd!" Kyra shook her head. "By that logic, Nigel

could be Tallus reborn . . . and before you ask, Demitri is nineteen and won't be twenty for a few months."

That didn't conclusively rule the Astral out, as Batty had said exact timings were difficult to pin down in Vaneklus, but my peerin vibrated and since it was most likely Dunston reaching out to let us know when to arrive for the party, I pulled it from my pocket. As I flipped the device open, I was surprised to see Eslee's face instead of her father's and pressed my fingertip against the lens, accepting the communication.

"I know you'll be disappointed to hear this, given how chatty you are," she said, her red-painted lips twisting into a smirk, "but I actually called to speak with Kyra."

I handed the peerin to Kyra, who accepted it with a surprised expression.

"I'm so excited about the party tonight!" trilled Eslee. "Daddy's gone completely overboard, and Mother's using it as an excuse for new jewelry, not that she ever needs an excuse. I don't know what you're doing this afternoon, but do you want to come over early and get ready together? I'm guessing you probably didn't bring any ball gowns for a weekend with Sebastian, and I have tons of things you can borrow."

Before Kyra could respond, Eslee's voice grew louder.

"Sebastian, I know you're lurking close by. You can get ready with Devlin while I help Kyra prepare for her debut in Nocenian society."

As if this party couldn't get any worse.

Still, Kyra looked so excited as she glanced at me for confirmation, I couldn't say no and disappoint her. Instead, I gave a slight nod.

"We'd love that!" Kyra assured Eslee, who squealed with delight. "Thank you so much!"

Watching Kyra and Eslee make plans together, an idea began

to form. I didn't want Kyra spending time with Demitri, but in order to put an end to that, I needed to replace her current best friend with a new one . . . and who better than Eslee? While she was vain and shamelessly manipulated her father and to a lesser extent, her uncle, she was also a smart businesswoman with a brazen independent streak. Perhaps encouraging Kyra and Eslee to spend time together would show Kyra she had better options for friends than the ridiculous little Astral with the overly styled hair. While I still wasn't excited about the party, I now found myself approaching it with far less dread than I'd felt before Eslee's call.

Even though I normally didn't keep any sort of regular sleep schedule, I wanted to be mindful of Kyra's needs, as she was the one dealing with switching from Aelian to Nocenian time, so we took the opportunity to rest for a few hours. To my surprise, I actually managed to fall asleep this time; thankfully, I didn't have any nightmares, as I would have been mortified to wake Kyra with my screams or thrashing.

As we prepared to leave for the Dekarais' house, Kyra ran her hands over the front of her tunic. "This seemed like such a good idea at the time," she fretted. "What if I say the wrong thing and upset someone? I don't want to make relations between Astrals and Daevals worse than they already are."

"You won't," I assured her. "Just you being in Nocens and making an effort to interact will go a long way with my kind. Remember, Nocens never outlawed Astrals coming here or established anything like the Blood Alarm, so the realm clearly isn't intent on remaining separate. Based on their past actions, Daevals have shown they're more likely to react rather than initiate anything themselves."

Kyra nodded. "My plan is to ask a lot of questions and let whomever I meet do most of the talking. I don't want to come across like some self-appointed savior swooping in with all the answers. I want to find common ground and figure out how everyone can benefit from working together."

"That's definitely the smartest approach with my kind. Just be yourself, and you'll have Daevals lining up to talk to you." I had no doubt Kyra could charm even the most recalcitrant citizen of Nocens; after all, look at the effect she had on me.

"Thank you for doing this with me," said Kyra. "I know socializing at a party isn't even close to your idea of a nice night, but I couldn't do this without you. And," her smile managed to be both shy and excited at the same time, "it's our first social outing as a couple. I love the idea of being out in public—well, in the Dekarais' house—with you."

"Me too," I agreed, knowing everyone we met would instantly view me as the lucky one in the relationship, and of course they'd be right.

As I opened a portal, Kyra looked around. "Where's Batty?"

"Aside from LeBehr's, he doesn't go out in public with me." Even though I'd been intentionally vague, Kyra tilted her head to one side, interpreting what I hadn't said.

"You mean, you don't want to be seen with him in public," she surmised. "I don't think that's right after everything he's done for us. I'm sure the Cyphers will go off and keep their own company once the party starts, but until then, he can stay with me."

Batty appeared on the back of the sofa, his wings wrapped around his pear-shaped body, dark eyes wide with hope.

"He is *my* Cypher," I pointed out, unused to anyone taking the bat's side or criticizing my treatment of him, but Kyra merely tossed her hair over her shoulder.

"He was my royal advisor before he was your Cypher."

I didn't see how that changed anything, but as long as I

wasn't responsible for cleaning up any messes the bat inevitably made, I could pretend he wasn't there.

Kyra and Batty both sensed my acquiescence, and the bat materialized on her shoulder as Aurelius snorted unhappily, joining us from across the room and following us through the portal.

Emerging on the circular driveway in front of the Dekarais' mansion, I couldn't fault the look of amazement that spread over Kyra's face. The house was three stories tall in the center with two-story wings extending out on either side, and the polished black limestone shone in the light of the setting sun, every window gleaming with gold trim. You couldn't see it from where we stood, but the grounds were protected by a tall fence, as well as a multitude of spells to keep trespassers or curious Daevals away. Dunston had long ago made an exception and allowed me to bypass the anti-portal wards he kept in place, and even though I knew I'd earned it, I never took his trust for granted.

We made our way up the checkered black and white steps that had always reminded me of a chessboard, and Kyra marveled at the red tourmaline light fixture suspended from the overhang formed where part of the house jutted over the driveway. As I pressed the buzzer beside the oversized front door, Kyra drew a deep breath, and I squeezed her hand, hoping to reassure her.

The door swung open, and a blur of chestnut hair, red boots, and long limbs otherwise known as Eslee pulled Kyra into an embrace, prompting Batty to dematerialize until the two women pulled apart. He then reappeared on Kyra's shoulder, grinning as if he was already having the time of his life.

"It's so good to see you again!" Eslee exclaimed to Kyra. "I don't know what's crazier . . . that you're voluntarily walking into a houseful of Daevals or that you're here with Nocens' most reclusive citizen!"

She shot me a grin. "Always nice to see you, Sebastian."

I dipped my head towards her, letting her sarcasm roll off me, as I knew Eslee well enough to understand when she was teasing. "You too, Eslee."

Eslee took Kyra's hand and pulled her into the house. "Devlin! Mother! Kyra and Sebastian are here."

The fire stirred in my veins even as I told myself there was nothing to worry about. Of course I would have preferred to keep Kyra away from Devlin for the foreseeable future—or forever—given what an incorrigible flirt he was, but just because he was annoying didn't mean he was dangerous, and dealing with him was worth it for Kyra and Eslee to spend time together.

As we stood in the foyer, Kyra swiveled her head from side to side, clearly trying to take everything in. The inside of the house looked like a curated museum, albeit one that wanted you to be comfortable during your visit. Onyx floors, twisting copper and platinum sculptures, life-sized paintings, hand-carved tables, overstuffed sofas and claw-footed chairs, brocade curtains, hand-woven rugs . . . I'd spent so much time in this house, I didn't think anything of the extravagance, but I understood Kyra's reaction. Today, the house was filled with the usual staff, as well as florists, caterers, musicians, decorators, and a host of other Daevals whose roles I could only imagine, preparing for the party.

Footsteps drew nearer, and Devlin rounded a corner. At least he was wearing a shirt that wasn't see-through, and for once, I was happy to see his fitted leather breeches . . . knowing Kyra's stance on not wearing anything that came from an animal, his attire wouldn't endear him to her. His butterscotch eyes, identical to Eslee's, glowed brightly as he stepped forward and made a small bow towards Kyra.

"I'm Kyra," she said with a smile, extending her hand, which Devlin immediately pressed to his lips. Without entirely meaning to, I clenched my hand into a fist, imagining it connecting with

Devlin's mouth before Batty's voice piped up between my ears reminding me *annoying* behavior wasn't the same as *inappropriate* behavior.

"I'm Devlin, and it's an absolute pleasure to meet you," the imbecile practically purred. His Cypher materialized next to him, the large black panther looking equal parts bored and annoyed to find himself at a family gathering. "This is Onyx," added Devlin. "You know, I only saw you from a distance at my Uncle Caz's, but I've been dying to meet you ever since."

His gaze skimmed over Batty, but as he registered the bat's presence on Kyra's shoulder, a surprised expression crossed his face. Cyphers were notoriously standoffish with anyone they weren't paired with, so the fact that my Cypher was so comfortable with Kyra was no small thing. Ever the showman, Devlin quickly recovered and smiled at Batty.

"I haven't seen you in ages," he said. "I was beginning to think you'd given up on Sebastian and were trying to get the Cypher *Adran* to reassign you early."

Thankfully, before the bat could respond, Devlin and Eslee's mother entered the room, pausing in the doorway for dramatic effect, as was typical for her, before continuing towards us. Her chin-length black hair swayed sharply against her jaw as her dark brown eyes took in the scene. I'd learned a lot about gems through the Dekarais, as I frequently tracked down and reclaimed precious stones stolen from their mines, and the ornate diamond and pearl necklace the woman was wearing cost more than I made in a month . . . which was saying something, as my fees were routinely considered exorbitant.

"It's always lovely to see you, Sebastian." Our hostess for the evening smiled at me before fixing her attention on Kyra. "And this must be the Astral I've heard so much about! I can't tell you how grateful I am you convinced my husband to throw a party.

I'm Rennej, darling, and it's a pleasure to meet you." Her Cypher, a lemur named Loris, materialized on her shoulder, much to Kyra's delight.

"I'm Kyra, and this is my Cypher, Aurelius. It's such a pleasure, Mrs. Dekarai. I've heard so many lovely things about you, but none of them did you justice."

Rennej made a tittering laugh as she pressed a hand to her chest, clearly pleased, and I had to admit, Kyra's social skills never failed to impress me. She certainly had a way with folks, charming them as if it was the easiest thing in the world instead of a valuable skill I could practice every day and still never possess.

"Well," said Rennej, "you never know what folks will say, especially those who can't be happy for someone else's success." She raised her hands in a helpless gesture. "It's not always easy, dealing with the constant pressures that go with a certain lifestyle, but I bear it as best I can."

"That's Mother . . . always the martyr," chirped Eslee, earning herself a scowl from her mother who quickly turned to Devlin and began fussing over him, brushing an imaginary speck of lint from his shirt.

"I see you've already met Devy," she beamed. "The only one of my children who truly appreciates me."

Rennej doted on Devlin and treated him as the favored child, while Dunston adored Eslee and treated her as if she'd hung the moon. It had always been that way, and both Devlin and Eslee used their select favoritism to their advantage, frequently pitting their parents against one another. It wasn't my idea of how a family ought to function, but somehow the Dekarais made it work.

"Well, as much as I'd love to stay and chat, Kyra and I need to start getting ready," said Eslee, tugging Kyra towards the grand black marble staircase. Kyra flashed me a wide smile as Aurelius walked beside her and Batty rode happily on her shoulder, and I did my best to return the expression before following Devlin deeper into the house.

While Kyra wasn't alone in wanting to reunite the realms, it was clear she was far more eager than I was . . . perhaps because she focused on the good that might result from reunification, whereas I was more concerned with the dangers and difficulties inherent to bringing two diametrically opposed realms together. I hoped she wouldn't be disappointed by the events of the evening. Wanting to do everything I could to ensure her time with my kind was successful, I offered a quick prayer to Rhide, the Fate associated with the past, asking for their blessing and assistance in bringing about the peace Astrals and Daevals had enjoyed before.

I also made a much more selfish plea to Ga'lie, the Fate who governed the present, entreating them to help me face whatever would be involved in preparing for the party with Devlin.

15

KYRA

*E*slee's bedroom was part of a suite of rooms, and after walking through her black and gold living space, I stepped into her bedroom and gazed around in amazement, having never seen anything like it. Red walls were covered in cascading strings of spelled red lights, some short, others reaching all the way down to the ground. A massive black four-poster bed was fitted with red curtains that matched the thick red rugs strewn across the floor. An ornate black wood and iron vanity was strewn with vials of cosmetics, and numerous paintings covered the walls while metal sculptures seemed to grow right out of the floor.

Eslee's Cypher, a mink named Sasha I'd met outside Caz's office, appeared on the bed, exclaiming happily over Batty's unexpected presence before welcoming Aurelius. As the Cyphers spoke amongst themselves, Eslee closed the bedroom door and turned to me.

"I have *so* many questions!" she exclaimed.

"What do you want to know?" I smiled, grateful for the chance to practice talking about potentially charged topics before the party.

"How in the burning realm did you end up in a relationship with Sebastian?!" Eslee gestured towards her Cypher. "Sasha will vouch that it takes a lot to shock me—a *lot*—but when Daddy told us about you being in a relationship with Sebastian, I literally almost fell out of my chair."

"Because I'm an Astral?" I hadn't expected Dunston's daughter of all Daevals to harbor ill will towards my kind.

"No, because he's *Sebastian*!" Eslee waved her hands as if trying to grasp invisible words. "Look, I've known him my entire life. His mother was close friends with my parents, and he was over here all the time as a kid. Most years, we had nearly every class together in school. I'm no expert, but I also know him better than probably anyone else in the realm, and he's the absolute last Daeval I would ever expect to be in a relationship with anyone! As far as I'm concerned, the only thing he loves more than his privacy is working for Daddy and Uncle Caz, although I don't know what he spends his money on. It's definitely not clothes— you've seen what he wears—and he's never once invited Devlin or me to wherever he lives. It's a true miracle of the Fates if he says more than ten words in a single evening, and I don't even know the last time I saw him smile . . . until today when you came upstairs with me."

I didn't know what to say to all that, but it didn't matter, because Eslee wasn't done.

"Daddy told us you the two of you accidentally met when Sebastian went to Aeles for work. I can't believe you didn't report him, much less stayed in touch with him! Don't get me wrong . . . he's not bad looking, if you like high cheekbones with a side of brooding. I'm just surprised, that's all."

"I feel like I've known him my entire life," I said, which wasn't a lie. "I think . . . he's definitely everything you described, but there's also so much more to him. He's brave and selfless and sees angles and possibilities I never even think to look for. He built a successful business by himself." I thought of his shower system in the cave, as well as how he'd piped turmaxinase gas and installed lighting fixtures throughout the cavern. "He can do anything with his hands. I mean, he can *build* anything with his hands," I corrected myself as Eslee arched a perfectly sculpted eyebrow, causing my cheeks to burn. "He also loves books and reading as much as I do," I added somewhat belatedly.

"Well, I couldn't be happier!" grinned Eslee. "Clearly you're the only one capable of getting him to socialize more than twice a year, and I'd love to take the two of you to all my favorite places in Vartox."

"I'd love that too," I replied eagerly. While I would take any opportunity to become more familiar with Nocens, I was also thrilled at the idea of making a new friend. "And how about you? Is there a special ma . . . Daeval . . . in your life?" I silently cursed myself, glad I'd caught my insensitive slip, but annoyed to find I'd unconsciously internalized my realm's position that courtships were always between a man and a woman even though I whole-heartedly disagreed with such nonsense.

Eslee shook her head. "I actually realized a few years ago I have no interest in being in a relationship with anyone." A mischievous grin spread across her painted lips. "Mother was initially heartbroken over the idea of never planning a wedding or bartering me off to secure some political alliance, but eventually she came around. Daddy and Uncle Caz have always supported me without question. Devlin, too, for all his other faults."

She clasped her hands under her chin in a gesture that reminded me of her father. "Now, as much as I would love to spend the entire night up here with you all to myself, we have a party to attend. Not to mention, I suspect Sebastian will kick down the door if he has to go too long without seeing you. Which brings us to the all-important question of what are you going to wear?"

Eslee crossed the room and threw open a pair of double doors, and I found myself gazing into the largest closet I'd ever seen in my life. It looked as if a clothing store had relocated itself just off Eslee's room.

"This is amazing!" I said, following her into the closet and turning around in a slow circle, taking in the floor-to-ceiling shelves filled with shoes and handbags. There were cedar drawers overflowing with silk scarves and cashmere tunics, as well as numerous racks offering everything from plain breeches to jewel-covered gowns.

"You should see Devlin's," chuckled Eslee, plunging her hands deep into a row of dresses and examining them one by one. "Now, let's think about what we want to convey. While I'd love to put you in something that would turn Sebastian's internal fire into an inferno, we'll save that for another time. Tonight, we want diplomatic. Elegant but not elitist."

Eslee continued to rummage through dresses before pulling one down from the rack. "Aha! Just what I was looking for."

I slipped out of my own clothes and stepped into the dress, grateful for Eslee's help with the buttons, but I almost laughed as I studied myself in the mirror. The garment was clearly meant for someone much taller and managed to be loose across my chest while stretching tight across my hips.

"Just wait," offered Eslee before whispering a spell I'd never heard and running her fingers over various parts of the dress. I stared at my reflection in awe as the dress began to change, fitting itself perfectly to the contours of my body and looking as if it had been made according to my specific measurements.

"In addition to being an artist," explained Eslee, "I happen to be *quite* gifted at tailoring spells."

Batty materialized next to a pair of boots and clapped his wings as I stared at my reflection in the large mirror. I'd never seen myself look more lovely. The bodice of the sleeveless ivory gown was covered with hundreds of silver and gold teardrop-shaped pendants. Silver and gold . . . like the blood that ran through the Astrals and Daevals I so desperately wanted to unite. The shimmering decorations extended all the way down to the bottom of the dress, and in some places, the tiny pendants were clustered together, creating a silver flower with a gold center or a golden bloom with a silver middle. From the waist down, the dress was an airy tulle, and I couldn't resist swaying from side to side, feeling like a princess from one of my favorite fantasy novels.

More like a queen from a once-united realm, remarked Aurelius, and I smiled my thanks to the Cypher who'd come to stand beside me.

Although I couldn't imagine what my family would think of me being in Nocens, surrounded by those we'd been taught our entire lives to fear, part of me wished my mother and sister could see me. Of course, that would require me telling them my secrets, and while I certainly hoped they'd be supportive of my relationship with Sebastian and my efforts to reunite the realms, there was always a chance they wouldn't agree with my decisions. If that turned out to be the case, I preferred to work through my grief when I didn't need to focus on so many other things. Plus, even though I loved my mother and siblings dearly, things had felt different between us since my father's death, making our interactions somewhat stilted. It was hard to grieve for him the same way they did, remembering all his wonderful qualities, when there was a side of him they didn't know about, a side I was only beginning to uncover.

Eslee waved for me to follow her back into the bedroom, pulling me from my thoughts.

"Now for your hair," she said, and I carefully sat down at her vanity as she ran a brush through my hair, leaving most of it down while pulling a few strands back and securing them with an ornate silver and gold comb. Batty strode between the numerous cosmetic containers before pressing the nozzle of a small white bottle, spraying himself in the face with perfume. Thankfully, it didn't seem to bother him, aside from making him sneeze.

"I remember you said something about making a sculpture when I first met you," I said to Eslee. "Is that the kind of art you like to create most?"

"Sometimes I like to paint, but working with metal is definitely my favorite," Eslee shared, her entire face lighting up. She pointed to an object across the room, twisted sheets of silver that had been melted together at odd angles and scorched in various sections. "That was one of my first pieces. There are more throughout the house, but most are at my studio. You should come by and pick out something for Sebastian's place; I can't imagine it's overflowing with art."

I thanked her, excited at the prospect of seeing her studio, even though I wasn't certain how Sebastian would feel about me offering decorating suggestions for his cave.

"Our living space could certainly use more art," agreed Batty, picking up a long, thin brush and brandishing it like a sword towards Sasha, who twitched her pink nose, unimpressed. Turning to me, Batty added, "Is there anything else that might make the times you are with us more comfortable?"

"Clever Cypher," chuckled Eslee approvingly.

"It might be nice to have more room for my things," I said to Batty. "Just so Sebastian doesn't have to clear out his dresser to make space for me."

"I shall see what I can do," nodded the bat, and I patted the top of his head.

"Daddy said he met you in a morgue of all places," said Eslee. "I'm used to not knowing everything my family members are up to but is there anything you can tell me about what you were doing there?"

Careful not to reveal Sebastian's past, as that wasn't mine to share, I told Eslee about Gregor and trace memories and Astrals experimenting on Daevals in Aeles. When I finished, I bit my lower lip, waiting for her reaction. I certainly didn't want her to treat me any differently than she had since I'd entered her home, but I could also understand if she saw Astrals in a new light after such a terrible revelation.

"That's awful," she said, shaking her head before fixing her butterscotch eyes on me. "But just because some Astrals are evil doesn't mean all of them are. I, for one, wouldn't want to be judged by the actions of just any Daeval."

"Are all Daevals so open-minded or is it just your family?"

"I'm sure I'd feel differently if I'd ever been directly harmed by an Astral," Eslee said, "but I think a major difference between our kinds is that Daevals don't automatically think something is bad just because it's different. I'm different from almost everyone I know, but that just makes me unique, not a mistake or someone who needs to be altered." Her eyes met mine in the mirror. "If you repeat what I'm about to say to my mother, I'll deny it left and right, but I've learned a lot watching her over the years. She gets just as much done through relationships and collaboration as Daddy and Uncle Caz do through threats and intimidation. That's how I prefer to operate and why I think you're so brave for trying to improve relations between the realms. I'll do whatever I can to help."

"I don't feel brave," I admitted. "I feel terrified."

"Look at it this way," suggested Eslee. "We'll start with efforts at cooperation, but if that fails, we can always resort to Daddy's preferred method and just take out anyone who doesn't agree with us." She grinned. "Rumor has it you're in good with a highly capable assassin. I bet he'd give you a great discount."

My shock must have shown on my face, because she laughed.

"I'm just teasing." She patted my shoulder. "Well, mostly teasing, but in all seriousness, anytime you feel nervous tonight, remember this: You can't fix a painting until it's on the canvas. Meaning, you have to start somewhere and do something and even if it doesn't turn out exactly as you hoped, at least you have something to work with."

"Thank you," I smiled. "Is that something your Fates say? In Aeles, we have Gifters but Sebastian's told me a bit about the Fates."

"Forget the Fates!" snorted Eslee. "That's my brilliance, and I want every bit of credit!"

As we laughed, I was surprised to hear Aurelius join in, and my heart soared at hearing his deep rumble. If my Cypher, who had spent lifetimes devoted to those with golden blood, could enjoy himself in a houseful of Daevals, there was hope yet for those in the divided realms.

16

SEBASTIAN

I followed Devlin into his suite of rooms and started to make my way towards a sofa when he shook his head.

"Oh, no!" he said. "We need to get you ready for the party, and I have a feeling that's going to take a while."

"What do you mean?" I looked down at my grey tunic and black breeches. "No one is going to care what I'm wearing."

"Kyra might." A devilish glint shone in Devlin's eyes. "I'd wager she's seen you in nothing but variations of that particular outfit since the day she met you. Wouldn't it be fun to wear something different for a change?"

"No."

Devlin let out an exasperated sigh. "Do you know how many Daevals would kill for an opportunity to borrow whatever they wanted from my closet?"

"I can honestly say that's one thing I would *never* kill for," I assured him.

"I told Eslee she had the easier job," Devlin muttered, stroking the gold hoop in his nose. "Listen, tonight's a big deal and it's important for you to look the part. I'm not trying to do the impossible and turn you into me. I'm just trying to make you the best version of yourself."

I couldn't deny the Dekarais were going to an extraordinary

amount of trouble to help Kyra, and while I thought the entire family cared far too much about how they looked and what they wore, I also didn't want to make them regret their generosity.

Reminding myself I would do anything for Kyra, I managed to ask, "What did you have in mind?"

Devlin grinned before disappearing into his closet and returning with a black suit that immediately made me cringe. While many Daevals favored tailored suits over the looser-fitting tunics and breeches I usually wore, I avoided suits because the jackets inhibited my movements and a tie only made it easier for an opponent to grab me.

"Just try it on," Devlin urged. "I'll fix anything that doesn't fit."

Taking the suit, I stepped into the bathroom and closed the door. At one time in my life, I hadn't given a second thought to being unclothed in front of someone else. But after being tortured in Rynstyn, my chest and back were covered with scars. I would never forget the day my eleven-year-old self had started to undress in the locker room of the school gymnasium—as I'd pulled off my shirt, the other boys around me had gone silent. Some hadn't remained silent long enough, peppering me with questions I'd ignored. Others had teased me, which I'd responded to with my fists, leaving bloody noses and one broken jaw in my wake. That had put an end to the taunts, but it hadn't stopped me from feeling self-conscious around someone when I wasn't wearing a shirt.

I heard Devlin lean against the bathroom door and braced myself for an onslaught of questions about Kyra.

"Based off what my father said," he began, "Kyra is really intent on improving relations between the realms. Have you spent any time in Aeles?"

"Definitely not." I stepped carefully into the black pants.

"I wonder what it's like," Devlin mused. "I've heard stories from Father and Uncle Caz, but I'd like to see it for myself. I know what you're thinking, and while of *course* I'd love to visit a realm full of women I've never met before, it's not just that."

I slipped on the long-sleeved shirt and began fastening the ridiculously small buttons. "What else is it?"

Devlin hesitated before responding, which was entirely out of character for him. "There might be opportunities there . . . you know, working for myself . . . somewhere that isn't here."

I certainly hadn't expected that. Devlin had never shown any interest in the family business waiting to be handed to him. Why would he consider starting a new venture when he had no desire to accept a role in something already established and wildly profitable?

Not even attempting the tie, I opened the bathroom door. While Devlin and I were roughly the same height, he was bulkier than I was, with muscles earned in the comfort of a gymnasium rather than the streets and alleyways of Nocens, and the shirt hung from my shoulders as the pants threatened to slide off my hips.

Devlin motioned me forward and took the tie from my hand. Slipping it around my neck, he began knotting it.

"If Astrals decide to stop being so isolated and Aeles lets our kind in, don't you think there would be good business opportunities?" he pressed.

"I suppose. Are you thinking of expanding the family business?"

He grimaced. "You'll probably think I'm crazy, but there's a lot of pressure that comes with being my father's son . . . and Caz's nephew. Everyone expects me to be just like them, to know exactly what to do and to never make any mistakes that might cost the business. Sometimes I think it might be nice to do something on my own. No one in Aeles would know who I was and it wouldn't matter if I did something my father disapproved of because no one would be comparing me to him."

Finished with the tie, he whispered a spell and ran his fingertips lightly over certain parts of the shirt and pants. I gazed down as the clothes began to shift, fitting themselves to my body as if they'd always been my size. Devlin grinned at his handiwork, then handed me a black belt. "Tuck the shirt in and put this on."

I did as instructed and as Devlin walked over to retrieve the suit jacket, I couldn't help asking, "Why are you telling me this?"

"Well, for one thing because I know you won't go blabbing to all of Nocens," he smirked. "But also because I want you to know I'm supportive of what Kyra is trying to do . . . and not just because she's gorgeous and I'm easily swayed by a pretty face, but because I'm personally invested in better relations between the realms." He held up the jacket. "I think it makes it easier to trust someone when you know they're acting in their own self-interest."

Slipping on the jacket, I couldn't disagree with his reasoning, but as I turned and saw my reflection in the full-length mirror, I suddenly wasn't interested in Devlin's reasoning. The combination of the black suit, black shirt, and black tie made my blonde hair seem brighter and my dark eyes even darker. While I still maintained clothing didn't matter, even I couldn't deny the suit gave me presence, and the fire stirred happily in my veins as I imagined Kyra's reaction.

"I can honestly say you look worthy of being seen with me," grinned Devlin. "Now for shoes."

"No need," I said, retrieving my black boots from the bathroom. I would compromise on my clothes but if for whatever reason Kyra and I needed to make a fast getaway, I wasn't about to be sliding all over the place in soft-soled dress shoes.

Devlin scowled, but then shrugged. "I can live with that.

Listen, I know you're close to my father, but don't tell him what I just told you, alright? I don't have any actual plans, I'm just thinking out loud."

"I won't say a word," I assured him, and I wouldn't. What he did with his life was up to him. Right now, I had far more important things to worry about . . . like how the Daevals Dunston had invited to socialize would react to Kyra's plans for the future of the realms. While I was glad to know Kyra had Devlin's support, the Dekarais had never been afraid to act however they wanted, sheltered by their wealth and status. Hopefully other Daevals would be equally supportive, motivated by the idea of new business opportunities even if the possibility of better personal relationships with Astrals wasn't especially enticing.

17

KYRA

I smoothed the front of my dress, doing my best to keep my hands from shaking as Eslee emerged from her closet wearing some sort of emerald-green body suit. The clothes were so fitted, they looked as if they'd been painted on, leaving very little to the imagination, even though she was technically covered from her wrists to her ankles.

"Judging by the look on your face, my outfit will definitely make a statement," she grinned, and I couldn't help smiling back, even though butterflies were fluttering in my stomach.

"How many Daevals do you think will show up?" I asked.

"Mother and Daddy run in very different circles, but between them and Uncle Caz, they know everyone who's anyone or trying to be anyone in Vartox. But don't worry," she added as I felt the blood drain from my face, leaving me momentarily lightheaded. "One of my family members will be with you at all times tonight, introducing you to the folks they know best and believe will be most helpful moving forward."

I let out a shaky exhale and managed to nod.

"I'm going to go tell Sebastian to come see you now so his jaw doesn't drop and break on the floor in front of the guests," Eslee said. "And then I'm going to tell Daddy you're ready. I think it'll make the best impression for him to escort you into the party . . . show everyone we support you and are committed to better relationships with Astrals."

"Thank you for everything, Eslee," I said, giving her a hug. "If there's ever any way I can repay you, please let me know."

"Once Aeles is open to my kind, I'd love to learn about the art in your realm!" she said. "Who knows? Maybe I can even set up a gallery in Celenia and expand my customer base."

I thought of Demitri and his work in the *Donec Auctoritas*, choosing artists to promote and organizing cultural events around various types of artwork. "I know just the Astral to help you, and he happens to be my best friend, so his help is guaranteed."

Eslee squealed and clapped her hands before striding out of the room, and I took the opportunity to rehearse answers to possible questions until there was a knock on the door, and Sebastian stepped inside.

For a moment, my body forgot how to breathe.

I loved everything Sebastian wore, but I'd never imagined him wearing something like what he had on now. The black suit fit him perfectly, highlighting his broad shoulders, narrow waist, and long legs. I felt hot all over, as if I'd suddenly acquired his pyromancy abilities and found my body filled with fire.

"You look amazing," I said somewhat breathlessly as I moved towards him.

When he didn't respond, I realized he was staring at me.

His eyes were wide, and his mouth was slightly open, and two streaks of red were spreading across his sharp cheekbones.

"Do you like it?" I asked, suddenly worried I didn't look as nice as he did.

"I feel like I'm back on our wedding night and I'm seeing you for the first time all over again." His eyes took me in from head to toe. "I can't believe you're real . . . and I can't believe I get to be with you."

I could feel myself blushing furiously and rather than attempt a response, I rose on my tiptoes and pressed my lips to his, surprised but excited at the force with which he returned my kiss. In fact, had we both not known Dunston was on his way to the bedroom, there was a very good chance the clothes we were admiring so much might have ended up on the floor.

Reluctantly pulling apart, I quickly fanned my face, trying to make it seem as if I hadn't just been picturing myself undressing Sebastian and exploring what was under that suit. It seemed we'd separated at just the right time because a knock sounded.

"Come in," I called, grinning at Sebastian, who ran a hand through his hair as he drew a steadying breath.

The door opened and Dunston stepped inside, his dimples on full display. As he took in the two of us, tears suddenly appeared, and he pulled out a white handkerchief.

"I wish Grace could see this," he said in a tight voice, dabbing his eyes. "She'd be so proud." I reached over and squeezed Sebastian's hand as a look of longing flashed across his face. Dunston quickly collected himself, clearing his throat and tucking away his handkerchief before offering me his arm. "Shall we?" he wiggled his eyebrows.

Heart pounding, I threaded my arm through his, and together we made our way down the wide hallway as Sebastian walked closely behind us.

"I'm not going to be ridiculous and say there's nothing to be nervous about tonight," said Dunston. "There's plenty to be nervous about, but the greatest rewards are born of the greatest risks. I admire your passion and your bravery. And hopefully next time, you won't be the only Astral at the party."

"Hopefully the next party will be in Aeles," I said, "although it won't be nearly as grand as this."

Dunston waved away my words. "You might be surprised to

learn I didn't grow up with money. I had the smarts and the drive, but what I needed were connections and opportunities . . . which was where Rennej came in. Her family wanted to make sure their generational wealth was in good hands, and I wanted to establish myself as a powerful figure in Nocens. We both got what we wanted and along the way, we even managed to become fond of each other." He let out a surprised laugh. "I haven't thought about that in *years*! Funny time to be remembering it now."

Even though I could never predict when my recovrancy powers would affect someone outside of Vaneklus, I had no doubt they'd contributed to Dunston's recollection. Part of me felt bad that just my presence could cause folks to unintentionally resurrect old memories, but I pushed my impulse to apologize aside. If the Dekarais could accept my golden blood, they shouldn't have any problem accepting me being a Recovrancer, even though now wasn't the time to share something so personal.

"Anyway, tonight the focus isn't on the past," Dunston continued, "interesting as it may be. Tonight is all about the future." He paused as we reached the end of the hallway, which opened onto a balcony, and I gasped as I surveyed the scene below.

The entire household had been transformed, becoming even more dazzling, if such a thing was possible, and it took me a moment to realize the décor matched my dress. Everything was silver and gold, side by side, intertwined, overlapping, each color shining brighter for being near the other. High overhead, miniature silver and gold fireworks began to explode, spelled to remain silent but providing a stunning backdrop as Dunston and I began our descent down the staircase. The faces below were a blur, but there were so many more than I'd expected, and I clasped Dunston's arm a little tighter.

Musicians with painted faces softly played silver and gold

instruments in a corner, and the numerous chandeliers shone, crystals spelled to cast tiny silver and gold rainbows on everything below. Twinkling gold lights were wrapped around the banister of the staircase and draped over numerous silver sculptures, each designed by Eslee, no doubt. Tables were covered with heavy gold cloths embroidered with silver stars enchanted to shimmer and sparkle, and silver-rimmed goblets overflowed with fizzy gold champagne.

Here we go, I said to Sebastian through the bracelet.

You can do this. I'll be beside you or behind you the entire time, his deep voice reassured me.

My breathing was shallow, but I held my head high as I stepped off the final stair, hoping I appeared excited, as opposed to terrified. While I once would have been afraid of being around so many Daevals, now I barely even noticed my body's internal buzzing; in fact, the more time I spent around Sebastian and others with silver blood, the less my body perceived them as a threat, proving yet again things didn't have to remain as they'd been. No, tonight my fear lay in saying or doing the wrong thing . . . of being the reason Daevals decided Astrals weren't worth their time after all.

Trying not to dwell on such thoughts, I lifted my eyes and found myself face to face with LeBehr.

"You're here!" I exclaimed, a rather silly statement to make, but I was so surprised to see the shopkeeper outside of her bookstore, the words rushed from my mouth.

She grinned before giving me a hug, which led her to readjust the black corset she'd laced over a purple dress whose skirt and sleeves appeared to be made entirely of ruffles. "I thought you might appreciate a familiar face. Plus, a watched potion never boils."

I took that to mean she'd already started brewing the potion to find the Chronicles, and excitement sped through me. We were one step closer to yet another goal that had previously seemed impossible, and I thanked her again for her support.

"Good luck," she said, dipping her head at Sebastian before making her way towards a table filled with silver oysters and gold caviar.

I was stunned at how many Daevals had turned out, and while I suspected many were merely curious or wanted the chance to attend a Dekarai party, I hoped at least some were genuinely interested in the fact that someone with golden blood wanted a better relationship with those in Nocens.

Dunston steered me towards a man with curly blonde hair pulled back in a ponytail.

"Ms. Valorian," the man offered me a bow. "It's a pleasure to meet you. I'm Camus." He shook Dunston's hand, then grinned at Sebastian. "Always nice to see you, Mr. Sayre."

"And you, Major DuFray." Sebastian reached out to shake the man's hand. "How's the military these days?"

"Sorely missing your skills." Camus gave a wry shake of his head. "I'll always wonder what might have happened had your feet been placed on a different path." As Dunston spoke to the major, I heard Sebastian's voice in my head.

I met Camus when I briefly attended the Nocenian military academy as a child.

I recalled the dream we'd shared and how Sebastian's father had wanted him to train with an elite Daeval military squad. Now wasn't the time to ask questions, so I simply nodded my understanding, but I also noted how happy Camus was to see Sebastian. Was there a possibility Sebastian might trade being an assassin for a role in the Nocenian military, as had apparently been his plan at one time? It was certainly worth mentioning when I wasn't attempting delicate diplomatic negotiations.

"I'm surprised to see someone from the military here," I admitted to Camus. "But I'm very grateful."

"Yes, I suppose we would know more than most about the brutality Astrals are capable of," he nodded, and the straightforward manner in which he said such a thing made a faint chill run down my spine. *Was* the Astral military brutal? I assumed they spent their days patrolling Aeles and practicing training drills on the off chance they were called to battle, but were there fights between the Aelian and Nocenian militaries regular citizens of Aeles weren't aware of? While I still didn't think Sebastian's concerns about Adonis or Nigel being Tallus were correct, Camus's words made me wonder . . . how much did I really know about what the soldiers did on a daily basis?

"Do you see a day when members of our respective militaries might work together?" I asked the major.

"I think both sides could certainly benefit from sharing information," he replied, his gaze steady. "I can't honestly say I'm here with the blessing of the highest military commanders, but I *can* say improved relations between the realms is a welcome idea . . . especially since I've been concerned for some time about a potential invasion."

"Invasion?" I stared at him. "I'll be the first to admit I know very little about Aelian military activities, but there's been absolutely no talk in my realm of starting a war with Nocens."

"Probably all the more reason for you to remember this conversation," Camus said. "Something's changed in Aeles over the last few months. Simply because we don't prevent Astrals from entering our realm doesn't mean soldiers can come in whenever they want. We don't hesitate to protect what's ours. Your military knows this and the fact that they keep testing our borders says they don't value the lives of those who fight for them, and that means there are bigger plans in place."

"I had no idea the Aelian military was doing such a thing," I shook my head, "and it's not the choice I want to see my realm make. Please know there are Astral soldiers who feel the same as I do and want to build a coalition with Daevals."

"I'm glad to hear it," smiled Camus, "and I'll pass it on."

We spoke a few moments more before Dunston guided me onwards, although Camus and Sebastian stayed back, and while it was odd to see Sebastian voluntarily conversing with someone, I also doubted he would pass up an opportunity to discuss any sort of fighting tactics.

After introducing me to numerous other Daevals, most of whom were involved in the Nocenian government or banking, Dunston rose on his tiptoes and scanned the room.

"I know Caz wants a turn introducing you to folks, but of course he's nowhere to be found . . . probably naked in a fountain somewhere." Dunston sighed irritably, and his reaction to his brother's absence made me suspect such a thing had actually happened before. "Are you alright by yourself while I go find him?"

"Of course," I said, glad to have the chance to get a drink. As Dunston walked away, I caught Sebastian's eye and gestured towards a table. Making my way across the room, I chose water over the free-flowing champagne, wanting to keep a clear head during such an important event. Someone tapped my shoulder, and I turned, nearly dropping the heavy silver goblet as I found myself looking into the golden-brown eyes of Minister Sinclair. While I probably ought to have said something clever, I opted for the truth.

"I did *not* expect to see you here. But I'm certainly glad to."

He shrugged. "I wouldn't be here if things had gone differently at the morgue. But it's clear I don't know as much as I thought, so being open to learning more about your kind seems the wisest course of action."

"My father clearly wanted Astral and Daeval healers to work together," I said. "And while I'm happy to share what I know, I'm also incredibly eager to learn from you and other Nocenian healers. I'm certain you know spells and healing techniques I've never heard of that would benefit those in Aeles."

"Should you take your father's place as your realm's next *Princeps Shaman*, are you willing to publicly champion such cooperation?" Minister Sinclair fixed his eyes intently on mine. "It will not be a popular position to take."

"I don't care about being popular," I replied. "I care about doing what's right for everyone who lives in either realm. Those of us with the ability to wield power have to be the ones to step out first. If we're too afraid to take a stand, how can we expect those without influence to do the same?"

I suddenly felt the weight of a slim crown on my head, and my shoulders straightened as I recognized the authoritative tone I'd used when speaking as Kareth. While I wasn't exactly the same woman, it was wonderful to know some part of who I'd been as the Felserpent Queen would always be with me.

"You have my vote . . . not that the opinion of a Daeval will do anything for you in Aeles," Minister Sinclair offered the barest hint of a smile. "But when you assume the position and publicly announce your support for working with Daevals, know I shall respond in kind."

"Thank you!" I was so happy, I wanted to reach out and hug the man, although I refrained, as I didn't dare risk wrinkling his dove-grey suit. "I can't tell you how much I appreciate that, and I look forward to working with you."

Caz appeared at my side, fully dressed and not looking as if he'd been in any fountains, and as we continued our rounds, I took the opportunity to ask as many questions as I could of the Daevals I met, trying to remember everything I was told.

While Astrals engaged with our government through voting and electing senators as representatives, it seemed Daevals were much more comfortable directly influencing government officials through large-sum donations or Caz's preferred currency of favors. Although Daevals were certainly not planterians, they were adamant about proper nutrition and living space for the animals ultimately intended to be used as food. While I found that odd, I secretly hoped I could eventually direct their concern for animal welfare to preventing animals from being seen as commodities in the first place.

I also learned Daevals despised the Astral laws regulating romantic relationships, finding us primitive in our thinking and seeing such bureaucracy as evidence of the government being too involved in the everyday lives of citizens. Overall, the mindset of the Daevals I met appeared to be, "Get what you can, when you can, because you can't trust others to look out for you," whereas the general thinking in Aeles could be described as, "You'll be taken care of as long as you do as you're told." There were problems with both views, but with each conversation, I found myself understanding Daevals better, if not always agreeing with them.

One thing was abundantly clear . . . Sebastian had been right in his assertion that reuniting the realms wasn't the same as bringing peace between Astrals and Daevals. Still, between my former position as the Felserpent Queen and my future position as the *Princeps Shaman*, I was determined to do both.

Eventually, the party came to an end, and after changing back into my regular clothes, I thanked the Dekarais for their unbelievable support and promised to find a time to visit Eslee's studio. Sebastian and I returned to his cave, and as the portal winked out of sight, I hugged him close, thrilled over the success of the evening.

"Tonight went so much better than I ever dared hope," I said, excitement and relief buzzing through me as I told him about my conversations with Minister Sinclair, LeBehr, and some of the other Daeval attendees. "It's so encouraging to know we're not alone in wanting to improve relations between Astrals and Daevals."

"I wasn't certain what to expect, but it was definitely a successful event," he agreed. "You were incredible. You're a born diplomat. At times I felt like I was watching you hold court back in Velaire."

I felt heat rush to my cheeks as a smile exploded across my face. "Tonight wouldn't have been nearly as successful without the Dekarais," I reminded him, wanting to give credit where it was due. "I'm lucky you have such welcoming—and powerful— friends. I can't wait to see Eslee again!"

"I can take you to her studio the next time you're here," offered Sebastian. "I don't always understand her art, but she's very passionate about it."

Given how much Sebastian preferred us spending our weekends alone in his cave, such an offer felt like huge growth on his part, and I grinned at him, pleased he was so supportive of my new friendship. "Thank you. I'd love that."

As the energy of the party began to dissipate, I looked at my bag near Sebastian's couch. While I hated passing up the chance to spend another night with him, it seemed best I return to Aeles, as I didn't want to accidentally oversleep or risk having something unexpected keep me from internship.

Sebastian scowled as I gathered my things, but when he spoke, his annoyance over me leaving wasn't for the reason I'd expected.

"I'm still worried about you going back to Aeles with Tallus potentially being there."

"I agree it's a risk, but it's a calculated one," I reminded him.

"Yes, Tallus could be somewhere in Celenia, but he could also be in hundreds of other locations across Aeles, and we're not even certain he's returned or managed to retain his past-life memories. I have my schedule for the week, so I know what to expect and if anything changes, we can discuss it before I agree to participate."

Aurelius ran an oversized paw over one ear. "I shall also be accompanying Kyra everywhere she goes."

"You don't need to do that," I protested. "Cyphers aren't child-minders. You're supposed to enjoy time by yourself, not—"

"—As your Cypher, your well-being is my utmost responsibility," interrupted the lynx. "And it's only until we learn whether Tallus has, in fact, returned."

While Cyphers couldn't fight by virtue of their positions as guides, I supposed the lynx could send a message to Batty if something happened and I, for whatever reason, couldn't access the bracelet to contact Sebastian, although such a scenario was troubling to contemplate.

"Thank you," Sebastian said to Aurelius, who dipped his head in response.

"Well, it's nice to see the two of you agreeing on something," I sighed. "Alright, Aurelius will be with me anytime I leave my apartment. Does that make you feel better about me going back?"

"Marginally," Sebastian replied, and while it wasn't the answer I necessarily wanted, I also understood it was a large concession from his point of view, and I stepped closer, taking his hands in mine.

"I already can't wait to come back," I said. "I love every moment I'm with you, and I love sleeping in the same bed."

"My bed's going to seem far too big without you in it," he said, his dark eyes fixed on my face before he leaned forward and pressed his lips against mine. For someone who seemed built of hard planes and sharp angles, I still couldn't believe how soft his lips were. I wrapped my arms around his neck, rising on my tip-toes as his hands circled my waist, pulling me closer with a quickness that stole my breath in a way I'd never experienced. I ran my fingers up his neck, letting them sift through his thick hair, and as he breathed a soft moan against my mouth, I knew in my shade I could kiss this man a million times in a million lives and still never get enough of him.

I had no idea how long our kiss lasted, but when we finally pulled apart it seemed far too soon, and I found myself more moti-vated than ever to reunite the realms. Once Daevals were allowed in Aeles, Sebastian and I could divide our time between Aeles and Nocens, falling asleep every night and waking up every morning where we belonged . . . together.

18

Rain drummed on the tin roof, and Sebastian lay in bed, watching the heavy drops slide down the windows, unable to sleep. The shock of seeing his father for the first time in over a year was still so fresh. It didn't escape his notice that his father hadn't come looking for him until he wanted something, and while that hurt, Sebastian had never experienced anything but pain from his father, so in a way, he was prepared rather than shocked.

Not liking the direction of his thoughts, Sebastian focused on the test he was supposed to take the following day. Would it involve needles? Would he be asked to demonstrate how fast he could run or how strong he was in a fight? Or would it be an academic test? He cringed at the thought of reading out loud in front of complete strangers.

What if he failed?

More importantly, what if he passed?

Part of him very much liked the idea of being an elite warrior in the Nocenian army. But at the same time, he knew he'd never be able to go along with anything his mother didn't like.

When it became clear his mind wasn't going to settle anytime soon, he decided if he couldn't control his thoughts, he also didn't have to be alone with them. He grabbed his stuffed toy dragon, slipped out of bed, and tiptoed to his mother's room.

"Mother?" he called, pushing the unclosed door open a little wider.

His mother rolled over from where she'd been curled against a pillow and smiled, although her cheeks looked wet in the moonlight shining through the rain-splattered window. "Come on in, sweetie," she said, patting the bed.

Sebastian crawled between the covers and let his mother pull him close as he settled his dragon beside him. She brushed his hair back and rested her cheek against his head as thunder rumbled.

Numerous thoughts fought for Sebastian's attention, but he kept coming back to one in particular. "Father talked about you being pregnant and wanting to keep me." He angled his head so he could see his mother. "He didn't want me, did he?"

His mother's silence told him he'd correctly understood the situation, and when she eventually spoke, she sounded both sad and frustrated.

"Your father has always wanted certain things for you," she explained, "and I've wanted different things for you. Unfortunately, that means you're caught in the middle, and it's not fair."

"He wants me to fight," Sebastian surmised, "and you don't want me to."

"There's nothing wrong with fighting," replied his mother. "I want you to fight for the Daevals and causes you care about. You have a very strong sense of fairness, and I love how quick you are to defend what you believe to be right. I just don't want strength to be the only thing you believe matters. You are so much more than your pyromancy and your portaling and your incredible reflexes." She placed a hand on the covers, right above his heart. "You aren't special because of what you can do. You're special because of who you are."

Even though his mother was saying nice things about him, she still sounded sad, and Sebastian searched for what he could say to make her feel better. "If you want me to fail my test tomorrow, I will."

His mother hugged him so tight, for a moment he couldn't breathe.

"The fact that you would even consider that is what makes you different from everyone you'd be around in that program. I'm so worried they'd change you." She hesitated. "But I also know there would be a lot of things you'd like about it. And they'd certainly be lucky to have you." She kissed his forehead and arranged the covers around him. "You just do your best, and let things work themselves out."

He nodded and drifted off to sleep, clutching his dragon as the rain pattered a lullaby.

The next morning, Sebastian tried to stand tall as he walked into the classroom where he would complete his testing.

Two Daevals were already sitting behind a table, and he felt their eyes settle on him. The older of the two, judging by the man's white goatee, stifled a yawn and looked like he'd rather be elsewhere. The younger man had curly blonde hair pulled back into a ponytail and looked very pleased to be there.

"You must be Sebastian," he said, standing up and smiling as he extended his hand.

Sebastian walked over and shook it the way he'd been taught. The Daeval gestured to his partner. "This is Vorens, and I'm Camus."

Vorens gave a quick nod, then turned back to the paperwork in front of him. Camus indicated a chair, and Sebastian sat down.

"Now," Camus said, "we're going to start by getting to know more about you. Then we're going to play some strategy games and give you some puzzles to solve. Nothing too difficult, based on what I've read about you. Do you have any questions before we begin?"

Sebastian had more questions than he could count, but there was one that mattered more than the rest.

"Are there going to be any needles?"

Camus shook his head. "No needles," he replied with a reassuring smile, and Sebastian let out a soft sigh of relief. He would do his best, partly because he didn't like to fail, but also because he didn't want his father to think he hadn't tried and end up blaming his mother.

"I'm ready," Sebastian nodded.

Hours later, Sebastian was exhausted. His head hurt and, even though they'd taken a break for lunch, he was hungry again. For the first time in a while, he really wanted a nap. He watched as Camus closed a thick folder and exchanged a brief glance with Vorens, whose miserable-looking demeanor hadn't changed much over the day.

Camus then turned to Sebastian. "Well done, young man. Clearly we need to review your results with our colleagues, but we'll be in touch. You can leave now."

Sebastian managed a weary, "Thank you," before making his way out into the hall. His mother was sitting in a chair reading and looked up from her book with a big smile. He stopped next to her and rested his head against her shoulder, too tired to talk, and she wrapped an arm around him.

"Let's go home," she whispered.

As they made their way out of the school, Sebastian couldn't help replaying Camus's words in his head. While he normally would have been proud of himself for earning such a compliment, in this instance, he had the sinking feeling doing well wasn't going to make things any easier.

19

KYRA

I rubbed my forehead as I woke, trying to ease the apprehension I felt from Sebastian's dream. Before I could tell Aurelius what I'd witnessed, the gold bracelet vibrated, and I pressed my fingertips against it.

I hate not being able to control when I'm going to share a memory, Sebastian groaned.

Knowing how much he despised feeling helpless, I ensured my response was gentle and not directly focused on him.

Camus clearly liked you from the moment he met you, I said. *He seemed as nice then as he was when I met him. He had the same hairstyle too.*

He's always been nice, agreed Sebastian, *even when—*

He stopped abruptly. *I don't want to get into it while we're apart and you've got to leave for internship soon. Can we discuss it when we're back together?* His next words were so muffled, it was clear they were directed more to himself than me: *If I limit my sleep, I should be able to avoid any more dreams until then.*

Of course we can wait. While I would support his wishes of when we talked about his past first and foremost because I cared about him, I could also easily imagine how terrible it would be not having control over when and how your deepest secrets were shared. If Sebastian had learned of my father's work with silver blood through a dream, I would have been mortified, not to mention angry and anxious, as well.

We spoke about other things as I readied for the day ahead, and I soon found myself heading to my appointment with Healer Omnurion. I'd interacted with her multiple times while working with my father, so it wasn't like meeting a stranger for the first time; still, walking up the familiar steps to the building housing my father's former office, tears pooled in my eyes. Thankfully, Aurelius was beside me, and he gently bumped his head against my knee, offering support I greatly appreciated.

Knocking on Healer Omnurion's door, I took a deep breath and forced a smile to my face as she welcomed me, kissing each cheek before motioning me inside. As I entered the office, I tried not to pay too much attention to the new pictures on the walls, as well as the different books, bottles, and other items filling the shelves. I nodded to the healer's Cypher, a pileated woodpecker named Picus, sitting on a tree stump near the healer's desk . . . which, I noticed, wasn't the same desk my father had used. Healer Omnurion gestured for me to take a seat, and her hazel eyes were sad as she offered me a kind smile.

"I can't even imagine how hard this is for you," she said. "Please let me know if there's anything I can do. I considered having us meet elsewhere, but I wasn't certain delaying your return here would be helpful." She grimaced before patting the rounded bouffant her strawberry blonde hair had been shaped into. "I'm sorry if I made the wrong call."

"I'd always rather face things as they are," I assured her, even though it was hard to draw a full breath and at least part of me wanted to rush out of the room. "Postponing the inevitable never makes it easier."

The healer smiled. "You're so like your father. No time for nonsense, and thank the stars, because we've already got enough of that." She straightened in her chair, and I appreciated her willingness to get down to business.

"Now," she said, "it's no secret I only agreed to be the realm's *Princeps Shaman* until you've completed internship and can formally accept the position. I'm not entirely certain what you can learn from me, as I suspect you're far more advanced than I am, but I'll help however I can. Is there any area of healing you feel you know less about compared to others?"

It was jarring hearing someone older than myself and well-respected in the healing community admit my skills surpassed theirs. Part of me wanted to explain my competency was due to who I'd been in a previous life, as well as my position as a Recovrancer, but I couldn't safely share either revelation. Many of my most vexing questions were more suited for Senator Rex than the kindly woman across from me. And while I desperately wanted to know about the potential side effects of recovering a shade from Vaneklus and placing it in a new body, that certainly wasn't an acceptable field of study, seeing how recovrancy was outlawed in my realm.

"I'd love more practice combining my *alera* and my *sana* bracelet in healing," I finally said, thinking of the trauma Sebastian had suffered and continued to suffer in the form of recurring nightmares. "I'm comfortable combining the two when working with the body, but I'd like to become more skilled at healing the mind."

"Ah, the difference between using a loom versus a needle," smiled Healer Omnurion. "*Aleric* alteration of the mind is quite advanced, and not something every healer is capable of, even if they aspire to do so." She pulled a silver flute from a drawer and placed it on top of the desk. "I use this in healing the same way you use your *sana* bracelet. How comfortable are you with various sound combinations?"

In addition to being involved with recovrancy, my *sana*

bracelet also helped me direct my *alera* when I healed someone. While the instruments healers used varied, the notes produced by the instruments were the same, whether you used beads, bells, pipes, a flute, or your voice. Each note had a name, as well as a personality. On my *sana* bracelet, Mwyaf was the first and largest bead. Made of black onyx, he was known as The Forgetful and was used to erase memories. Beside him was a slightly smaller diamond bead, Glir, The Clarifier, who brought clarity and focus, helping those who heard him make wise decisions. Tawazun, The Balancer, was a dark blue sapphire who established equilibrium in all things. The grey agate bead beside her was Zerstoren, The Destroyer. Next was Rheolath, The Controller, a bright red carnelian stone capable of controlling living and inanimate objects. Saund, The Soother, was a stunning pearl who brought peace and calmness to all who heard her. And finally, there was Lleiaf, a citrine bead that shone like a miniature sun against my wrist. As The Rememberer, she helped folks recall events that happened long ago or things they were, for whatever reason, unable to remember on their own.

"I've used two-tone combinations quite a bit," I said, as I used Tawazun and Rheolath every time I went in and out of Vaneklus. I thought back to the time I'd used Rheolath to take control of Laycus's boat, refusing to let him leave my sight until he'd answered my questions about Sebastian's mother. "I have more experience using Rheolath on inanimate objects than living creatures," I added. "I've only used Zerstoren twice, to destroy abnormal growths in a patient's body, and that was under my father's supervision."

Healer Omnurion pointed to various keys on her flute. "*Aleric* alteration of the mind will require the coordinated use of Lleiaf, Rheolath, and Mwyaf . . . and possibly Zerstoren. Lleiaf will bring whatever is troubling the patient to the forefront of their mind,

Rheolath will allow us to assume control of their mind, and Mwyaf will help them permanently forget such pain. Some Astrals, however, struggle to forget certain things, even with help and even though they want to, and in those instances, we'll use the additional power of Zerstoren to ensure whatever thoughts are traumatizing them are destroyed for good."

I nodded. I still wasn't comfortable with the idea of permanently destroying someone's memories, but at the same time I thought how much happier Sebastian would be if he wasn't constantly forced to relive the trauma he'd endured in Rynstyn.

"I'm certain you already know this," continued Healer Omnurion, "but two things bear repeating—first, we never erase memories without the explicit consent of the patient we're treating. We conduct a lengthy interview alongside a counselor to ensure the patient truly understands what they're asking us to do. And second, there will be times when no matter how well we perform our work, the mind simply will not release a memory. While skill is necessary, it's also no guarantee of a successful outcome, as we still have much to understand about memories and how the mind functions."

I clasped my hands tightly in my lap. I didn't like doing things correctly only to ultimately fail at a task, and my unease must have shown on my face because Healer Omnurion leaned forward and smiled.

"It's more than a little overwhelming, especially in the beginning, but with practice and care, you'll do the best you can and that's all you can do," she said warmly.

It's not all that different from your recovrancy work, Aurelius pointed out. *You don't know everything about shades and likely never will—I doubt anyone could, aside from Laycus and his sister—but that doesn't prevent you from doing the best you can with the information you have.*

You're right, I agreed, before turning my attention back to Healer Omnurion.

"Where should I start?" I asked.

"Let's make sure you're fully comfortable with each bead on its own before we try combinations. You mentioned having more experience using Rheolath on inanimate objects, so let's start by having you use her on me." She placed a hand on the desk, palm facing up. "Take control of my hand and make me lift it off the desk."

I took a deep breath and ran my finger over the carnelian bead, focusing on the healer's hand as I whispered, "*Bana sevap ver-akessin*." I quickly felt myself connected to her hand, able to sense the calluses on her palm, the length of her nails, and the faint throb of arthritis. Although I concentrated hard and kept the connection, Healer Omnurion's hand didn't so much as twitch.

"You're treating my hand as if it's a stand-alone object," she noted. "How would I move my hand, if *I* was the one who chose to do so?"

"With your mind," I realized somewhat sheepishly. "Our minds control our movements." Changing my focus, I sought a connection with Healer Omnurion's mind, imagining tendrils of *alera* floating out from Rheolath and establishing connections that allowed me to assume control of the voluntary motor center. Rheolath hungrily latched on to the healer's mind, and I tightened my focus, limiting the bead's power to one discrete act. Slowly, I lifted Healer Omnurion's hand off the desk, first one inch, then two . . . her hand hovered in the air, but I couldn't maintain the connection and her arm dropped, the back of her hand thumping gently against the desktop. Even though the whole thing had only taken a moment, I was surprised to find myself breathing harder, and small beads of sweat clung to my hairline.

"Very good," nodded Healer Omnurion. "I'm glad you're not overly enthusiastic about assuming control of anyone. I'll recommend some books to give you a foundational understanding of emotional and mental healing. I'll also send you a list of exercises to improve your skills using Mwyaf, Lleiaf, Rheolath, and Zerstoren individually. You can continue practicing on me, as well as shadowing me, of course."

I thanked the woman, and we outlined the rest of my training curriculum for the next few weeks. When our time together was finished, the healer ran a hand over her Cypher's feathered back as I gathered my things.

"What's next on your schedule?" She smiled.

"I'm meeting with Senator Rex." When the senator had first told me I'd been matched with the *Donec Medicinae* for internship, he'd also mentioned speaking to Healer Omnurion about being involved in my training. I hoped the healer was still supportive of the idea, and to my relief, she nodded.

"If you're interested in climbing the political ladder, he's certainly one to take notes from. Of course, anything he says these days will be preceded and followed by a long exposition on the evils of Daevals." A frown crossed her face, and casting a quick glance at Aurelius, I seized the unexpected opportunity.

"That pretty much describes his internship orientation speech," I shared, keeping my tone light. "He seems quite passionate about reminding all of Aeles why we should remain separate from Daevals." Not wanting to go too far, but also wanting to give Healer Omnurion a chance, since she'd been almost critical of the senator, I added, "Father always said it's easy to overlook similarities when you're focused on differences. I know violence is sometimes necessary but as a healer, my duty is to preserve life. Cooperation can bring change just as easily as fighting."

Healer Omnurion went very still, her eyes scanning my face.

After a moment, she said, "There are those in the healing profession who would agree with you."

I didn't want to risk saying more, but I smiled at the woman, feeling as if we'd shared a small but important moment that would hopefully grow into something larger.

20

KYRA

*L*eaving my father's former office, I cast a locator spell I'd learned as a child, then said Senator Rex's name out loud and watched as lights glowed on the marble floor beneath my feet, guiding me down various corridors and indicating when I should turn.

At last I found myself walking down a quiet hallway with a few corridors branching off on either side, ending in a small open office. A large desk sat in the middle of the room, and bookshelves lined the walls, paneled in dark wood at the bottom and painted a deep blue at the top. A blue and gold carpet covered most of the floor, and a delicate crystal and citrine lighting fixture hung from the ceiling. At my approach, Lionel looked up from the papers he'd been reading, and a smile sprang to his face almost as quickly as he rose from his seat.

"Ever the punctual one, Ms. Valorian. Can I get you anything to drink?"

I declined, and he waved for me to join him as he stepped towards an imposing door. Numerous eight-sided stars, the symbol of Aeles, were carved deep into the wood.

"I'm so pleased you'll be joining our little team," he said, grasping the shiny brass doorknob. "We might be few in number, but you won't find two Astrals more dedicated to serving our government."

I smiled and made what I hoped was an appropriate reply even as my heart began to beat faster. Lionel rapped smartly on the door before opening it, enthusiastically stepping inside to announce my arrival. I followed, wiping my suddenly damp palms over my thighs.

You don't have to do this, offered Aurelius as he padded along beside me. *You could always make an anonymous report about Senator Rex and let others look into whatever he's doing with silver blood.*

Then I might never know about Father's involvement, I reminded him. *Also, I'm not certain who I can trust in Aeles, especially in the government. I know you and Sebastian don't like it, but right now I'm our best option for getting into the Rynstyn facility.*

Aurelius flattened his ears but didn't argue.

"Welcome!" said Senator Rex with a smile, turning from where he'd been standing in front of a fireplace. "I trust you were able to find my office without too much difficulty?"

"No difficulty at all," I assured him.

Lionel excused himself, and even though I knew he would be right outside the door, now that I found myself alone with Senator Rex, I momentarily worried he'd somehow become aware of my secret plan to end the Astral experimentation program. Fortunately for me, Astrals didn't expect to be deceived by someone else with golden blood, as we were raised to give one another the benefit of the doubt, always starting from a place of trust rather than suspicion. While I still didn't like lying, I also thought telling small falsehoods in the service of discovering a larger truth made my actions admissible, if not entirely commendable.

Senator Rex gestured to one of two dark blue armchairs

arranged in front of the fireplace, and I took a seat as Aurelius settled near my feet. Senator Rex took the other chair, and a beautiful barn owl suddenly appeared on the arm, ruffling its white and brown feathers.

Senator Rex smiled at the creature.

"Kyra, may I introduce my Cypher, Mendax. Mendax, this is Kyra Valorian and Aurelius."

"I apologize it's taken so long to meet you both," said the owl. "I've heard so much about *you*, in particular, Kyra, I feel as if I already know you." Aurelius and I returned the greeting as Senator Rex leaned forward and interlaced his fingers, resting his elbows on his knees.

"I was so pleased when you expressed interest in continuing your father's research," he said gently. "It can't be easy for you, though, so please tell me if there's anything I can do to help."

"Thank you," I replied. "Right now, I feel like the best way to honor my father is to continue where he left off. If he was working on something, it had to be important, and I don't want to see his progress lost, not when it might help other Astrals."

A faint gleam shone in the senator's pale blue eyes. "I'm pleased to hear that . . . probably because I agree." He settled into the armchair, his previously stiff posture relaxing and making me glad of the answer I'd given.

"I'm certain you have questions," he said, "and I'll do my best to answer them, but perhaps it makes sense to start with an overview of what your father was working on."

"That would be nice."

"Our research is highly classified," began Senator Rex. "Had your father been at liberty to tell you about it, I'm certain he would have; however, a condition of working on this project was that he maintain absolute silence about his involvement."

"I still have trouble believing he went to Nocens and spoke

with Daevals." I allowed some of my real feelings on the subject to make their way into my voice. "I know he did it for a good reason, and with the government's approval, but it's still hard picturing him doing something I grew up thinking could never—and *should* never—happen."

Senator Rex nodded. "Given what we know of Daevals, that makes perfect sense. I can certainly relate to growing up believing those with silver blood are vile creatures who cause harm without the slightest provocation. I still maintain such a belief, mind you, but over the years, my thinking on the cause of their evilness has, shall we say, shifted."

Senator Rex crossed one leg over the other, running a hand over the sharp crease in his navy blue trousers as he chose his next words with obvious care.

"With regards to the work your father was doing, he was studying Astral blood to identify and quantify the unique properties that make us who we are. He'd just begun to compare it to Daevalic blood, since as I mentioned before, Daevals tend to live longer than our kind, and he and I both felt passionately about working to extend the average Astral lifespan. I'll provide you with the research notes he left behind, which I'm certain will explain things far better than I can; however, I do ask that the notes remain in your office, first and foremost because they're government property, but also because they might be misconstrued, should they fall into uneducated hands."

I nodded my understanding.

"Now," continued Senator Rex, "that being said, my interest in comparing gold and silver blood isn't *just* limited to figuring out how to help our kind live longer."

Brace yourself, urged Aurelius, even though by all outward appearances the Cypher had settled into a comfortable position and was on the verge of falling asleep in front of the fire.

I held my breath, hoping I'd be able to hear the senator's words over my pounding heart.

"Unlike most Astrals, you've actually interacted with a Daeval," he said. "While I know your time with one was limited, may I ask what you thought of his intellectual capacity?"

Thankfully, this was a question I could answer honestly. "I was always told those with silver blood were mindless brutes, but the one I fell through the portal with was clearly in control of himself. He considered different options and made logical decisions, so I can't say he was unintelligent."

Senator Rex nodded eagerly. "Your experience only provides further evidence of what I've suspected for a while now . . . when it comes to understanding Daevals, our knowledge is incomplete and in some instances, incorrect."

I couldn't fathom Senator Rex secretly wanting to improve relationships with Daevals, even though such a revelation would certainly be welcome, so I blinked a few times and did my best to appear surprised.

"I'm not used to hearing someone with golden blood admit they were incorrect about anything involving Daevals," I said, causing Senator Rex to laugh.

"Yes, our kind are quite stubborn when it comes to changing their minds about something like Daevals," he agreed. "The thing is, I've started to believe those with silver blood don't always have a choice in how they behave. They have the ability to make *some* choices, of course, as the one you fell through the portal with did in choosing not to harm you. But making those choices is difficult and goes against the grain of who they are. Their natural disposition leads them to darkness and depravity."

"I'm not certain I see how this relates to the research my father was doing," I said.

"In addition to comparing gold and silver blood to discover

differences about lifespan length, your father was also studying Daevalic blood to identify the properties that make Daevals who they are . . . to discover the basis of their greed, callousness, and violent dispositions," explained the senator.

"Why would you want to know so much about Daevals?"

Senator Rex fixed his eyes on mine. "If we can identify what makes them different, there's a chance we can change them. You see, unlike some of my colleagues who think we'd be better off exterminating everyone with silver blood, I believe there's another option. If the recipe for who we become lies in our blood, it's reasonable to assume altering silver blood would quite literally change a Daeval from the inside out."

"You want to make Daevals more like us." I fought to suppress a shudder. Just because he didn't want to kill every Daeval didn't make Senator Rex's plan any better . . . he still thought the ideal scenario was a world without Daevals.

"Yes," replied Senator Rex firmly. "Either we find a way to alter their silver blood, or we find a way to replace it with something better."

I thought of Gregor, his body drained of silver blood. Based on his trace memories, his captors had attempted to transfuse golden blood into him, but his organs had shut down from the shock of being filled with a foreign substance they couldn't process. Anger flooded my torso, hot and thick, and I tried to draw a deep breath as I ran my hands over my breeches, desperately working to keep myself composed. I wanted to reach for my *sana* bracelet and let Saund's soothing voice calm me, but that would prompt questions about why I was distressed. How in the falling stars could Senator Rex consider such a thing? What gave him the right to say Astrals were perfect as they were while Daevals would never be acceptable as they'd been born?

"I can't imagine Daevals willingly lining up to have their

blood altered," I finally said, wishing my voice didn't so sound strained. Thankfully, my comment merely prompted Senator Rex to sigh, his normally straight shoulders drooping.

"Yes, figuring out how to deploy such an intervention will certainly be a challenge, one I don't currently have a solution to . . . which means we shall simply focus our attention on what we presently have the power to control," he said.

"Do you still have silver blood available to study? You mentioned before you weren't certain how my father acquired it, other than it came from the Nocenian government. What if we run out?"

"The Nocenian government was apparently quite generous with how many vials they gave your father," replied Senator Rex smoothly. "We're in no danger of running out of silver blood."

Thank goodness for kidnapped Daevalic children, muttered Aurelius, and I pressed my lips together, lest I accidentally convey the lynx's words.

My silence didn't go unnoticed by Senator Rex, but thankfully he assumed he knew where it was coming from.

"I understand this is difficult information to process," he said. "Please don't think I'm a Daeval sympathizer. You would be hard-pressed to find someone who despises them more than I do. I simply believe they don't have to remain a cause for concern. I've been working with the military, since no one keeps a closer eye on Nocens than them, and while some still favor destroying the entire realm, others are open to addressing the Daevalic problem through change on an individual level." A frown flashed across his face. "Of course, some officers still don't understand how truly dangerous Daevals are and question the need for any intervention, but they'll come around. After all, if Daevals can become like us, they're no longer a threat and there's no reason we can't all live in peace. Studying their blood is a means to an end, and knowledge is *always* worth whatever the cost to acquire it."

I thought back to what Camus had shared at the Dekarais' party about his concern over a potential Astral invasion. While I was glad to hear not everyone in the military supported fighting with or altering Daevals, I hated being reminded at least some powerful Astrals viewed silver blood as something to be gotten rid of. Senator Rex's plan sounded like a kinder, gentler option than war, but he still wanted to see Daevals erased from exist-ence. Rather than using weapons or spells, he envisioned a genocide brought about through blood.

"I completely support peace between the realms," I said, which was true. "Where would you like me to start?"

"I think it would be best to familiarize yourself with your father's notes," said Senator Rex. "Everything you need should be in your office, but if there's anything else you require, simply name it and I'll ensure you have access to it. Once you're ready to start working with silver blood, I'll deliver it to you."

"Thank you." I tried to keep a neutral expression on my face even as my stomach churned at the idea of doing anything with blood forcibly taken from children. I had no desire to help Sena-tor Rex figure out how to change Daevals into Astrals, but I also had to play along, at least until I obtained the information I needed about my father and the experimentation program.

As I reached down to grab my knapsack, Senator Rex cleared his throat.

"Before you go," he rested his elbows on the arms of the chair and steepled his fingers, "it behooves me to say this, although it's rather awkward . . . one of the areas in which your father excelled was his ability to maintain the utmost secrecy regarding this project. Even though I'm certain it goes without saying, I hope I can expect the same from you. I remember being an intern, and I know there's always comparison of who's doing what work with whom. While we are by far engaging in the most cutting-edge research, we must keep it to ourselves for the time being."

"Of course," I agreed, clutching my knapsack between my hands to keep them from shaking out of anger, anxiety, or some combination of the two. I didn't need to be reminded how good my father had been at keeping secrets, given how many he'd kept from me.

"Lionel is aware we're studying Astral blood, but he's unaware we're comparing it to Daevalic blood," added Senator Rex. "Healer Omnurion believes I'm guiding you through the ins and outs of becoming a politician. Neither will ask questions."

The senator rose and walked to his desk. Opening a drawer, he withdrew a small purple pouch, which he peered into before handing it to me. Inside was a captum.

"I know you have your own personal recording device," he explained, "but this one will be just for your work and can stay in your office. It's best to maintain a separation between personal items and those used in your official position."

I thanked him and stepped forward, but before he opened the door, he turned to face me, making me stiffen ever so slightly.

"Please don't hesitate to come to me with any questions you might have, even ones that seem inconsequential. What we're attempting is unheard of but together, I have no doubt we can achieve what others believe to be impossible."

I forced a smile to my face that would no doubt be taken as my agreement, and as the senator opened the door and made his way to Lionel's desk, Aurelius flicked his tail.

What he means is, once you're the Princeps Shaman *you can ensure the entire realm supports invading Nocens and turning every last Daeval into an Astral.*

Given Aurelius's disdain for Daevals, I was surprised to find him so opposed to the idea of altering them. Was being around Sebastian, or possibly Eslee, softening his outlook on those who lived in Nocens? I certainly hoped so.

"Lionel will take you to your office," said Senator Rex. "And allow me to say again how excited I am about our partnership."

"Thank you so much for this opportunity," I said. "I appreciate it more than I can say."

21

KYRA

"I did my best when it came to decorating," Lionel offered, "but we can change anything you don't like." He glanced down at Aurelius. "I wasn't certain whether you would prefer a cushion on the floor or a chair of your own, so I included both."

"That was quite thoughtful," replied Aurelius, the black tips of his ears pricking upwards. "I do like having options."

Lionel shot me a relieved smile, then guided me down the hallway, turning into one of the corridors that branched off to either side before coming to a stop and gesturing at a door.

"I oversaw the lettering of your nameplate myself." His chest puffed outwards ever so slightly.

I stared at the brass plaque on the door, surprised to see my name in swirling letters: *Kyra Valorian, Intern.*

"I thought interns shared an office when they weren't out on field placements." I turned to Lionel. "Why am I receiving such special treatment?"

The man's smile was just shy of a smirk. "Kyra, you are the future *Princeps Shaman* of Aeles. You can't be expected to concentrate in some cramped basement room surrounded by chatty trainees destined for no more glory than signing papers. Your work is *far* too important."

"Oh . . . thank you." I wasn't entirely certain what else to say, having never expected such a luxury.

Lionel smiled before explaining that offices in the *Donec Legibus* didn't use locks and keys. "After I leave, you'll hold the doorknob, it doesn't matter on which side, and your handprint will be recorded. You can grant others access to your office by allowing the door to record their handprints and approving the recording, but I don't recommend such a thing."

He opened the door, and Aurelius and I stepped inside a room much larger than I'd expected. The front part resembled a laboratory, complete with high counters, open shelves, and storage cabinets. There was also a sink, as well as numerous burners, vials, and beakers.

At the back of the office was a sturdy desk, in front of which were two armchairs identical to those in Senator's Rex office, and a small table was situated between them. The lower half of the walls was paneled in dark wood, with the upper half painted a cheery goldenrod yellow I found quite welcoming. While the floor in the front part of the office was tiled to make for easy cleaning, the back was covered in an oversized Montemian carpet with a repeating leaf motif in shades of blue, green, and gold.

"You're welcome to bring in your own decor," Lionel explained, "but I didn't want it to feel barren in the meantime."

"It's wonderful!" I assured him. "I'm still trying to get used to the fact that I have my own office. I can't imagine what the other interns will say."

"Who cares what they think?" scoffed Lionel. "I doubt you'll see them much anyway. Between your work with Senator Rex and Healer Omnurion, you're going to be far too busy to worry about a little gossip from those who are merely jealous. It's not as if you haven't worked exceptionally hard to be where you are. You deserve this."

While I appreciated his words, at that moment I didn't feel like I deserved anything. Senator Rex was only working with me because he wanted me to continue my father's research, not because of anything special about me. And while it was true my father hadn't cast a vote to select the intern matched with the *Donec Medicinae* to avoid charges of favoritism, given that I was his daughter, had my obtaining the position ever truly been in doubt outside of my own insecure fears? Everyone in Aeles had adored my father, and their love for him had to have contributed to me receiving preferential treatment. Would things be different if they'd known about his work with silver blood obtained from captive Daevalic children? Would such knowledge have kept me from internship or—my stomach tightened—would other Astrals have been unconcerned about him harming those from a different realm?

Realizing I'd lapsed into silence, I quickly smiled at Lionel, hoping he'd thought I was merely overwhelmed by recent events.

"Thank you for everything," I said. "I'm looking forward to working with you, and I can't thank you enough for making my office so welcoming. At this rate, I'm never going to want to leave!"

Lionel winked. "That's the idea." Bowing from the waist, he asked if there was anything else he could do to help me settle in and when I told him I was fine, he took his leave, reminding me he was always available to answer questions.

After recording my handprint on the doorknob, I pressed my fingertips against the bracelet.

Ask Aurelius if he thinks anyone's been following you, Sebastian said without preface, but before I could reply, he cleared his throat. *I mean . . . I'm worried about you, and I miss you. Can you ask Aurelius if he thinks anyone's been following you? The sooner we identify Tallus, the better.* Something about him making an effort to communicate more clearly broke the tenuous hold I'd been maintaining on my emotions.

I'll ask him, I replied, although the words came out choked. Tears rose unbidden, burning the backs of my eyes, and I looked upwards, blinking furiously to keep them from falling.

What's wrong? Sebastian's entire demeanor changed, his voice sharp as the blade of a knife. *Where are you?*

I'm safe, I said, trying to ease his concern. *I'm with Aurelius in my new office in Celenia, but I just . . .* I wiped away a tear that had managed to escape. *Senator Rex all but confirmed my father was part of the experimentation program. I can't believe he would do such a thing . . . it goes against everything he taught me and everything I thought I knew about him. And even though I probably shouldn't, I still miss him so much. Everything here is a reminder he's gone and never coming back.*

I could tell Sebastian would have been far more comfortable responding to an actual threat. While he'd been excellent at providing comfort in our previous life, in this one, he had practically no experience taking care of anyone but himself.

That's a lot for you to process, he finally said. *Is there anything I can do to make it easier for you?*

Talking to you and knowing I'm not alone definitely helps. I sniffled, then drew a deep breath before straightening my shoulders. No matter how hard this was, I could do it, because it wasn't just for me . . . this was for Sebastian and Gregor and others like them, locked away and experimented on simply because my kind thought they didn't deserve to exist as they were. I would be strong for them, and I would use my position, whether I deserved it or not, to stop such torture.

I spoke with Sebastian a while longer, then, feeling much better, promised to contact him later and touched my fingers against the bracelet to end our connection. Aurelius hopped up onto one of the blue armchairs and blinked at me.

Where are you going to start? he asked.

I gestured at the neatly arranged stack of notebooks waiting on one of the counters. *I think it makes sense to read everything Father left behind.* Gazing at a row of empty test tubes, I made a face. *Hopefully I won't need to make an actual breakthrough for Senator Rex to trust me enough to take me to the facility in Rynstyn.*

I am still not certain attempting to visit the facility is the wisest course of action, cautioned Aurelius.

I have to know if Father went there. I have to—

—You can uncover what your father was involved in without retracing every step he took, Aurelius interrupted, which only happened when he felt especially strongly about something. *Falling stars, Kyra, this is serious!* His cerulean eyes bored into mine. *You're talking about something supported by the highest levels of the Aelian government. Should you manage to obtain evidence of Daevals being tortured, that still might not be enough to end the program. Plus, Daevals are becoming aware of what's happening in Rynstyn and even Caz and Dunston won't be able to keep it quiet forever. Once more Daevals know, it could mean war!*

His thick silver whiskers twitched unhappily. *This has the potential to reshape the entire realm . . . both realms. How will that bring you any closer to reuniting the two?*

I studied the lynx. *I wasn't certain you supported our plan to reunite the realms.*

I'm not in favor of anything that puts you in danger, he admitted, *but if your plan is truly to reunite Aeles and Nocens, don't you think telling everyone what's been going on in the mountains of Rynstyn will only make your task more difficult?*

Then, what do you think I should do? I can't just let the program continue, not now that I know about it.

Of course not, agreed Aurelius. *But it seems to me you could just as easily stop it from a position of power, after you and Sebastian have reunited the realms and have a say in things. You could shut it down without anyone else ever knowing it existed.*

There was a great deal of wisdom in Aurelius's words, yet one part of his plan bothered me. *Ending it quietly doesn't do justice to the Daevals who were victimized there.*

Making a big deal of it simply creates more animosity between those with silver and gold blood, the lynx argued. *Why bring up things that will only be divisive?*

Because it's the right thing to do, I replied. *Those Daevals who were tortured or lost their lives at the hands of Astrals deserve to be recognized and remembered. I don't want to sweep this quietly aside just because it could potentially make things harder . . . I want all of Aeles to know what Astrals are capable of—what they've been doing for years— and I want Daevals to know not everyone with golden blood supports such awful practices. Once everything is out in the open and we're all working with the same information, then we can chart a way forward* together.

Aurelius sighed and gazed at his furry paws before lifting his head. *I just worry that bat places reuniting the realms above everything else, including your safety.* His gaze softened. *I am aware you've known him for far longer than we've been paired, but in this lifetime, I am your Cypher, Kyra, and I want to see you live a long and happy life.*

I stepped forward and wrapped my arms around the lynx. *No one could love me more or take better care of me than you.* I rested a cheek against the top of his soft head. *I trust you, Aurelius, and I need your insight and advice. I know your only goal is to keep me safe,* and the fact that you don't have any ulterior motives makes you one of the most important voices in my life. I love you.

I love you too, replied the lynx, leaning into my embrace and even purring slightly as I ran a hand over his back. *You know, for all his faults, Sebastian does seem to value your safety almost as much as I do.*

Sometimes I think the two of you would be happiest if I lived in Sebastian's cave and never ventured outside without taking Nerudian as my bodyguard. While I hadn't meant the suggestion seriously, Aurelius merely shrugged a black-spotted shoulder.

I can't say that's a bad idea. But at least you know where I stand on things.

I do, I nodded, *and I think before we even consider what we're going to do with anything we discover, we need to see exactly what Father was working on.*

Aurelius settled into his chair as I picked up the pile of notebooks. Part of me wished I could burn them and save myself from facing whatever truths they held, but I would never do such a selfish thing.

As you like to say, Aurelius, knowledge changes you. You can't go back to who you were before you knew something. I have to keep moving forward.

The lynx gave a solemn nod, and I braced myself for what I might uncover in the pages of my father's familiar handwriting.

22

SEBASTIAN

While the week passed slowly, it also provided me time to purchase an additional dresser and wardrobe. Batty had suggested Kyra might like having more space for her things, and for once his unsolicited advice made sense—the more comfortable she was here, the more frequently she would want to come over. I hoped she'd be pleased with the purchases. I also took the opportunity to complete a few contract assignments, which helped me stay busy, and while Kyra likely had her suspicions about how I was spending my time, she didn't mention it. When we finally reached Gwener on the Aelian calendar, I was so happy to be near her again, I didn't even care our time together would start with dinner at Adonis's. Besides reuniting me with Kyra, the evening would also provide an opportunity to observe her Astral friends for any indication one of them might be Tallus reborn.

Standing outside Adonis's cottage, I felt as if I was seeing the setting for every childhood bedtime story my mother had ever told me. The sun was sinking behind distant mountains, and the fading light provided an invitation for fireflies to flicker over the well-kept grounds, hovering above the flowers growing around the wood and stucco structure.

"It's so lovely," remarked Kyra as Aurelius sniffed a yellow daffodil. "I've only been here once, a few months ago when Adonis first moved in and threw a housewarming party, but he's clearly done a lot of work since then."

Stepping up to the cream-colored door, I rapped my knuckles against the wood, the sweet scent of honeysuckle tickling my nose. My mother had loved climbing vines, always maintaining how important they were to the bees, insects, and birds that enjoyed their nectar.

Many bats enjoy their nectar too, huffed Batty, speaking through our connection since he was back in the cave. He'd wanted to attend the dinner party, but I'd refused; it was enough for me to be here without worrying what he might say or do. While Kyra understood what a big deal this was for me, she'd also been adamant about Batty joining us for future events in Aeles once I was more comfortable around her friends.

The front door swung open, and there was Adonis, his grin stretching so wide, I thought the corners of his mouth might actually touch the lobes of his ears.

"You're here!" he exclaimed. "I'm so glad!" He pulled Kyra into a hug, but I was pleased to see his arms didn't linger, and he quickly turned to me, extending a hand as he did.

"I'm going to assume you're not a fan of hugs," he grinned, "but it's great to see you again, and under much less stressful circumstances this time."

I nodded and shook his hand, impressed at the strength of his grip.

"We're still waiting on Demitri," Adonis said, "but come in! Make yourselves comfortable."

"Knowing Demitri, he'll be late because he couldn't decide what to wear," Kyra chuckled, and even though Adonis smiled too, something at the edges of his expression made it seem forced. I wasn't certain what to make of it, but I'd keep an eye on it, nonetheless.

As we moved into the living room, I noted the placement of the furniture, as well as a door that opened into a backyard. Obviously if we needed to leave quickly, I'd open a portal, but if that failed for whatever reason, it was always wise to have a back-up escape route.

The wooden cottage walls were painted white, and the sofas and chairs looked well-used but inviting. The cheerful yellow, blue, and white color scheme made the space feel more welcoming than I'd expected for an Astral's home, and large windows framed by blue and white checkered curtains let in the remainder of the waning sunlight. Footsteps hurrying down the hallway caught my attention, and turning around, I found myself face-to-face with the unicorn sanctuary guard who'd sent me to my untimely death. I knew Kyra had befriended him and trusted him at least as much as she trusted Adonis, but it was still odd to see the soldier standing across from me without brandishing a sword. An otter I took to be his Cypher appeared by his boots.

Kyra quickly interlaced her fingers through mine. "Sebastian, this is Nigel," she gestured towards the soldier. "Also known as Lieutenant Coran. Nigel, this is Sebastian."

I couldn't fault a soldier for following orders and protecting the territory he'd been assigned, so I extended a hand, and Nigel gave a relieved grin before stepping forward and shaking it.

"I've already apologized to Kyra," he said, "but I'm sorry for what happened in the sanctuary. It wasn't anything personal."

"No hard feelings," I assured him.

Nigel pointed at the otter. "This is Otto." He smiled before turning back to me. "I also told Kyra if you're ever open to offering a fighting lesson or two, I'd certainly sign up! I've never seen anyone move the way you did. Where did you learn to fight like that?"

I was about to reply when a knock sounded, and Adonis rushed to open the front door.

"There you are!" he practically shouted as he ushered Demitri inside, nodding to the red-tailed hawk perched on the man's shoulder. "I was worried you might have received a better dinner offer."

"I wouldn't have missed this for anything," replied Demitri as his Cypher flew across the room to settle on the back of a chair. He handed Adonis a bottle of wine. "For our gracious host. The flowers outside look amazing; you've done so much since the last time I was here!"

Adonis beamed, and I recalled how my mother had always loved compliments about her flowers.

"I couldn't have done it alone," Adonis said as he closed the door. "Nigel's been a huge help since he moved in."

Demitri's eyes widened in a somewhat unfriendly manner, and I found myself more fascinated than I cared to admit. Did Demitri have some grudge against Nigel I didn't know about? I'd have to ask Kyra later.

"Nigel is *living* here?" Demitri asked, tugging on the ridiculous black suspenders he was wearing, although they were no more ridiculous than his burgundy pants. "Did the Astral military suddenly run out of housing?"

"No," laughed Nigel, as if Demitri had said something clever. "I could have stayed in the barracks in Celenia, but seeing as how we've been partnered, Adonis was kind enough to let me stay with him while I'm looking for a place of my own."

"Well, hopefully you'll find something soon!" said Demitri. "I'm sure living out of a trunk is exhausting."

"I feel as if I've lived here for years." Nigel clapped Adonis on the back. "The problem is going to be finding a place as comfortable as this."

"There's no rush," assured Adonis. "Before it was just Gordon and me, and he certainly didn't take up much space." He caught my eye as a large toad suddenly materialized on the table in front of the sofa. "Gordon is my Cypher," he explained.

I'd expected someone like Adonis to have a far more intimidating Cypher than a toad, which made me wonder if he'd ever wanted to be paired with a more powerful animal, as I had. Perhaps I'd ask him someday, but at that moment, Demitri smiled at Kyra and crossed the room to give her a hug, driving all other thoughts from my mind.

Demitri appeared completely oblivious to the fact that Kyra and I were holding hands, and as he embraced her, I made no move to loosen my grip, prompting Kyra to return his hug using only one arm, which in my estimation was more than enough. As Demitri released her, his eyes ran over our interlaced fingers, and he scowled.

"Are we certain the Blood Alarm won't go off?" he demanded, prompting Kyra to sigh.

"You could start with, 'Hello Sebastian, nice to see you again,'" she said. "He's taking a huge risk coming where he's not allowed, surrounded by Astrals . . . and members of the military no less!"

I moved closer to her, and while my words were meant for Kyra, I stared directly at Demitri as I spoke. "Coming here tonight was important to you, which means it's important to me."

Demitri's eyes flickered angrily, but from my peripheral vision, I could see Kyra gazing happily at me, and Demitri saw it too, which was likely the only thing that made him hold his tongue.

"I, for one, think it's fantastic you came!" interjected Adonis. "You're always welcome in my home, Sebastian; in fact, anytime I invite Kyra over, please know the invitation includes you too, and I'll just assume you're coming." He grinned at the other Astrals. "If being a good host can improve relations between the realms, I'm happy to lead the way!"

"Adonis, now that we're all here, can we help you with dinner?" asked Kyra, clearly wanting to keep the conversation moving, perhaps worried my next response to Demitri's rudeness wouldn't be so polite.

"Everything's waiting in the kitchen," said Adonis, beckoning us to follow him.

"It smells amazing!" noted Kyra appreciatively, and as someone who only used my kitchen to reheat food I'd purchased elsewhere, I was surprised at the size of the room. There were two masonry ovens and a six-burner cookstove heated by frictional matches, as well as two large iceboxes and more cabinets and drawers than many stores had. I had to admit, it did smell good.

"I thought we could eat outside in the garden," Adonis suggested. "We can cast a warming spell if it gets too chilly. Let me just take the lids off a few things."

After piling our plates high with food, everyone moved outside, and I admired the twinkling strands of lights crisscrossing the wooden scaffolding overhead. As I took a seat at the wrought iron table, I was annoyed but not surprised to see Demitri practically leap into the empty chair on the other side of Kyra.

"Before we talk about anything else," he said, "Kyra, I really need you to sign some sort of paperwork or write an official memorandum, *something*, so Lionel will let me visit you."

"What do you mean?" asked Kyra, placing her napkin in her lap.

"I mean, I tried to visit you yesterday, and I ended up being escorted into Lionel's office, and no matter what I said to him, he seemed to believe you didn't want to be interrupted and that I should visit with you after work hours." Demitri pursed his lips as he shook his head. "The *nerve* of him, saying I didn't have the proper access! He literally shooed me away."

Adonis offered him a sympathetic smile. "If it makes you feel better, it's not just you. He's like that with everyone."

While I still wasn't pleased about Kyra working so closely with another man, my opinion of Lionel rose significantly, as I very much appreciated knowing there was a protocol-obsessed gatekeeper limiting anyone's access to my former wife.

"Well, just find out what sort of permission I need," Demitri whined to Kyra. "Otherwise, I'll never be able to come visit you."

"And what a pity that would be," I said just loud enough for Demitri to hear. He glared at me as Kyra gave me a warning look I knew I deserved and wasn't sorry to receive.

Adonis quickly changed the subject, and while he or Nigel occasionally asked me about Nocens, I appreciated that no one tried to gather information about me. I doubted Kyra wanted any of them to know what I did for a living, so perhaps she'd suggested they refrain from more personal questions.

Towards the end of the meal, Demitri snapped his fingers and turned to Kyra. "I almost forgot! I went through the different locator spells I know, and I think the best one to use when you're looking for more suppressor medallions is an *Inventum* spell. Only the caster receives an alert when they're near the object they're searching for. You can make it more like getting a little shock than setting off a loud alarm."

Kyra's eyes widened with excitement. "So, I could cast that type of spell on the medallion we have, carry it around Aeles— hidden in a pocket or bag, of course—and then I'd get a vibration when I came near another medallion?"

Demitri nodded, and Kyra smiled warmly at him.

"Thank you so much for figuring this out!" Her words caused Demitri to sit up straighter as he clearly enjoyed the moment.

"I've said it before, but I'll say it again . . . there's nothing I wouldn't do for you," he quipped, leaning over so he could rest the side of his head against Kyra's shoulder. His eyes met mine as a smirk flitted over his lips.

Before I could say something cutting or simply flip the table over onto Demitri's lap, Adonis rose to his feet. "I'm going to get dessert," he announced. "Sebastian, would you mind helping me?"

I very nearly refused, but Kyra gave me such a hopeful look, I swallowed down my refusal and settled for gathering dishes before following Adonis inside. Setting the dinnerware down in the oversized sink, I focused on my breathing, allowing the fire in my veins to cool.

"Thank you for helping," said Adonis, closing a cabinet door. "Honestly, I just needed a moment . . . and from the look of things, so did you."

I moved away from the sink, crossing my arms over my chest as I turned to face the Astral. It was frustrating how someone as pathetic as Demitri riled me up so fast, but I couldn't deny that he did. Part of me didn't want to ask the question perched on the tip of my tongue, but I also never passed up an opportunity to do reconnaissance.

"Was Demitri like this towards Kyra's other partners?" I asked.

Adonis appeared deep in thought as he filled the sink with soapy water.

"I didn't spend a lot of time with Kyra growing up," he finally said. "We knew each other, but our parents weren't close, and we were two grades apart in school. Since I've been spending more time with her, I've only seen her on a couple of courtship outings, and Demitri was perfectly pleasant to the guys she was with."

I scowled but forced myself to ask, "What about anyone she had a more serious relationship with?"

"I never met anyone she was seriously involved with." Adonis shook his head.

"You mean besides Demitri," I muttered.

Adonis dropped the plate he'd been holding, but thankfully it simply slid into the soapy water rather than breaking.

"It's true?" His eyes were wide. "They *were* romantically involved at one point?"

I shrugged, not entirely comfortable having this conversation but appreciating that Adonis was clearly affected by it, although I knew his reasons were different from mine. While I wanted to know everything I could about the woman I'd been married to in a previous life, he obviously didn't want to be lied to by those who claimed to be his friends.

"Kyra told me they've always been best friends and that's it, but . . ." I let my voice trail off, and Adonis nodded vigorously.

"But you watch them together and it's almost *impossible* to believe they weren't a couple at some point," he said, waving a hand and sending soap suds flying. "Sometimes I want to tell one of them to be still while the other moves . . . it's like one can't do something without affecting the other. They always know what each other is going to say, and they have years of shared life experiences together. No matter how close you get, you're always on the outskirts and they still have something you're not quite a part of."

I nodded slowly, more than a little surprised to hear Adonis's heated words expressing many of the same thoughts I'd had. Something inside me thawed towards the soldier, which led me to venture another question.

"Why do you think Demitri can barely say a civil word to me when he was perfectly pleasant to Kyra's other partners?"

"Oh, that's easy." Adonis wiped his hands on a blue towel. "He knew she wasn't really interested in them, the same way he knows you're different."

"What do you mean?"

Adonis made his way to one of the iceboxes and pulled out a beautifully decorated chocolate cake, which he carefully placed on the white and grey stone counter. "I mean, it's obvious what you two have isn't some casual fling. I don't know your entire backstory, but it's clear you have a connection that defies understanding. I've certainly never seen anything like it."

For a moment, the soldier's expression turned wistful, and he gazed down at the cake before sighing and reaching for a knife.

"I never expected to meet her," I said. If Kyra and I were going to reunite the realms, we'd have to tell those who knew us the truth about our past at some point, and while now wasn't the time, I also wanted to offer Adonis something in exchange for listening to my concerns.

"I expected to be alone forever, but then I accidentally opened a portal to the wrong place, and now I can't imagine my life without her. Things happen when you least expect them, and if a relationship between the two of us can work, it can work for anyone."

Adonis looked at me for a moment, then slowly smiled. "That's true." He nodded. "Thank you for the reminder. There's always hope."

I'd never imagined someone thanking me for inspiring hope, but I ducked my head in acknowledgment. It felt good knowing Adonis and I were united on the issue of Kyra and Demitri, even though I hadn't expected to feel so comfortable around the soldier so quickly. The only man my age I'd ever been close to was Farent, and that had been in my previous life as Schatten. Farent had been an incredibly capable soldier who had quickly risen through the ranks to become captain of the guard, but more than that, he'd been my closest friend and confidant, aside from Kareth. Something stirred in the back of my mind, and I thought a memory might be forthcoming, but nothing flashed before my eyes and whatever I'd felt remained too vague for me to do more than notice it as I helped Adonis carry slices of cake outside.

23

KYRA

Thankfully, we made it through dessert without any more uncomfortable incidents. Adonis had brought his spectacular chocolate cake out after everyone had clamored for seconds, and I leaned forward and cut off a large slice to take back to Batty. Before I could ask Adonis to borrow a container for the cake, Nigel dropped his napkin beside his plate and grinned at Sebastian.

"I bet I could get us out of clean-up duty if you agree to show me some techniques with a sword," he said, his grey eyes bright with excitement.

I wasn't certain it was a good idea for Sebastian to be near anyone with a sword, even if it wasn't a real fight, especially considering his history with Nigel. But as he glanced at me, I could see a rare excitement stirring in his dark eyes.

"We don't need to rush off," I said hesitantly, "but are you sure this is a good idea?"

"Of course!" Nigel jumped to his feet. "Come watch, and if anything seems too dangerous, we'll stop." He smiled brightly at Adonis. "I guess that leaves you and Demitri to clean up . . . hopefully that's alright."

"It's fine," Adonis replied, although I thought I heard something catch in his voice, and he quickly took a drink before waving Nigel away. "Go have fun, and we'll join you when we're done. Unless you want to watch," he said to Demitri, who immediately shook his head.

"Washing dishes sounds *far* superior to watching a sword fight," he assured Adonis.

I did my best to study Nigel without being noticed. Was he trying to find a way to give Demitri and Adonis time alone together? Normally that was something I did, but only because I knew about Demitri's feelings for Adonis. Did Nigel, being Adonis's roommate, know something about the man I didn't? Did he have feelings for Demitri he was unable to act on, given the laws of Aeles, prompting Nigel to help where he could? I didn't know, but the idea was certainly intriguing, and clearly I needed to pay better attention to Nigel's behavior where Adonis and Demitri were concerned.

Nigel hurried indoors, and I took the opportunity to ask Adonis about taking a piece of cake with me. He happily offered to box up my slice as Nigel returned carrying two swords, and Sebastian and I followed him to the side of the house, where there was a flat expanse of grass. Casting a few orbs of light into the air, he offered one of the swords to Sebastian as I found an out-of-the-way place to stand. Aurelius and the other Cyphers were keeping their own company in the living room, and I wished again Sebastian had invited Batty. While I understood his concerns, given that this was his first time socializing with Astrals, next time I'd ensure the bat was included.

Sebastian twirled the sword a few times, getting a feel for it, and my heartbeat quickened as I remembered the way he and Nigel had fought in the unicorn sanctuary, up until he'd crashed through the ice and entered Vaneklus before his time. And now Nigel was encouraging him to wield a weapon again. Was the soldier trying to lure him into a fight? Was it possible Sebastian had been right and Nigel *was* Tallus reborn? I considered the possibility before putting it aside. My intuition said no, Nigel was simply eager to learn from a swordsman as skilled as Sebastian. If it turned out I was wrong . . . well, we would deal with that when the time came.

Sebastian raised and lowered his shoulders, then rolled his head from side to side before settling into a fighting stance. Nigel did the same, stretching his arms and kicking his legs before facing Sebastian.

"Now, I do have to work tomorrow," the lieutenant grinned, "so I'd like to keep all my limbs intact, but I also don't want you to go easy on me."

"I won't," Sebastian assured him, and I wrapped my arms around myself as the two men lunged towards one another, blades ringing beneath the night sky.

While Nigel was skilled with a sword, it was obvious even to untrained eyes like mine that Sebastian was the better fighter. I was surprised, however, to see what a good instructor he was, as well. He frequently stopped Nigel, demonstrated a certain grip or stance, then walked the soldier through practicing it before moving at a speed more akin to an actual fight. Soon Nigel's cheeks were red, and he ran a sleeve over his damp forehead. Sebastian, on the other hand, didn't appear to be breathing any faster than normal, much less sweating.

"Do you have any tips on throwing a sword?" asked Nigel. "I can't ever seem to get the landing right."

Choosing a spot a few yards away, he threw the weapon forward. While the blade was supposed to stick in the ground, the sword careened wildly and smashed into a window, breaking the glass before clattering to the ground.

"Oops." Nigel clasped a handful of his unruly ash blonde hair. "Maybe no one heard."

Our Cyphers suddenly appeared around us, and footsteps sounded on the patio, followed by Adonis and Demitri hurrying around the corner of the cottage, worry replacing Adonis's usually cheerful expression.

"Everything's fine," Nigel quickly explained. "I was just practicing throwing my sword and didn't get the aim quite right."

He walked closer to the broken glass and said a spell, causing the fallen shards to rise from the yard and reform in the window frame.

"Is that all we ran out here for?" huffed Demitri. I knew he hated having time with Adonis interrupted but still, it had been an accident. "I thought Sebastian had thrown Nigel through a window." Shaking his head, he turned to go back to the kitchen when Sebastian spoke.

"Keep assuming the worst about me, Demitri, and it won't be a sword or Nigel flying through a window."

I tried to catch his eye to indicate he needed to stop, but either Sebastian didn't see me or he purposefully ignored me. Instead, he walked closer to Demitri, twirling his sword in a wide arc.

Demitri spun around, an equally rude remark likely on the tip of his tongue, but his eyes widened at the sight of Sebastian moving closer. I stepped forward, ready to intervene, when Sebastian's sword stopped mid-spin, clanging against the blade of Nigel's sword.

Except Nigel wasn't holding the sword.

Adonis was.

I'd been so busy watching Sebastian and Demitri, I hadn't seen Adonis pick up the sword, nor had I noticed him positioning himself so he could move in front of Demitri, blocking Sebastian's view of the other man.

Sebastian tilted his head to one side, weighing the situation, and to my relief, Adonis grinned at him.

"Now that Nigel's gotten to see what you can do, it's my turn. Care to spar a few rounds?"

Sebastian never would have harmed Demitri—at least that's what I told myself—and I was surprised Adonis hadn't recognized that. Perhaps it was simply his training as a soldier, but for a split second, he'd acted as if Sebastian had been a real threat. At least he seemed to have sorted things out.

"Why not?" shrugged Sebastian, taking a few steps back and widening his stance to balance on the balls of his feet. "Are we keeping score?"

Adonis shook his head. "Let's just have fun. No drawing blood and bodily contact with hands and feet only."

"Works for me," replied Sebastian.

And with that, he darted forward, sword raised.

I held my breath as the two men faced off. Even though I knew neither was actually trying to harm the other, I also knew from watching my younger siblings how quickly play fighting could turn dangerous.

After a few moments with no bloodshed, I started to relax and it wasn't long before I found myself enjoying the exhibition. Of course it didn't matter who won, since we weren't keeping score, but part of me felt the tiniest bit smug knowing Sebastian's true level of skill, given who he'd been before.

Adonis swept a leg forward in a wide arc, very similar to a move I'd seen Sebastian use to catch the Formari creatures in Vaneklus off-guard. He then spun around and kicked out with his other leg, forcing Sebastian to take a step back to avoid catching a boot in his chest. Surprise registered on Sebastian's face, and he narrowed his eyes. Feinting to one side, he shot around Adonis, forcing the soldier to turn in a tight half-circle just as he delivered a well-placed jab with his palm to the captain's sternum.

Adonis grunted and acted as if he was going to take a step

backwards, then pivoted into a sweeping roundhouse kick that clipped the edge of Sebastian's shoulder. Sebastian ducked into a forward roll, and before Adonis could jump out of the way, he grabbed one of the soldier's legs, pushing Adonis backwards and making him lose his balance.

To my surprise, though, Adonis threw himself into a backflip, using his boot to push off Sebastian's back and landing, albeit shakily, a few feet away. Sebastian rushed towards him and for a moment, the two were little more than a blur of arms, legs, and swords until they eventually separated.

I could tell Sebastian was breathing harder and as he studied Adonis, the expression on his face was a mixture of surprise, annoyance, and what might have been pure enjoyment.

Adonis, too, was breathing faster, but he also wore a huge smile. "For being left-handed, you're really good at protecting your right side," he said to Sebastian. "You don't leave any openings, and you're almost impossible to get behind. Sometimes you overshoot your punches, though, which means you're using your arm too much; let more power come from your shoulder."

I bit the inside of my lip, expecting Sebastian to pin Adonis to the ground before providing him with a personal demonstration of overshot punches. Instead, he nodded.

"You balance equally well on both legs," Sebastian said, "and you don't favor one side as a starting point, which makes it harder to predict what you're going to do. But you're using mostly your legs in your flips, which is why you're not sticking your landing. Lead with your chest and follow through with your hips, then your legs . . . you'll flip with more force and be upright faster."

Adonis considered Sebastian's feedback. "Alright. Come at me again so I can try that."

Sebastian seemed only too happy to oblige, but rather than moving quickly, he took his time, and everything inside me jangled with nervous anticipation. Without warning, he kicked out at the same time he sliced his sword downward, prompting Adonis to move to one side before using his blade to pin Sebastian's sword to the ground. As Sebastian crouched to wrap both hands around the hilt, he nodded, and Adonis stepped forward, pushed off Sebastian's shoulder with one foot, and threw himself into a truly beautiful backflip, landing gracefully without the slightest bit of swaying.

Sebastian set his sword down. "Much better. Now, try to hit my chest while I work on not overshooting my punches."

Adonis tossed his sword to Nigel before zig-zagging forward in a flurry of movements, throwing uppercuts, punches, palm thrusts, and jabs. While Sebastian initially focused on defending himself, blocking and ducking, he quickly went on the offensive, his fists reaching for Adonis's chest. After a moment, the two pulled apart.

"My accuracy was more consistent," Sebastian noted with a self-satisfied nod, pushing his hair off his forehead.

"I could feel the difference this time," agreed Adonis. "Plus, your arms won't tire out as fast." Ruffling his hair, he studied Sebastian. "I'm not exaggerating when I say you're the best fighter I've ever sparred with. That was a real treat . . . I always think I know my own tendencies, but it's good to be reminded of them, especially when I'm really challenged."

"I'd spar with you again," said Sebastian. I hadn't expected him to say that, and clearly neither had Adonis, who appeared genuinely surprised. "If you ever want to take a break from baking, that is," Sebastian added in what for him was a rare attempt at teasing, although I wasn't certain Adonis would recognize that.

Adonis placed his hands on his hips.

"I'll have you know fighting skills translate quite nicely to baking!" His eyes sparkled as he fought unsuccessfully to repress a grin. "Speed, flexibility, and focus are *just* as important when you're wielding a spatula as when you're wielding a sword."

"If you say so." Sebastian shrugged, but I didn't miss the smile that flitted over his face.

24

KYRA

*B*ack in Sebastian's cave, Batty was thrilled over his unexpected piece of chocolate cake, and I was surprised to see a new dresser and wardrobe situated against the rock walls. I was even more surprised when Sebastian gestured to them and said, "I thought you might like to have more space for your things."

"Thank you!" I gave him a hug. "I'd love that."

Sebastian returned my hug, then headed off to shower, and I thanked Batty, who had clearly recalled our conversation in Eslee's bedroom and prompted Sebastian to make the purchases. As I transferred my shifter cloak, *The Book of Recovrancy*, and a few other things from the drawer I'd been using into my new dresser, I couldn't help feeling excited—I'd never lived with anyone other than my family. I'd considered moving in with a roommate a few times, but I'd always decided against it, not wanting to deal with them being loud when I wanted to study or not cleaning up after themselves.

Changing into my sleeping clothes, I made my way to the bed, trying to decide how best to discuss the dinner party. Just because things hadn't gone smoothly between Sebastian and Demitri didn't mean the entire evening had been a disaster.

Sebastian soon joined me, his hair damp, and I was pleased to see him slide under the covers this time.

"Thank you again for going tonight," I began. "I'm sure it wasn't easy, being in Aeles around so many Astrals, but I think this was a really good start. Adonis was clearly thrilled to host us, and you seemed to have a good time sparring with him. Are you still worried he or Nigel might be Tallus reborn?"

Sebastian turned to face me, resting an elbow on his pillow and propping up his head.

"I did have a good time sparring with him," he agreed. "I've been thinking about it ever since we got back . . . while I want to say I can't remember the last time I had so much fun training with someone, that's not entirely true. I don't think Adonis is Tallus reborn—Nigel, either—but I *do* think I knew Adonis in a previous life." His eyes sought mine. "I think I knew him as Farent."

I blinked as memories washed over me, filling me with sadness . . . when I'd been Kareth, Farent had been married to my brother, Donovan. After Tallus had murdered Farent, I'd entered Vaneklus to recover his shade, but to my dismay, I'd discovered the stalwart soldier had died at his appointed time. I'd been devastated, but that had paled in comparison to what Schatten had felt.

"I feel ridiculous even saying this," continued Sebastian, some of his hair falling into his eyes, "but if we've returned and Tallus has most likely returned . . . do you think it's possible . . ." his voice trailed off, as if saying the words out loud would ruin the hope he was secretly holding.

"Of course it's possible," I assured him. "Rebirth is a normal part of life. The only difference between us and everyone around us is we've managed to keep most of our memories from a previous life intact. Those who didn't use a spell won't have any knowledge of who they used to be."

"So, you're saying the next time I see Adonis I probably

shouldn't tell him how good it is to have my favorite training partner back?" A wry smile crept over Sebastian's mouth, momentarily distracting me from our conversation. While he was certainly smiling more frequently than when I'd first met him, it was still a rare enough event to make me pause and take notice. There was no question Sebastian was handsome regardless of his facial expression, but when he let down his guard enough to smile . . . my head swam, and I couldn't look away, captivated by his lips. I was also profoundly grateful he felt safe enough to share something so personal, and I almost leaned over and kissed him, until I remembered we hadn't discussed all the events of the evening.

I returned his smile. "Probably not, but if Adonis was Farent in another life, it makes sense he'd be drawn to you as you clearly are to him." Rearranging my pillow, I added, "It's too bad Farent couldn't have come back as Demitri. That would make things so much easier. I think—"

"—He acts as if I have no right to be with you," exclaimed Sebastian, his almost-happy demeanor darkening, "when really, I have more right than anyone!"

"I want to tell him about our past," I explained. "I think if he understands our connection, it'll be easier for him to accept us as . . . well, *us.*"

"I don't need him to accept anything," snapped Sebastian. "We're together whether he likes it or not."

I stiffened at his tone and was about to reply when Aurelius spoke.

While there's no denying Sebastian's conversational etiquette leaves much *to be desired, perhaps you ought to consider where he's coming from.*

"Aurelius wants to talk to me for a moment," I said. Speaking to Cyphers was so common, folks usually didn't get upset when someone unexpectedly lapsed into silence, but I didn't want Sebastian to think I was pulling away or ignoring him. Fortunately, he nodded.

What do you mean? I asked Aurelius, sitting up and peering out of the alcove. The lynx was laying with his chin propped on the arm of the sofa, and his blue eyes were bright as they met mine. While I was used to him sharing his perspective, this was also the second time in two days he'd taken Sebastian's side on something.

I mean, this is a man who has lost almost everyone and everything he's ever cared about, said the lynx. *He views relationships, especially important ones, as things to be guarded against losing. You see relationships as positive, fulfilling, and adding to your life . . . his experience has taught him anyone he cares about can be taken away from him.*

But Demitri is never going to take me from him.

You and I know that, said Aurelius gently, *but all Sebastian has to go on is your word. He's jealous of the life you had before you found one another again. And he's afraid the promise of building a future with him won't be as attractive as continuing what you've already established with Demitri.*

I tucked my hair behind my ear. *Do you think it would be better if he knew Demitri wasn't attracted to women?*

I think he needs to take you at your word when you say you have no romantic interest in Demitri . . . but at the same time, yes, it would likely make him feel better.

I'll talk to Demitri this week. Thank you, Aurelius.

A Cypher's work is never done, yawned the lynx before I felt him drifting off to sleep.

Turning back to Sebastian, I reached out and took his hand in mine.

"I wish I would have known you my entire life," I said softly.

"I wish I would have grown up knowing who I used to be and who we were, and that it hadn't taken years for us to find one another again. But I'm forever grateful we did, and now we can focus on building a life together. I don't want to say goodbye to everything in my old life as I build a new one, but I also want you to know nothing in my past compares to my present or my future with you, Sebastian."

His gaze was unblinking, and I could tell I had his complete attention.

"I have never had the slightest romantic thought towards Demitri," I continued. "I want you to trust me when I say he will never come between us, and while I promise he's never had any romantic inclination towards me, even if he did, it wouldn't matter because you're the only one I want to be with. You don't have to worry about who I'm around or how they're acting towards me because you don't have to worry about *me*."

I leaned closer to him. "I only want you."

And with that, I pressed my lips against his, trying to convey everything I felt for him, everything that had burned inside me during our past life together and everything I treasured about him now.

Sebastian reached up and pressed his palm against the back of my head, pulling me closer and letting his fingers tangle in my hair. I moved towards him, running a hand over his shoulder and down his chest, which even beneath his sleeping shirt somehow managed to be both hard and soft. For someone who generally despised physical touch, albeit with good reason, I was glad he didn't so much as flinch at the pressure from my hand. His kisses were equal parts insistent and tender and sent my senses spinning in all directions, making me feel dizzy and weightless and like I might drift up into the air if I released my hold on him.

At almost nineteen years old, I'd kissed exactly three boys, but none of those kisses had been even remotely close to what I was experiencing now. While I'd always tried not to compare myself to others my age, I'd also secretly assumed I was something of a late bloomer when it came to romance, and that someday I'd care enough about someone to want to go beyond simply kissing them.

Lying in bed, kissing the man I'd already been lucky enough to spend a lifetime with, I decided today was that day. Unfortunately, as Sebastian wrapped his arms around me and pulled me closer, my mind was suddenly flooded with the memory of the first time Schatten and I had seen each other unclothed.

My breath caught somewhere between my lungs and nose, and my limbs stiffened as my heart skipped a beat before racing forward. Sebastian sensed the change immediately, and we pulled apart just enough to look at one another; his eyes were wide, and it was obvious he'd seen the memory I'd unwittingly recovered.

"I'm sorry," I groaned. "I was loving everything we were doing, and I thought about doing more, and then . . . well, you saw what I remembered. I just got a little overwhelmed."

Sebastian rolled onto his back before wrapping an arm around my shoulder and pulling me against him. As I pressed the side of my face to his chest, I was secretly happy to discover his heart was pounding as hard as mine, and I enjoyed the thrumming for a moment before continuing.

"I know we've been together before, and while that ought to make it easier, sometimes I think it makes it harder," I tried to explain. "I want us to know each other now like we did then, but . . . what if your new body likes different things I don't know about or whatever I do to you doesn't feel good or—"

"—Anything you do to me feels wonderful," Sebastian insisted, his deep voice vibrating in his chest and tickling my ear.

"When you so much as smile at me, I feel like I could conquer all of Nocens without even needing Rhannu."

I squeezed his torso where my arm was draped across it.

"And," he added, "just so you know . . . I worry about that too."

"Really?" I pushed myself into a sitting position to look at him.

"Of course," he replied. "I worry I won't be able to make you happy or meet your needs like I used to."

I'd never imagined Sebastian making such an admission, and hearing that he, too, was worried about being intimate made me feel much better.

"We'll figure things out," I assured myself as much as him. "It's not as if we don't have anything else going on . . . I'm learning to be a Recovrancer again, you're getting reacquainted with Rhannu, we're trying to shut down an evil experimentation program, and we're working to reunite the realms, not to mention trying to figure out what to tell Astrals and Daevals who've known us our entire lives about who we used to be. Before, all we had to do was get married."

"At least the first time we met, we had three uninterrupted days and nights to ourselves." Sebastian sighed. "I meant what I said before, though . . . I'll never pressure you. There's no rush. It's whatever works for us."

While I was grateful for Sebastian's patience, I also fought down my own disappointment. Hopefully whatever worked for us would present itself sooner rather than later, as I wanted to make new memories with the man beside me, not simply recall previous ones, incredible though they'd been.

25

KYRA

When we woke, I used Sebastian's peerin to contact Eslee to see about visiting her studio. Accepting my call, she grabbed her hair and pantomimed a scream before apologizing and explaining her father had insisted the entire family go to Dal Mar to surprise his sister for her birth anniversary. Eslee was certain her aunt Minerva would have preferred celebrating her birth anniversary alone, but her father so rarely demanded the family do something together, she didn't want to risk upsetting him by returning to Vartox. While I was disappointed, I also understood, and we agreed to meet the next time I was in Nocens.

Sebastian headed off to train with Rhannu, and I made a quick breakfast from the supply of planterian food Batty showed me in the icebox and cabinets. I then settled my shifter cloak over my shoulders and made my way to Vaneklus.

Standing in the cheerless waters of Death, I smiled as the Shade Transporter's boat appeared.

"I find myself quite unable to predict when you'll be visiting these days," Laycus said by way of greeting.

"I'm staying with Sebastian on the weekends when I'm not at internship," I explained. "I know it doesn't actually matter, but I'm still too scared to come here when my physical body is in Aeles.

So, you'll see me quite a bit for a short period for time, then have a long break until I return."

Laycus sighed as if he was already exhausted. "What do you wish to work on?"

"I want to figure out if Sebastian's mother is still in Ceelum, so I can speak to her and find out if she wants to be recovered. I'd also like to recover another shade, since as of right now, I've only recovered Sebastian."

Laycus's garnet-red eyes flickered. "I have no awareness of shades until they appear on my dock, so with regards to recovering one, we shall simply have to see if one appears while you're here. As for Sebastian's mother, surely that book told you a shade in Ceelum can choose whether or not they appear to a Recovrancer. If you seek Grace Sayre and she doesn't appear, what then? She might simply be ignoring you or she might have already gone to Karnis for rebirth."

"The book did tell me that," I nodded. "And you're right, starting in Ceelum won't provide conclusive answers . . . which is why I want to go to Karnis and speak with your sister."

Laycus let out a barking laugh, and the river rippled against my knees as if it was somehow laughing with him.

"Why in the grey waters of Death would you think I'd do such a thing?" exclaimed the Shade Transporter. "I am obligated to transport shades, not Recovrancers."

"I think you'll do it because you agreed to be my mentor, and in this case, you truly are the *only* one who can help me," I said. "You also know if you refuse, I'll start looking for ways to contact your sister without involving you and there's a good chance I'll disrupt all of Vaneklus in my attempts."

Laycus's expression turned from incredulous to angry. "Not even as Kareth did you ask such a thing!" he hissed. "If you had, I would have given you the same answer—there's little chance you'd survive the journey. Once a shade begins the trip to Karnis, they cannot come back up the river; there's no traversing it as you please."

I returned his glare, my frustration rising. There had to be something he wasn't telling me. Pulling *The Book of Recovrancy* from my bag, I silently begged it to share anything that would prove Laycus wrong. Black text began to rise on the white page, and I read the words out loud:

> *The river of Death runs in only one direction, carrying shades ever forward. Once a shade reaches Karnis, they must progress on to rebirth and cannot go back the way they came; however, this does not apply to a Recovrancer who has established a relationship with Death. Simply because a Recovrancer cannot recover shades from Karnis does not mean she cannot venture there and still safely return to the land of the living.*

I looked up at Laycus, who appeared to be contemplating snatching the book out of my hands and ripping it to shreds.

"What does that mean, establishing a relationship with Death?" I asked.

The Shade Transporter clenched his jaw before responding. "In order to know what is taking place in Death without actually being here, a Recovrancer may form a relationship with this realm, permitting them to know when a shade has arrived. Such a relationship allows them to do other things, as well, but it is not an easy undertaking."

More words appeared on the page.

> *A bond with Death is not easily managed. Death is insistent and will demand attention at the worst and most inconvenient*

of times. It cannot be tamed, but a relationship can be formed with it, although the success of such an endeavor will depend entirely on the willpower of the Recovrancer. If she cannot manage to divide her attention, she stands to become consumed by Death, fixated on the dead and failing to truly live. This is not a life, and she will find herself spending more and more time in Vaneklus until she eventually forgets the spell to return to the land of the living.

A trickle of anxiety slipped down my spine, and I looked up at Laycus, who shrugged.

"I told you it would be challenging."

Additional words appeared on the page, and I hoped they were more promising:

In order to establish a deeper relationship with Death, a Recovrancer must stand in the waters of Vaneklus. She must introduce her blood into the river while saying:

Chan eil beatha agus bas nan aghaidh
Is iad a' ghrain agus a' ghealach
Aon an-comhnaidh a 'leantainn
an te eile.

"Life and Death are not opposites," translated Laycus. "They are like the sun and moon, one always following the other."

"I did this as Kareth, didn't I?" I asked. "That's why I was such a good Recovrancer. I established a bond with Death."

Laycus exhaled loudly before nodding.

"If I'm going to share my blood with Vaneklus, I'll need a knife," I said. "I'll go borrow one from Sebastian, but I'll be right back."

"Blades made in the realm of the living will disintegrate upon entering Vaneklus," the Shade Transporter replied haughtily, as if I should have known such a thing. "Only certain items can withstand Death, such as your cloak, Rhannu, and that infernal book."

"Do you have a knife I can borrow?" When Laycus remained silent, I shook my head. "Well, then, I'll go ask Batty. He'll know of something I can use. In fact, he probably has daggers stored in one of his wing pockets."

"There is no need to involve Bartholomew," scowled Laycus, obviously unhappy I'd thought of a way to work around him. Reaching up one of his billowing sleeves, he withdrew a dagger. The blade was so dark, it looked like a piece of the sky on a moonless night had been cut from the heavens and attached to the silver hilt. While he didn't say as much, his actions made me wonder if Batty truly did carry hidden daggers in a secret wing pocket, even though I found such an image more adorable than terrifying.

I took the proffered knife and made a careful incision along my forearm. Returning the weapon to Laycus, I then shifted *The Book of Recovrancy* into one hand, which made it difficult to grasp, but I suspected if I asked my disgruntled mentor to hold the book, he'd toss it into the water or worse. Crouching down, I lowered my arm into the river until the water reached my elbow, and the current picked up as it sensed my blood. I read the spell aloud, then withdrew my arm from the water and healed the cut. Slipping the book back into my pack, I stood up . . . and found myself swaying so violently, I nearly fell over.

Images exploded before my eyes . . . terrible, gruesome images . . . a knife driving into a chest. Someone screaming as flames rose around them. Arms flailing beneath water. Hands squeezing around a throat. Bones breaking. A body falling from a peak. A rope tightening around a neck, and military-issued electrum sticks pressing into flesh as shrieks rent the air.

"Make it stop!" I screamed, pressing my palms against my eyes, although that did nothing to slow the flood of images. "Laycus, what's happening?"

"Death is insatiable." His voice sounded far away. "When it is not actively feeding, it savors memories of past consumption. You must learn to control your attention."

"How?" I wailed, my knees knocking as my entire body trembled.

A cauldron of water boiled as someone fought the restraints tying them to a chair. An ax sank into the back of a head. A sword slipped between ribs.

"Focus on the images you don't find so terrible," Laycus said.

A bag was put over someone's head, muffling their terrified screams.

"I can't!" I doubled over as more horrible images filled my mind: vile, heartbreaking stories of pain, suffering, and loss.

Something hit my left shoulder, hard, and I gasped, pulling my attention away from Death's memories enough to see Laycus moving his staff from one hand to the other. "Ow," I winced, rubbing my shoulder, but for a moment, the terrible images were gone.

"Pain has a way of helping us prioritize," said Laycus. "You've done this before. Now, focus!"

As the images washed over me again, I tried to sift through and focus on those that weren't so gruesome . . . a woman squeezed someone's hand, then smiled as she exhaled her last breath. A man patted a child's head, coughing so hard his body shook, then lay back against a pillow before closing his eyes, his chest stilling. A young girl shivered beneath the ice and snow of an avalanche, surprised to find herself feeling so sleepy when before she'd been freezing, closing her eyes and exhaling through blue-tinged lips.

It took all the strength I possessed to focus on the scenes of my choosing, and I lost control numerous times, allowing more disturbing images to rush in, but in each instance, I forced my attention onto something less horrible. Time passed, and I had no idea how long I stood there, fighting to maintain a sense of control without losing myself entirely to Death.

I've done this before, I told myself. *I did it as Kareth. I can do it now.*

"Do I need to hit you again?" called Laycus.

"No," I groaned through clenched teeth. "I can do it."

And I could . . . slowly but surely, the more I shifted between images, the easier it became to control the thoughts filling my mind. Eventually, I could let certain ones flow past with barely a glance, aware of them without being affected by them. After what felt like an eternity, I placed my hands on my thighs and pushed myself upright, panting as sweat slid between my shoulder blades.

"Well done." Laycus nodded. "That went much better than the first time you attempted such a thing."

I was about to reply when a woman appeared on the dock. My head ached and my limbs felt sluggish, but I also wasn't about to pass up the opportunity. Laycus looked at the shade, then back at me, tilting his head inside his cowl as he waited for my response.

Taking a deep breath, I ran my finger over Glir, immediately feeling my senses sharpen, although the feelings of rightness and peace I'd experienced the last time I'd used my *sana* bracelet in Vaneklus didn't appear.

I looked up at Laycus. "It's not her time."

"Are you certain?" he demanded.

"Yes."

Laycus's eyes flashed, and he made a dismissive wave with his hand.

"Send her back, then," he said, but before I could ask how to do that, his boat pulled away, quickly disappearing inside the perpetual fog. I pulled out *The Book of Recovrancy*, desperately hoping it would share the information I needed. I'd recovered Sebastian's shade, but I suspected that process had been unique, given how our shades were bound to one another. Also, his physical body had been in his cave, right next to mine . . . did it matter I had no idea where this woman's body was?

Thankfully, words rose quickly on the page:

Once you have determined your right to claim a particular shade, take the shade's hand and repeat:

Chan e an t-am agad (It is not your time)
Tilleadh gu beatha (Return to life)

The shade will return to their physical body with no memory of encountering you.

I appreciated the book was kind enough to translate for me since Laycus wasn't there, and memorizing the words, I returned the book to my pack before sloshing forward to the dock. Focusing on the middle-aged woman in front of me, I sensed she was an Astral, although given that her shade was no longer tethered to a physical body containing golden blood, I had no idea how I knew such a thing.

The woman eyed me warily, so I offered her what I hoped was a friendly smile.

"Am I . . . dead?" Her blue-green eyes searched mine.

"Yes," I replied gently, "but you don't have to stay that way. It isn't your time." I extended my hand, and while she initially hesitated, a splash somewhere farther down the river caused her to jump, and she quickly grabbed my hand.

"You've been given a second chance. Make the most of it," I admonished her before saying the spell from my book. The woman gazed incredulously at me, then opened her mouth, but before she could say anything she winked out of sight, vanishing as if she'd never been there. I wasn't certain what I'd expected—a popping sound, thunderous applause, a happy chiming noise—but the silence following her departure was a bit of a letdown. I assumed if I'd done something incorrectly, the shade would have reappeared, but I remained alone on the dock. To my surprise, my newly established connection with Death allowed me to feel Vaneklus's disappointment, and that more than anything confirmed my recovrancy had been a success.

"It wasn't her time," I reminded the realm as respectfully as I could. "You and I are going to have to learn to work together, because like the sun and the moon, we each have a role. We're not opposites . . . and one is no better than the other."

A breeze wafted over my face, which should have been impossible, as there were no winds in Vaneklus, but I'd felt the gentle caress, nonetheless, and even though there was no one around to see me, I smiled.

26

A week went by without word of the test results, and Sebastian supposed that meant he hadn't qualified for the military program. While a small part of him was disappointed, most of him was relieved. He hadn't liked the idea of attending a school where he couldn't live with his mother, even if it meant learning more about weapons and battle strategy.

Sebastian and his mother ate dinner on the porch that evening, and he showed her how he'd perfected his standing backflip. She clapped and praised his hard work, then played the cello as he rocked on the porch swing and watched the fireflies come out. Verbena buzzed around his head as Batty ate licorice while hanging upside down from the porch railing.

His mother later told him a bedtime story featuring his favorite character, a fat red dragon who had all kinds of adventures, and then she sat beside him and played with his hair until he fell asleep.

Sebastian woke sometime in the middle of the night and rubbed his eyes. The sound of voices reached his ears. Raised voices. One of them belonged to his mother, and the other, unfortunately, belonged to his father.

He wished he could pull the covers over his head and go back to sleep, but he couldn't. Slipping out of bed, he crept to his door, which he never closed all the way at night, and listened.

"Do you have any idea what an incredible opportunity this is for him?" his father shouted. Papers rustled, and his father spoke again.

"*We are pleased to inform you that your son has not only met but exceeded the requirements we deem necessary to guarantee success in the Special Initiative Program. His ability to analyze situations, creatively meet objectives, and adjust course when faced with obstacles is impressive in one so young. Under the guidance of our esteemed instructors, we are confident he will become a formidable presence in the Nocenian military.*"

Sebastian didn't know how the other Daevals had figured all that out from doing games and puzzles with him, but he had to admit, what he understood sounded like he'd done well.

"I don't care!" his mother replied. "I don't want him to do this."

"I don't care what you want," retorted his father.

"What if Sebastian doesn't want to change schools?" asked Grace.

"If he doesn't, it's only because you've convinced him it's a bad idea," said Malum.

"I let him do the testing, didn't I?" His mother's voice was sharp. "I'm the one he's been living with as he's become so incredible at things. No one wants to see Sebastian happy more than I do, but I know him, and this won't make him happy. If you'd spent more than ten minutes with your son this past year, you'd know that too!"

Sebastian heard his father's boots crossing the hardwood floor, followed by the sound of his mother gasping before a loud slap rang out. The fire inside him roared to life, and without another thought, he rushed downstairs.

His father's hand was wrapped around his mother's throat, and her eyes were wide as she tried to break free from his grasp. One side of her face was red from where he had hit her.

"Let her go!" Sebastian yelled, flames swirling over his hands.

His father turned his head. "Glad to see you're awake. We were just talking about you."

"Sebastian, go back upstairs now!" cried his mother. Malum tightened his grip around her throat, and she winced.

Sebastian glared at his father, letting the flames wind up his arms. "Leave her alone, and I'll talk to you."

Malum let go of Grace and turned to face Sebastian. Crossing his arms over his chest, he raised an eyebrow. "So? What do you think? It's an amazing opportunity."

Sebastian swallowed, wondering how his father could go from hitting his mother to casually having a conversation. Breathing deeply and pulling his fire back inside, he considered what he was about to say, aware the choice he made would change his life forever. At the same time, there really wasn't a choice . . . as long as his mother was safe, he could handle anything else that came his way. Plus, it was obvious his father wanted him to do this, so if there was ever a time to bargain with the man, it was now.

"If I agree to this," Sebastian said, looking directly at his father, "I don't want you near my mother ever again. You leave her alone, and I'll do the training. I can't be the best in the program if I'm worried about you hurting her."

"Sebastian, no!" said his mother, taking a step forward. She was stopped by his father, who shoved her back against the wall, pinning her in place.

Looking at Sebastian, his father grinned proudly. "I'm pleased to see you already have such strong negotiating skills. And you make an excellent point . . . you won't be able to concentrate to your full potential in that program if you're constantly thinking about your mother."

Malum reached into his jacket and withdrew a silver dagger. Time seemed to stop, and Sebastian screamed as he ran forward, just as his father drove the blade into his mother's chest.

"You should have stayed mine, Grace," Malum said quietly,

wrenching the knife free. "If you don't belong to me, I have no use for you."

As his mother sank to the floor, Sebastian watched as his father drew the blood-covered blade across her throat. His mother collapsed to one side, and Sebastian fell to his knees, reaching for her hand as his father's arms engulfed him.

"Let me go!" he shrieked, trying to summon his fire as tears streamed down his face and sobs shook his entire body. He screamed and kicked and fought against his father with all his might, but it was no use.

"Mother!" he cried, his throat constricting around the single word. Malum tightened his grip, then opened a portal and carried Sebastian through, bringing them out next to a tall iron fence topped with stone gargoyles. Rain ran down their hideous faces, making them look like they were screaming and crying at the same time.

Malum kicked the heavy wooden door, which quickly opened, and someone escorted them to a room, where he finally released his grip. Sebastian immediately bolted towards the door, but his father stood in front of it. Sebastian threw himself at his father, who took his pounding fists and kicking feet without so much as blinking. He screamed and cried and tried to claw his way out, but Malum was immovable and after a while, Sebastian could feel himself tiring.

Finally, he sank to the floor and wrapped his arms around himself, too exhausted to do more than simply lie there.

"It had to be done, Sebastian," his father said matter-of-factly. "You would have always been thinking about her, and you can't afford distractions here." The door opened and before his father let himself out, he added, "I'll be back in a few weeks to check on your progress."

Sebastian stared at the wall across from where he lay, barely blinking. He kept seeing the knife sinking into his mother's chest. Closing his eyes didn't make the image go away.

Batty materialized and gently put a wing on Sebastian's leg. For once, Sebastian didn't kick at him.

His father hadn't let him get any of his clothes or toys, and he didn't even have a picture of his mother. Nothing.

Eventually someone came to show him to another room. He didn't even consider trying to escape. What was the point?

His mother was dead.

Classes started the next day, but he made no effort. He didn't care when instructors yelled at him, threatening to contact his father and report his poor performance. His father had taken away the only thing that mattered; he couldn't hurt Sebastian anymore.

Days turned into weeks. He lost weight and when he wasn't in class, he lay curled up on his bed, facing the wall and wishing he could be with his mother, wherever she was now.

Sebastian knew something was different when Camus, one of the Daevals who had been involved in his testing, came into the dormitory.

"May I?" he asked politely, but Sebastian didn't answer, so the man sat down on the edge of the bed anyway.

"I think you know why I'm here," said Camus. "You are failing to live up to your potential."

Sebastian didn't disagree with him.

Camus sighed, and when he spoke again, Sebastian heard both anger and sadness in his voice. "I told your father he ought to use your mother as an incentive. Do you know what that means? It means using her as a reward; for example, if you did something especially well, you'd be allowed to visit her. I saw you with her before testing, and it was obvious how much you cared for her."

Sebastian didn't miss the frustrated hiss in Camus's voice as he muttered, "Clearly, your father disagreed with my assessment, and now I've been proven right." He didn't sound happy about it.

"I want you to know," Camus added, "I fought to keep you here. Your potential is astounding, and we are suffering a considerable loss by seeing you go."

Sebastian turned his head towards the man. "Where am I going?"

Camus shook his head. "I don't know, but your father is on his way to pick you up." The soldier rose slowly and offered a sad smile. "I do hope to run into you again someday," he said. "If you're ever in need of work or want to revisit career options, please don't hesitate to contact me."

Sebastian nodded, even though he doubted he would ever do so.

Camus walked out of the room just as Sebastian's father entered, and he could feel the tension between the two men as they purposefully ignored one another.

Sebastian pushed himself into a sitting position and looked up just as his father's fist crashed into his face. He fell over backwards and tumbled off the bed, crying out as his father reached down, wrapped a hand around his shirt, and lifted him off the ground.

"I never should have let Grace keep you," Malum growled. "First you took her from me, and now you've failed me completely!"

Sebastian closed his eyes, thinking his father was going to rip his head from his shoulders, but instead he heard him whisper the spell to open a portal. Still holding Sebastian so his boots dangled in the air, Malum stepped through the doorway before releasing his grip; dropping to the ground, Sebastian only just managed to land on his feet.

Looking around, he found himself in the foyer of a fancy mansion that reminded him a little of the Dekarais' house, the nicest house he'd ever been in. Thick tapestries hung on the walls, and two white marble staircases rose gracefully in opposite directions. The lights were too bright, though, and the sharp lemon scent reminded him of the products his mother used to clean house.

He blinked a few times, trying to get his bearings, and as he noticed a tall woman walking towards him, an alarm sounded in his head—the woman was an Astral, the most hated enemy of his kind. To his surprise, she smiled at his father.

"This must be Sebastian," the woman said. If she hadn't been the most vile creature Sebastian could think of, he might have found her quite lovely, with her long silver hair and intense green eyes.

He glanced from the woman to his father, but his father didn't return his look.

"You've bought the right to do whatever you want with him," snapped Malum. "Just make sure he never sets foot in Nocens again."

The woman's smile widened but there was nothing friendly about it. "It's been a pleasure doing business with you," she said. "Hold him, please."

Malum pinned Sebastian's arms behind his back as the woman produced something that looked like a collar with a small medallion hanging from it. Clicking it quickly around his neck, she nodded, and his father released him.

"Any special abilities we should know about?" the woman asked.

"He's a Pyromancer, but there's nothing special about him," spat his father. Then, without so much as a backwards glance, Malum stepped through a portal and closed it behind him, leaving Sebastian alone with the Astral. She introduced herself but he wasn't really listening, too focused on the collar around his neck, which was just tight enough to be uncomfortable.

He was vaguely aware of the woman mentioning something about a "rehabilitation program," but it wasn't until he was in class the next day and stumbled while reading out loud that he realized what she'd meant.

"*The ability to read well is one of the things that sets us apart from animals,*" *said his teacher.* "*If you cannot read, you are clearly no better than a beast. We shall have to improve upon your nature.*"

She then took him to a room where two Astrals held his arms behind his back and plunged his head into a tall bucket of water. He tried to scream but only succeeded in swallowing the water, his efforts to free himself nothing against the strength of those holding him.

Batty immediately sought help from Dunston and was gone for so long, Sebastian began to feel worried. When the bat eventually returned, he was in tears.

"I told Dunston everything that happened. He contacted your father and demanded he come over and explain himself." Batty shook his head, causing a tear to splash on his foot. "As we know, your father can be incredibly convincing when he chooses to be. Apparently after he took you to the military academy, he set fire to the scene of his crimes. He burned down your house."

Sebastian felt as if someone was carving a fissure across his heart with a dull knife.

"According to the story your father spread, you lost control of your pyromancy and started a fire that ultimately took your life, as well as your mother's." Another tear dripped off Batty's nose. "He said the fact that I was in Nocens without you was proof our bond had been severed. I pleaded with Dunston to come to the Cypher Adran with me, to see for himself that I could not be bonded with anyone else because you are very much alive, but your father said I was delusional, among many other things."

The bat's wings drooped, and he hung his head. "I have failed you."

Everything inside Sebastian hardened. He was on his own now, and he would look after himself.

The next day he got in trouble for fighting, and his shirt was taken off before he was chained against a wall, where an Astral whipped him until he passed out. He soon learned whipping was a favorite punishment of the Astrals. Other days, they attached small devices to his scalp and face and asked him questions; if they didn't like his responses or thought they were "too much like what a Daeval would say," they sent painful shockwaves into his head that made it feel like his entire skull was vibrating.

Most nights he lay in bed wishing he could just die and put an end to his suffering, but the one thing that gave him strength was knowing his Astral captors weren't aware of his ability to make portals. He and his mother had never told his father Sebastian had inherited his portal-making skill, and while there were anti-portal wards in place, wards could be overcome. Someday someone wouldn't be paying attention, and that would be the day Sebastian escaped.

27

KYRA

*W*aking up alone in my bed in Celenia, I wasn't surprised to find my cheeks were wet from crying in my sleep. Everything inside me ached at what I'd witnessed. I recalled Dunston saying he hadn't always been there for Sebastian the way he should have been; he must have been referring to not believing Batty about Sebastian being held captive in Aeles. My hand shook as I touched the golden bracelet.

Sebastian opened the connection, but while I could sense him, he didn't say anything.

I'm so sorry, I whispered. *Is there anything I can do?*

Part of me expected him to say I could pretend like I'd never seen the dream, but instead he sighed. *You can keep working with me to shut that program down.*

I will. I sat up and brushed my hair off my face. *I promise, Sebastian . . . we'll end that program for good.*

And then I realized there was something else I could do.

I'm supposed to be completing assigned readings in the Archives for Healer Omnurion today, I said, *but she's in Iscre, so no one will be checking on me. I'm still not comfortable entering Vaneklus while I'm physically in Aeles, so I need you to pick me up. I'm going to see Laycus, and I'm going to find your mother.*

Sebastian was silent for a moment. *Are you sure?*

Yes. Just give me a few minutes to get dressed.

My heart was racing as I changed out of my sleeping clothes into a tunic and breeches. Was I ready for this? I'd volunteered, which meant I *had* to be ready; I couldn't let Sebastian down, not after everything he'd endured. Feeling far from confident, I was nevertheless determined to do my best.

A portal soon appeared in my living room, and as I joined Sebastian in Nocens, I didn't miss the apprehension in his eyes or the tightness around his jaw. He kissed me, then headed to his weapons vault after explaining that training would help keep him distracted until I returned.

Sitting down in an open space, I waved goodbye to Batty and Aurelius before entering Vaneklus. My fingers reached for the edges of my shifter cloak, and something about wearing the garment I'd been gifted as the Felserpent Queen made me a little less anxious about what I was attempting.

Laycus's boat arrived shortly, and he leaned against his ever-present staff. "Are you certain you are up for this?" he asked, correctly guessing why I was there.

"Yes," I said, trying not to sound as scared as I felt. This was for Sebastian, and I would do anything for him. "Will you help me?"

Laycus nodded. "I will."

I'd been so prepared to argue my case, I was surprised at Laycus's concession. "What made you change your mind?" I couldn't help but ask.

"You wouldn't give me a moment's peace if I refused," he replied. "But, in addition to that motivating bit of knowledge, not even as Kareth did you do such a thing." He shrugged before extending a skeletal hand. "It's nice to know I can live as long as I have and still be surprised."

Taking Laycus's cold hand, I planted a foot on the side of his boat and allowed him to help me up, trying not to kick his beloved vessel. Thankfully, the boat didn't so much as rock, and I sat down on the single wooden bench.

Since I hadn't done this before, not even in another body, I had no memories to guide me, which was unnerving after having them for so many other things, but I tried to put my fear aside. This was how everyone else did things, how I'd done things until a few weeks ago, acting without knowing how my decisions would turn out.

"Away we go," said Laycus, and by some invisible command, the boat began moving forward. Part of me expected to feel a breeze on my face, like when I was out on the ocean in my kadac, but the air was still. The only sign we were moving was the passing landscape, which consisted of enormous boulders marking the edges of the realm and preventing a shade from wandering too far from the dock.

"If Ceelum falls within your domain, why don't you interact more with the shades there?" I always tried to make the most of my time with Laycus, learning everything I could, but talking also made me less nervous, or at least made it easier for me to ignore my nerves.

"The entire point of being in Ceelum is to rest," replied Laycus. "How well do you rest when someone is constantly interrupting you?"

"Not well," I admitted. "Vaneklus is just so different from what I thought it would be."

"Death is always surprising," agreed the Shade Transporter. "Everyone has died numerous times, yet they always act like each time is the first. I often think it would be easier if shades remembered they'd been here before and will inevitably return again."

"Did your sister begin overseeing Karnis the same time you

became the Shade Transporter?" Perhaps Laycus might let something about his background slip.

Laycus grinned. "An admirable effort, Recovrancer, but not information you need to complete your quest today."

I scowled at his obvious glee over my failed attempt to learn more about his history.

"Batty believes Sebastian and I aren't the only ones who've returned," I said, "so I also want to ask your sister about Tallus."

Laycus's eyes flickered with interest, and I told him what Batty had said about Velaire, Rhannu, the *Cor'Lapis* stone, and reuniting the realms.

"It's frustrating to remember certain things about my past but not others." I sighed. "I feel like there's so much I *ought* to know that would be helpful, but I can't recall it."

"It's shocking you remember anything at all," said Laycus. "Clearly you prioritized your memories with Schatten, so I'm not surprised you remember those best." He shook his head as if he couldn't believe what a foolish choice I'd made.

"What do you know of Tallus?" I asked. "You must have ferried him at least a few times." Deep down, some part of me wished Laycus had claimed the man's shade for himself at some point, consuming him and ending his existence.

Laycus smirked as if he knew what I was thinking, and given the odd properties of Vaneklus, as well as my stronger connection to the realm, it was entirely possible he was somehow aware of my thoughts.

"Tallus has always appeared on my shores at his appointed times. I could not have claimed him, even if I'd wished to."

"Would you? If you could have?"

Laycus gazed into the distance. "I have always been biased when it comes to you," he finally said. "If there was a way to keep Tallus from harming you, I would have done it by now."

"Why me? Out of all the shades you've met and ferried, why take an interest in me?"

"Well, for one thing because you're a Recovrancer. I know I'm going to see you in my domain whether I want to or not." Laycus made no effort to hide the exasperation in his tone. "Much as I would love to bar your kind from ever entering Vaneklus again, that isn't how it works, hence, I must be at peace with it as best I can. But you've always been different, every time I encountered you."

I sat up straighter, Laycus's words sparking something inside me. "You knew me in other lives, didn't you? Not just as Kareth." Excitement sped through me at the prospect of learning more about my own history.

Laycus studied me closely. "Forgetting can be a kindness," he cautioned. "There are very real difficulties associated with remembering every day of every life. I worry about telling you too much and overwhelming you. I am not saying we will never have this conversation, but I think it best to focus on the task at hand."

While part of me wanted to insist I could handle anything Laycus shared, the rest of me considered his words, as they were surprisingly similar to things I'd read in *The Book of Recovrancy*. I was more fortunate than most, able to remember at least parts of a past life and reconnecting with the man I'd been married to in that life. Anything else I'd done, or anyone else I'd been, surely paled in comparison.

At the same time, I hated not having information that involved me . . . although Laycus's measured response had made at least one thing clear.

"You *did* know me in other lives, then," I said. "Not just as Kareth and who I am now."

"I did," nodded Laycus. "And you'll be pleased to know you always strove to improve relations between Astrals and Daevals.

I've never seen you more livid than when the Blood Alarm was established."

Something tugged on the edge of my attention, the awareness of a memory I knew I'd made but couldn't quite remember how to access.

"When was the Blood Alarm established?"

"Approximately nine hundred years ago, give or take a decade," said Laycus.

I thought back to the other Recovrancers I'd read about while visiting the Aelian Archives with Demitri after my first trip into Vaneklus. One of them had been a woman named Jaesian, and she'd lived roughly nine hundred years ago.

"Did I always come back as a Recovrancer?" My heartbeat sped up. I felt like I was standing on the edge of a precipice, about to lean over and see something important down below.

Laycus was silent, clearly weighing his response. Trying to make it easier for him, I asked, "Was I Jaesian? I came across her in my research. She used a tuning fork the way I use my *sana* bracelet. Was that me?"

"Yes," said Laycus, "but no more questions about your past lives. I don't want to be responsible for damaging your mind by burdening you with information you're not fit to process."

Telling myself I would do more research on Jaesian later, both in Aeles and using *The Book of Recovrancy*, I turned my attention to the front of the boat. A fog bank parted, allowing us to slip through a narrow opening, and the current of the grey water picked up, causing me to sway a little on the bench.

The scenery on either side of the river was slowly changing, dark and ominous boulders giving way to shining white quartz formations. While there was still no grass, clusters of pearls lined the banks like sea anemones, glinting occasionally in a light whose source I'd never been able to determine.

Time stretched on, and Laycus stopped the boat at three different points, saying words in a language I didn't know and making complicated gestures with his hands before we continued on.

"There are gates here," he explained. "The river only flows *towards* Karnis, but that hasn't stopped some shades from changing their minds partway through the journey and trying to swim back to something familiar. Gates were installed to prevent such a thing from happening."

I nodded, appreciating the unexpected information, before noticing the color of the river had changed. Instead of a dull grey, it was clear . . . so clear, in fact, I could see all the way down to the riverbed, dotted with smooth white stones. Slender snow-colored trees lined the river's edges, their white boughs beckoning gently onwards; instead of leaves, though, clear crystals hung from their branches.

The river took a sharp turn, and while I couldn't wait to see what was around the bend, Laycus placed his staff into the water, drawing the boat to a stop.

"Hello, Suryal," he called. "I have someone who wishes to speak with you."

A boat of bleached wood suddenly appeared from a hidden cove. A figure stood at the front, dressed in a shroud and cowled hood like Laycus, but while he wore all black, this figure was clothed in white. As the pale boat pulled up beside us, the figure lowered the hood to reveal a woman with garnet-red eyes. While her face was similar to Laycus's—little more than a skull covered in skin—she also had long white hair and a kind smile.

"Welcome to Karnis." She dipped her head in greeting. "This must have been extremely important if you were willing to make the trip confined in a boat with only my brother for company."

"I'm grateful he brought me," I replied, "just as I'm grateful to you for meeting with me. I'm Kyra."

"I am Suryal," the ruler of Karnis smiled. "How may I be of service?"

"I'd like to ask you about two shades. The first is Grace Sayre. She died thirteen years ago but it wasn't her time. Has she passed through your waters since then?"

Suryal closed her eyes and appeared deep in thought. I was so nervous it was difficult to breathe, and I dug my fingertips into the wooden bench. This was it . . . this would determine whether or not I truly had a chance of recovering Sebastian's mother.

Suryal finally blinked her eyes open. "No," she said. "Grace Sayre has not crossed my waters in the time period you are describing."

I couldn't believe what I'd just heard. "That means she's still in Ceelum."

"So it would seem," Suryal nodded. "I've been expecting her for a few years now, but she seems disinclined to return to the land of the living." Sweeping her long white hair over one shoulder, she added, "Or perhaps she is merely disinclined to return to the land of the living through *me*. She must wish to preserve the memories she made in her last physical body."

"I think she doesn't want to forget her son, Sebastian," I offered. "She'd rather stay in Ceelum than be reborn in another body without her memories of him."

"Many shades struggle to let go of what they last knew in favor of moving on to the unknown," agreed Suryal. "She is certainly not the first." Her eyes shimmered, but whereas Laycus's gaze was most often malicious or disdainful, Suryal's was curious. "Who was the second shade you wished to inquire after?"

"Tallus. I'm not sure what his name was during his last life, but when I was Kareth, I knew him as Tallus."

Suryal used her staff to draw a circle along the surface of the river before gazing intently into it. I leaned forward and tried to see what she was studying, but it was only clear water to my eyes, much to my disappointment.

"Tallus does not linger," said Suryal. "He has never rested in Ceelum and always makes his way to me as fast as he can. The last time I returned him to the land of the living was twenty-eight years ago."

I glanced at Laycus. "And he hasn't returned to Vaneklus since, because you would have ferried him."

"He has not returned to my shores," confirmed Laycus.

"That means he's somewhere in Aeles." Anxiety sloshed in my stomach even as I tried to ignore it.

"Yes." Suryal shifted her staff from one hand to the other. "If your first life was as an Astral, you will return as an Astral in all subsequent lives."

I thought back to when Aeles-Nocens had been one realm. "What about when Astrals and Daevals had children together? Did their children have gold or silver blood or some mixture of the two?"

"Blood will always be silver or gold," replied Suryal, "although I cannot say what causes one parent's blood to be passed on instead of the other's. Children inherit some things from one parent, some things from the other; so it has always been and likely will always be."

I thought of something else Batty had said. "Suryal, are you allowed to tell me whether Tallus returned as a man or a woman in his most recent life cycle?" Even one more piece of information would make him easier to identify.

"I am allowed," she chuckled. "Tallus chose to be reborn as a man, the same choice he's always made. Personally, I think changing it up every now and then would be far more interesting, but some folks *do* have their preferences." She gestured towards me. "You, for example, have almost always chosen to come back as a woman."

"*Almost* always?" I leaned forward, clutching the side of the boat. "You mean I came back as a man at some point? When? What was my name?"

"That is quite enough," interjected Laycus. "You've asked your questions and received your answers. Our time here is finished."

He was right. I had the information I needed. Sebastian's mother was in Ceelum, which meant I stood at least a chance of recovering her. And Tallus was alive and approaching his thirties as a man.

"Thank you," I said to Suryal. "It was an honor to meet you, and I can't tell you how helpful you've been."

"I look forward to seeing you again, Kyra," she smiled. "Not for a long time, though. Enjoy your life."

Suryal cast a fond glance at Laycus, who shook his head but nevertheless offered her a wave as his boat turned around, putting Karnis behind us as we headed back up the river.

"Well," said Laycus, "on to Ceelum, then?"

"Yes, please. And thank you again for doing this. I know it's an imposition, but there's no one else who can help me."

"You're right on both counts," he sniffed. "And to think, at one time I thought dealing with shades would be the most tiring part of my work."

"Well," I countered, "you *did* say it was nice to see you could still be surprised after living for so long. Perhaps Recovrancers exist at least partly to keep you from getting bored."

Laycus gave me such a look at using his own words against him that I pressed my lips together and chose to remain silent as we began the journey to Ceelum.

28

KYRA

*L*aycus made fast work of guiding us back up the river before drawing his boat to a stop.

"This is as far as I am allowed," he explained. "You will have
to go forward on your own, Recovrancer."

Swallowing hard, I carefully made my way over the side of
the boat, glad the water only reached my knees. "Will you wait
for me?"

"I shall," Laycus assured me, "if for no other reason than the
sooner this is all finished, the sooner I can return to my usual
routine."

Nodding my thanks, I made my way forward, one cautious
step at a time. After a few moments, my skin began to prickle, and
the air became heavier. Extending a hand, I was surprised to feel a
pressure against my palm even though I couldn't see anything
around me except the river. Perhaps just as there had been gates I'd
been unable to see, there was an invisible barrier separating
Ceelum from the rest of Vaneklus. Pushing my palm against the
pressure, I hoped it could somehow sense I was a Recovrancer.

There was a soft hiss, like steam escaping a kettle, then the
pressure against my palm disappeared, causing me to stumble
forward a few steps. When I righted myself and looked back, I
could no longer see Laycus. Everything around me was still grey,

but a darker grey more akin to the onset of a storm or an early twilight. Lights flickered on either side of me, a bright glint here, a glimmer there, but nothing lasted long enough for me to make it out.

The Book of Recovrancy had made it clear I would only be able to see those shades who chose to reveal themselves, and thinking about the invisible gates we'd passed through, I wondered what else might be around me I was unable to see. Were there landscapes here, a sky overhead filled with a sun, moon, or stars? Were there shades nearby, watching me this very moment? It was irritating and quite unsettling to think I was surrounded by things I was powerless to see.

"Hello?" I called in a loud voice. "My name is Kyra Valorian. I'm a Recovrancer, and I'm looking for Grace Sayre." Everything around me was silent aside from the water lapping against my legs.

Turning in a slow circle, I waited, blinking each time a light sparked against the dusk-like atmosphere that somehow never drew any nearer to complete darkness. Perhaps it took a while for a shade to receive a message here, supposing that shade wanted to receive messages in the first place. It was at least conceivable Grace wouldn't want to speak with me; after all, she didn't know me.

"I'm here about Sebastian," I added, thinking if anything would tempt Grace to interact with me, it would be the mention of her son. "He asked me to come here and speak to you."

Something splashed behind me, and I spun around, nearly jumping out of my skin as I found myself face-to-face with a woman I'd only seen in dreams.

"I'm Grace Sayre," she said. "You know my son?"

Even in Death, there was no mistaking the note of protectiveness in her voice.

"I do," I said, staring at the woman and struggling to believe this was really happening even though I'd fervently hoped for such a moment. "I'm Kyra. And you're probably going to think I'm crazy, but I promise everything I'm about to tell you is true."

Grace studied me intently before nodding, causing her blonde hair to brush the tops of her shoulders. Like Sebastian, she was tall and lithe, although her eyes were a lighter shade of brown than his and her face wasn't as angular.

"Tell me everything," she said.

And so I did.

I had no idea how long I spoke, since time ran differently in Vaneklus, but eventually I'd shared all I wanted to say. Grace hadn't done more than nod or shake her head, and when I fell silent, she stared off into the distance.

"I can't believe it," she finally said. "I'm relieved to hear Sebastian is still alive. I was worried his father might have ended his life the way he did mine." Her jaw trembled. "I wish I'd been there for him. What you described . . . what he went through at the hands of Astrals . . . my poor boy. I can't imagine."

She closed her eyes as grief, anger, and regret came and went across her face. I knew all too well the horror of hearing what Sebastian had endured, and I wished I could ease Grace's pain, just as I wished I could erase Sebastian's memories of his trauma. Eventually Grace brought her gaze back to mine, smiling as she did.

"Sebastian always loved stories about Rhannu. And now I see why . . . he was drawn to what was rightfully his." She stepped closer. "My greatest fear when I died was that Sebastian would always be alone, blaming himself for my death. You can't imagine how happy I am to hear he has you. Whatever he did to deserve your love, to have made you willing to bind yourself to him in order to find him again . . . thank you." Her voice broke. "For loving him that much."

While Sebastian and I hadn't said we loved each other yet in this life cycle, there was no question we did. Our love for one other was a constant, an unbreakable bond that defied both death and time. While I'd known this on some level since remembering who we were, I let myself savor the rush of happiness that swept through me at Grace's words, aware of how truly fortunate I was. Sebastian and I had overcome impossible odds to find one another again, and I would never take such love for granted. "He would be here with me now if he could," I assured his mother. "He misses you terribly."

Grace beamed. "And how's Batty? Is Sebastian any nicer to him?"

"He's making a concerted effort to be nicer to Batty." I appreciated her concern for the Cypher.

"Where does he work?" Grace's eyes brightened with curiosity. Inwardly, I cringed, quickly directing my gaze down to the water as I searched for the right thing to say. I didn't want to ruin the woman's good mood, but I also couldn't lie to her.

"He has his own business," I ultimately settled upon, "and he does a lot of work for Dunston and Caz Dekarai."

At the mention of the Dekarais, Grace clapped her hands and laughed excitedly. "Oh, I'm so glad he still keeps in touch with them. How are they? Devlin and Eslee must be grown by now."

I told her what I knew of the Daeval family, and she smiled wistfully when I described the party they'd thrown.

"I wish I could have been there. What sort of work does Sebastian do for Dunston and Caz?"

My efforts to avoid discussing Sebastian's occupation had clearly failed. Bracing myself, I said, "He's an assassin. Apparently a very sought-after one."

Grace winced. "Well, I can't say I'm surprised. He was always a gifted fighter." She looked closely at me. "And you support his chosen profession?"

"No," I assured her. "I want to convince him to try a different profession, but it's challenging. He's made a very good living for himself and likes the reputation he's built. I'm certain he can find something he enjoys that doesn't involve ending lives . . . we just have to figure out what."

"Sebastian can be very stubborn," warned Grace, "but if anyone could convince him to change careers, I have no doubt it would be you."

"I'll certainly do my best," I said, before drawing a deep breath. It was time to get to the real reason for my visit. "When I spoke to Sebastian about the possibility of recovering you, he said the decision was up to you and he would respect whatever you chose."

Lest she not make an informed choice, I told her what I knew of the complicated procedure, as well as the possibility that she might not adjust to a new physical body even if we were able to obtain one in the manner described by *The Book of Recovrancy*.

Grace's eyes briefly widened, but she quickly straightened her shoulders.

"If there's even a chance of being reunited with my son, it's a risk worth taking."

I let out a deep breath, relieved because I knew that's what Sebastian wanted, but also anxious over what her decision would require of me. "There's still a lot I need to figure out to make this happen, but now that I know what you want, I'll work as fast as I can," I said.

"Thank you." She smiled. "I'm not going anywhere. When you see Sebastian, please tell him I love him and I've never stopped thinking about him."

"I will," I returned her smile, "and I'll be back soon."

Grace waved goodbye before disappearing, and I walked in

what I hoped was the direction I'd come from, reassured when I felt the air growing heavier around me. Extending my palm against the pressure, I heard the same hissing noise as before, and as if a curtain had suddenly been pulled back, I saw Laycus standing in his boat.

My relief must have shown on my face, because Laycus gave me a look as he reached down and helped me back into the boat. "Surprised to see me?"

"Happy to see you," I clarified. "Thank you for waiting. I found her."

As Laycus ferried us away from Ceelum, I told him about my conversation with Grace. Eventually, we reached the dock, and he shook his head.

"I don't know why I'm surprised," he said. "Every time you return to life, you come back stronger and more determined. At this rate, in a few hundred years you'll figure out how to keep the living from dying altogether, and my ferrying days will be over."

"That wouldn't be so bad." I shot him a teasing grin. "Think of all the things you could do with that extra time . . . you could write a tell-all book about what it was really like to be the Shade Transporter. You could hold a book signing at LeBehr's shop."

Laycus made a snorting noise that might have been his version of a laugh, and I hopped over the edge of the boat back into the river before looking up at him.

"I still don't necessarily like it," I said, "but I understand now, more than ever, that Death is a part of life. One chapter ends, and another begins. Besides," I rested a hand affectionately on Laycus's boat, "I suspect you might not be able to exist for long outside of Vaneklus, so doing away with Death would mean doing away with you. Aside from Sebastian and Batty, you're my oldest friend, and I'd miss you terribly. You've helped me become who I am, and I'm fortunate to know you, Laycus."

The Shade Transporter's eyes flickered as he processed my words, likely searching for sarcasm, but he eventually offered me the kindest expression I'd ever seen on his skeletal face.

"I'm fortunate to know you too, Recovrancer."

"So you're fine if I'm able to visit more frequently?" My question caused Laycus to groan and command his boat to pull away from me.

"One more thing," I said before he could disappear into the fog. "I asked you before why you made an exception for Sebastian's mother and ferried her to Ceelum instead of . . . you know . . . and you said your reasons were your own. I know you don't mindlessly consume every shade who appears in Vaneklus early, but I think there's more to it than that. Your sparing her feels important, and since it involves Sebastian, I'd really love to know why."

Laycus's boat drew to a stop as he stared down into the water. Eventually, he replied, "I suppose it was because of you."

I was certain I'd misheard him, but his next words confirmed I hadn't.

"If this was the life cycle in which you and Schatten found one another again, I didn't want to have ended his mother's existence for good and be forced to tell you that." He scowled. "But it was *only* because I knew you'd start looking for a way to prevent me from ever consuming a shade again, and I simply couldn't deal with the hassle."

Laycus could try and make it seem as if he'd only been acting in his own self-interest, but I knew otherwise, and I was deeply touched that his care for me outweighed his disdain for my chosen partner.

His boat began to move farther away, and I waved at him. "I'll let you know when I'm ready to recover Sebastian's mother."

"I shall wait with bated breath," he sneered, and while at one time such a rude comment would have hurt my feelings, now it simply made me smile, as I knew Laycus cared for me as I did for him, merely in his own way.

Jogging to Sebastian's weapons vault, I rushed inside, the soles of my boots sliding on the stone floor as I came to a stop.

"I found your mother."

Sebastian was pulling a dagger from a training dummy, but at my words, his head whipped towards me so fast, it was a wonder he didn't wrench his neck even as the rest of him went completely still.

"Her shade is still in Ceelum," I assured him, before sharing the details of my time in Vaneklus.

When I finished, Sebastian placed the dagger on a table and began pacing back and forth, alternating between running a hand through his hair and shaking his head.

"I can't believe it," he said. "If it was anyone other than you telling me this, I *wouldn't* believe it." He paused in his pacing and stared at me. "You really spoke to her?"

"I did." I gave him the message his mother had asked me to share.

Sebastian seemed to stop breathing, absorbing every word I said, and when I was done, he closed his eyes before pressing his palms against them. His chest was rising and falling in increasingly faster intervals, and while I knew he had to process things in his own way, I ached to somehow make it easier for him.

"I can't believe some part of her still exists," he said after a moment, his voice tight with trapped emotion. "I thought . . . after what happened to her . . . I never dreamed there was a chance she might not truly be gone." His dark eyes shone with unshed tears, and he quickly turned away as he ran the long sleeve of his black tunic over the upper part of his face. I wanted to hold him and allow him to cry as much as he wanted, but when he turned back towards me, the wetness was gone from his eyes, replaced by a steely determination I instantly recognized from having seen it so frequently in our past life together.

"What do we do next?" he asked.

"The stronger connection I have with Death will allow me to know when a shade has entered Vaneklus," I explained. "I can also tell the difference between a shade who died at their appointed time and a shade who can be recovered. *The Book of Recovrancy* was clear we need a new physical body for your mother, but it has to be from someone who died at their appointed time. It also has to be from someone with silver blood."

I fingered the serpent-shaped clasp of my cloak. "Obviously, that's not all, since *The Book of Recovrancy* said more will be revealed with time, as it determines my readiness. I'll keep reading and hopefully whatever else is required won't be too complicated."

I had no idea how I was going to visit Vaneklus more frequently, given that I only went into Death when I was in Nocens . . . plus I still had my training with Healer Omnurion, and I needed to work on my father's research so Senator Rex would allow me to visit the facility in Rynstyn. Thankfully I didn't have to actively focus on reuniting the realms, as LeBehr's potion wouldn't be finished for a few more days, meaning she couldn't locate the Chronicles until then.

Sebastian spoke, pulling me from my worries, and I lifted my gaze to his.

"If anyone understands the importance of proper preparation, it's me," he said, "so there's no rush. It's enough to know there's a chance of seeing my mother again." He fell silent before adding, "If it turns out you can't bring her back or you bring her back and it doesn't work out, I won't blame you." He stepped closer. "It's incredibly important to me you know that."

"Thank you," I said as he reached out and tucked my hair behind my ear, one of my favorite gestures of his. "If I can't recover her, I'll take you to Vaneklus so you can say goodbye."

Confusion flickered across Sebastian's face. "I thought the living couldn't be in Vaneklus without becoming ill."

"Laycus said the living can't be in Vaneklus *for long* without suffering consequences." I smirked. "He's never explained how much time that entails, but I took you to Vaneklus before and you came out fine."

"I came out better than fine," he said quietly. "That's where I learned the truth about myself, and Rhannu, and us."

Leaning forward, Sebastian pressed his lips against my forehead, and while the kiss was one of the more chaste ones we'd shared, it was also incredibly intimate, causing the hair on my arms and neck to rise.

"Thank you," Sebastian whispered, his breath warm against my skin. "I knew this before, but I'm even more aware of it now . . . I truly don't deserve you."

Resting my head against his chest, I hugged him tightly.

"We deserve to be together," I said, "and we deserve to be happy."

After a moment, even though I hated to do so, I pulled back.

"I would much rather stay here with you, but I need to make every moment count these days. Can you open a portal back to my apartment? I'm going to go to my office and figure out how to get invited to the experimentation facility in Rynstyn." I unclasped my cloak and handed it to Sebastian. "We'll come up with a plan for how to actually do that together, but I'm the only one who has a chance of getting an invitation."

Sebastian frowned, so I added, "It's no different than having LeBehr start the process of finding the Chronicles. We're gathering the pieces we need so that when it's time to make a move, we're ready."

One side of Sebastian's mouth rose upwards. "That sounds like something I would say."

"I told you before," I grinned, "it's possible you're rubbing off on me."

29

❦

KYRA

*B*ack in Celenia, I stared into the box of glass test tubes. As soon as I'd reached my office, I'd sent a message to Senator Rex letting him know I was ready to begin working with silver blood. He'd soon appeared outside my door, holding a small wooden crate filled with vials of the bright substance and flashing me a knowing grin before wishing me favor from the Gifters.

I wonder if any of this came from Gregor, I said to Aurelius. My stomach rolled, and I took a deep breath, quelling my revulsion over the tubes of stolen silver blood and trying not to picture it being forcibly extracted from a terrified child. I didn't want to be anywhere near blood taken without permission, but if I wanted Senator Rex to think I was fully on board with his project, I had to play the part and play it convincingly.

My father's notebooks were nearby in case I needed to reference something, and while nothing he'd written had specifically confirmed his involvement in torturing Daevalic children, nothing he'd recorded had refuted such a thing, either. I'd read his notes until I'd memorized them, desperately looking for a clue that would explain his behavior, but I'd come up empty-handed every time.

Obviously, the fastest way to earn myself an invitation to the experimentation facility was to make an important breakthrough, but that was also the last thing in the realm I wanted to do, giving

Astrals any chance of successfully altering Daevals. At the same time, if it *was* possible to somehow transform a Daeval into an Astral through their blood, I wanted to know about it before anyone else.

Talking out loud always helped me think, so I cast a silencing spell on the room, ensuring no one in the hallway would overhear what I said to Aurelius.

"Let's start with what we know." I rested my hands on the counter. "With Sebastian, the Astral researchers tried behavioral modification, but that didn't prove effective, so they turned to studying blood. They had just started exploring the differences and similarities between gold and silver blood when Father became involved. Based on his notes, Daevalic blood is identical to Astral blood in almost every way . . . both are made up of liquids, which contain water, salt, and important nutritional components, and solids, which are mostly immune-related cells. There's also a third component, and that determines whether your blood is gold or silver."

Taking the captum Senator Rex had given me out of its bag, I placed it flat on the table and summoned one of the *Donec Medicinae*'s analysis programs. I then carefully removed the cork stopper from a test tube and used a dropper to place a bead of silver blood on the captum. Picking up a clean scalpel, I pressed the blade against my fingertip, then placed a drop of my own blood on the glass-like surface.

"The body recognizes blood based on various combinations of proteins on the outside of each blood cell," I said. I watched as the captum analyzed the components of the two blood samples, projecting images and chemical formulas into the air above the table. "If you alter the protein combinations, you alter the blood. There are four types of golden blood, B1 through B4, and if you reconfigure the components, you can turn one type into another to make it compatible with a particular Astral's body. Since we know blood can be altered, let's start there and see if we can turn silver blood into golden blood."

Reaching my hand out to one of the projected images, I began rearranging proteins along the outside of the silver blood cell, substituting, repositioning, adding, and removing pieces until the two magnified blood cells before me were identical.

"It's definitely possible to change silver blood into golden blood," I said, wondering if the Astral researchers already knew this. It seemed the process also worked in the other direction and with enough changes, I could make golden blood silver. While I could transform one blood type into the other, however, nothing I did allowed the two types to mix; regardless of the changes I made, gold and silver blood remained distinctly separate and unable to work together. I hoped this wasn't somehow symbolic of Astrals and Daevals in general. Closing my eyes briefly, I tried to think like Sebastian, imagining every worst-case scenario and planning for any possibility.

"Ultimately, it doesn't matter if we can change silver blood into golden blood because a Daeval's body won't accept it," I concluded, thinking of Gregor's trace memories and how his captors had filled his body with golden blood only to have his internal organs shut down, due to their incompatibility with the substance.

"If I were the researchers and I couldn't alter golden blood to be accepted by a Daeval's body, I'd turn my focus to the body itself," I decided. "Then the question becomes, is it possible to alter a Daeval's body so it accepts golden blood? And, going one step further, is there a way to alter the blood production centers within a Daeval's body, ensuring their body not only accepts golden blood but produces it?"

"That would require extensive alteration of a Daeval," noted

Aurelius. "How would you change a living being so completely?"

How, indeed?

The beads on my *sana* bracelet glinted in the overhead lighting, and my stomach clenched even as I forced myself not to shy away from the answer.

"Healers already use Rheolath to alter certain aspects of Astrals' bodies," I reminded the lynx. Healers didn't use The Controller to make superficial changes for vain Astrals, but they did use the bead's powers for more serious reasons, such as removing scars from those who had been badly burned or healing a cleft palate that prevented someone from eating or speaking. "Just because we've traditionally only used Rheolath to make certain physical alterations doesn't mean she can't be used to make others. She could certainly be used to assume control of a Daeval's body and alter it to produce and accept golden blood."

"Even if the Astral researchers went so far as to alter the internal workings of a body, remember what Laycus and Suryal said," cautioned Aurelius. "Shades always return as the same blood type. I can't imagine a shade who's been a Daeval all their life suddenly taking to a body that now only produces golden blood."

I nodded, my mind racing until it settled on something so terrifying, I didn't want to say it out loud. "What if altering a Daeval's body isn't enough?" I asked softly. "What if you have to alter their shade, as well?"

I'd never heard of *aleric* alteration of a shade, but that didn't mean it wasn't possible. At the same time, if using *alera* to alter the mind was difficult, I couldn't begin to imagine how much harder controlling and manipulating a shade would be.

"Even in my many centuries of existence, I've never heard of *any* healer being able to alter a shade." Aurelius frowned.

I stared directly at him. "What about a healer who was also a Recovrancer?"

Aurelius's eyes widened with the same horror I felt contemplating such a thing, but I pressed on, forcing myself to see my hypothetical musing through to the end. "What if, as a Recovrancer with a unique connection to shades, I could alter a Daeval's shade and make them believe they've always been an Astral?"

"Such a transformation would be far too lengthy." Aurelius shook his head. "For the sake of argument, let us say Aeles invades Nocens and conquers the realm, holding all the Daevals who live there captive. Even if every Astral with healing powers is recruited to alter Daevals' bodies, there's no telling how long the process would take to complete . . . not to mention no one knows a Recovrancer might be capable of altering a shade, or that there is once again a Recovrancer in Aeles. Even if you willingly agreed to participate, which you would never do, it's not feasible to turn Daevals into Astrals one by one."

"If the biggest obstacle to altering Daevals is how long the process will take, that won't be nearly enough to dissuade Astral researchers from attempting it," I replied darkly. "I agree it's not practical, but it's also at least *possible*."

I gazed at the silver and gold blood on the captum. "Thankfully, as you said, I'm the only one in all of Aeles who could even attempt such a thing, and since I'd never do it, it seems Daevals are safe from being turned into Astrals, at least for now."

Shutting down the analysis program before cleaning off the captum, I made up my mind. "I'm going to tell Senator Rex I've explored all the possibilities I can think of and I can't find a way to make Daevals more like us through their blood. I'm going to make a case for studying living Daevals instead and hopefully he'll invite me to the experimentation facility to study them."

"I still worry he is far too clever to be tricked into divulging anything." Aurelius twitched his whiskers.

"You're probably right," I agreed, "but he wants me involved, which means at some point he's going to have to tell me more or the project will stall. I'm valuable to him, and that has to count for something."

Tidying up the laboratory, I then used my peerin to compose a message to Senator Rex, asking to meet with him at his earliest convenience.

Lionel looked up and smiled as I stopped before his desk.

"Go on in," he said. "Senator Rex is expecting you."

I smiled back, hoping my expression masked the butterflies fluttering in my stomach. While I'd expected Senator Rex to set up a meeting in a day or two, I'd been pleased when he'd replied and said his next appointment had unexpectedly rescheduled, leaving him free to meet now. Aurelius shook his head as I opened the senator's door but kept his thoughts to himself.

"Ah, Ms. Valorian!" exclaimed Senator Rex, rising from his desk and motioning towards the blue armchairs in front of the fireplace. "Make yourself comfortable, please. Would you care for anything to drink? Tea, perhaps? Coffee?"

"I'm fine, thank you," I replied as I settled into the chair.

Senator Rex tipped a small vial over the logs in the fireplace, causing a flame to spark, and once a fire was crackling cheerfully, he sat down and gave me a welcoming grin. "I'm so pleased you wanted to meet! How can I help?"

"I've worked my way through my father's notes," I began, "and I've reproduced the experiments I could, with the same results. I've used all the knowledge I possess about healing and bodies, and I can't find a single way to have golden blood be accepted by a Daeval's body."

Senator Rex drummed his fingers on the arm of the chair, his earlier enthusiasm disappearing. "That is disappointing," he finally said. "I was convinced if anyone could figure this out, it would be you. If you're saying it's not possible, I have to believe it truly can't be done." He let out a long exhale.

Now was my chance. A few weeks ago, I never would have been bold enough to try and trick Senator Rex into believing me, but I was so close to getting myself to Rynstyn, to knowing the truth about my father and stopping the experimentation program, I had to take the risk.

"I'm not saying Daevals can't be changed." I tried my best to sound reassuring. "At this point, it just seems like blood isn't the best way to change them. But I'm a healer, so there might be other ways I could affect a body . . . but I'd need access to a living Daeval and not just blood in a test tube."

It was a stretch, because most Astrals would never volunteer to go near a living, breathing Daeval. But I hoped since Senator Rex knew I'd been near one before he wouldn't be surprised by my willingness to be close to one again, especially in the name of continuing my father's research.

"I realize that might sound callous," I added, "treating a Daeval as something to be studied, but I've also heard knowledge is *always* worth whatever the cost to attain it."

I prayed to Bellum, the Gifter of Victory, that using the senator's own words would strengthen my case, and Senator Rex studied the dancing flames in the fireplace before speaking.

"I do hope you'll forgive me for what I'm about to say. You see, it made sense to keep certain things to myself until I was better acquainted with you, but you've made it clear you want to be involved . . . and it's obvious this project will move faster with you onboard."

Everything inside me began vibrating with nervous excitement, but I tried to appear calm as I nodded for the senator to continue.

"While it's true we receive silver blood from the Nocenian government, that's not the *entire* truth . . . you see, we have an arrangement whereby certain Daevalic criminals are given the option of coming to Aeles for a short period of time. In exchange for donating blood and participating in other research, they receive time off their imprisonment sentence."

Based on the evidence I had from both Sebastian and Gregor, children were the focus of the experimentation program, not adults, but Senator Rex's words were delivered so smoothly, they invited belief without question. Rather than let my disgust show, I widened my eyes in mock horror.

"Criminals?" I gasped. "Isn't that dangerous?"

"They're kept under strict guard in a secluded facility far away from our kind," Senator Rex explained in a soothing tone. "And in order to participate in the program, none of the crimes they committed can be of a violent nature."

"But how are Daevals able to be in Aeles without setting off the Blood Alarm?" That seemed like the logical question anyone in my place would have.

"There are ways," replied Senator Rex evasively, much to my frustration.

I lowered my gaze to the ground, trying to seem as if I was struggling to overcome disbelief. "Why would the Nocenian government agree to a program like what you're describing? They can't be doing it out of the goodness of their hearts."

"Well, it helps keep their prison population down, which is a focal point for specific Daevalic politicians," replied Senator Rex. "But more importantly, certain Daevals are paid exceedingly well for each criminal who participates in our program."

While I could actually envision such an arrangement working, I had no reason to believe it was happening, although I'd certainly have Sebastian mention it to Caz and Dunston, just to make sure no Daevals were profiting from selling off their own kind.

"That makes sense," I said. "Money can be very motivating."

"I've always been grateful it's not a motivating factor for me." Senator Rex smiled. "It's a trap far too many politicians fall into, regardless of the color of their blood."

"What does motivate you?" I was genuinely curious to hear his answer, even though I suspected it would be another lie. To my surprise, though, when his light blue eyes met mine, they were overflowing with sincerity.

"A desire to do what I believe to be right," he replied in a steady voice. "I want Astrals to be the best we can be, to live safely and happily with those we love. Everything I do springs from my love of our realm and our kind." He leaned forward, firelight glinting off his red-gold curls. "And what about you, Ms. Valorian? What motivates you?"

"Truth," I said, holding his gaze. "I want to know the truth, whether it's about an Astral, a Daeval, a situation, or something that might seem trivial to others . . . even if it's painful, I want the truth."

A smile spread across the senator's face. "You're so like your father. I believe he would have given a similar answer."

Given what I'd learned about my father these past few weeks, I wasn't as sure, but I couldn't think about that right now. "Thank you for telling me where the silver blood comes from."

"Thank you for handling such a shocking revelation so well," Senator Rex replied. "And you're right . . . knowledge is always worth whatever the cost to acquire it. And on that note," he crossed one leg over the other, "what would you think of seeing our research facility for yourself?"

Even though I'd secretly hoped for such a thing, I hadn't expected to find it offered to me on a proverbial golden platter.

"Are you serious?" I managed to reply.

"I am," he said with a nod. "Given how invested you are in this project, it only makes sense for you to see the facility first-hand. Would that be of interest to you?"

I wanted to shout *yes* but tried to temper my excitement so as not to seem overly enthusiastic. "Is it safe?"

"Absolutely," assured the senator. "It's a quick trip to Rynstyn via intersector, and you'll be with a capable escort at all times. For your first visit, there won't be any interacting with the prisoners, but I can foresee a time when you are able to study a living Daeval in its entirety."

Thinking it might seem odd or suspicious if I insisted on speaking with any Daevals during my first visit, I didn't push the issue. "That sounds wonderful! Thank you."

"Oh, it's my pleasure!" Senator Rex rose from his chair, prompting me to do the same. "I'll speak with Healer Omnurion and clear your schedule for tomorrow afternoon. Does that work for you?"

"Absolutely." The sooner I visited the facility, the sooner I could obtain the evidence I so desperately needed. Before walking towards the door, however, I paused. My excitement over getting invited to Rynstyn had almost made me forget to ask the question whose answer would most likely break my heart once and for all.

"Senator Rex . . . did my father know about the facility in Rynstyn and how silver blood was actually being acquired?"

The senator nodded, the single gesture making everything inside me go numb. "He did. He even visited the facility a hand-ful of times."

I thanked Senator Rex and took my leave, focusing on putting one foot in front of the other until I reached my office. Closing the door behind me, I leaned against it, staring up at the ceiling. Clenching my hands into fists didn't stop them from trembling, and the shaking quickly spread throughout the rest of my body. My chest seemed caught in an invisible vice, making it impossible to breathe, and I dropped my face into my hands. Part of me wanted to scream, releasing the anger I'd been pushing down ever since my father's death, while the rest of me wanted to cry at how badly I'd been betrayed. I couldn't help feeling as if I'd lost my father all over again, only this time, *he* was to blame for my loss. Aurelius bumped his head against my knee, and I crouched down, wrapping my arms around him.

Father knew. I confined the conversation to my mind, even as a tremor shook my body. *He knew what our kind was doing to Daevals, and he didn't even try to stop it! How could he? He was the* Princeps Shaman . . . *his life was dedicated to healing, not torturing!*

We don't know all the facts of his involvement, Aurelius insisted. *From the outside looking in, you're cooperating with Senator Rex while secretly trying to end this terrible program. Isn't it at least conceivable your father might have been doing something similar?*

I can't imagine that's the case, but . . . I suppose there's always a chance. Deep down, I didn't feel as if I could allow myself the luxury of maintaining any hope when it came to my father. Releasing the lynx, I gazed into his eyes. *Still no word from Flavius?*

No, and now I'm concerned, said Aurelius. *I've never been unable to reach another Cypher for so long. Once we return from our expedition, I'll arrange a meeting with the Cypher Commission and see if they know anything.*

Perhaps he changed his mind about remaining a Cypher, I suggested. *It's possible he decided to return to being a mortal animal rather than being bound to someone else.*

It's possible, Aurelius's whiskers drooped, *but it's not like him to simply vanish with no trace. I think he would have said something if he'd changed his mind. I'll keep searching. He'll turn up eventually.*

Pressing my fingertips against the bracelet, I wasted no time telling Sebastian about my conversation with Senator Rex and my upcoming trip.

He groaned. *Do you have any idea how dangerous this is?*

It's also the opportunity we've been waiting for. This is my chance to get the evidence we need to prove what Astrals are doing to Daevals. I have to do this.

He was quiet for a moment, and while I could sense a variety of emotions churning inside him, his next words surprised me. *I want to see you before you go. Can I portal to your apartment and pick you up?*

Everything's going to be fine. I'll only be there a few hours, if that. He was making it seem as if I was headed off on a venture I might not return from even though I wouldn't be leaving my realm.

I know, he said. *And I realize you were just here, but . . . I would feel better seeing you again.*

I smiled, hearing a tone he only rarely used, a tone that was gentle and hopeful at the same time. *I always want to see you,* I replied. *I'll let you know when I'm home, and you can come get me.*

30

SEBASTIAN

"What's your plan?" I asked Kyra after retrieving her from Aeles.

"I'd love to bring a captum, but I'm sure I won't be allowed to record," she said. "I'd also love to get my hands on one of the collars you wore, if they still use them, but I doubt I'll see one on my first visit." Her expression brightened. "At least I can take the suppressor medallion and try to locate others."

"I don't think that's a good idea. If something goes wrong while you're there, that medallion is the only way I can come get you. In a dangerous situation, it's safer to focus on one thing at a time; you can search for the other medallions later."

"What if I'm not invited back?"

"Then you can use whatever evidence you're able to obtain to show Aeles what's happening to my kind, and you can look for other medallions as you're helping dismantle the program," I said.

Kyra considered my words, then nodded. "Even if I can't bring back anything tangible, just seeing what's happening with my own eyes will make for excellent testimony."

"Have you thought about who you plan on testifying to?" I pressed her. "We don't know who we can trust in the Aelian government."

"I believe Healer Omnurion would be appalled at anyone

being tortured and experimented on, regardless of the color of their blood, so I think she would support us. Demitri's mother holds significant political power; she's in charge of litigation between the provinces and could bring attention to what's happening. But more than that," Kyra drew a deep breath, "I've realized Astrals will listen to me. They loved my father, and everyone expects me to take his place as the next *Princeps Shaman*. I'll speak out publicly about whatever I see in Rynstyn and Astrals will listen because of who I am. It's one thing for my kind to dislike Daevals. It's another thing entirely for them to support Daevals being kidnapped and experimented on; I have to trust there are others in Aeles who won't stand for that."

I wasn't nearly so certain. Should Kyra openly announce what she'd learned, Nocens would without a doubt be listening. We'd have to tell Dunston and Caz before we went public and hope they could prevent the Nocenian government from immediately declaring war and launching a rescue initiative into the golden-blooded realm.

"Aurelius will be with me the entire time I'm at the facility," Kyra added.

I glanced at the lynx.

"I will not leave her side," he said, which made me feel slightly better.

"Do your best to memorize the layout," I instructed. "When you arrive, notice how many steps it takes to reach certain landmarks . . . pay attention to when you make turns or how many doors you go through."

"Why?" Kyra gave me a confused look.

"It's a good safety practice. If I have to come in and get you, that information could make the difference between a fast, clean exit, and having to fight our way out."

"Alright." Her blue eyes widened slightly. "I'll do my best."

"It probably goes without saying, but I also think we should keep the connection through the bracelets open," I added.

Kyra made a face. "I've learned it's really hard to pay attention to what's happening in front of me when we're talking in my head. I'm worried I might miss something because I'm listening to you or telling you something." She clearly anticipated I would disagree, because she added, "As you said, in a dangerous situation, it's safer to focus on one thing at a time."

A part of me briefly wished Kyra didn't pay such close attention to the things I said, even though deep down, the fact that she did made me feel special in a way I'd never before experienced. I thought back to shortly after I'd first met her, and how she'd reached out through the bracelets while I'd been completing a contract in Falmayne. It had been incredibly difficult to engage in a fight and a conversation at the same time, to the point that I'd severed the connection as soon as I'd been able to lay down my weapons.

"Alright," I consented. "I'd rather you pay attention to what's happening around you. But I want you to reach out the second you're out of that facility."

We had a quiet dinner, helpfully supplied by Batty, and I was pleased Kyra didn't ask me to take her back to Aeles, instead borrowing some of my sleeping clothes and crawling into bed. I pulled her close as she curled up against me.

"LeBehr's potion to find the Chronicles should be ready any day now," she said. "Assuming we find our book, what do you think it'll be like if we actually reunite the realms?"

I gazed up at the stone ceiling. Even though I knew that's what we were working towards, it still seemed so unlikely we would succeed.

"I don't know," I admitted. "All my earlier questions still stand, even though we've seen there *are* Daevals and Astrals who are open to the idea of better relationships with one an-other. But a few folks who aren't opposed to peace isn't the same as everyone putting aside their differences and seeing each other as equals. We ruled last time because things were so terrible, everyone was willing to find a compromise. In this life, I don't want to rule anything. But I don't see how we can keep from being involved when we're the ones pushing Astrals and Daevals together again." I shifted, prompting Kyra to lift her head and look at me. "When we first became king and queen, we had to sacrifice a lot. You gave up becoming the *Princeps Shaman* in order to rule. Are you willing to do that again?"

Kyra was silent for a moment. "I'll do whatever it takes to put an end to the feud between Astrals and Daevals," she said, but I didn't miss the reluctance in her tone. "I'd rather be the *Princeps Shaman*, but perhaps I'm not meant to be." I could sense her turn-ing over her next words. "Are you willing to give up your work in order to facilitate a united Aeles-Nocens?"

I'd known I would face this question eventually in my relation-ship with Kyra, but I appreciated she'd asked and given me the chance to answer rather than simply telling me what I "ought" to do.

"I think I'd have to give it up," I said. "While we could easily establish peace through fear, I'm not certain that's the best way to maintain it. The thing about being feared is you always have to remind others why they should fear you, which means con-stantly escalating the things you do to inspire fear. That works fine in my profession, but I don't know if it's the smartest way to govern a realm. At the very least, no one would trust someone in a position of power who was also an assassin." Even though it was the logical decision, a heaviness settled inside my chest at the thought of giving up everything I'd worked so hard for.

"Perhaps there's another way you could use your . . . skills," offered Kyra. "You know how you told me healers can choose the direction they work in—they can use their knowledge of the body to heal or hurt—perhaps you could do something similar. Instead of being the one breaking into places and harming Daevals, you could help others prevent those things from happening. You could go into a home or business, analyze the security, and point out any weaknesses, based on your own experience. If you didn't work for Dunston, I'm certain he'd hire you to ensure someone *like* you didn't steal from him or cheat him or worse."

I considered Kyra's words. I'd never thought of such an option, but hearing her say it, I couldn't deny it was at least interesting.

"I'd basically be helping folks protect themselves from someone like me."

"You could offer your services as an independent security consultant." Kyra smiled. "Or, perhaps there's an opportunity for you in the military. Ideally, once the realms are reunited and Astrals and Daevals are working together, we'd have a combined military made up of soldiers from both Aeles and Nocens. Being a soldier was your plan at one time. I'm certain Adonis and Nigel would support it. Camus as well."

If Kyra was willing to give up the position she'd spent her life working towards, it was only fair I be prepared to do the same.

"Those are both good ideas," I told her. "I'm not ready to decide anything now, but if you can change careers, I can too. As long as I'm with you, I can do anything."

Kyra nodded. "We'll just keep doing the next right thing, and we'll figure it out together, like we always have. There's also no reason we have to do things exactly like we did before. I want to be involved in improving relations between the realms, but I don't want to be responsible for making *all* the decisions. I actually like the idea of a coalition, something where both Astrals and Daevals are represented and can make decisions together, rather than the two of us just doing what we think is best."

I couldn't imagine how such a thing would work, but I agreed it would be nice.

Kyra gazed directly into my eyes.

"I've almost said this to you so many times." Her cheeks reddened. "I've been waiting for the right moment, but I don't know that there is one. Or maybe there won't be a right moment until I just say it. You already know how I feel about you, but I want to tell you . . . I love you, Sebastian."

"I love you too," I replied without a moment's hesitation, reaching up and stroking Kyra's hair. "Even though it's not the eternity we'd planned, I will always find you, and I'll do whatever it takes for us to be together."

Kyra leaned forward, pressing her lips against mine, and while part of me considered suggesting we go beyond kissing, I didn't want our first time together to be associated with her going off to the place I'd been tortured. We had the rest of our lives to be with one another, and I'd never felt as content as I did in that moment, replaying Kyra telling me she loved me and knowing I loved her in equal measure.

At the same time, I couldn't stop the anxiety trickling into my stomach. It was one thing for Kyra to share my dreams and see what had occurred in the mountains of Rynstyn; it was quite another for her to physically enter the place responsible for some of my worst nightmares. I knew we didn't have an alternative to obtaining the evidence we needed to shut the program down, and when there wasn't a good decision to be made, you often had to select the least terrible choice from the available options. Still, just because I knew it was the logical decision didn't mean I had to like it . . . how could I, when it involved the safety of the woman I couldn't live without?

31

KYRA

*T*he following afternoon, I met Senator Rex at his office, where he gestured to an intersector embedded in the floor near his desk. As I walked to the platinum plate, my heart was beating so loud I worried the senator might hear it.

"Not just anyone is allowed in the facility," Senator Rex explained, "so the intersector will require my authorization before sending you. Are you ready?"

I nodded before stepping onto the thick plate, Aurelius at my side. Senator Rex briefly closed his eyes, likely holding the facility coordinates in mind, then crouched down and pressed a finger against the intersector. The last thing I saw before I was whisked away was his light blue eyes gazing up at me as a triumphant smile spread across his face. Of course he was happy . . . he thought I was going to help him achieve what he wanted most, ending the existence of Daevals.

I blinked as I arrived in the facility, taking in the twin white marble staircases rising gracefully in opposite directions, as well as the tapestry-covered walls. As I turned around, a woman who had clearly been waiting for me stepped forward.

"You must be Kyra." She offered me a welcoming smile. "My name is Zenden. I had the pleasure of working with your father for a bit. We all miss him dearly, and I'm so sorry for your loss."

"Thank you," I replied, trying to place where I'd seen her before. I knew I'd never met her, yet her silver hair and intense green eyes were somehow familiar. And then it struck me . . . she was the Astral from Sebastian's dream, the one who'd greeted him when he'd first arrived in Rynstyn with his father. She was older now, soft lines creasing the corners of her eyes and mouth, but there was no question it was her. Anger rushed into my chest, but I pressed my palms against my breeches and shoved my feelings down. "I'm happy to be following in my father's footsteps."

"Before we begin," said Zenden, "I do need to remind you that anything seen or heard here is strictly confidential and not to be discussed with anyone other than Senator Rex. Do you have a captum or peerin on you?"

I shook my head, glad I hadn't tried to sneak either in. "I assumed I wasn't allowed to bring any devices with me."

"Wonderful!" she said cheerfully. "Then off we go." She motioned for me to follow her as she turned and headed towards a nearby hallway.

"What can you tell me about the history of the facility?" I asked as we walked down the wide corridor. The overhead lights bounced between the white slate floor and the stark white walls, and I found myself squinting against the artificial brightness.

"Our program was started approximately eight hundred years ago," explained Zenden. "The founder, Errubus, was a visionary thinker who realized there was more than one way to address the Daevalic problem. He conducted the first study into the differences and similarities between Astrals and Daevals. Since then, we've built from his original research, while also expanding the scope of the program far beyond anything he likely ever imagined."

She smiled at me, clearly expecting me to be impressed, and I forced myself to smile back, even as my mind reeled. I hadn't expected the facility to have existed for so long; it was almost as old as the Blood Alarm, at least according to what Laycus had told me.

"Errubus's studies would be considered quite primitive now, but they were groundbreaking at the time," continued Zenden. As we reached the end of the hallway, she pressed her palm against a tile in the wall, and the doors in front of us groaned as a lock slid out of place, allowing her to push them open. This hallway looked similar to the last, except there were closed doors at regular intervals on either side, and while I wondered what was behind them, I knew better than to ask.

"There were times when the program was almost shut down, usually due to difficulties recruiting research subjects," lamented Zenden, "but dedicated Astrals managed to keep it going, and eventually researchers moved from studying things like appearance and food preferences to focusing on observable behavior . . . the choices Daevals made when placed in certain situations."

I glanced at Aurelius. That sounded like what Sebastian had experienced.

"Almost a century was spent attempting behavior modification." Zenden turned left at a branch in the hallway and, remembering Sebastian's advice, I realized I hadn't been counting steps. It was difficult memorizing my surroundings while also paying attention to what my guide was saying. At least I'd been noting doors and turns.

"Our researchers thought if we could teach Daevals to make better choices, they could become more like us. Alas, that particular area of research proved unfruitful and was eventually abandoned in favor of what we're working on now . . . understanding Daevals from the inside out."

Making a sharp right, Zenden suddenly stopped and gestured to a wall made entirely of glass. I stared at the metal chairs on the other side, each one bolted to the floor and fitted with numerous arm and leg restraints. Beside the chairs were cylinders with long tubes snaking out from them.

"This is where we collect the blood samples from our volunteers," Zenden explained, and I wanted to simultaneously cry and shatter the glass before me, imagining seven-year-old Sebastian strapped to one of the chairs. My body shook as the emotions I was keeping in check sought an outlet. Thankfully, there were no Daevals in the room, otherwise, I wasn't certain I could have stopped myself from attempting to free them.

"Where do the Daevals stay when they aren't participating in research?" I asked, trying to distract myself.

"They have their own quarters," replied Zenden. "They are still criminals, after all, so we can't allow them unrestricted freedom, but they each have their own room and are given three meals a day, which is more than they'd receive in a Nocenian prison."

The way she lied, so effortlessly, was infuriating, but I nodded, hoping if I seemed unsettled, Zenden would attribute it to my fears of having Daevalic criminals in Aeles.

We continued into another hallway, where the black floor and black walls made it seem as if we'd entered a tunnel. Zenden grasped the slick steel handle of a door and pulled it open before gesturing inside. "This is a typical prisoner's room."

I stepped into the room, my heart racing. Had Sebastian stayed in something like this? There was a small bed, a desk and chair, and a bucket in the corner for toiletry needs, which was demeaning if not downright barbaric. As I turned to ask Zenden how many Daeval prisoners were currently in the facility, she stepped back into the hallway and pulled the door shut in a single swift gesture. I stared at the back of the metal door, not believing what I'd just seen even as some instinctive part of me knew I needed to act. Hurrying forward, I tried to turn the door handle, but it didn't move, so I pounded on the door with my fist.

"Hello?" Was Zenden trying to give me a sense of how prisoners lived?

Or, was I trapped?

My heart thudded without any discernible rhythm and just before I reached over to touch the bracelet and contact Sebastian, the door handle began to turn. I stepped back, shifting my weight onto the balls of my feet. I wasn't strong like Sebastian, but I was a fast runner, and if I could slip past Zenden, I could make my way to the nearest intersector and leave. The door swung open, and even as I told myself to run, I stood rooted in place, unable to take so much as a single step forward.

There, in the doorway, stood Senator Rex.

And he was smiling.

"I'm sorry it had to come this. But there was no other way to get what I wanted." His eyes glowed with happiness. "*You*, Ms. Valorian."

That didn't make any sense. "Me? I'm already helping you study silver blood. Why would—"

"—You're only involved because you're trying to put an end to my research," interrupted the senator.

I glanced at Aurelius, each heartbeat ringing in my ears, making it hard to form a thought. I'd played along so well. How had Senator Rex figured it out? And why did he have to appear now, when I was so close to getting what I needed?

Senator Rex pulled a captum from his pocket and angled the device towards the wall. A projected image appeared, the blood cells I'd simulated with the *Donec Medicinae*'s program, and I heard myself say to Aurelius, "What if altering a Daeval's body isn't enough? What if you have to alter their shade, as well?"

No.

My voice continued to play from the captum: "What about a healer who was also a Recovrancer?"

Begging any Gifter listening to please distort the captum feed, I cringed as I heard myself say, ". . . I'm the only one in all of Aeles who could even attempt such a thing, and since I'd never do it, it seems Daevals are safe from being turned into Astrals, at least for now."

"I was incredibly disappointed you kept this from me," said Senator Rex. "But perhaps it's only fair . . . you see, I didn't fully trust you, either, so I put a spell on the captum I gave you, ensuring anything it was used for was recorded and shared with this device." He tapped the captum he'd just used before returning it to his pocket. "I'm impressed, but not at all surprised. I knew it would take someone with your particular skills to figure this out."

"This entire trip was a set-up." The realization made my knees buckle, and I wished I could sit down.

"Yes," nodded Senator Rex. "I'd wanted to bring you here for a while, but first I needed you to find a way to alter Daevals. Once you'd done that, it was time. Now, if you'll be so kind as to follow me. You too, Aurelius. And just so you know, Cyphers can't dematerialize within the walls of this facility. They also can't establish contact with other Cyphers, although you've likely already figured that out."

Aurelius pinned his ears against his head and growled, low and menacing, but I placed a hand on his back. I didn't want to be separated from him, which meant the less attention Senator Rex paid the lynx, the better. Following the senator out of the room, I noted anything that might be a landmark as we wound our way through various corridors.

"Why do you hate Daevals so much?" My boots clicked against the floor as I worked to keep pace with Senator Rex.

"You know the answer to that better than anyone," he replied. "After all, you and I have *quite* the history together."

32

KYRA

$\mathcal{I}$ stopped so fast, it was as if an invisible wall had sprung up and I'd crashed right into it.

"What did you say?" My voice came out as a hoarse whisper.

"I said, you and I have quite the history together. And now I've saved you the trouble of forcing me to reveal myself." Senator Rex turned to face me, then shook his head. "You know, I've never been able to return looking anything like my former self. I'm quite jealous, although I'm not sure why you chose to do so this particular life cycle."

It couldn't be. But even as part of me protested, the rest of me recognized the truth. I'd been working alongside a Daeval-hating Astral without ever once suspecting he might be the very Daeval-hating Astral Sebastian and I were searching for. Guilt and anger fought for control of me, and I wished I could disappear into a crack in the floor. How had I missed this? Even as I asked the question, though, I knew the answer . . . I'd missed what had been right in front of me because I hadn't been looking for it. If I hadn't been so focused on uncovering what my father had been doing, perhaps I would have seen Senator Rex for who he really was.

"Tallus," I croaked, uncertain whether I meant it as a statement or a question. "You're Tallus."

"I am. I'm glad to hear you remember me."

"How could I forget?" I clenched my hands into fists and recalled smoke pouring from the castle windows as Schatten and I stood on the mountainside, watching our home burn. "You're the reason Schatten and I were forced to flee! You killed Farent and countless others! You're the reason the realm was divided . . . why Aeles and Nocens became unstable and why my father's dead! You ruined *everything!*"

"No," he replied in a tone as if he was correcting a child. "I was merely seeking to undo the damage *you* did by partnering with a Daeval and allowing those filthy silver bloods to live as equals among our kind."

"How did you keep your memories intact? It's nearly unheard of for a shade to recall details from a previous life."

Tallus grinned proudly. "You're not the only one capable of extraordinary spell-casting. I remember details from every life I've lived since I was Tallus, and I must say, it's been nothing but a constant struggle with you, one I intend to end *this* life cycle once and for all."

"What do you mean, a constant struggle?" I asked. "I haven't seen you in more than a thousand years."

Tallus blinked, clearly caught off guard. "You've never been one for falsehoods, so I have to believe you're telling the truth . . . you really don't remember?"

I shook my head, unable to speak as everything in me dreaded whatever I was failing to recall.

"Interesting," he said. "Well, then, allow me to be your guide through history."

Tallus started walking again, and I noted each turn we took until he stopped and opened a heavy door, gesturing for me to step inside. A furnace blazed on one side of the room, flames crackling loudly, and I winced at the heat.

A long metal stretcher was fitted onto two elevated rails that led directly into the furnace, and I suddenly felt ill. Judging by the size, the stretcher was intended to hold a body . . . a body that could be slid into the fire where it would be reduced to ash.

I was standing in the facility's crematorium.

My heart began to beat wildly, and I glanced down at where my *sana* bracelet was hidden beneath my sleeve, recalling my training with Healer Omnurion. I wasn't experienced enough to assume control of Tallus's mind, making him forget who he was or what he wanted with me, but I might be able to wield Rheolath well enough to control his body, keeping him from following me while I escaped.

Contact Sebastian! Aurelius shouted between my ears. *I cannot reach Batty, so you must use the bracelet!*

Not wanting to draw attention to what I was doing, I slowly reached for the gold bracelet, but before I could pull up my long sleeve, Tallus's next words caused my hand to freeze in mid-air.

"This marks the sixth time I've encountered you," he said. "I first met you as Kareth. I now know you as Kyra. In between, I knew you as Jaesian, Lochlyn, Fazeera, and Yerpa. Do those names sound familiar?"

I stared mutely at him, recognizing the names from the research Demitri and I had done in the Archives. "They were all Recovrancers," I finally said. There was no point in denying it, not when I'd incriminated myself in the recording Tallus had.

"They were all *you*," he clarified, "and they were Recovrancers because you are a Recovrancer."

"I can't be the only Recovrancer to have ever lived!" That directly contradicted things I'd read about junior and senior Recovrancers in *The Book of Recovrancy.*

"Of course not," he said. "Those were merely the ones I was concerned with. You must possess the most persistent shade to *ever* exist! Once it became clear you would never stop looking for

Schatten, I directed my efforts towards preventing his return. When you came back as Jaesian, I oversaw legislation outlawing Daevals in Aeles and establishing the Blood Alarm. I couldn't prevent Schatten from returning to Nocens, but I could at least keep him from simply walking into Aeles. Or portaling, more accurately . . . for all his faults, he was always quite skilled at crafting portals."

Tallus shook his head before reaching into a jacket pocket. Pulling out a handful of metal pieces, he separated them across the stretcher. "Do you recognize these?"

Before me lay six suppressor medallions identical to the one I'd found in my father's medical kit, now residing in Sebastian's dresser drawer. I held my tongue, though, not certain what Tallus knew I was aware of, and what he only suspected I knew.

"I have spent lifetimes tracking these down," he continued. "There's one missing, and I doubt you're going to tell me if you have it, but ultimately it doesn't matter."

Turning and grabbing a bowl from the counter behind him, he scooped up the medallions, tossed them into the container, then placed it on the stretcher before shoving the metal gurney into the furnace.

"No!" I shouted, reaching for the stretcher, but it was too late . . . flames surged upwards, crackling and sparking, and I didn't need to see inside the bowl to know the heat was already melting the metal.

"As much as I despised those medallions, I'm also grateful for them," said Tallus. "Without them, who knows how long it would have taken me to create the collars Daevals wear here? And now, aside from the single medallion I'm assuming you have, there's no way for a Daeval to be in Aeles unless they're wearing one of my collars."

I gaped at him. "*You* created the collars used here?"

"Yes. When you returned as Lochlyn and had the medallions made, I retaliated by establishing the very facility in which we now stand. I was known as Errubus at the time, and I realized if you were never going to stop searching for Schatten, I needed to end the existence of Daevals altogether . . . no Daevals meant no Schatten. If I'm being honest, the fact that this facility even exists is your fault."

My head spun, trying to process so much information at once. "I . . . I oversaw the creation of the medallions?"

"Yes. You see, I spent years trying to change Daevalic behavior, to make them more like us, but it wasn't particularly fruitful. While I continued exploring that particular area of research, I also turned my attention to you. When you and Schatten abdicated your thrones and took Rhannu, seeing as you're a Recovrancer, I assumed you hid the sword in Vaneklus. Since you were the only one who could retrieve it, the logic was simple . . . without you, Schatten would be useless even if he returned and even if he somehow made it into Aeles. So, I focused my efforts on outlawing recovrancy and ensuring anyone who might possess the ability was killed."

"How did you know when a certain Recovrancer was me?"

"I didn't always," Tallus admitted. "But if there was even the slightest chance she *might* be you, it was worth ending her life."

"How did you know it was me this time?" I wrapped my arms around myself.

"Well, for one thing, you look exactly as you did before, and while that could have simply been a coincidence, I've kept an eye on you since I saw your picture in your father's office. When I heard you'd fallen through a portal with a Daeval, I insisted on accompanying Lieutenant—excuse me, *Captain*—Prior to hear your story. Then, when news of a Daeval breaking into the unicorn sanctuary reached me, I knew it couldn't be a coincidence.

So many years with nary a peep from Nocens and then all of a sudden two attempts by Daevals to infiltrate our realm and both involving you."

"You're the one kidnapping Daevalic children from Nocens," I said with disgust. "You wanted to establish an orphanage to have access to as many silver-blooded children as possible."

"I still think it's a brilliant idea," Tallus said with a toss of his head. "Unfortunately, I couldn't devote as much time to it as I wanted. Stoking anti-Daeval sentiments in Aeles turned out to be much more difficult than I'd expected, likely thanks to your work in past life cycles. I was forced to spend an inordinate amount of time as a concerned senator writing bulletin briefs and giving speeches reminding Astrals how dangerous those in Nocens really are."

While it was encouraging to hear not everyone in my realm agreed with Tallus's views, my mind jumped back to the orientation speech he'd given, as well as what Sappho had felt and Aurelius had mentioned. "Is that your gift? Controlling minds?"

"I wish!" he chuckled. "I can influence, but I cannot control. My gift lies in assessing probabilities and understanding the statistical likelihoods of things happening or not happening. I then act to influence those probabilities, increasing or decreasing them. The weaker the mind, the less influencing I have to do, and most Astrals merely require a nudge or two. With you, however . . ." He sighed. "I've never had success affecting a single one of your thoughts. Schatten's, either. I was never certain whether you cast some sort of spell to protect yourselves or if there were other things at play."

"We never cast any spells to protect ourselves from you," I said. "Perhaps you're not as powerful as you believe." My assertion sounded braver than I currently felt, and I swallowed to wet my dry throat.

"Perhaps," Tallus agreed, his gaze falling to where my long sleeve hid my left wrist. "Or perhaps you were protected and didn't even know it. I always wondered what those bracelets were capable of. I went searching for them the first time I returned after dividing the realms." His top lip curled upwards. "I'll spare you the details of digging through corpses more than a hundred years old, but suffice to say the bracelets weren't there, leading me to think you either destroyed them before you died, or they were far more powerful than I'd imagined, able to come and go of their own choosing."

I thought back to what Batty had told us about the bracelets and his fears Tallus would try to locate them. While I was grateful for the Cypher's foresight, I didn't like Tallus's obvious interest in my bracelet. What had he meant about me being protected and not knowing it?

"I'm not certain if maintaining my memories also helped me maintain my gift," Tallus flexed his fingers, "but over the centuries, I've learned influencing thoughts largely depends on the type of thought I'm seeking to change. You see, when you try and make someone believe something, there's a chance they'll recognize the idea isn't coming from within themselves. Once they realize that, there's a stronger chance they'll disagree with the thought or come up with an argument against it. Fears, however, are different."

My breath caught, and I stepped closer to Aurelius.

"Fears *always* arise from within each individual," continued Tallus, "and are unique to every single Astral or Daeval. That makes them the easiest type of thought to influence because we typically don't even perceive them as thoughts."

He raised a hand, and purple smoke began to wind its way around his fingers. "Let's see if your mind is any less protected now that you're only wearing one bracelet instead of two."

The smoke from Tallus's hand sped towards me, and I closed my eyes, bracing myself and willing my mind to be as impenetrable as a tightly locked puzzle box. My torso thudded with each drumming heartbeat, and I jerked my sleeve up and ran a finger over Glir, letting the pureness of the diamond bead's voice help me maintain a clear head. Even as I focused on the peal of the bead, though, I could feel Tallus's power trying to work its way inside me, poking here, prying there, looking for the slightest weakness in my defenses. Sweat began to gather at my hairline and as the seconds ticked by, doubts started to form, even though I tried to ignore them.

Had wearing two bracelets somehow protected me in a way one bracelet couldn't? How long could I truly hold out against someone who had spent centuries strengthening their power while I was still becoming reacquainted with mine? While I was fairly certain I knew most of my fears, I now worried there were others hiding inside me, waiting to be freed so they could incapacitate me from the inside out.

I will not be controlled by my fears, I told myself, and just as I felt a particularly strong attempt by Tallus to force open the door of my mind, Death suddenly yanked so hard at our connection I nearly fell to one side. Images poured into my mind, the gruesome mixed with the less horrendous, and a newfound strength surged through me, making it almost easy to repel Tallus's attempts at manipulation.

Thank you! I cried, relieved I wasn't alone in my struggle. Recalling what Laycus and *The Book of Recovrancy* had revealed, I suspected Death didn't like the idea of sharing my mind with anyone else, and for once I was immensely grateful for its selfish nature.

After a moment, I didn't sense anything trying to force its way inside my mind, and I carefully turned my attention from

Death to Tallus, standing in the doorway, arms crossed, tapping his fingertips against the sleeves of his jacket.

"Well, that is frustrating," he said, nostrils flaring. "It seems your mind is still protected no matter how many bracelets you wear. But now we know. Do the bracelets work in other ways as they did before?"

I stared at him, and he made a scoffing sound. "You forget I watched you and Schatten use them every single day of your reign."

Sweat dampened my palms. If Tallus knew I could communicate with my former husband through the bracelet, would he try to remove it by force? Cut off my hand?

My fear must have shown on my face because Tallus smiled. "I have no interest in taking your bracelet, as I'm more certain than ever it wouldn't work for me. While I ensured Cyphers can't communicate from inside this building, *you* have no such restriction, and I fully expect you to reach out to Schatten or whatever his name is this time around and tell him everything you've been through."

The final piece of this terrible puzzle clicked into place, and I felt as if someone had struck me.

"You want him to come here and rescue me."

33

KYRA

"I don't just want it," Tallus corrected me. "I'm counting on it."

"So you can fight him? He'll kill you."

"Oh, without question, especially if you've recovered Rhannu for him, which you most likely have," agreed Tallus. "No, I won't be fighting him, and his visit here will not be a rescue, although I'm certain he'll try. After he fails to free you, the three of us will have a conversation, and in exchange for his safety, you will agree to continue the work I've started transforming Daevals into Astrals."

I felt as if someone had upended a bucket of ice water over my head.

"You don't even know if that will work!" I exclaimed.

"That's why experiments must be conducted," Tallus nodded, "although I believe it *will* work, due to your unique combination of abilities as both a healer and a Recovrancer."

"I've just started working on *aleric* alteration of the mind." I dug my fingertips into my scalp. "I wouldn't even know where to start when it comes to altering a shade."

"Lucky for us, you're a fast learner."

"Even if I was capable of doing such a thing, what's your plan—kidnap every Daeval one by one and bring them here to be altered?"

"No, the choice to be altered will be up to them," replied Tallus. "Aeles is so on edge, all it needs is a push in the right direction. Once I spread the story of how the future *Princeps Shaman* was attacked by a Daeval, the realm will be in an uproar and the military will agree to invade Nocens. After we have control of the realm, Daevals can become like us or they can die. The choice will be up to them, which is more than they deserve, but let it never be said I forced anyone into anything."

"That could take ages!" I protested.

"I'm not concerned with a quick solution," retorted Tallus. "I'm concerned with a permanent one. I don't care how long it takes. You and I will continue to be reborn and if need be, I'll share the spell I used to keep my past life memories intact . . . that way you'll know what's required of you each life cycle until silver blood no longer exists."

There was no way I would let myself be reborn with any kind of connection to Tallus, and as he opened the door, I drew a deep breath. Loosening my hold on the fury that had been building inside me, I ran my finger over Rheolath, the carnelian bead smooth against my skin. If ever there was a time to control a living being, it was now.

"*Bana sevap verakessin*," I said as Tallus moved to step through the open door, only to stumble as the stone glowed and Rheolath took control. Straightening, Tallus slowly turned around, his furious expression assuring me he was fighting me every step of the way. If I could just get past him, I could use Rheolath to engage the locking mechanism on the door, trapping him in the crematorium as Aurelius and I made our way to the first intersector we could find.

Glaring at me, Tallus managed to lower his chin towards his chest and closed his eyes. I could feel my control slipping, and I strained with all my might to maintain the connection. I forced him to take a single halting step away from the door, my muscles as tense as if I was physically fighting him, and I slid one boot forward, willing him to step backwards again. Just when I thought I'd succeeded, he rolled his shoulders and lifted his head. My control snapped, causing me to sway where I stood.

"While I might not be able to control others' minds, I am particularly skilled at protecting my own," he said. "Now that you've gotten that out of your system, follow me."

Defeated, I followed Tallus back to the room Zenden had locked me in earlier. He didn't offer any parting words, nor did I, and as the door closed behind him, I lowered myself to the floor and pulled my knees to my chest, resting my forehead against them. I wanted to burst into tears, but I couldn't, too overwhelmed to do more than replay Tallus's words in my mind.

Aurelius rubbed his head against my shoulder, and I looked up.

This is all my fault, I said. *If I hadn't had those medallions created, Tallus wouldn't have used them to make collars . . . he wouldn't have founded this facility . . . Sebastian never would have been tortured.*

My chest began to rise and fall faster as my breath came in uneven bursts.

It's my fault Gregor is dead. It's my fault Daevals have been experimented on. So many terrible things have happened because of me, and I don't even remember being those other women!

None of this is your fault! insisted Aurelius. *You've only ever tried to do good, and your enemy has met you at every turn. But this time you're not alone . . . you have Sebastian. Now, reach out to him so he can get us out of this miserable cell. We can figure things out after that.*

It's a trap, I argued. *Tallus wants him to come here. I can't let him get hurt because of me.*

Kyra, there is nothing that man wouldn't do for you, and there is no one better equipped to break you out. The hard part will be keeping him

*from destroying everyone and everything in the process. I can't commu-
nicate with Batty, so while I never imagined saying this, Sebastian is
truly our only hope.*

Aurelius was right, but I hated asking Sebastian to return to
this terrible place. This was where he'd been tortured, where he'd
fought daily to escape from. What would it do to him to come
back?

How am I going to tell him what I learned from Tallus? I whispered. *What if he hates me for being the reason this facility exists?*

*He won't hate you, because you didn't do anything wrong. Things
you intended for good were twisted and used for evil, and that is Tallus's
doing, not yours.*

Doing my best to believe Aurelius, I pressed my fingertips
against the gold bracelet.

Before you say anything, I said to Sebastian, *I need you to listen
and stay calm.*

34

SEBASTIAN

$\mathcal{I}$ tightened Rhannu's scabbard around my chest, forcing myself to take deep, controlled breaths, lest the fire in my veins explode through my skin and set everything around me ablaze. Normally, I derived immense satisfaction from being right, and while I'd known from the start it was a terrible idea for Kyra to visit the Rynstyn facility, this time I didn't feel the slightest pleasure at having my worst fears confirmed.

Actually, of all the worst-case scenarios I'd imagined, none of them had involved her being kidnapped by an Astral senator who turned out to be our oldest enemy returned. As someone who was typically quite skilled at planning for the absolute worst, I was disappointed I hadn't considered that particular possibility. Hopefully I wasn't losing my edge.

Kyra's voice was strained inside my head. *Sebastian, this is a terrible idea. Tallus wants you to come here.*

I pinned the suppressor medallion to my shirt, then tucked it behind one of the scabbard straps so it couldn't be pulled off me.

It doesn't matter. I'm coming.

"Tallus does indeed expect you," said Batty from his perch on the back of the sofa. "But perhaps that will work in our favor."

Hold on, Batty's saying something, I said to Kyra. *Don't close the connection, just wait a moment.*

I turned to Batty. "Make it fast."

"I know you prefer to operate by yourself, but in the interest of rescuing Kyra, I believe it makes sense to involve others . . . specifically, Adonis, Nigel, and Demitri."

"Tallus will know Kyra is friends with them," I countered. "If we include anyone, it ought to be Dunston and Caz."

"If a Daeval suddenly appears in Aeles so close to Kyra being kidnapped, Tallus will know you had something to do with it," Batty replied, and I clenched my jaw, even though I knew he was right.

"Tell me what you're thinking." I shifted my weight from one foot to the other.

"We dress Adonis as you, then have him create a distraction to buy you time to get inside the facility."

"That's too expected," I shook my head. "It's an obvious ploy."

"I agree Tallus will think it's most likely a distraction," Batty nodded, "but even with his unique powers, he cannot be in two places at once. If he is paying attention to Adonis, he cannot be focused on you rescuing Kyra."

"Even if Adonis buys me enough time to get inside, I don't know that I'll have enough time to get Kyra out." I ran a hand through my hair. "It wouldn't be an issue if I could open a portal, but we know from experience they have wards in place to prevent that."

"That is where Nigel comes in." Batty edged closer to me. "If you recall, he used to have a machine that prevented the creation of portals . . . until you destroyed it, of course."

I pressed my lips together, preferring not to think about the time I'd died.

"I'm certain he's been given a new such device or at least has access to one, and with the proper guidance, he is clever enough to perform basic reprogramming," continued Batty, his dark eyes shining. "And that is where I come in. I shall help him reconfigure the device to allow for *creating* portals instead of preventing them. I will then materialize into the experimentation facility and locate Kyra; once I have found her, you will use the device to portal in, rescue her, and portal out."

"Kyra said Cyphers can't materialize in and out of the facility," I reminded him. "That's obviously a new development since I was there."

"Cyphers have never been able to materialize in or out of that facility." Batty shook his head.

"*You* came and went as you pleased the entire time I was there." Was all the sugar the bat ate affecting his memory? "If—"

"—Yes, but did you ever see another Cypher dematerialize during the two years of your captivity?" Batty asked.

I considered that. "No, I never saw another Cypher appear or disappear at will, but I just assumed they didn't want to leave whoever they'd been paired with."

"They were unable to leave," said Batty. "That is why they never brought help, even though they very much wanted to."

I'd been under the impression the other Daeval children in the program were unwanted, as I'd been. It hadn't occurred to me until this very moment they might have had families desperately wondering what had happened to them, possibly even searching for them.

"If what you're saying is true," I crossed my arms over my chest, "and Cyphers have always been unable to dematerialize inside the facility, how did *you* manage to come and go for two years?"

"I told you before, a Cypher is only one of many things I have been in my life," Batty smiled, "but that story is *not* as important as freeing Kyra."

"Tell me why I need to include Demitri in this," I said. Normally any mention of the whiny Astral made the fire in my veins stir unhappily, but if he could be useful in rescuing Kyra, I certainly wasn't above working with him.

"He will ensure Kyra's family is safe," said the bat, "as Tallus will no doubt focus on them next."

Gazing across the cavern, I knew what I had to do.

"Contact Gordon," I said. "Tell him I need to meet with Adonis, Nigel, and Demitri as soon as possible."

I lifted my hand to knock on the door of Adonis's cottage, but the soldier must have been watching through the window because the door swung open, and he waved me inside. Nigel was standing by a chair while Demitri sat on the sofa and as Adonis closed the front door, all three men turned to face me.

I suddenly felt ridiculous, given what I was about to say. But if others were going to risk their lives to help me, they deserved to know the truth. Besides, Kyra and I had known this moment would come . . . I just hadn't anticipated I would be the one telling the truth about who we were.

"This is going to sound ridiculous," I warned them, "but hear me out. I promise what I'm about to tell you is the truth." Batty materialized on my shoulder and patted my cheek, which did nothing to improve my mood.

The others nodded, so I took a deep breath and told them the story of how a Daevalic warrior had wed an Astral healer to bring peace to the realm, only to be betrayed, and how they'd bound their shades using an ancient spell, promising to return together when the time was right to reunite the divided realms. I told them about Kyra being a Recovrancer, about Batty's involvement, and Tallus's endless quest to undo whatever good we did.

When I was done, the three Astrals were so quiet, I heard a bird call from a tree outside. Adonis began pacing back and forth, occasionally ruffling his hair. Nigel had taken a seat and wasn't moving, aside from the occasional blink. Demitri sat in stunned silence that, unfortunately, didn't last long enough.

"I *wish* I could say I was surprised," he hissed, an angry flush spreading over his face, "but all this proves is you've been terrible for Kyra no matter what your names are or what life cycle you're on!"

I clenched my hands into fists, more stung by his words than I wanted to let on.

"At least I only have to put up with you in this life cycle," I retorted. "You just hate I get to be with Kyra forever and you only get to be her friend now."

"What about after you reunite the realms?" challenged Demitri, rising to his feet. "The spell was to ensure you came back together when it was time to reunite the realms, but what then? Once you've fulfilled your purpose, there's no reason for your shades to stay bound across future life cycles. Then you'll be without her too!"

A flame flickered over my palm before I could stop it, and I quickly retracted the fire; it had been years since I'd lost control of myself in such a manner. Demitri couldn't be right . . . could he? Much as it bothered me, I pushed the thought from my mind. Kyra and I would figure out our eternity together later.

Adonis placed a hand on Demitri's shoulder. "I know you're worried, but the best thing we can do right now is focus on rescuing Kyra."

The anger quickly drained from Demitri's eyes, and he nodded as he let out a shaky exhale. Whether it was Adonis's words or his touch, I was glad at least something had succeeded in calming Kyra's excitable friend.

I turned to Adonis. "Does that mean you'll help me?"

"Of course," he replied, and I found myself able to breathe the slightest bit easier.

"I'm in too." Nigel nodded. "How do we help?"

"Did the Aelian military replace your portal disruptor after Sebastian destroyed it?" asked Batty. Nigel darted off to his room, then returned waving the cursed device, and Batty flew over to his shoulder, causing the soldier to startle.

"Together, I believe we can reprogram this to allow for the creation of portals," explained the bat. "However, I always think better with a little something in my stomach. Is there any of that delicious chocolate cake left?"

"Adonis made banana bread yesterday," offered Nigel as he headed towards the kitchen with my Cypher, leaving me alone with Adonis and Demitri.

"What can I do?" asked Demitri.

"You can ensure Kyra's family is safe." Much as I hated it, I knew they'd listen to her best friend, even if they didn't understand what was happening. "Most likely, they're going to need to leave Aeles, but we'll worry about that after we rescue Kyra."

Demitri nodded. "I'll take them to my parents' house. My mother wields a lot of influence, and my father's a beloved celebrity, so they'll be safe there, at least for a while."

I dipped my head in acknowledgment, and Demitri hurried out the front door towards the intersector; to my surprise, Adonis rushed after him. I doubted the two realized I could see them through the window and what with my excellent hearing, I heard every word they said.

"We'll get her back," Adonis said. "I'll do everything in my power to ensure she's safe. I promise."

"Thank you," said Demitri. "I . . . I hope . . . I want you to come back safely too." He dropped his eyes to the ground, which meant he missed the ear-to-ear grin that sprang to Adonis's face, although I didn't, even though the soldier quickly assumed a more neutral expression.

"I'm glad to hear that," Adonis said. "It makes it both harder and easier to leave, knowing there's someone waiting for me to return."

I thought back to the conversation I'd had with Adonis at his dinner party. Was *this* the reason he was so concerned about the exact nature of the relationship between Demitri and Kyra . . . because he had feelings for Demitri? In his past life, Farent had been married to a man, so if Adonis truly was Farent reborn, falling for Demitri certainly wasn't out of the question. In fact, the most pertinent question seemed to be if Demitri returned the captain's romantic interest, but I'd have to figure that out later.

Adonis looked as if he wanted to say more, then thought better of it and extended a hand, which Demitri took. Adonis suddenly pulled the other man into a quick hug, but by the time Demitri realized what had happened, Adonis had already released him and was walking back inside the cottage, a determined expression on his face.

"What do you need from me?" he asked, closing the front door as Demitri disappeared on the intersector.

35

KYRA

*K*nowing Sebastian was working on a plan to free me meant there was nothing I could do except wait, and since I had no desire to be alone with the thoughts pounding inside my head, I lowered myself into a cross-legged position.

Aurelius pricked his ears. "Do you really think it's wise to visit Laycus now?"

"Tallus knows who I am. There's no point in pretending I'm not a Recovrancer." Missing my shifter cloak, I hoped I could keep my clothing dry; the room was quite chilly, and returning from Vaneklus with soaking wet clothes would be incredibly unpleasant. "I need answers. I'll be back soon."

Aurelius nodded, and I touched Tawazun and Rheolath before closing my eyes. "*Bidh me a'dohl a-steach.*"

Striding through the water lapping gently against my legs, I shouted, "Laycus! I need to speak with you!"

Within seconds, I heard the familiar slap of oars against the river, and Laycus's boat emerged from behind a curtain of fog that disappeared as he pulled into view. He scowled and was likely going to say something unkind about my admittedly rude entrance, but I spoke first.

"I found Tallus. He's been posing as a senator in my realm, but he revealed himself, and he knows who I am. He's keeping me trapped in a secret facility and using me as bait so Sebastian will come and he can force us to work with him."

Laycus slumped against his staff as if the strength to stand had suddenly left him.

"I've already contacted Sebastian through the bracelets and he's working on a plan to free me, but while I'm waiting, I need answers." I gazed up at the Shade Transporter, not even trying to hide the fear coursing through me. "Tallus told me terrible things, and I need to know if they're true."

I swallowed hard before forcing the next words out.

"Tallus said the four Recovrancers I read about—Jaesian, Lochlyn, Fazeera, and Yerpa—were all me coming back and looking for Schatten. Is that true?"

"Yes."

"Tallus also said I was the one who oversaw the creation of the medallions . . . the medallions he used to create the collars Daevals wear when they're brought to Aeles. Is that true?"

"That is also true," Laycus replied. "There was a metallurgist living in Aeles centuries ago who possessed extraordinary knowledge involving the fusion of blood and metal. Her name was Izabela, and it was she who created the medallions. After she died, she left information on how to recreate her work but alas, it was destroyed by Tallus during one of his numerous returns."

"So many lives have been altered or ended because of me." I gazed into the distance as the river lapped at my knees. "It has to stop, Laycus."

"It will," he assured me. "You and your consort will reunite the realms and bring peace between those with gold and silver blood. Now go back to your body and—"

"One last thing." I told him how, because of my unique powers, it might be possible for me to force a shade to be housed in a body altered to produce and accept golden blood. "When someone dies, they always return as the same blood type . . . if everyone in Nocens is filled with golden blood and I make their shades believe they're an Astral, what happens when they die? They were born Daevals, so they can't be reborn as Astrals. How will their shades return for another life cycle if silver blood no longer exists?"

Laycus was silent, staring down into the water. Finally, he raised his head, his garnet eyes flickering uncertainly.

"I do not know." While his voice was quiet, his words sent a thunderclap of fear through me. If Tallus succeeded, not only would he rid the realms of silver blood, he would also ensure no Daeval ever passed through Karnis for rebirth again, effectively bringing about the genocide he so desperately wanted. Given that he wasn't a Recovrancer with an intimate knowledge of shades, I wasn't certain he was aware of such a consequence, but he'd no doubt be pleased.

"I will speak to Suryal," said Laycus. "*You* will have Bartholomew inform me the moment you are out of that place. Now go back to your realm and keep your eyes open!"

I nodded and quickly left Vaneklus behind, grateful to have had my questions answered as something else suddenly occurred to me.

Even if Sebastian and I reunited the realms, as long as Tallus was able to return, there would never be peace. He would never stop working to undo any good the two of us did. He would always be looking for ways to destroy the relationships we built, sowing fear and discord between those with different blood.

Leaning back against the wall of my cell, I summoned my *alera* to my hands and gazed at the golden light swirling over my fingers.

Could I become skilled enough at *aleric* alteration of the mind to make Tallus forget his own past, removing his memories of who he'd been and what he'd done? I doubted it. I hadn't been able to successfully affect his mind using one bead on my *sana* bracelet, and destroying his memories would require a three- or four-bead combination. Healer Omnurion had said there were times when, regardless of a healer's skill, the mind simply refused to let go of a memory. Tallus's memories were obviously well-protected, certainly by whatever spell he'd cast but also by his own willpower. If we couldn't stop him from returning with his memories intact, we had to stop him from returning at all.

Sebastian no doubt believed he would be the one to end Tallus's life, likely with Rhannu. But ending a life wasn't the same as ending a shade, similar to how destroying a building wasn't the same as truly stopping the Astral experimentation program. I wouldn't stand by while Tallus threatened those I loved. I'd stumbled upon the idea of controlling shades purely as a thought experiment, but now that I'd imagined such a thing, I knew what I had to do. I would learn to control a shade so completely I would have the power to do the unthinkable and remove it from a physical body. I would then remove Tallus's shade and take him to Vaneklus, forcing him to appear in Death before his appointed time. There, Laycus could consume him, ensuring Tallus ceased to exist once and for all.

36

SEBASTIAN

"You're going to be a distraction," I said to Adonis before explaining what I needed him to do. The soldier went to his room, then returned wearing all-black clothing. He'd secured a black cloth around his neck he could use to cover his face and head, leaving only his eyes visible.

"Just to be clear, I'm not going to permanently harm another Astral," he said, "even one doing something as terrible as guarding the experimentation facility. They'll face the consequences of their crimes, but I'm not the one to punish them."

"That's fine," I said. "The main point of you being there is to distract Tallus while I'm inside rescuing Kyra. Initially, you'll throw the facility into chaos, but Tallus won't leave Kyra unless he's certain I'm there . . . at least I wouldn't if I were him, so after you set off a few explosives, I'll come out and engage him. Then I'll portal to wherever Kyra's being held, and you can keep wreaking havoc so he won't be certain if I've gone after Kyra or if I'm still attacking the facility."

"Is your plan *just* to rescue Kyra?" asked Adonis.

I glanced at him, not certain what he meant.

"You're going back to where you were tortured," he said. "Do you have other plans beyond rescuing Kyra?"

"Rescuing her is my first priority. Once she's safe, I'll free any Daeval children being held captive. If I have the chance, I'll destroy the facility and kill Tallus."

"You have to give the Astrals working there a chance to get out before you destroy anything!" insisted Adonis.

"The Astrals working there are knowingly participating in torture and murder," I argued. "A quick death is more than they deserve, but it might be what they get."

Adonis made a face but didn't argue. "Where will you take any children you find?"

Where, indeed?

I opened a portal back to my cave, retrieved my peerin, and rang Dunston, but he didn't pick up. Neither did Caz, and while I knew they'd return my call when they could, I was running out of time. I tried Eslee next, and thankfully, she answered. I didn't have time to go into my full backstory with Kyra, so I kept my explanation brief.

"Kyra dug too deep into what Astrals are doing to Daevals in Aeles, and she's been kidnapped. I'm going to get her out, and if I can, I'll rescue any children being held prisoner. Can I bring them to your house?"

"Of course," she replied without hesitation. "I was just heading to the studio, but I'll stay here instead. Devlin's home too, so I'll wake him up if I need help, although I can't imagine things getting *that* desperate."

"Talk to your father and uncle. I'm betting any children I find will be orphans, but if they have families, figure out how to reunite them. If any of them need healing, contact Minister Sinclair at the Meddygol *Adran*. Thank you, Eslee."

That settled, I returned to Adonis's cottage.

"Can you draw the layout of the facility?" he asked. "At least the outside of it?" Grabbing some parchment and a pencil from a drawer, he offered them to me. At the thought of returning to a place I still strove to forget, the fire writhed angrily in my veins, and a terror I hadn't felt since childhood stirred in the pit of my stomach. Pushing it down, I took the drawing supplies and used the nearby table to recreate what I remembered. I was no longer a prisoner, and I was no longer powerless; Kyra needed me, and I wouldn't allow my past experiences to keep me from rescuing her.

"The facility is enclosed by a high fence that's spelled to shock you on contact," I said. "If it were truly me attacking the facility, I would know this and wouldn't touch it. I *would*, however, come prepared."

I pulled a small box from my weapons belt and offered it to Adonis. "Throw this against the fence, and it'll counteract the shock spell for as long as it stays in place." I handed him a tiny glass vial filled with an explosive potion. "This will blow the main gate off its hinges. After you do that, you'll run to a different section of the fence and scale it."

Adonis nodded as he carefully slipped the glass vial into a pocket.

"Do you know how to cast any fire spells?" I asked.

"I can make a fire larger or smaller, but I can't create it from nothing," said Adonis.

I'd expected as much and produced a cylinder holding small silver discs, each coated in various chemicals, as well as a few spells. "Put one of these down, and you'll have roughly ten seconds to get out of the way before it bursts into flames," I explained. "Tallus knows I'm a Pyromancer, so if there's not a significant amount of fire, he'll be suspicious. Put one at the front entrance, then run around back." I pointed to a spot on the drawing I'd made. "Drop another disc here."

"You've really thought this out," noted Adonis. "Not that I

don't appreciate good planning, but aren't you worried the more time we take, the more danger Kyra is in?"

"Tallus wants me in Rynstyn," I said, "and he knows Kyra is the only reason I'd go back there. Plus, he can't end the existence of Daevals without her help. He won't harm her because he needs her. That gives us some time, and I want to be as organized as possible because we're only going to get one shot at this. If we fail, Tallus will most likely move her to a new location, and we'll have to start all over."

Adonis and I continued to work our way through the distraction he would create, and while I could tell he was impressed at the array of tools and potions I produced, I appreciated he didn't ask where I'd acquired them or how I'd known to make them.

Adonis's Cypher, Gordon, appeared on the table and volunteered to place some of the smaller explosives around the perimeter, spreading them out so they would detonate at odd intervals.

"You place them and then you dematerialize," Adonis instructed the toad. "I don't want to risk you being seen."

"That's one of the nice things about being me," Gordon croaked in a gravelly voice, a smile brightening his dark green face. "No one expects anything of something so small. They won't even know I'm there."

Once Adonis had memorized the plan, I told him to grab a sword, which he did. I then led the way outside.

"Now we need to make sure you move like me," I said, withdrawing Rhannu from my scabbard. The sword felt so right in my hand, I immediately found myself relaxing, a calmness sweeping through me, even though I could also feel the sword's eagerness to fight. Marks flowed up and down the silver blade, and Adonis's eyes widened.

"Now *that's* a weapon," he whistled. "What do those symbols mean?"

"They're Shthornan, an ancient Daevalic language. When you say their names, Rhannu performs additional actions. I'll show you another time."

I handed him a silver button I'd magnetized and coated with spelled ingredients. "When you put this on your sword, it'll create flames to cover your blade. They're not real, and they won't burn you," I assured him, "but one of my preferred methods of fighting has always been to cover my sword with fire."

Summoning the fire inside me, I let it flow through my hand, enveloping Rhannu until the weapon appeared to be made entirely of dancing red flames.

"It won't last forever," I warned Adonis, "but it'll certainly be memorable."

Adonis nodded, then took up a position behind me, mimicking my movements as I made my way through various sword-fighting forms. We practiced until he could do a rather impressive impersonation of me, and as I watched him move as I would, gliding from one position to another, my chest tightened. This was so like working with Farent that had Kyra's safety not been on the line, I would have thoroughly enjoyed myself.

"Good," I said when Adonis turned and raised his eyebrows, seeking my approval. "You learn fast."

He grinned just as Nigel opened the door and joined us, the portal disruptor in one hand and Batty on his shoulder.

"I think we did it!" the lieutenant exclaimed. "I changed some of the wiring on the inside, because that's easier to do with hands than wings, then Batty added some spells—ones I've never even heard of—and now when you press this button," he gestured towards the top of the device, "you can *make* a portal rather than preventing one from opening. Give it a try. Adonis, cast an anti-portal ward."

Adonis did, and when I tried to open a portal, nothing happened. The air around me sizzled and snapped, but no doorway opened.

"Now, I'll just press this button," Nigel held a finger against the top of the device, "and you should be good to go."

"*Fosgail*," I said, and a portal immediately snapped open, much to my relief and Nigel's delight. Batty clapped happily before wrapping a wing around the back of Nigel's head and hugging the side of his face.

"I see many collaborations in our future," said the bat. "You follow directions extremely well."

Nigel blushed at the compliment but seemed pleased as he handed me the portal device, which I secured in a pocket. The sun had already sunk below the horizon, and Adonis's spelled garden lights twinkled on as we reviewed the plan once more. Then, it was time to leave. Adonis and Nigel exchanged a hug, clapping one another on the back and engaging in friendly banter about how next time Nigel would be the one acting as a distraction.

Batty provided the coordinates to the facility, and I opened a portal, the apprehension inside me crackling almost as loud as the shimmering gateway. As I watched Batty fly through the doorway, followed by Adonis, I couldn't help marveling over this unexpected turn of events. I'd *never* imagined trusting Kyra's life to my bat, nor working with an Astral to break into an Aelian facility. But just because they weren't who I necessarily would have chosen to work with didn't mean they weren't skilled in their own ways, and as I stepped after them, for the first time in years, I found myself grateful I wasn't alone.

37

SEBASTIAN

The night air was cold, and snow covered the ground outside the fence separating the experimentation facility from the rest of the heavily wooded area. As I gazed through the pine trees, inhaling the scents of sap and ice, I struggled to believe I was back *here*, of all places, facing the terrors of two very different pasts.

"Thank you again for this," I said to Adonis, keeping my voice low. "It's difficult for me to admit, but I'm not certain I could do this on my own."

Adonis grinned. "You're welcome, and I'm glad you recognize that . . . this is what friends are for."

I nodded and extended a hand, which earned me a raised eyebrow from Adonis.

"Surely you know me better than that by now," he scoffed, and I couldn't entirely keep myself from smiling as I allowed him to pull me into a hug. While it wasn't anything close to comfortable, it also didn't feel as terrible as I'd expected.

"Let's go ruin Tallus's night," said Adonis, and then he was off, slipping through the trees almost as quietly as I moved.

Kyra, I said. *I'm outside the facility. Adonis and Batty are with me, and we're going to get you out.*

Please be careful, she implored, and even though my safety wasn't as important as hers, I assured her I would be.

Batty hopped from one tree branch to another, bringing himself eye level with me.

You cannot kill Tallus, he said. *At least not yet. We must first break the spell he cast to remember his past lives . . . if you kill him now, he'll simply return and continue sowing hatred between the realms, even if you reunite them.*

I hadn't thought of that, and I ran a hand through my hair. Unfortunately, it made sense, and if I'd learned anything in my career, it was the necessity of patience. Letting go of my frustration and disappointment, I nodded my understanding.

Let me know the instant you've found Kyra, I instructed my Cypher. *Once you send me the coordinates, I'll activate the portal device and come to you.*

The bat gave me a smart salute, followed by his usual dopey grin, then dematerialized as I touched a pocket, reassuring myself the portal device was there. I also took the chance to offer a quick prayer invoking all three Fates, as my past, present, and future were each at play here.

Adonis had left the tree line and made his way to the closed gate. He lobbed the glass vial at it and a terrific explosion rang out, filling the air with dirt and metal and rocking the ground beneath my feet.

I am inside, said Batty, *and an alarm has just sounded, no doubt due to Adonis's attack.*

I wasn't certain if the bat was flying around or simply materializing in and out of rooms, but as Kyra repeated what she remembered from the routes she'd taken, I passed on the information to my Cypher.

After what seemed an interminably long time, during which I watched Adonis place the explosives I'd prepared along the perimeter fence, Batty spoke.

I have found Kyra. There are four guards outside her door, as well as the Astral who must be Tallus.

What's he doing? A fire suddenly exploded towards the back of the compound. That had to be Gordon's work, and I sent a silent message of thanks to the toad.

He is pacing back and forth and keeps looking down the hallway, said Batty. *Now he is talking to the guards . . . he is saying there is no chance you would make such an obvious attack and it's clearly a ploy . . . but he appears quite anxious and does not seem to believe his own words.*

Time to draw him out.

Striding forward, I made my way through the twisted remains of the front gate, my boots crunching against the snow as another explosion sounded and flames danced along the fence. Reaching the inner courtyard, I pushed back my hood, revealing my face, and pulled Rhannu from its scabbard. The entire building was under heavy surveillance and Tallus had to be watching the feed from the captums placed at strategic intervals; this would prove who I was beyond any shadow of a doubt.

Tallus is leaving, said Batty, *and most likely heading your way.*

A few moments later, a man stepped through the heavy front door, not bearing any resemblance to the Tallus I remembered.

"I'm almost disappointed at how predictable you are," he said, studying me. "I take it you aren't going to come quietly?"

"No."

Purple smoke began to twist around Tallus's hands as he moved them in a complex spell-casting gesture. "I wasn't just a historian, you know. My true passion has always been research, which means I can't pass up the opportunity to conduct an experiment. Let's see if you're also protected with only one bracelet."

A plume of smoke sped towards me, and even though I

stepped to one side and easily avoided it, everything around me changed. I was standing inside my childhood home. There was the dining table with the mismatched chairs, and my mother's cello stood upright in a corner. I spun in a circle, trying to make sense of what I was seeing. It had to be a hallucination, but how had Tallus done it? Footsteps sounded on the porch, and I turned to face the front door as it swung open and a man stepped into the living room.

Everything inside me, including my fire, froze.

"What a shame you're so inept at protecting the women in your life," said my father as he adjusted his black silk tie. "You failed to protect your mother. And now you've failed to protect Kyra."

I knew both accusations were blatantly untrue, but my father appeared so lifelike standing there before me, it was difficult to doubt what my senses were assuring me was very real.

"You killed my mother," I replied. "And I'm going to rescue Kyra."

"You talk as if you're some sort of hero," snorted my father, "but we both know you're not. You never will be." He stepped closer. "You're a villain, Sebastian. You're darkness and sharp blades, burned bodies and ended lives. The silver blood you've spilled is almost as bright as the gold you received for your work, and you live only for yourself." He shook his head. "You don't deserve Kyra. And we both know she could do *far* better than you."

The sharp retort I'd been forming melted in my mouth. Deep down, some part of me *didn't* believe I deserved Kyra, and hearing the apparition before me so casually mention one of my greatest fears made me feel like I'd been kicked in the stomach.

As if sensing he'd gained an advantage, my father offered me a smile that was both sad and pitying.

"It was always going to be like this," he said. "You can't fight who you are. You're half me. You won't be able to keep from hurting her."

"I would never hurt Kyra," I spat, even as I tried to remember this wasn't real and there was no point in arguing.

"You tell yourself that," my father agreed, "but deep down, you're terrified you're more like me than you want to admit. Deep down, you know how easy it would be to become me."

"No." I shook my head, but even as I denied it, the scene before me shifted and I saw myself yelling at Kyra, saw myself drawing back a hand and slapping her across the face, saw myself kicking a door shut before forcing her onto the bed.

Fear rushed through me, and I lowered Rhannu to my side, my hand shaking around the sword's hilt. Was this some horrible vision of the future? It couldn't be. I would never hurt Kyra. If this was a glimpse of what was to come, I wouldn't let it happen.

The scene shifted back to the farmhouse, and my father stood before me again, the ever-present smirk twisting his thin lips.

"You can change your name," he said, "but you can't change who you are."

"I would never do those things!" I insisted, telling myself as much as him. As he began to laugh, I recalled my mother's words from childhood: *I know it might not feel like it, but you always have a choice in how you behave.*

I had a choice. And I would always make the same one, no matter how many times I had to do so.

"I'm not you!" I shouted at my father. "And I *never* will be!"

My heart racing, I raised Rhannu, prepared to run the sword through my father's chest . . . but I stopped. Resorting to violence was exactly what he would do, what he had done countless times. The best way to prove I wasn't like him was to avoid acting as he would.

I lowered my sword.

"I'm not you," I said again, and this time my voice was steady, not because I was keeping myself in check but because I *knew* I was different from my father. The choice I'd just made not to attack him proved that. "I don't have to be afraid of turning into you, because the choice has always been up to me. I'll never be you."

The scene around me suddenly shifted, and I found myself standing outside the experimentation facility as Tallus summoned the purple smoke back to himself. As the smoke vanished, I was overcome with dizziness, and I swayed where I stood, trying to maintain a sense of which way was up and which was down.

I could tell Tallus was saying something to me, probably about the lingering effects of his spell, but I couldn't make it out, and I pressed a hand against my head, disoriented and feeling as if everything around me was happening in slow motion. Blinking and trying to breathe, I became aware of Batty screaming at me, and it took all my effort to focus on what he was saying.

—the coordinates! the bat shouted. *Here are the coordinates to Kyra! Open a portal!*

Ears ringing, I nevertheless managed to open a portal, and as I turned my attention to rescuing Kyra, the fire inside me roared back to life, burning away the fears I'd just faced and filling me with a new resolve. Even if Tallus ran as fast as he could, he was limited by doors and hallways, which meant there was no chance he could catch me.

The first two guards outside Kyra's room didn't see what ended their lives. The other two were clearly startled as I stepped out of thin air, but Rhannu made their ends swift as well.

I pounded on the door. "Kyra?"

"I'm here!" she called.

"Stand back and make yourself as small as possible."

I'm ready, she said through the bracelet, and I tightened my grip before plunging Rhannu straight into the center of the metal door.

"*Toe'dye!*" I said, causing a mark on the sword to glow bright gold. The metal began to quiver, and then the entire door melted, pouring down like a grey waterfall. Thankfully, holding Rhannu protected me, and the molten metal didn't even touch my boots as it flowed into the hallway, where it shimmered under the flashing red emergency lights.

Darting through the open doorway, I grabbed Kyra and kissed her hard before opening a portal and shoving her into my cave. Aurelius leaped after her, and I closed the portal as soon as his short tail cleared the gateway.

Batty appeared in front of me, flapping his wings to stay aloft.

There are five Daeval children being held here, he said, *and as I was searching for them, I found something else. There is a wolf here too, and while he is presently unconscious, he might be the Cypher Kyra is looking for.*

Neither Kyra nor I had closed the connection through the bracelets, which meant she could follow along with my thoughts. As I considered why a wolf would be held captive at the experimentation center, she cried, *Please, Sebastian! It might be Flavius. That would explain why Aurelius couldn't reach him. You have to save him!*

I need to get the Daeval children out first, then I'll get the wolf. Batty shared the location of the first child, and I pushed the button on Nigel's device, opening a portal.

The room was exactly as I remembered: white walls, a small bed, a desk and chair, and a toiletry bucket in the corner. I could hear heavy breathing coming from under the bed, so I crouched down, bringing myself face-to-face with a terrified boy.

"I'm not going to hurt you," I assured the trembling child. "I'm a Daeval, just like you, and I'm here to take you home."

Given that the suppressor medallion would prevent the boy from sensing my blood, I quickly pulled up my sleeve and pressed one edge of Rhannu's blade against my forearm, revealing my silver blood. Even though the effects of the medallion made my blood look more white than bright silver, at the very least it was obvious I wasn't an Astral.

The fear in the boy's eyes instantly gave way to relief. He scrambled out from under the bed and wrapped his arms around my leg as if to ensure I wouldn't leave without him. I didn't know anything about comforting children, but I patted his back a few times, the way my mother had done to me when I'd been upset, as I conjured another portal. Some part of me couldn't believe what was happening, and I felt as if I was standing to one side watching myself take action. How many times during my imprisonment had I wished for this very thing? No one had ever appeared and set me free, but being here now, it felt good knowing I could give these children the rescue I'd dreamed of.

I pointed to Eslee on the other side of the portal. "She's a Daeval, just like us, and she's going to keep you safe while I rescue the others, alright?"

The boy nodded and stepped through, taking Eslee's hand as he did. Thinking of Eslee's gift for manipulating metal, I caught her attention. "Find a way to get that collar off him," I said, and although her eyes widened in horror at the device around the child's neck, she managed a nod, and I hurried to the next room.

Three of the other children responded similarly to the boy, readily cooperating once they realized I possessed silver blood, but the last child, a girl who couldn't have been more than five or six, shrieked hysterically over my sudden appearance and wouldn't stop screaming, so rather than attempting to explain things, I simply swept her into my arms and handed her to Eslee, who took her like she dealt with terrified children every day.

Running footsteps sounded outside the door, and Batty quickly shared the coordinates to where he'd seen the Cypher, allowing me to portal into a sterile room where a timber wolf was lying on a low cushion. The creature was hooked up to various monitors beeping at regular intervals, and the tubes going into the animal's body had to have been delivering a potion to keep it unconscious.

I gently withdrew the tubes, careful to avoid the large needles at the ends, then cradled the creature and conjured a portal. Kyra practically jumped through to join me but stepped back when she saw the wolf, the blood running from her face.

"It's Flavius!" she exclaimed. "Is he—"

"He's unconscious, but he's breathing," I said, setting the creature down on the cavern floor. "I need to get Adonis home, and then I'll be back."

Kyra nodded, dropping to her knees beside the wolf and stroking his fur.

Can Gordon tell where Adonis is? I asked Batty.

Batty reached out to the Astral's Cypher. *He is currently fighting guards near where the front gate used to be.*

Opening a portal, I hurried through to where Adonis was engaging a group of guards. In addition to wielding a sword covered with fire, he was also casting an impressive array of spells. Tallus was nowhere to be seen, which meant he was probably searching for me inside the facility.

"*Newwl!*" I said, causing another rune along Rhannu's blade to glow gold, and suddenly Adonis and I were enveloped in a bank of fog that had risen from nowhere. I could hear the guards shouting to one another, unable to see past their own limbs, and I quickly opened a portal to Adonis's cottage.

"Kyra's safe, and so are the Daeval children," I told him. "It's time for you to leave. Thank you."

He nodded, then darted through the portal, and I closed it as the fog around me cleared.

"Schatten!"

I turned toward the facility as Tallus reemerged, and while everything inside me yearned to attack the man, I stayed where I was. Just because I couldn't end his life didn't mean there weren't other things I could destroy. This place had stolen my childhood and traumatized me in ways I was still working through. I'd dreamed of ending this program for years, and now that the Daeval children were safe and I knew who was truly behind the experimentation, there was only one thing left to do.

"*Dieargryn*," I said, causing the rune to glow. "*Frry'doe!*" I added, causing a second rune to burn bright gold. I'd just activated the runes for an earthquake and an explosion, and as I raised the sword high over my head, I summoned every ounce of fire in my veins and directed it to the weapon. "*E'mstyn!*" I shouted, commanding the actions to spread outwards.

And then I plunged Rhannu's blade into the ground.

The result was immediate . . . the snow-covered earth rolled like a giant creature was stirring beneath it, and the fire spread outwards, racing towards the building and latching onto anything it could find. The entire complex shuddered and groaned before collapsing in on itself. Metal screeched and beams snapped as fiery debris rained down, causing some of the guards to run to the nearby woods for cover. Others ran back into the building, shouting about rescuing those still inside.

I conjured a portal but stopped and looked over my shoulder. Watching the place I'd been so desperate to escape burn was immensely satisfying. Tallus would likely be more dangerous than ever, furious over his failure, but at least we knew who he was and had put an end to his vile program.

Tallus studied me from across the lawn, shadows from the firelight flickering across his face.

"Those who don't learn from the past are doomed to repeat it," he called, "and I remember the past *far* better than either of you. I know what you and Kyra plan to do!"

I stepped through the portal and closed it quickly behind me, silencing the sounds of the destruction I'd wrought. Kyra rose from her crouched position near the wolf and rushed towards me, hugging me so hard I wouldn't have been surprised to hear a rib crack. Replacing Rhannu in my scabbard, I returned the embrace, relief washing over me as I struggled to believe everything that had just occurred.

38

SEBASTIAN

*H*olding Kyra, I gazed at the toffee-colored walls of my cave, chest heaving as I tried to process all that had happened. Kyra was safe. The Daeval children were safe. Adonis was safe. Even though Tallus had somehow conjured my deepest fears and manipulated my mind, I, too, was safe.

Our breathing began to slow, and after a moment, Kyra lowered her arms and looked up at me. "I knew you would rescue me, but I'd love to know how you did it."

I told her what I'd shared with Adonis, Nigel, and Demitri, and her eyes widened as she alternated between shaking her head and covering her face with her hands.

"I can't believe they know!" she said when I was through. "I can't believe they believed you."

"We need to get your family out of Aeles," I told her. "If I was Tallus, I'd target them next. I'm certain the Dekarais have a place they can stay." Clearly I would be in the family's debt forever, but it was worth it to help Kyra.

She let out a troubled breath as she wrapped her arms around herself. "Before we contact my family, there's something I need to tell you."

If Tallus had somehow hurt her, I didn't care what Batty had said . . . I'd portal back and end the man's life that instant.

"Tallus told me a lot of things about who I used to be in my past lives," Kyra continued, looking at a spot somewhere over my shoulder. "He told me . . . he said it's my fault the experimentation facility was established. I know it's not, but I still feel so responsible!"

A pained expression crossed her face as she recounted what she'd learned about herself, including her returns as other Recovrancers, how she'd overseen the creation of the medallions as Lochlyn, and how Tallus had used them to create the collars worn by Daevals secretly brought to Aeles. When she spoke of how Tallus had started experimenting on Daevals as a way to prevent my return, she trembled and her voice broke.

I put my hands on her shoulders, gently shaking her until she brought her eyes to mine.

"You didn't do anything wrong," I assured her. "Tallus is the one at fault here; you were simply trying to ensure I had a way into Aeles. Everything you did was to find me, and I would *never* fault you for that. No one else would fight as hard for me as you have every life cycle you've lived. If anything, I'll never deserve what you've done for me."

"I know Tallus can't control minds, but sometimes the things he says make so much sense, it's hard not to believe them." Kyra sniffled.

"He did something to me, when I first saw him." I explained about having to face my deepest fears.

"He tried that on me, too," she nodded, "only Death didn't take kindly to sharing my mind and helped me shut him out. I'm so sorry for what you experienced, though."

She pressed her lips against mine.

"Thank you for not hating me," she murmured.

I pulled back and cupped her face in my hands. "I could never hate you. I love you. My shade is bound to yours." I suddenly remembered what Demitri had said. "And speaking of that, do you have any idea what will happen to us after we reunite the realms? If that's what we bound ourselves to do, and we do it, will we still continue to find one another in future life cycles?"

Kyra stared up at me, uncertainty spreading through her eyes. "I don't know," she said quietly. "I never considered that." She hesitated before asking, "What if reuniting the realms means the end of us being able to find one another again?"

I very nearly replied, "Then we won't reunite the realms," but I caught myself. "We need more information," I said instead. "Perhaps Laycus can help."

"That'll be the first thing I ask him when I go back to Vaneklus," agreed Kyra. She then turned to where Batty was sitting on the sofa and scooped up the bat, hugging him to her chest. "Thank you for everything! You helped rescue me and the Daeval children, and you found Flavius. You're amazing."

To my surprise, Aurelius cleared his throat. "I, too, would like to offer my most sincere appreciation for your hard work, Bartholomew. I can't say I never doubted you, but I will say I've never been so happy to have been proven wrong." He gazed up at Batty in Kyra's arms. "Kyra is everything to me, and I will never forget your devotion to her."

Batty squealed and floated down from Kyra's arms. Landing on the stone floor, he scurried over to wrap his wings around one of Aurelius's legs, and while the lynx couldn't keep from stiffening, he did manage to pat Batty's back with a large paw.

Kyra caught my eye and gave me an imploring look, obviously wanting me to express my appreciation to the bat, as well.

"I have something to say too." At my words, Batty let go of Aurelius and gazed up at me.

"We wouldn't have returned, and we certainly wouldn't have found one another again, without you," I said to the bat. Stepping closer, I crouched down, resting my weight on my heels. "You've always done everything you could to help us. This rescue mission never would have succeeded without you and . . . I've never truly appreciated you. Thank you for everything."

I wasn't prepared to have Batty launch himself at me, leaping against my chest in his version of a hug. While I would have been happy to have him simply accept my thanks, I was able to pet his leathery wings a few times without feeling too uncomfortable.

Thankfully, Batty didn't linger; he dematerialized before reappearing on the dining table next to a package wrapped in brown paper. Before I could ask him about the package, though, Flavius stirred, flicking the tip of his tail before stretching his paws, and Kyra immediately hurried to his side.

Lowering onto her knees, she rested a hand on the wolf's head. "It's alright," she stroked his fur. "You're safe now."

As the wolf blinked open his amber eyes, Kyra told him how Batty and I had rescued her and, in the process, discovered him being held captive. "Aurelius has been trying to contact you for weeks! Were you being held in Rynstyn the entire time?"

"I was," nodded the Cypher, slowly pushing himself up into a sitting position.

"After your father's passing, I took some time to myself, then returned to the Cypher Commission when I felt ready for reassignment. I was told by Senator Rex to go to the facility in Rynstyn, but when I presented myself, I was locked in a room. I couldn't make contact with other Cyphers, so I couldn't tell anyone where I was, and then I was drugged into unconsciousness."

"I have to know, Flavius," said Kyra, fear and determination vying for space in her eyes, "why was Father involved with that terrible program?"

"He became aware of the project by accident," explained the Cypher. "Once he realized what was happening, he offered to be of service on the condition no one outside the program could know of his involvement. He was trying to gather evidence of what was happening to put a stop to it. He found a medallion the researchers used to develop the collars they put on Daevals to keep them from setting off the Blood Alarm and managed to smuggle it out."

Kyra nodded. "I found it in his medical kit."

Batty suddenly materialized with a dish of water, spilling half of it before successfully placing it beside the wolf, who drank gratefully before continuing.

"Once your father realized Astrals were kidnapping Daevalic children to experiment on, he knew he had to act. He was such a fixture at the facility, no one thought anything about him coming and going, and he managed to take one child's body from the crematorium before it could be destroyed, although he fixed the paperwork to appear otherwise. The day before Arakiss died, he secured permission to visit Nocens under the pretense of scouting for new research subjects. He took the boy's body with him and left it in an alleyway, with the hope someone would find it and use trace memories to uncover what had happened."

I reached over and placed a hand on Kyra's shoulder as she momentarily closed her eyes. Opening them, her voice trembled as she said, "Father is the reason Gregor's body made it back to Nocens."

Flavius nodded. "He was going to give it a few days and let someone find the body, then he planned to reach out to a Nocenian healer he'd spoken with before—Minister Sinclair—to ensure Daevals knew about trace memories and how to detect them. Unfortunately, he died before he was able to do so."

At this revelation, Kyra buried her face in her hands, rocking back and forth as sobs shook her body, and I knelt beside her, wrapping my arms around her.

"He *was* trying to shut the program down!" she cried. "I wish I'd never doubted him."

"We know the truth, and that's what matters," I consoled her, resting my cheek against the top of her head and holding her until her sobs quieted.

My peerin suddenly vibrated, and even though I hated letting go of Kyra, I pulled it from my pocket and flipped it open, thinking it might be Eslee with an update on the children. The message wasn't from Eslee, however, and I had to read the words on the screen twice before I could say them out loud.

"LeBehr sent a message," I said. "The potion for locating the Chronicles is ready."

In spite of everything she'd just experienced, Kyra's tear-stained face shone with happiness.

"I also have good news to share," Batty called from the dining table, gesturing to the package beside him. "It seems an elderly dragon who only rarely leaves her home in Oexiss heard of Nerudian's search for a particular cloak. After some digging through her accumulated treasure, she found herself to be in possession of such a garment and was more than happy to collect her reward."

My heart leapt into a racing beat as I made my way to the table and pulled back the wrapping paper. As my fingers made contact with the black and grey scales, something inside me stirred, as if a puzzle piece had suddenly been turned to a different angle, allowing it to easily snap into place. I had been chosen to rule Aeles-Nocens, selected by the last of the Great Beasts . . . me, out of every other possible Daeval. These scales gave me that right as much as possessing Rhannu.

Picking up the cloak, I shook it out, smiling at the familiar swishing of the scales as I fastened the silver clasp shaped like a serpent around my throat.

Turning to face Kyra, I drew myself up to my full height and straightened my shoulders.

"First we find the Chronicles," I said. "Then we gather our allies, reunite the realms, and end our fight with Tallus forever."

Acknowledgments

Starting a new book is equal parts thrilling and terrifying. It's thrilling because you get to go back into the world you've created and spend time with characters you love, but it's terrifying because you can't imagine exactly how you're going to go from a blank page to a three hundred–page book . . . and yet somehow, with persistence, inspiration, support, and a dash of magic, the book begins to take shape and before you know it, you're writing the Acknowledgments section.

Thank you to my publisher, SparkPress, for another amazing publishing opportunity, and to Brooke Warner for giving me so much creative freedom on this project. Many thanks to Lauren Wise, Samantha Strom, and Shannon Green for their hard work . . . I know I don't see half the things you all do, but I see the results, and they are greatly appreciated. Julie Metz, you have my thanks and deepest appreciation for yet another wonderful cover. Anne Durette, thank you so much for your sharp-eyed copyediting . . . your love for the story and attention to detail made this book significantly better, and I'm forever grateful.

A huge and heartfelt thank you to the best PR team in the galaxy, the always amazing BookSparks, including Crystal Patriarche, Hanna Lindsley, and Rylee Warner. Thank you for your enthusiasm, your support, your industry knowledge, and for never making me feel like a pest for emailing you. It's a true honor to be part of the BookSparks family, and working with you all was without a doubt one of the best writing-related decisions I ever made.

And speaking of my best writing-related decisions . . . AR Capetta, I will be forever grateful that Fate or the Gifters or some other inexplicable force gave me the chance to work with you.

There is no better feeling than having an editor who "gets" your story and your characters and is excited to help you write the best book you possibly can. I live for your margin notes and often refer back to your kind words when I'm feeling low. Thank you for loving my little #foundfamily.

Much of this book was written during daily writing hours with Together Alone, the greatest writing group to ever exist (no, I'm not biased), and I'm so grateful to have been welcomed in with open arms.

To Nicole Valentine—sitting outside with you at the Highlights Foundation retreat is an experience I will never forget. Our conversation was a turning point in how I saw myself, not just as a writer, but as an author, and your openness and willingness to share your knowledge and experience meant more to me than you'll ever know.

Huge thanks to the Highlights Foundation for providing a spectacular place to write (and for feeding me so well I barely fit into my clothes by the end of the retreat!). I was finishing up edits to this book even though I was technically at the retreat working on a middle grade novel, and as a result, I know some of that amazing Highlights' magic is running through these pages. I'm so fortunate to have met, learned from, and been supported by Sarah Aronson, I.W. Gregorio, K.X. Song, and Nancy Werlin, and I'm so excited to be expanding my writing family.

To all the bloggers, Bookstagrammers, Booktokers, and book lovers who shared pictures and posts featuring *Reign Returned*, you have my undying appreciation. It's a dream come true to be able to say, "Sounds like something Batty would do!" and have people know what I'm talking about!

To all my family and friends who showed up for book events, wrote reviews, gave my book as gifts, and supported me in ways big and small . . . thank you so incredibly much! Writing might be a solitary process, but authors need community, and you've given me the best community anyone could ask for.

To my husband, Cameron—to truly thank you for everything you've done for me would require a separate book. Thank you for always being so excited about whatever book-related news I zoomed down the stairs to tell you. I love that you know me well enough to read my books and point out where you see me in a character or recognize us in a conversation. Kyra and Sebastian share a love story almost as incredible as ours, and I can't imagine doing any of this without the love, laughter, and hugs you give me on a daily basis. Your unfailing belief in me still amazes me at times, but I'm so grateful for it.

About the Author

Photo credit: Cameron Bowman

KATIE KERIDAN made her literary debut at ten years of age when she won a writing contest by crafting a tale about her favorite childhood hero, Hank the Cowdog. After that, Katie continued to write, through college and graduate school and during her career as a pediatric neuropsychologist. While Katie enjoyed being a doctor, scientific research didn't bring her nearly as much joy as did creating her own characters and worlds, so she slowly left the medical world behind to focus exclusively on writing. Her debut YA fantasy novel, *Reign Returned*, was published by SparkPress in 2022, and her work has been featured in *Highlights Hello Magazine*, *The Blue Nib*, *Youth Imagination Magazine*, *Red Fez*, *The Red Penguin Review*, *Sand Canyon Review*, and *Every Day Fiction*. She loves sharing her writing with others who feel different, misunderstood, or alone. Katie lives in Northern California with her husband and two very demanding cats.

SELECTED TITLES FROM SPARKPRESS

SparkPress is an independent boutique publisher delivering high-quality, entertaining, and engaging content that enhances readers' lives, with a special focus on female-driven work. www.gosparkpress.com

The Blue Witch: The Witches of Orkney, Book One, Alane Adams. $12.95, 978-1-943006-77-9. Nine-year-old Abigail Tarkana has a problem: her witch magic has finally come in, but it's *different*—and being different is a problem at the Tarkana Witch Academy. Together with her scientist-friend Hugo, she face off against sneevils, shreeks, and vikens in a race to discover the secrets about her mysterious magic.

But Not Forever: A Novel, Jan Von Schleh. $16.95, 978-1-943006-58-8. When identical fifteen-year-old girls are mysteriously switched in time, they discover the love that's been missing in their lives. Torn, both want to go home, but neither wants to give up what they now have.

The Alienation of Courtney Hoffman: A Novel, Brady Stefani. $17, 978-1-940716-34-3. When 15-year-old Courtney Hoffman starts getting visits from aliens at night, she's sure she's going crazy—but when she meets a mysterious older girl who has alien stories of her own, she embarks on a journey that takes her into her own family's deepest, darkest secrets.

Caley Cross and the Hadeon Drop, J. S. Rosen, $16.95, 978-1-68463-053-0. When thirteen-year-old Caley Cross, an orphan with a dark power, is guided by a jumpsuit-wearing mole into another world—Erinath—she finds a place deeply rooted in nature where the people have animal-like powers and she is a Crown Princess—but she soon learns that the most powerful evil being in *any* world is waiting for her there.

Eye of Zeus: Legends of Olympus Book 1, Alane Adams. $12.95, 978-1-68463-028-8. Finding out she's the daughter of Zeus is not what a foster kid like Phoebe Katz expected to hear from a talking statue of Athena. But when her beloved social worker is kidnapped, Phoebe and her two friends must travel back to ancient Greece and rescue him before she accidentally destroys Olympus.